THE GREAT
SANTA SEARCH

JEREMY P. TARCHER/PENGUIN

a member of Penguin Group (USA) Inc.

New York

THE
GREAT
SANTA SEARCH

As Told to JEFF GUINN
by Santa Claus himself

ILLUSTRATIONS BY MARK HOFFER

JEREMY P. TARCHER/PENGUIN
Published by the Penguin Group
Penguin Group (USA) Inc., 375 Hudson Street, New York, New York 10014, USA •
Penguin Group (Canada), 90 Eglinton Avenue East, Suite 700, Toronto, Ontario M4P 2Y3, Canada
(a division of Pearson Penguin Canada Inc.) • Penguin Books Ltd, 80 Strand, London WC2R 0RL,
England • Penguin Ireland, 25 St Stephen's Green, Dublin 2, Ireland (a division of
Penguin Books Ltd) • Penguin Group (Australia), 250 Camberwell Road, Camberwell,
Victoria 3124, Australia (a division of Pearson Australia Group Pty Ltd) • Penguin Books
India Pvt Ltd, 11 Community Centre, Panchsheel Park, New Delhi–110 017, India • Penguin
Group (NZ), 67 Apollo Drive, Rosedale, North Shore 0745, Auckland, New Zealand
(a division of Pearson New Zealand Ltd) • Penguin Books (South Africa) (Pty) Ltd,
24 Sturdee Avenue, Rosebank, Johannesburg 2196, South Africa

Penguin Books Ltd, Registered Offices:
80 Strand, London WC2R 0RL, England

First trade paperback edition 2007
Copyright © 2006 by 24Words, LLC

Most Tarcher/Penguin books are available at special quantity discounts for bulk purchase
for sales promotions, premiums, fund-raising, and educational needs. Special books or book
excerpts also can be created to fit specific needs. For details, write Penguin Group (USA) Inc.
Special Markets, 375 Hudson Street, New York, NY 10014.

The Library of Congress catalogued the hardcover edition as follows:

Guinn, Jeff.
The great Santa search / as told to Jeff Guinn.
p.   cm.
ISBN 1-58542-513-3
1. Santa Claus—Fiction.   I. Title.
PS3557.U375G74   2006   2006046365
813'.54—dc22

ISBN 978-1-58542-599-0 (paperback edition)

Printed in the United States of America
1   3   5   7   9   10   8   6   4   2
This book is printed on acid-free paper. ♾

BOOK DESIGN BY AMANDA DEWEY
ILLUSTRATIONS © 2006 BY MARK HOFFER

For Felix Higgins

Lunch is on me.

Foreword

YOU DON'T LIVE as long as I have—more than seventeen hundred years so far, and counting—without becoming something of a philosopher. After all the things I've seen and the people I've met, I've concluded it's true that most problems are really opportunities. Everyone's life includes moments of crisis when everything seems to be going wrong, and we feel discouraged or even helpless. But if we are determined enough, we can find ways to make the best of these situations, and afterward find ourselves happier than we were before. The story I'm about to tell is proof.

Let me set the scene.

Sometimes, during the few quiet moments we have at the North Pole, I reflect on how lucky I've been. Of course, my greatest privilege has been to help so many children all around the world celebrate Christmas, and the other holidays of St. Nicholas Day and Epiphany. The presents that they've received from me and my wonderful friends have always been intended as symbols of caring, a sign that on the most special of holidays someone loved them enough to leave a gift, just as on that happiest of days some two thousand years ago God demonstrated his love for us all with the gift of his son Jesus. I have never meant for my mission to divert attention in any way from that. As Santa Claus, I want to contribute to the celebration without being mistaken for the cause of it.

This is what I have tried to do for many centuries, and I hope I've mostly been successful, though I'm aware that there have always been and will always be those who twist the traditions of Christmas to suit their own selfish purposes. Part of my good fortune is that I've encountered so few of them. Instead, I've known many fine people whose actions were sparked by generosity of spirit, and some of them live and work with me now at the North Pole. You've heard of several: Benjamin Franklin, Amelia Earhart, St. Francis of Assisi, Leonardo da Vinci, Attila the Hun, and Theodore Roosevelt. There are others who should be better known than they are: Sarah Kemble Knight, who wrote the first books about traveling in colonial America, and Bill Pickett, the great African-American cowboy. One has a colorful reputation that has very little to do with the actual facts—King Arthur, who was really a British war chief rather than a crowned head of state. Then there are three dear people whom popular history has never noted at all, because they have never sought the fame they so richly deserve—Willie Skokan, the fine Bohemian craftsman; Felix, the former Roman slave who became my first companion in this gift-giving mission; and Layla, my beloved wife, whose courage and common sense have meant so much to all of us for so very long.

You may be wondering what all this has to do with problems actually being opportunities. Well, in 1841 an acquaintance of mine had an idea that eventually threatened to ruin Santa Claus and the spirit of Christmas altogether. His name was J. W. Parkinson, and he owned a dry-goods store in Philadelphia. Though the story I want to tell is concerned with what happened more than 160 years later, we can trace everything back to J.W.'s plan to drum up a little extra holiday business at his shop.

He had no inkling, and would never have believed, that because of his marketing brainstorm the entire nature of Christmas celebrations throughout America would eventually change forever, and that the generous spirit of the holiday and reputation of Santa Claus would one day hang in the balance. Everything I've tried to represent came very close to being destroyed forever.

But it wasn't. In the end, some wonderful people refused to let this happen. In the process, they taught me that "Santa's helpers" are even more numerous than I had realized, and reminded me that the only time it's certain there can't be a happy ending is if we give up trying to make one happen.

I hope you enjoy the story, and learn from it, too. No one, including me, is ever too old to learn.

—*Santa Claus*
The North Pole

THE GREAT
SANTA SEARCH

He only managed to lower himself as far as his waist before getting stuck tight.
Standing beside me, Layla and Sarah dissolved into helpless giggling;
Felix and Ben chuckled, too, but I felt sorry for the fellow.
I'd gotten stuck in a few chimneys myself over the years.

CHAPTER

One

 don't see why you won't agree, Santa Claus," said J. W. Parkinson, pacing in front of the stone fireplace in the living room of his home. "It would be great fun for you, and extra holiday profit for me. We'd both be benefiting."

"That's just it, my friend," I replied, taking another sip of the delicious hot chocolate he'd just served. "I would enjoy myself, and your general store would sell extra toys. But what about the other merchants in Philadelphia who have toys for sale? Wouldn't they feel you had an unfair advantage because Santa Claus invited children to meet him at J. W. Parkinson's? I know you've promised to use some of the additional income to buy gifts for needy children, but I still can't do it. I love and treat everyone equally, you see. In anything regarding Christmas, I can't favor you over your competitors. I suppose the best way to put it is that Santa Claus doesn't endorse any store or product, and never will."

J.W., a slender middle-aged man with so much nervous energy that he twitched even while sitting down, wasn't willing to accept my decision.

Born to a poor German immigrant family shortly after the so-called Revolutionary War freed the American colonies from England, he'd worked hard to earn enough money to open his own store that sold what we then called "dry goods"—mostly clothing, tools, and toys. Once he had his shop, he labored tirelessly to make it successful. J.W. sold products of good quality at reasonable prices and made a point of memorizing all his customers' names so they could be greeted warmly whenever they came in. I'd made his acquaintance when I learned that each Christmas Eve he would personally take sacks of toys and candy into the poorest neighborhoods of Philadelphia, distributing gifts to those children who never dared hope they might celebrate the holiday with presents. Of course, my companions and I had the same mission, and on a worldwide scale, but we always realized we could never brighten the Christmas of every deserving child and so welcomed those kind souls like J.W. who didn't simply sit back and assume it was only Santa's responsibility to provide holiday happiness. As was often the case with those fine people I would personally meet and thank, J.W. recognized me immediately. For almost a dozen years, he had gladly kept our friendship secret. But now, in October of 1841, he'd come up with a new way to encourage Christmas trade at his store, and it involved me making a well-publicized personal appearance there. He'd nail posters to every tree in Philadelphia, J.W. vowed, each urging parents to bring their children to J. W. Parkinson's at noon on December 18, one week before Christmas. There, the little ones would have the thrill of meeting Santa Claus, and at the same time their parents could purchase all the Christmas toys needed—J.W. would have available an especially big selection of dolls, whistles, hoops, and wooden blocks, among other playthings.

"Business has been a bit slow of late, and so I want to do something to stimulate sales," J.W. told me, his eyes flashing with excitement. He was someone who got so worked up about his own ideas that he couldn't understand it when others didn't share his enthusiasm. "I know you like to keep your presence in Cooperstown, New York, a secret"—until we moved to the North Pole in 1913, that was where my friends and I lived and made toys—"but I'll protect your privacy. The children, of course, will be meeting the real Santa, but I'll tell their parents I simply hired a stout bearded man to dress up in red-and-white robes to look like you. They'll never know they were in the same room with the actual Kris Kringle!"

I winced at the word "stout"—"burly" is so much more dignified—and held up my hand in a cautionary gesture.

"So you're not only asking me to endorse a specific store, you're also asking me to lie?" I said, keeping my tone gentle. "I never deceive anyone, J.W. Telling parents that I wasn't who I really am would be untrue."

"Think of the excitement in the eyes of the children you'd meet, Santa," he pleaded, neatly switching the topic to a safer subject. "We've spoken of how you've dedicated your life to children, and yet you never really have the opportunity to spend time with them. You regret that so much, you've said over and over. Well, here's your chance."

"And what of the children who couldn't be at your store that day?" I asked. "If their parents chose to shop somewhere else, wouldn't that mean they didn't have the same opportunity to meet Santa? No, J.W., it's out of the question. Let's not discuss it any further. I have to be leaving for Cooperstown soon, but do you suppose Mrs. Parkinson has some of her tasty home-baked cookies for us to enjoy before I go?"

In fact, she did, and for another half hour J.W. and I chatted about other things—the problems I sometimes had getting the proper feed for my reindeer, his endless efforts to find better brands of canvas work pants that would last farmers through more than one harvest—but I could sense he hadn't given up on his Christmas plan. For the next several weeks, I expected a letter from J.W. to arrive at our isolated farm property in Cooperstown, pleading with me to reconsider. But nothing of the sort came, and by early December I had completely forgotten about it.

Then one afternoon I was just going over my list of toys already in hand for Christmas Eve 1841—we had sufficient dolls crafted and stored in our massive Cooperstown barn, but there weren't half enough wooden tops; with just three weeks to go, we'd have to spend a few extra hours crafting them every day right up to December 24—When my wife, Layla, knocked on the door of my study. I was glad to see her, as always. After almost sixteen centuries of marriage, her smile still makes my heart beat faster. But on this occasion, she wasn't smiling.

"Here is something you need to see," Layla said, handing me a sheet of wrinkled paper. "Your friend J. W. Parkinson is going to have Santa at his store after all."

I put on my reading glasses and examined the paper, which turned out to be a promotional poster. In large letters, it announced *"Kris Kringle in Philadelphia! Bring the little ones to J. W. Parkinson's, 100 North Donovan Street, at noon exactly on December 18. Mr. Kringle himself will visit with the tots while Father and Mother take advantage of our store's unmatched selection of holiday toys. See him arrive down our chimney! Don't be late!"* There was also a cartoon on the poster. It depicted a *very* heavy bearded man in fur-trimmed robes, reaching into a large sack overflowing with toys. On the side of the sack was printed, *"My friends shop at Parkinson's!"*

I felt both frustrated and sad. Despite my refusal, J. W.—a good man, I believed, one who truly loved Christmas and meant no harm to anyone—was doing something that went against everything the holiday was supposed to be about. That was frustrating. The sadness came from knowing trusting children would be introduced to an impostor. Some, I knew, would believe they had truly met Santa Claus—or, in this case, Kris Kringle, a nickname by which I was known in some other parts of the world. Growing up in a German family, J. W. had undoubtedly called me Kris Kringle rather than Santa when he was a child. Now he was promising Kris Kringle to another generation of children. What if this Kringle-in-disguise was so obviously an actor rather than the real Santa that some children who'd come to meet him went away disillusioned, convinced that because he was a fraud, Santa Claus must not exist after all?

"Even though we still have a great deal to do here before Christmas, I'll go to Philadelphia at once and inform J.W. I simply forbid him to do this," I told Layla.

"I think it's too late for that," she replied. "One of our other friends in Philadelphia sent us this and added that the posters were already tacked up all over the city. Thousands of parents will have seen them by now, and many must be already making plans to take their children to J.W.'s store on the eighteenth. Perhaps you should appear as Kris Kringle after all."

"That is something I just cannot do," I said. "Santa Claus by any name does not endorse products or stores. We'll just have to hope that this promotion isn't too disastrous. We'll get the reindeer ready, and I'll fly down to Philadelphia to see what happens for myself."

I didn't go alone. Layla came along, as well as Ben Franklin, who'd lived much of his early life in Philadelphia. Felix, my oldest friend and helper, and historian Sarah Kemble Knight also decided to join us. Sarah was always a useful companion on such trips. In the early 1700s, she'd written the first book about traveling in the American colonies. Sarah had a fine memory for roads and rivers and could always suggest short-cuts that saved the reindeer considerable flying time.

So on the morning of December 18, 1841, the five of us secured ourselves in the sleigh, and our eight great sources of propulsion and flight leaped into the cold winter air and whisked us south. Dasher, Dancer, Prancer, Vixen, Comet, Cupid, Donder, and Blitzen were fine, intelligent animals who responded to my slightest tug on the reins. We flew faster than the human eye could follow and were kept warm by thick robes draped over our shoulders and across our laps. Normally on such trips, my passengers and I would talk and laugh and sing, but this time we spoke very little, and even then in hushed, worried tones. No good, we felt, could come of J.W.'s scheme.

After about fifteen minutes in the air, we spied Philadelphia far below. Though measured against modern-day Philadelphia it would have seemed a messy collection of cabins, dirt streets, and corrals, by the standards of 1841 it was a great city indeed. With almost ninety-four thousand residents, it was the fourth largest in all of America, ranking in population only behind New York City, Baltimore, and New Orleans. Still, the houses and farms on its outskirts dwindled down quickly, so it was no real problem for us to land the sleigh in an isolated area. We scattered some feed for the reindeer to enjoy while they awaited our return. We didn't have to worry about someone stumbling upon them and perhaps taking them away. The reindeer were trained to obey only those of us from the farm in Cooperstown. If any strangers approached, they would fly into the air and hover out of sight until the interlopers were gone.

J.W.'s store was on the west side of the city. Though we could have walked the three or four miles there in less than a minute—traveling much faster than ordinary humans was one of the powers granted to us in our gift-giving mission—we chose instead to stroll at a more ordinary pace. It was about eleven o'clock in the morning, a full hour before "Kris Kringle's" promised arrival.

"Philadelphia was one of the first American cities to pave some of its roads with cobblestones," Ben informed us. "That field over there was where I flew my kite in a thunderstorm to see if lightning carried electricity."

"I'll bet you were shocked to find out that it did!" Felix joked.

As soon as we reached the main part of town, we saw J.W.'s posters everywhere. They were tacked to trees and pasted on walls. No modern-day media like radio and television and the Internet existed, so posters were the accustomed means of promoting civic events. If you wanted people to know about some program or other, you put up as many posters as possible and hoped passersby would notice them.

As Layla had predicted, many people had seen J.W.'s posters. When we neared Parkinson's, we saw a crowd of several hundred all trying to get in the front door at once. Grown men and women herded ahead of them children who were shrieking with excitement. J.W.'s employees were trying in vain to get everyone lined up neatly.

"I expect they'll have to call the police to come and get this under control," Sarah said. "Some of those children may be knocked down by accident. How awful!"

Then J.W. himself emerged from the store, standing on its front porch and waving his arms to get everyone's attention. His costume alone could have accomplished that—J.W., who normally dressed quite conservatively, was wearing a long bright green coat and purple trousers, and on his head was a red stocking cap with white tassel. He must have ordered the clothes especially.

"I'm J.W., one of Kris Kringle's assistants, and I request that you all calm down," he shouted. "Our Christmas friend is on his way here"— there was loud cheering from all the assembled children and many of the grown-ups—"and if everyone will just give us some room, you'll be able to watch him arrive. Stand back, and in a few minutes keep a careful eye on the roof. Do you see the chimney there? Do you remember how Kris Kringle, or Santa if you prefer calling him that, likes to come into houses on Christmas Eve? Boys and girls, get ready to meet your hero! Mothers and fathers, prepare to purchase some of the best toy bargains in Philadelphia!" Then J.W. disappeared back into his shop. His employees were now able to convince the crowd to form a semicircle in front of the store, backed far enough away from the porch to have a good view of the roof.

"He means to have this false Kris Kringle jump down that chimney," Ben said. "He's keeping the crowd in front of the store because he's going to get him up there from the back. Let's go see."

My friends and I were always able to blend in when we visited cities. We dressed like everyone else and, without my famous red robes trimmed with white, no one ever seemed to realize this broadly built, white-bearded man was anyone other than an ordinary fellow. So the five of us edged our way along the fringes of the crowd to where J.W.'s workers stood to prevent anyone from going around to the back of the store. One of them stepped up and said, "Don't go any farther, please," but Layla calmly told her, "We're friends of Mr. Parkinson, and he invited my husband to be part of this," which was certainly true.

Behind the store, J.W. stood beside a heavy ladder that had been propped up against the back wall. A tent was pitched a few dozen feet away; inside we could hear someone grumbling about boots not fitting properly, and where was the cushion to be worn under his robes?

"No one is to come back here—wait! Santa, it's you!" J.W. blurted. "Have you decided to appear after all? The other fellow I've hired can just step aside!"

"I haven't changed my mind," I said firmly. "I'm sorry you haven't changed yours. You're about to do a terrible thing, old friend. It isn't too late to call this off."

"But it is, Santa," J.W. replied. "Did you see all the people out in front? This is going to be a great success. You'll see. Christmas and Kris Kringle will be more popular than ever!"

Layla placed her hand on my arm, a signal not to continue the debate. "He's going to go through with this," she whispered. "All we can do now is watch what happens."

One of J.W.'s employees hustled up and informed him that it was noon: "The crowd is just *bristling* with anticipation, Mr. Parkinson," he said.

"Then let's give the people what they want!" J.W. responded, his voice cracking from excitement or a guilty conscience or some combination of the two. "Mr. Kringle! You, in the tent! It's time!"

There was rustling behind the tent's canvas walls, and then the front flap flipped open. A short, portly man in expensive red robes emerged. His hair and beard were white, but some of the talcum powder used to make them so hung in a cloud above his head. He was jamming a pillow underneath his robes to give the appearance of additional stoutness.

"If I fall off the roof, I'll take you to court," he growled at J.W. "You never told me a chimney was involved."

"It will all be fine, Kris Kringle," J.W. promised. "Remember, you must be jolly. I won't pay you the other half of your fee if you're not." He gently pushed the impostor over to the ladder. "Go tell the people that Kris Kringle is about to appear," he instructed a subordinate, who disappeared around the corner. Moments later, a huge cheer was raised by the crowd.

The false Kris Kringle gingerly climbed the ladder, hauling along a massive, toy-filled sack with *"My friends shop at Parkinson's"* printed on the side. As he did, J.W. hustled around to the front of his store. We followed.

"Boys and girls, look at the roof!" he shouted. "He's coming . . . he's coming . . . *here he is!*"

The impostor in red robes had indeed appeared. He'd evidently had some trouble transferring his own weight and the hefty sack from the ladder to the roof itself, for he teetered for a moment before regaining full balance by throwing his free arm around the wide chimney. In doing so, he almost lost his grip on the sack of toys, and in his frantic attempt to get a firm new grip on the sack he nearly let go of the chimney, which might have resulted in a spectacular fall to the ground.

But he didn't fall, and, once confident that he wasn't about to tumble, the fraudulent Kris Kringle nodded to the crowd below. The response was loud cheering, and I began to hope that things might conclude without any real damage to the image of Santa and the beliefs of children. But then J.W. shouted out again.

"Now it's time to enter the store, everyone!" he instructed loudly. "After all, when Kris Kringle slides down a chimney, he ends up inside rather than out! Hurry, now—he's about to come down!"

This encouraged a mass rush to the front door of the shop, which of course wasn't wide enough to accommodate so many people at once. There was much resulting confusion, with parents grumbling and children screeching and J.W. and his employees trying very hard to keep things as orderly as possible. At least the struggle to get inside distracted onlookers from the stumblings of the red-robed figure on the roof, but the five of us from Cooperstown had stayed back from the crush and so kept looking up at him with a sense of fascinated horror.

As I had learned over several centuries, "sliding down a chimney" is not the easiest thing to do. Even the largest fireplaces have relatively narrow chimneys through which smoke is meant to escape; they have never been built with the idea that a full-grown man—all right, a somewhat overweight man—might attempt to slide down them. Add a large sack of toys to the mix and it's quite easy to get stuck before you've dropped even a few feet. That's why I have always preferred using doors or windows. Cooperative parents usually make available to me more convenient ways than chimneys to get in and leave my gifts. But J.W. obviously wanted Kris Kringle to come into his store by the chimney route and no other, so his impostor Santa tried to slide down. He only managed to lower himself as far as his waist before getting stuck tight. Standing beside me, Layla and Sarah dissolved into helpless giggling; Felix and Ben chuckled, too, but I felt sorry for the fellow. I'd gotten stuck in a few chimneys myself over the years.

"Take a deep breath and suck in your stomach!" I called out helpfully. "Hold your toy sack over your head!"

He looked down at me, and even at that distance I could see the panic in his eyes. "I'm sucking in my stomach and I'm still stuck!" he cried, and I was glad all the children had finally gotten inside J.W.'s store so they couldn't hear the man they thought was me sounding so forlorn.

"Tell him to pull the cushion out from under his robe," Layla whispered, and that's what I did. He managed with great difficulty to push one arm down between the chimney wall and his body; we watched his shoulder twitch as he struggled to yank the cushion free. Evidently he succeeded, for suddenly his whole body dropped down out of sight, and the sack of toys fell right behind, with man and sack tumbling, I was certain, onto the hard floor of the fireplace itself. I hoped for the fraudulent Santa's sake that J.W. had remembered to put out the fire.

We hurried inside to find that he had—but he'd forgotten to provide some sort of padding to cushion "Kris Kringle's" fall, so the unfortunate fellow had the wind knocked out of him on impact. The toy sack landed on top of his head, knocking his red tassled hat askew and littering the floor by the fireplace with tin whistles and soft cloth dolls. Some of the crowd gasped in concern, but J.W. announced cheerfully, "In just a moment, Kris Kringle will sit on that bench over there and visit with the kiddies! Parents, this way to a display of the finest toys in all of Philadelphia!" All the mothers and fathers trooped off obediently, though Layla, Ben, Felix, Sarah, and I stayed behind. The poor pretend gift-giver was helped to the bench by a pair of J.W.'s employees, dragging his half-empty toy sack behind him while another of J.W.'s workers scurried to pick up the other scattered playthings. His red robes were streaked with soot—J.W. had also forgotten to have the chimney cleaned beforehand—one elbow of his costume was torn, and, without the cushion at his waist, the red robes hung loosely. White powder still smoked from his hair and beard. I was certain that none of the children could now believe he was really me.

And yet it seemed that all of them did. Later, Layla reminded me how people of all ages usually see whatever it is they expect: "Because they so badly wanted to meet you, Santa, it didn't matter that robes were dirty or a beard was obviously dark rather than white. The boys and girls were just thrilled that Santa in any form was there for them to see and talk to and perhaps touch."

The frazzled fellow pretending to be Kris Kringle slumped on the bench and eyed the children surrounding him with the same nervousness that a mouse might have exhibited in the presence of a pack of lively cats. The boys and girls, in turn, wriggled with excitement and waited for their beloved Christmas friend to say or do something.

After perhaps two full minutes of silence, one little girl asked, "Is your name Kris Kringle or Santa Claus? I've heard people call you both."

The proper answer would have been that his name was Santa to some and Kris Kringle to others, and that either name was entirely acceptable to him, but the bruised, sooty impostor was apparently not educated enough in the history of Christmas to realize this.

"Mr. Parkinson calls me Kris Kringle," he replied. "I guess that's good enough for me."

"Where are your reindeer?" a boy wanted to know.

"I came by wagon today."

"But why not fly with the reindeer?"

"One of them had a cold."

"Which one?"

"Um." The false Kris Kringle's brow furrowed. "Remind me of their names."

I was positive the children would realize the terrible fraud being perpetrated—how could Kris Kringle or Santa Claus not remember the names of his faithful reindeer friends? Instead, they laughed in delight and started calling out "Dasher!" and "Cupid!" and "Blitzen!," all eight names in every possible order, until finally the pretender said, "It's the first one."

This vague response luckily satisfied the children on the topic of reindeer, but of course they had many more questions—about where Kris Kringle lived, how he decided which children got what toys, and, over and over, what each individual child there at Parkinson's might expect to find in his or her stocking on Christmas morning. In every instance, the fellow pretending to be me had no plausible response.

"This would be the perfect time to tell them that presents are really the least important part of Christmas," I muttered to Layla. "He should explain that the real pleasure of the holiday comes from giving thanks to God for sending Jesus and from the companionship and love of family and friends!"

And perhaps he would have said something of the sort. I doubt it, but it might have happened. Instead, J.W. suddenly burst back into the room, with package-laden parents trailing behind him.

"Boys and girls, it's time for dear Kris Kringle to return to his secret toy factory!" J.W. said. "He's most pleased to have met you, and now you must bid him farewell. When you have, you may want to visit the toy displays here to make certain your mothers and fathers know exactly what you want Kris Kringle to bring you on Christmas Eve!"

Having been expertly goaded into a frenzy of greed, all but one of the youngsters galloped away to the far side of the store, where shelves groaned under the weight of almost every toy imaginable. But one boy, a rather pale child with red hair and countless freckles, stayed where he was.

"Mr. Kringle is leaving now, sonny," J.W. said. "Wave goodbye, and go help your parents look at the toys."

The youngster didn't budge. He pulled one of the wrinkled event posters out of his pocket, along with a pencil. "I want his autograph," he said. In 1841, autograph-collecting wasn't the widespread hobby it would later become, but some people did like to ask famous individuals to sign their names as keepsakes. The fake Kris Kringle tried to inch toward the door and escape, but J.W. caught him by the elbow.

"I'm sure he'd be delighted to oblige," J.W. said, and swung the reluctant fraud back toward the boy. The child held out the poster and pencil. The impostor took them, scribbled, and handed them back. Then he rushed through a back door, with J.W. right behind.

"Gosh," the freckled boy sighed. "I got his signature."

"May I see your poster?" I asked. He handed it over. Underneath the cartoon, there was scrawled "Cris Cringle," with capital *C*s where *K*s should have been.

"The fool can't even spell!" I grumbled, and the little boy looked alarmed. Layla took the poster from me and handed it back to him, saying, "How wonderful for you! Merry Christmas!" He ran off, brandishing the paper.

Layla, Ben, Felix, Sarah, and I went out the same back door where J.W. and his impostor had exited. That unfortunate fellow had already disappeared, undoubtedly hoping to make his getaway before any more children asked awkward questions. J.W. was folding up the torn, soot-stained robes.

"I suppose the costume shop will charge me extra, since these things will have to be washed and mended," he said. "Well, Santa, the children were excited and their parents are buying almost every toy in my shop. Would you agree this was a great success?"

"Absolutely not, J.W." I said, and proceeded to tell my well-meaning friend gently but firmly about the pretend Kris Kringle's foolish answers in response to the children's questions, and how he couldn't even spell his name correctly when asked for an autograph. "Is any amount of profit worth the risk of even one child having his or her belief in Santa Claus ruined forever? Even if that didn't happen today, it could have, and it will surely happen sooner or later if you host any more of these appearances by men pretending to be me."

"What if I made certain the next Kris Kringle I hired was a better actor who knew the names of all eight reindeer?" J.W. asked. "I admit I didn't choose this first one very carefully, but next time I would know better."

"He still wouldn't be the real Santa," I said. "Look into your heart instead of your wallet, old friend. Do you truly think what you did today was right?"

J.W. looked first indignant, then sorrowful. He was, as I have noted, a decent man who loved Christmas for the best of reasons.

"You're right, Santa Claus," he said. "The fellow I hired to portray you was simply disgraceful, and it's a mercy none of the children in my store today had their belief in you ruined. You have my word that until the *real* Santa agrees to appear, I'll never attempt such a thing again."

I hugged him—after all, no lasting harm had apparently been done—and then my companions and I returned to where the reindeer were waiting. Soon afterward, we were back in Cooperstown, enjoying a delicious meal of fried chicken.

"We still need a thousand more wooden tops, and Leonardo predicts there will be snowstorms along the East Coast on Christmas Eve, but at least we don't have to worry about impostor Santas any longer," I said, finishing my fourth piece of chicken and wondering if Layla would notice me reaching for a fifth.

"Don't sound so certain," my wife responded as she moved the chicken platter just beyond my reach. "Offering the chance to meet Santa is a foolproof way for merchants to bring extra holiday customers into their shops. Some Christmas season in the future, ten stores might simultaneously present the 'real' Santa, or even a hundred. What will we do then?"

I thought for several moments before replying: "I have no idea."

Occasionally, when I believed there was cause for special concern, I did act. The best example of this came in 1931. So many poorly disguised impostors were ringing bells on street corners or pulling children onto their laps in stores that I decided it was time for everyone to know at least what Santa actually looked like.

CHAPTER

Two

 n 1843, just over a year after the disaster at J.W.'s dry-goods store, Layla and I set sail for England. Before we moved to the North Pole in 1913, my companions and I worked and lived in three different locations—Cooperstown in America, Nuremberg in Germany, and London in England. Because our gift-giving mission had grown so dramatically, it was impossible for us to maintain a single gigantic toy-making facility in secret until Leonardo da Vinci designed what he accurately described as "a self-contained environment" beneath the snows of the most isolated spot on the planet.

But prior to that, we had the three separate toy factories. Arthur was in charge in London; Attila ran the operation in Nuremberg; Felix kept an eye on things in Cooperstown; and Layla and I were free to live and work in turns at each facility.

We decided to go to London for a while because Christmas in England still had not recovered from events in the 1640s, when the king was driven from his throne. The antiholiday Puritans took control of British government and banned Christmas forever. They didn't succeed—my wonderful wife Layla had much to do with that—and by 1660 the monarchy was restored and Christmas was again a legal holiday. But much of the traditional spirit had been lost. Most English business owners insisted that their employees come to work as usual on December 25. A nation that had long loved singing carols and exchanging gifts and feasting on holiday goose and pudding now hardly celebrated Christmas at all.

So in 1843 Layla and I crossed the Atlantic Ocean. In London we encouraged a fine author named Charles Dickens to write a short holiday story he called *A Christmas Carol.* The tale of how miserly, holiday-hating Ebenezer Scrooge learned to appreciate all the wonderful things Christmas stood for warmed the hearts of everyone in England. At the same time, the young English queen Victoria married Prince Albert of Germany, and Albert, like most of his countrymen, not only loved Christmas but celebrated it in public with all his heart. He introduced Christmas trees to England; this in turn encouraged people to place gifts under them and children to hang their stockings again. As Father Christmas—this is what British children called me—I was thrilled to be part of the renewed Christmas enthusiasm that spread to every part of the nation.

Of course, I didn't lose touch with my friends back in America. The reason I was able to concentrate on fully restoring Christmas in England was that belief in Santa Claus had finally taken hold in the United States. It had been quite a tussle to bring this about—the English Puritans had originally banned celebrating Christmas in their American colonies, too—but thanks in great part to the stories of Washington Irving and *A Visit from St. Nicholas* (later known as *'Twas the Night Before Christmas*) by Clement Clark Moore, in America children and their parents gradually embraced the idea of my gift-giving mission. On Christmas Eve, Felix and my other American-based companions traveled thousands of happy miles, leaving gifts for sleeping boys and girls to discover in the morning. Now, you may wonder why I was so opposed to J. W. Parkinson hiring someone to pretend to be me, yet had no problem with my friends acting in my stead. It's quite simple: they did their good deeds at night and in secret. They did not dress up in red robes and try to trick children into believing they were Santa. Any reindeer hoofbeats detected on rooftops were, however, quite real. My flying sleigh was part of Christmas tradition in America, but not yet in other parts of the world. So Dasher and the other seven reindeer stayed in Cooperstown, and on Christmas Eve they whisked Felix through the skies in my place.

Layla and I did not hurry back to America. In our many centuries of gift-giving, we had spent a considerable amount of time in England. Because of her ultimately successful efforts to prevent Christmas from being lost to that lovely green land forever, Layla had grown to love the country in a very special way. So we spent a few extra years revisiting places that had unique meaning for us, like the old barn where we had discovered the wounded Arthur around 500 AD, and the town square in Canterbury where in 1647 Layla and ten thousand brave working-class men, women, and children defied Parliament and declared they would keep celebrating Christmas whether the Puritans in power liked it or not.

Letters from Felix back in America assured us that acceptance there of Santa Claus, as well as love for and celebration of Christmas, continued to flourish. I frowned a little when I read J. W. Parkinson was honoring the basic truth of the promise he made, but not the spirit. After 1841, he did not hire impersonators to pretend they were me. But he did annually festoon his dry-goods store with banners proclaiming that the shop was *"Kriss Kringle Headquarters"*—with the extra *s* added to "Kris," it was obvious J.W. could not spell any better than the fraud he had originally hired to portray me. I considered returning to Philadelphia to confront J.W., but I already knew how he would respond. He'd promised not to hire any more false Santas, and he hadn't. Nothing had been promised about pretending I endorsed his store by having my "headquarters" there. Such borderline deceptions are all too common,

I'm afraid. Out of obligation rather than any hope he'd change his ways, I planned to see J.W. after I returned to America and ask him again to keep any form of direct or indirect Santa endorsement out of his holiday advertising, but when Layla and I finally did sail back to the United States in the spring of 1860, we were told that J.W. had recently passed away. Since then, I have remembered him with qualified affection. He loved Christmas and he generously helped poor children have happy memories of the holiday. But he also used the joy and symbols of Christmas for his own financial benefit. Of course, he was certainly not the last to do this.

Layla and I had a lovely reunion with our friends in Cooperstown. We drank hot chocolate, took the sleigh and reindeer out for lengthy spins, and caught up on all the local and national news. Some of it was very bad, and not unexpected. The young American nation was being torn apart by racial and political strife. Many white residents of Southern states owned African-American slaves. In the Northern states, slavery was not only illegal but also considered immoral. A political compromise temporarily prevented war; new states joining the Union were alternately "free" and "slave." When pressure mounted from Northern politicians to end slavery forever, Southern leaders promised they would leave the Union rather than give up their right to own slaves if they pleased. They meant it.

All of us in Cooperstown hated the concept of slavery. Felix in particular despised the idea of any human being owning another—he knew firsthand the horror of being considered property rather than a person, since he had been a Roman slave.

Civil war did break out, and the loss of lives and destruction of property was awful. It took four years for the North, which had more citizens and manufacturing plants—which meant more soldiers and weapons— to wear down the South and free slaves in America forever. It wasn't the end of slavery everywhere in the world, sad to say. In some parts of this planet, slavery still endures in various forms. But it was eradicated in

America, and we were glad of it, though this came at such a terrible, bloody cost.

Curiously, public devotion to Santa increased during the war. A cartoonist had a great deal to do with it. Thomas Nast was the son of German immigrants to America; he arrived with his family in 1846, when he was six years old. From the time he was a teenager, Thomas wanted to draw cartoons for popular magazines. It took him several years to find much work, but like all talented, committed artists, Thomas simply kept trying until he succeeded. He joined the staff of *Harper's Weekly*, one of the most prominent publications, just as the Civil War commenced.

Thomas was immediately assigned to travel to battlegrounds and draw what he saw there, which mostly consisted of horrible scenes of carnage. The young man—still in his mid-twenties—was repelled, as he should have been, by the violence and blood. Feeling discouraged, in 1862 he was trying to think of some hopeful, happy theme he could work into his sketches of war.

By coincidence or fate, at exactly the same time Clement Moore and his poem *A Visit from St. Nicholas* were back in the news. At the age of eighty-two, Clement was asked by the New York Historical Society to provide them with a handwritten copy of the great work. *A Visit from St. Nicholas* had been printed in various newspapers every year since 1823, but on this particular occasion more people than ever wanted to read it and to learn about the wonderful man who had written it. There were more stories about the poem, and Thomas Nast read some of them.

So it was that in the 1862 holiday edition of *Harper's Weekly* Thomas Nast had an amazing cartoon of Santa as Moore had described him, complete with beard, pipe, robes, and a sleigh pulled by eight flying reindeer. The unique thing about the Nast cartoon was that it showed Santa passing out gifts to troops of the Union army. Some people felt this cartoon was inappropriate since it depicted me favoring one army over another—and, indeed, though I hated slavery I did not hate the young men who fought for the South. But mostly, people in the Northern states who read *Harper's Weekly*—and most of them did; remember, there was no television or radio yet, so everyone read when they wanted entertainment—fell in love with Santa as drawn by Nast. He immediately began drawing many more cartoons with Santa in them, most of them published at holiday time, and all of them generating widespread public comment. More people in America welcomed Santa into their lives than ever.

Because war limited our powers to move about at amazing speeds, my companions and I were not able to distribute as many gifts in America during the years 1861 to 1865. Though Nast depicted me handing out presents to Union soldiers, in fact I focused most of my efforts on sneaking through the Southern lines and bringing small gifts to slave children. It was a dangerous process, and I had several close calls, but the risk was acceptable; these innocent boys and girls desperately needed proof that they were loved for themselves, and not just valued for the labor they could provide to their masters.

When the war finally ended, I wondered if the country's fascination with Santa Claus might lessen, but it didn't. Nast's cartoons remained popular, and copies of them soon hung in homes throughout the re-united land. I was pleased by that, though not with how Nast chose to present me to the world. *His* Santa Claus was an elf, though he couldn't really be blamed for thinking I was. Clement Moore's poem did describe me as "a right jolly old elf," which gave the erroneous impression that Santa and his friends were short little creatures straight out of some imaginary fairyland. I asked Felix to go New York City, where he could find Nast and offer a private meeting with me, so the cartoonist could see I was a full-grown man. Nast also had me living and working at the North Pole, which at the time I believed would be physically impossible. I had become friends with my earlier chroniclers Washington Irving and Clement Moore, so I had no doubt Thomas Nast would prove to be a pleasant acquaintance who would correct his errors in future cartoons. But Felix reported back that Nast did not want to see me.

"He believes this would damage his artistic integrity, Santa," Felix said. "He wants you to know that he believes in you, but he says that if he met you he would lose his freedom to draw you exactly as he imagines you to be."

"Did you at least inform him I'm a man and not an elf?" I asked.

"Yes, but he said the public prefers you as an elf, and so he would continue to draw you that way."

I reluctantly accepted this. It has always been my custom to try to be whatever children wanted. That is why, in different countries, I have so many names and varying gift-giving customs. We managed to incorporate flying reindeer into our American activities because Clement Moore's poem caused so many boys and girls to believe in my sleigh and soaring steeds. But I couldn't turn into an elf. Even holiday magic has its limits.

As the nineteenth century moved along, Americans continued to love Santa, and, of course, I loved them. It was a happy time for me and my companions. One special highlight came in 1889. Layla had been an indispensable part of my mission for many centuries, but never received any credit for her efforts. Nobody who wrote about me or drew cartoons of me ever seemed to imagine that I might have a wife, let alone one who was an equal partner.

Katharine Lee Bates was a fiercely intelligent woman from the American northeast who spent much of her life proving that scholarship and writing ability was not limited to men. Miss Bates earned a master's degree in arts at a time when many women did not even have the opportunity to go to high school. She served on the faculty of several distinguished universities during a long, honorable academic career, and in the 1880s she became particularly intrigued by the whole idea of Santa Claus and Christmas gift-giving. Surely, Miss Bates thought, Santa couldn't do everything all on his own. He must have a wife, and not one who was content to stay home doing chores while her husband soared around having all the fun. So she wrote a poem about it, using some popular terms of the day, especially "goodwife." This was a way many people in the 1880s would refer to a married woman. "Goodwife" was often shortened to "goody."

The poem Miss Bates published in 1889 was titled *Goody Santa Claus on a Sleigh Ride.* It was a long, rollicking collection of verse, one that involved a great deal of colorful imagery. Taking her cue from Thomas Nast, she had my wife and me living at the North Pole, and added some whimsical details of her own. Santa and "Goody" Claus, besides making toys, presided over flocks of Thanksgiving turkeys and magical "rainbow chickens" that laid brightly colored Easter eggs. That is, Santa presided from the comfort of his favorite chair. Goody had to actually tend to the menagerie and take care of groves of Christmas trees as well.

The part Miss Bates got exactly right was that Santa's wife was not content to stay at home while her husband enjoyed the great privilege of gift-giving. How Layla laughed when she read the verse describing Goody's showdown with her husband:

You just sit there and grow chubby off the goodies in my cubby
From December to December, till your white beard sweeps your knees;
For you must allow, my Goodman, that you're but a lazy woodman
And rely on me to foster all our fruitful Christmas trees.

Goody insists that she accompany Santa on his Christmas Eve sleigh ride, and even tells him to wait once in a while on a rooftop while she goes down the chimney for a change:

Back so soon? No chimney-swallow dives but where his mate can follow
Bend your cold ear, Sweetheart Santa, down to catch my whisper faint:
Would it be so very shocking if your Goody filled a stocking
Just for once? Oh, dear! Forgive me. Frowns do not become a Saint.

When every slumbering child has had his or her stocking filled, Santa and Goody fly back to the North Pole:

Chirrup! Chirrup! There's a patter of soft footsteps and a clatter
Of Child voices. Speed it, reindeer, up the sparkling Arctic Hill!
Merry Christmas, little people! Joy-bells ring in every steeple,
And Goody's gladdest of the glad. I've had my own sweet will.

It was, and still is, a wonderful poem and caused people everywhere to start thinking of Santa as a man married to a *very* capable woman.

"Why, I believe I must meet Katharine Lee Bates," I said to Layla. "Perhaps she'd like to join our gift-giving company, though I hope she won't be too disappointed to learn we don't live at the North Pole with flocks of Easter egg–laying chickens."

"You can just stay home," Layla replied cheerfully. "Goody Claus herself is going to go see Miss Bates." She left that very day, and returned a week later to report that, though Miss Bates was a wonderful person who loved Christmas dearly, she did not want to give up writing for gift-giving.

"She says she believes she still has important work to do, Santa," Layla said, and Miss Bates was correct. Just a few years later, she felt inspired to write another poem. This one began,

Oh, beautiful for spacious skies, for amber waves of grain . . .

"America the Beautiful" was first published in 1895. Miss Bates revised it several times, and in 1910 the poem was combined with music called *Materna* by Samuel A. Ward. The resulting song, of course, has become a national standard and treasure.

Looking back, I believe that 1889 might have been the last year America enjoyed a simple, heartfelt Christmas. Santa was now a permanent part of the nation's holiday tradition. On Christmas Eve children did go to bed, as Clement Moore had predicted almost seven decades earlier, "with visions of sugarplums" dancing in their heads. Choirs strolled the streets singing carols; the essence of the holiday was appreciation for the gift of Jesus and the opportunity to extend warm good wishes to family, friends, and even strangers.

In 1890, this changed. I will not say I blame J. W. Parkinson, who was by that time long gone, and who had not meant any harm to begin with. But his hiring almost half a century earlier of a fraudulent Kris Kringle suddenly had an effect on the holiday that well-intentioned J.W. would never have expected or intended.

James Edgar was a thickset Scottish immigrant who lived in Brockton, Massachusetts. He was part owner of the Boston Store, which, like J.W.'s earlier shop, sold "sundries," things like buttons and thread and shoe polish and, yes, toys. Edgar had become quite successful, with enough money to indulge himself in an expensive hobby, which was collecting old posters. He owned hundreds, including a poster from Abraham Lincoln's first presidential campaign and one of the earliest advertisements for Buffalo Bill Cody's Wild West Show.

In early 1890, Edgar visited an antique store in Philadelphia. There he found for sale one of the posters J.W. had printed to advertise "Kris Kringle's" appearance at his store on December 18, 1841. As dozens of newspapers later reported, Edgar bought the poster, paying a dollar for it, which was a considerable sum at the time. He took it back to Brockton and hung it in his office at the Boston Store.

Now, Edgar certainly enjoyed Christmas, both for the holiday's own sake and for the extra customers who came to buy Christmas gifts at his shop. The more he looked at the old Parkinson's poster, the more he thought having "Santa" greet customers was an excellent marketing strategy. Unlike J.W., Edgar didn't hire an impersonator. He had his own long white beard and considerable waistline. On December 1, 1890,

Edgar put on red robes and announced Santa Claus had come to enter-
tain holiday shoppers at the Boston Store.

Up at the Cooperstown farm, we had no advance warning, but we
soon found out about it, as did much of the rest of the country. Unlike
1841, when there was very little way for news to spread rapidly, every
1890s town of any size had at least one newspaper that was widely read,
and major cities like Boston, which was quite near Brockton, had as
many as half a dozen. Someone tipped a reporter at one of the Boston
papers that Santa Claus himself was visiting a Brockton store and would
be there every day until Christmas! The reporter took the train to
Brockton, watched Edgar asking children what they wanted Santa to
bring them for Christmas, and wrote a long story about it that was
printed the next day, along with a sketch of the scene. Well, reporters
from all the other Boston papers felt obligated to come out and write
about this store-visiting Santa, too. This meant that, within a few days,
people all over Massachusetts and New England had read the stories. By
the time newspapers in New York and Philadelphia and other major
American cities picked up the story a few days later, there were already
long lines in front of the Boston Store from daylight until well after
dark. It was all Edgar could do to shake hands and briefly visit with
every anxious child, many of whom had traveled a long way to meet
with Santa. Parents in Providence, Rhode Island, even chartered a special train to bring hundreds of boys and girls from that city to Brockton.

I rushed from Cooperstown to see this latest pretender myself; Layla
and Felix came along. Though we arrived early in the morning, there
was already a line of waiting children that stretched for several blocks.
Because we were not accompanied by youngsters, we were able to go
right into the store, and what a sight it was! On one side there was Edgar,
resplendent in red Santa robes, sitting on a chair placed on a high platform, shuffling children on and off his lap as each leaned forward to
whisper gift requests into his ear. Mostly, the line moved briskly, though

every fourth child or so had a lengthy wish list and so needed a few extra seconds of Santa's time.

On the other side of the store were long counters displaying toys of every sort, and there was frenzied activity at those counters as well. Parents were practically shoving money in the hands of clerks who tried frantically to keep up with customer demand. All this was being observed by several well-dressed men, as well as a half-dozen other fellows in less expensive suits who were scribbling in notebooks.

"I know the men with the notebooks must be newspaper reporters, but who are the men standing next to them?" I whispered to Felix. He didn't know, but Layla thought she did.

"They must be owners of other local shops," she said. "It's obvious that having Santa appear greatly boosts holiday toy sales. You know what that means, of course."

When I said I didn't, she told me: "Within the next few days, there will be a Santa greeting children in every big store in Brockton and Boston, and perhaps in shops all over the country. When one merchant has an idea that works, it's copied by competitors."

"Surely not," I scoffed. "It's working out well in this instance because Edgar looks so natural, so Santa-like, with his white beard."

"And he's fat," Felix added, perhaps intending to be helpful.

"But there can't be that many Santa impersonators who really look and act the part," I said. "No self-respecting store owner would insult Christmas and risk disappointing children with an obvious impostor." Even as I spoke, I knew I was indulging in wishful thinking.

Layla was right. In the few weeks between Edgar's first appearance as Santa and Christmas Eve 1890, stores all over America began advertising appearances by Santa Claus. It happened everywhere, not just in Brockton and Boston. I can't be more specific about how often because we stopped counting after reaching two hundred. All over the country, the number of stores with pretend Santas continued to multiply every year after that.

In a few isolated cases, the impostors were, like Edgar, at least physically appropriate to the role. Any child tugging one of their beards was rewarded with a handful of real white whiskers. A few of the false Santas at least took the time to learn Christmas history, so they could intelligently answer questions from their young admirers. But so many of these men were unsuitable. All the red robes and *ho-ho-ho*ing in the world could not make them convincing. They might wear droopy fake beards, or become cross with boys and girls who didn't act exactly as they wanted, or, worst of all, tell trusting young believers that Santa would only bring them toys from a specific store.

Within a few years, there was a predictable result. Many children began to believe that Santa Claus must not even exist. How could he, when every Christmas they saw dozens of different "Santas," all looking and acting differently, each claiming to be the real person?

Some still managed to trust their hearts rather than their eyes. In 1897, a lovely eight-year-old girl named Virginia O'Hanlon wrote to the *New York Sun* asking if there really was a Santa Claus. A wonderful editor named Francis Church replied that "Yes, Virginia, there is a Santa Claus. He exists as certainly as love and generosity and devotion exist, and you know how they abound and give to your life its highest beauty and joy." Though he did not say so specifically, I believe Mr. Church was referring to the difference between pretenders in costume and me when he added, "Nobody sees Santa Claus, but that is no sign that there is no Santa Claus. The most real things in the world are those that neither children nor men can see . . ."

It was a perfect response, one that was reprinted and repeated all over the country. Virginia was reassured, and, by reading her letter and Mr. Church's reply, countless other boys and girls were as well. But the exchange between Virginia and Mr. Church could not in any way prevent or even postpone what a few generations later would be known as "the commercialization" of Christmas. Drawings of "Santa" began to appear in product advertisements. Supposedly I was now endorsing everything from soap flakes to hand tools. It was ironic that I had spent so many years wondering if America would ever accept Santa at all, and now I was afraid that I was too much a part of holiday commerce rather than heartfelt Christmas celebration.

"I remember, during my first days with the Pilgrims at Plymouth Rock, that I hoped one day even a few people in America would know my name and allow me to be part of their Christmas happiness," I said to Layla one night as we sat together in my study. It was 1913, and we'd just moved all our operations to the North Pole. We were still adjusting to the long nights there in the winter, where the sun never comes out.

"I have heard a saying about being careful what you wish for," Layla replied. "Considering how hard you've worked so people would know about you at all, aren't you at least in some way pleased that everyone in America seems to think about you during the holidays?"

"It's not *that* they think of me, but *how* they think of me," I said. "Until now, whether I was known as Santa or Kris Kringle or Father Christmas or any of dozens of other wonderful names, my gifts were understood to be symbols of caring, gestures of love. Now children are making up long lists of things they specifically want, instead of gladly receiving whatever Santa has brought them. I don't blame the boys and girls; adults who own stores and create advertising campaigns are encouraging them to act this way. Christmas is perhaps being celebrated more enthusiastically than ever, but now there's something calculating about it. I'm afraid the sweetness of the original holiday, the innocence, is being lost."

"Well, what do you intend to do about it?" Layla asked. "Sitting here complaining won't change anything."

"I think that, beyond continuing our mission, there's very little we *can* do," I said. "Even if I came forward and presented myself as the real Santa, I'd only be taken for one more impostor. This is all very frustrating, but we'll simply carry on and hope that things change again, this time for the better."

And, for nearly another hundred years, this is what we did. I don't mean to make it sound as though Christmas in America became all bad, or even close to it. There were still many, many adults who remembered the real reason for the holiday and who taught children that Santa symbolized love and sharing rather than grabbing and getting.

Occasionally, when I believed there was cause for special concern, I did act. The best example of this came in 1931. So many poorly disguised impostors were ringing bells on street corners or pulling children onto their laps in stores that I decided it was time for everyone to at least know what Santa actually looked like. The Coca-Cola company was planning a series of holiday printed advertisements for its soft drinks featuring "Santa." Artist Haddon "Hans" Sundblom was hired to paint the portraits. I left the North Pole to find Mr. Sundblom; when I did, I volunteered to be his model. He immediately realized who I was, and we became fast friends. He drew Coca-Cola's "Santa" ads for thirty-five years, and during that time always told anyone who asked that a retired salesman named "Les Prentice" posed for him. The Coca-Cola ads were a sensation, and, as I hoped, caused more employers to insist their pseudo-Santas at least looked the part.

There was another occasion when commercial efforts evolved into wonderful Christmas traditions. Few people today remember that "Rudolph the Red-Nosed Reindeer" was originally conceived in 1939 as a holiday advertisement for Montgomery Ward. But children and grown-ups alike fell in love with the story, and by 1949, when popular cowboy singer Gene Autry recorded a splendid Christmas carol—also titled "Rudolph the Red-Nosed Reindeer"—America had a new Christmas icon, though, unlike me, one that wasn't part of actual history. There was some consternation at the North Pole—Leonardo tried and failed to find or create a red-nosed flying reindeer—but we eventually decided Rudolph, who bravely struggled to prove himself to "all the other reindeer," was a worthy addition to Christmas lore. His never-give-up spirit was inspiring in the best holiday tradition.

There was another positive change. In the 1960s and '70s, even as so-called "shopping malls"—dozens, sometimes even hundreds of stores all located in single huge structures—began to appear, there also emerged several companies whose sole job it was to provide well-trained, more believable "Santas" to these gigantic malls during the holidays. This drastically reduced the number of pretenders who were presented to trusting children while wearing scraggly fake beards or drooping, pillow-stuffed paunches. I still wished the practice of hiring performers to portray me had never been initiated, but most of the malls had enough responsibility to ensure their fake Santas at least looked and acted authentic.

So the years passed, and it seemed, for a while, that the commercialization of the holiday in America had expanded as far as it could from its bumbling origins in 1841 at J. W. Parkinson's dry-goods store. Then, not many years after the beginning of the twenty-first century, one December day Felix returned to the North Pole from a trip to New York City and said he had to speak to me right away.

But the wild-haired man said, "Oh, there's no need to rush off, Miss Hathaway. We have some time before our meeting is supposed to start. Perhaps these nice people might like to join us for hot chocolate. They're selling some over there on the other side of the rink." He grasped Sarah's and Felix's arms and began steering them away.

Three

elix and Sarah Kemble Knight had married in 1994, following a two-and-a-half-century courtship. I was delighted that two of my dearest friends had found happiness together; besides Layla and me, they were the one of the very few married couples among our fellowship.

Accordingly, Layla insisted afterward that each year Felix and Sarah enjoy at least one short vacation together. She told them not to do North Pole–related work while they were away. "It's good for any husband and wife," she explained to me after we waved goodbye to Felix and Sarah as they departed on a trip to Tibet to celebrate their first anniversary. "While it's wonderful that all of us have been together for so long, it's also appropriate for a couple to occasionally have some time to be away by themselves. Don't you agree?"

Having been a married man myself for some sixteen centuries, I knew when it was in my best interest to agree with my wife completely.

"Yes, dear," I said.

"Do you happen to remember the last time *we* took a vacation to-gether?" Layla continued.

I frantically searched my memory. "Not *that* long ago," I muttered. "Surely no more than a dozen years, or perhaps twenty."

"Try almost two centuries," my wife said. She sounded exasperated. "In 1818 we went to Oberndorf in Austria to enjoy Christmas midnight mass at the Church of St. Nicholas, and while we were there we helped the priest and church organist compose 'Silent Night.'"

"And what a lovely song it was!" I exclaimed, hoping Layla's warm memory of that special moment might overcome her obvious irritation with me. It didn't.

"It would be very nice," she said, "if we had another vacation, just the two of us."

"It certainly would," I replied. "We'll have to do that."

"When?"

"Soon, I'm sure," I said, and I truly meant it. But there were always reasons I couldn't get away. Perhaps Leonardo and Ben and Willie Skokan had just invented new toys that needed thorough testing, or else I was urgently required to meet with the leader of some country whose government wanted help planning national Christmas celebrations. Layla would sigh and ask me to promise we'd definitely take a trip the next year, and meanwhile she made certain Felix and Sarah regularly enjoyed short vacations together.

On this particular trip, they'd left for New York City right after we'd finished our gift-giving in many parts of Europe on December 6, which is Saint Nicholas Day. There was an eighteen-day interim before Christmas Eve; all the necessary toys had been made, and so it was good for Felix and Sarah to relax a little in between those two special, but hectic, nights.

One of the lovely holiday traditions in New York is the display of a giant Christmas tree at Rockefeller Center. The custom had begun in 1933 and each year, it seemed, the tree was taller and decorated with more dazzling, multicolored lights. Every year the tree was at least eighty feet high, and occasionally it was a hundred. Its mighty branches extended as much as forty-one feet, and each Christmas the tree sparkled with a minimum of thirty thousand bulbs connected by five miles of wire. In all, this was a sight to gladden the heart of anyone who loved Christmas, as Felix and Sarah surely did. It had been decades since they'd last been to New York City to see the tree, so on December 7 they left the North Pole on dogsled and traveled to a railroad station hundreds of miles away. From there they continued by train into New York City, where they planned to stay for a few days to see the Rockefeller Center tree and happily stroll hand-in-hand along wide, snowy Manhattan avenues, taking in all the amazing holiday displays in store windows before returning to the North Pole and joining in final preparations for our Christmas Eve gifting-giving.

So I'd anticipated their return. It did surprise me that Felix wanted us to talk the moment he arrived. When friends have known each other for so many centuries, there usually is no hurry to catch up on each other's news.

"Surely this can wait until after dinner, Felix," I suggested. "I happen to know Lars, our chef, has prepared one of his special chocolate cakes for dessert."

"This is more important than cake, Santa," Felix replied, and I knew instantly that whatever he wanted to tell me was critical. In the seventeen hundred years we'd been together, there were very few things my overweight friend had ever considered more important than cake. It was one of the things we had in common. So I asked him to follow me to my cozy den, where a warm blaze crackled in the fireplace. Sarah came with us, and Layla, too. My wife and I settled back into chairs and waited for our friends to tell us their news. They scrunched together on the overstuffed sofa, wringing their hands and appearing rather nervous.

"Goodness, why do you look so worried?" I asked. "I can't remember the last time either of you seemed so upset!"

"It may be that there isn't any cause for concern, Santa," Sarah said. "But we had a conversation with someone we met in New York that you should know about. Something very serious might be happening."

"Something that affects you, and Christmas," Felix added. "Like J. W. Parkinson, I'm certain Bobbo Butler doesn't *mean* any harm, but still—"

"Bobo?" I interrupted. "What sort of name is that?"

"Not *BOW*-bow," Felix corrected. "It's pronounced *BAH*-bow. For Bob O. Bob O. Butler. That's his name, and he gets upset if it's pronounced incorrectly."

"That's whose name, Felix?" Layla asked.

"Bob O. Butler is a man we met in New York City, right in front of the ice-skating rink at Rockefeller Center," Sarah said. "We went there to see the magnificent Christmas tree, of course, and they were having this special skating program at the rink beside it. The program was being sponsored by the LastLong Toy Company." Layla and I groaned when she mentioned the toy manufacturer. At the North Pole we were all completely dedicated to crafting quality toys that would hold up for years of nonstop play, but LastLong's widely assorted products were always shoddily made and usually broke instantly upon use by children. The company spent millions of dollars each year on advertising, making their wagons and dollhouses and bicycles sound like things no child in America could do without. LastLong's promotions were every bit as catchy and effective as their products were terrible. Each year, the company sold twice as many toys as its closest competitor. In our snowbound workshops, any time we accidentally produced a substandard toy that wobbled when it should have rolled or flopped when it should have bounced, we'd cry out in unison, "Now, *there's* a LastLong toy!" But, inexplicably, the company thrived.

"It seems LastLong has a new line of ice skates," Felix explained. "There were banners everywhere advertising them. They read, '*Skate Like a Champion with LastLong*,' and some of the most famous skaters in the world like Michelle Kwan and Scott Hamilton and Kristi Yamaguchi were gliding around the Rockefeller Center rink on LastLong skates."

"What a treat for you to be there to see them!" Layla exclaimed. Ever since we'd been at the North Pole, she'd grown very fond of ice-skating, since we often needed skates or snowshoes for our occasional evening strolls outside. Without false modesty, we all believe the ice skates we make at the North Pole are the finest anywhere, and they're certainly among the gifts from us most requested by children. "Weren't you impressed with how well they could skate?"

"Actually, I felt sorry for them," Felix said. "Like all their other products, LastLong skates don't. Last long, I mean. The blades kept breaking off and all the famous skaters would fall down. And there was such a big crowd gathered around to watch, too. The whole thing was rather embarrassing. You'd think this would have convinced parents not to buy those skates for their children, but LastLong had a sales booth set up beside the rink and there were huge lines there afterward. Their advertising is so good, Santa. They know just how to make people think they have to have their products."

"Well, that's a shame, but we can't force parents to demonstrate good judgment regarding the toys and athletic gear they buy their children," I said. "Thank you for bringing this to my attention, Felix and Sarah, but we already knew LastLong toys were terrible. Shall we go in to dinner now? If we don't hurry, all the chocolate cake might be gone."

"I don't think the faulty skates were what Sarah and Felix wanted to tell us about," Layla observed. "They want to report their conversation with this man named Bobbo Butler."

Reluctantly—I could just *taste* Lars's delicious Hot Chocolate Cake, which was somehow spicy and sweet at the same time—I sat back down in my chair. "What did Bobbo—did I pronounce it right?—say that concerns you?" I asked.

Felix took a deep breath, which was always a sign that he had a great deal to say. I could forget dinner, and especially dessert, for some time.

It all started, my oldest friend explained, during the skating exhibition where the great champions took falls when their LastLong skates broke.

"They had attracted quite a big crowd, of course," Felix said. "The rink itself is not very large, and people were packed in on all sides. No one was in danger of being crushed, but everyone was jostled at least a little."

Felix had put his arm around Sarah so they wouldn't accidentally be separated. On the other side of his wife, he'd noticed an odd-looking pair who were jammed together, too. The man was of medium height, and quite wiry. He had a prominent, hooked nose and a fringe of dark hair circling an otherwise bald scalp—this hair bristled out in every direction. The woman was tall, extremely so, certainly several inches above six feet. While her companion had his eyes glued on the rink, she seemed determined to protect him from being bumped by anyone. At one point, she reached out with her left hand to gently prevent Sarah and Felix from being knocked off-balance into the short man with the wild fringe of hair. My North Pole friends nodded their thanks; the woman smiled and nodded back. Once or twice during the rest of the short program, her eyes met those of Sarah or Felix. Soon they were exchanging grins and waggling eyebrows in mock wonder at all the famous skaters who lurched on faulty skates.

The wild-haired man never looked at Felix or Sarah—or at anything or anyone else—until the program was over. Then, as the crowd thinned, he suddenly glanced at them and said, "Quite a show, don't you think? And entertaining, though not in the way the skaters wanted."

"I think it was the fault of the equipment rather than the skaters," Sarah pointed out.

"I know!" the fellow exclaimed. "LastLong Toys my, well, *foot.* They're junk, is what they are!"

"I wish they would go out of business," Felix said.

The other man's eyes widened. "Well, *I* don't," he replied. "They may make junk, but it's profitable junk, and I need them to sponsor my programs."

The tall woman looked alarmed. "We really don't need to talk about this, chief," she said hurriedly. "Program sponsors, you know, and specific company names, and . . . *junk*." She smiled at Sarah and Felix and said, "I'm so sorry if we jostled you. Happy holidays."

But the wild-haired man said, "Oh, there's no need to rush off, Miss Hathaway. We have some time before our meeting is supposed to start. Perhaps these nice people might like to join us for hot chocolate. They're selling some over there on the other side of the rink." He grasped Sarah's and Felix's arms and began steering them away. "I like to get out and talk to the public. I want to hear what you've got to say."

"Say about what?" Felix asked.

"Television, of course," the man replied. "Let's get our hot chocolate and sit down over by those tables. It's cold out, but not too cold. You'll be warm enough, won't you, if you've got the hot chocolate?"

"I'm *sure* these nice people have shopping to do, chief," Miss Hathaway protested, trailing after the other three.

"No, we're fine," Sarah said. In the centuries she and Felix had been part of our globe-spanning mission, they'd met lots of quirky, interesting people and usually enjoyed the experience.

So the man bought four cups of hot chocolate and pulled Sarah and Felix over to a nearby table, leaving Miss Hathaway to pay the vendor. When she got to the table, he discovered they had no napkins, and asked her to go find some. After that, he noticed they had no spoons to stir their drinks, and requested that she get those, too. He did not make these requests in any mean-spirited or even bossy way. His matter-of-fact tone indicated he was in the habit of asking, and expecting, her to perform these small tasks as part of an everyday routine.

"Ah, that Heather Hathaway," he said as she hurried off in search of spoons. "I can't tell her this because then she'd probably want a raise, but she's the best personal assistant any TV-network president ever had." He gave Sarah and Felix a sharp look over the top of his cardboard cup, trying to see if they were impressed.

More out of courtesy than astonishment—after all, she was close friends with such luminaries as Ben Franklin, Theodore Roosevelt, and Leonardo da Vinci, not to mention Santa Claus—Sarah politely responded, "A television-network president? Are you really?"

The fellow nodded. "Bob O. Butler. You can call me Bobbo. Not *BOW*-bow, mind. *BAH*-bow. That's how my friends know me, and I can tell you're both my friends." He said this with the same absolute certainty that a puppy demonstrates in thinking everyone he meets wants to play with him.

"We're pleased to meet you, Mr. Butler. Excuse me—I mean, Bobbo," Sarah replied. "I'm Sarah, and this is my husband Felix."

"Glad to make your acquaintance," Bobbo said. "Tell me, how old are you?"

Now, this struck my friends as odd. "I beg your pardon?" Sarah asked.

"Your ages are important to me," Bobbo replied, impatiently gesturing for his assistant to put the spoons she'd just fetched on the table, and to sit down herself. "Take out your notebook, Miss Hathaway. We may hear something important. Don't want to tell me how old you are? Can I try to guess? I'm very good at this. You, Sarah, are just about in your mid-thirties. Right? Of course, I'm right." He mistook Sarah's sudden wide smile for corroboration. Actually, she was smiling because she had just celebrated her 342nd birthday. We all like to think we look younger than we really are, and Sarah was pleased to have this proof. Then Bobbo turned his attention to Felix. "Now, you, my friend, have a few more years on you than your wife. I'd say, what—forty-two?"

During Felix's early life no one kept exact track of when slaves were born. He had no idea how old he was, only that he was at least seventeen hundred.

"Close enough, Bobbo," he replied. "What a good guesser you are."

"I have to be, in my job," Bobbo said. "Now, I want to know more. Felix, what do you do for a living?"

In modern times, our fellowship had developed a safe, traditional answer to this inquiry. "I'm a consultant," Felix said. "I work in manufacturing. Around the holidays I'm mostly involved in distribution." This description, though vague, was certainly accurate. All of us tried never to lie.

Bobbo wasn't done asking questions. Did Sarah and Felix have children? "No." Favorite hobbies? "Crafts and world travel." Miss Hathaway jotted down all these answers. Hometown? "We've moved a lot. Right now we live up north."

"Ah," said Bobbo. "You're from Boston."

"Why are you asking us all these things, Bobbo?" Sarah asked. "I know it's natural to be curious about new friends, but this is almost more an interrogation than a conversation."

"Demographics, Sarah," Bobbo replied, tossing out the word like they must certainly be familiar with it. The puzzled expressions on their faces convinced him they weren't. "In the television business, we try to know as much about every segment of the general public as possible. Where people live, what they do to earn their livings, what their hobbies are, especially how old they are—these are the things that help us decide what programs to put on the air. Each show is specifically created to please certain types of people; we pay to produce and broadcast our programs by selling commercial time to sponsors who want to bring the attention of the same market audience to their products. I hope that isn't too complicated an explanation."

"It isn't," Felix said. "To pay for your programs, you need sponsors. To get sponsors, you have to have the right audiences watching your programs."

"Exactly!" Bobbo exclaimed. Then his grin turned into a grimace. "Recently, I'm afraid, my network hasn't been succeeding as well as it once did. Now, I'm sure you've enjoyed many of our wonderful shows over the years. You do watch FUN, don't you?"

"Fun?" Felix asked, sounding puzzled, which he was. "How do you watch *fun?*"

"No, F-U-N," Bobbo said. "That's the name of our network. FUN-TV. It stands for Family Ultimate Network. That's been our special demographic. For decades we've produced wholesome shows that families can watch together—parents, children, grandparents, different generations gathered together in front of their televisions enjoying programs that never include anything sordid or violent or what kids today call *gross.*"

"That's very admirable, Bobbo," Sarah said.

"It may be admirable, but in recent years it hasn't been working very well," Bobbo sighed, and from the corner of her eye Sarah saw Heather Hathaway's eyes glisten suddenly with unshed, sympathetic tears. "Tell me, folks, what programs on FUN-TV have you seen lately?"

"None, I'm afraid," Felix said. "Don't take it personally, Bobbo. We never actually watch television."

"Of course you do," Bobbo snapped. "Everybody does. It's a fact."

"I'm sorry, but it isn't," Felix replied.

"Well, what do you do at night?"

"We enjoy visiting with old friends," Felix said. "Now, we often watch DVD movies. But we really don't watch television *shows* as such. The few times we've tried, there haven't been many programs that seemed to be worth our time."

"Exactly!" barked Bobbo. "People like you have been driven away from television by all that awful *reality* programming that's saturating the TV industry!" That wasn't precisely what Felix had told him, but Bobbo was obviously a man who heard what he wanted to hear. "The ones who watch it now want spectacle, not quality entertainment. What's involved in a modern-day hit show? Why, people pretending to be stranded on a desert island! People singing badly and being made fun of for doing it! People eating *bugs*! Yuck!" He was quite distressed; Miss Hathaway leaned over, patted him on the back, and had him take a sip of hot chocolate.

"He gets very upset when he thinks about this," she whispered.

Bobbo gulped a little more hot chocolate. "Holiday programming was always the most-watched part of our broadcast year," he said. "Our ratings doubled every other network's—heck, *tripled* 'em. Parents and children would wait all year to see whatever Christmas specials we'd have on FUN-TV. And we had some great ones, like our remake of *A Christmas Carol* starring Bob Hope as Scrooge and Bing Crosby as Marley's ghost. You must have seen that one. Millions did."

"Sorry," Felix said.

"Ah, well. Everything was fine until about ten years ago, when that so-called 'reality TV' got started. I believed it would never catch on. I mean, nobody was really going to starve on that *un*deserted island. For heaven's sake, they had a whole *camera crew* right there with them. But for some reason that kind of silly show got popular, and families stopped watching TV together because older people were disgusted with the programming. They could watch movies on DVD instead, like you two do. That left kids as the big audience, though not younger ones, because their parents wouldn't *let* them watch unsuitable shows. So it was down to the teenagers, who want to act cool and *not* watch family programming in favor of the nastier stuff, and so sponsors stopped buying many commercials on FUN-TV and things have been terrible for us since."

"That's actually why we're at Rockefeller Center today," Miss Hathaway added. "We still have commercial time to sell for our Christmas special this year, and we're hoping the LastLong Toy Company might buy some of it. They've got these new skates of theirs, though apparently they're not very good ones."

"Oh, that's because the heels of the skates above the blades are too short," Felix said. "To provide enough support for the foot and the blade, the heel on any ice skate has to be one and a half inches long. To save on production costs, I suppose, these skates of LastLong's appear to have only three-quarter-inch heels, which throws off the weight of the skater, puts too much pressure on the blade, and so the blade snaps and the skater falls. It's very obvious."

Bobbo Butler stared at Felix. "Now, how would you know a thing like that?"

"I've designed and built some ice skates in my time," Felix said. "All kinds of toys, too. The LastLong products are junk because the company cuts corners on materials, plus they're shoddily put together. They could manufacture fine toys if they wanted to, but clearly they don't."

"He's a toy expert, Miss Hathaway," Bobbo remarked. "You don't meet many of those at the Rockefeller Center skating rink. Well, it's been grand, folks, but Miss Hathaway and I have a meeting in a few minutes with Lucretia Pepper, the LastLong company president. Their headquarters is near Rockefeller Center. She hasn't bought advertising on FUN in years, but we're hoping she'll like the concept of this year's Christmas special."

"What is it about, Bobbo?" Sarah asked.

"We're calling it *Merry Monkey*. A monkey in the Central Park Zoo suddenly understands the spirit of Christmas and spends Christmas Eve distributing gifts to all the other animals there. We're using real animals, not cartoon or computer-generated ones. Do you like it?" Bobbo asked anxiously.

"It's certainly unique," Sarah said carefully.

"Well, it's the best we can do on a limited budget," Bobbo said. "The cost of renting monkeys has just skyrocketed. But maybe Lucretia Pepper will like it. I wish I had something better to tell her about."

"In the middle 1800s, toy monkeys were among the most popular Christmas gifts for children in France and Germany," Felix said. "It was one of the first times in history that material was sewn to look like animals. Before that, the stuffed toys children received for Christmas had mostly been dolls shaped like humans. Maybe you could do your special about toy monkeys in Christmas history. That would be interesting."

Bobbo had stood up, preparing to leave with Miss Hathaway for his meeting with Lucretia Pepper. Now he sat slowly down again.

"You're a toy expert *and* a Christmas expert? I wish I'd met you before we put *Merry Monkey* into production. It's too late to change the show now. But can I have your phone number, please? If FUN-TV can keep going, I'd like to have you consult on our next holiday special."

Sarah shot her husband a warning glance, but Felix had always been happy, even eager, to offer advice to anyone who asked and many who hadn't. Some years earlier Leonardo had insisted that all of us at the North Pole carry individual cell phones. It made it easier to stay in touch. Except for certain world leaders and a few other trusted friends who didn't live at the North Pole, we'd never given out the numbers before, certainly not to someone who was still almost a total stranger. Felix had taken a great liking to Bobbo Butler, though, and before Sarah could stop him he recited his cell-phone number. Without being asked, Heather Hathaway copied it down for her boss.

"If you want to start thinking about it, I've decided that next Christmas we're going to have to take a crack at reality TV ourselves," Bobbo said. "There's got to be some form of it that's family-friendly, that parents and young children *and* teenagers would all want to watch. I just need one can't-miss holiday show, one that pulls a huge demographic, and then I'm sure FUN-TV's reputation would be restored and people would start watching our wholesome programs again. Then we'll be beating sponsors off instead of going to them to practically beg, like I have to do right now at LastLong Toys. Reality TV and Christmas, though—that's a difficult combination."

Having told this much of the story, and having taken so very long doing it that every crumb of Lars's chocolate cake had certainly been gobbled up by the rest of our fellowship, Felix now began to fidget on the couch in my North Pole den. It was obvious he didn't want to tell me the rest of what happened with Bobbo Butler. We all sat for a moment in uncomfortable silence until Sarah finally said, "Go ahead, Felix. Tell Santa."

"Why don't *you* tell him?" Felix asked plaintively. But Sarah gave him a stern look. He sighed and said, "Remember, I didn't mean any harm."

"It's all right, Felix," Layla said soothingly. "I'm sure this is something we need to hear."

"Well," Felix said, looking everywhere but at me, "Bobbo said again that he had to be going to his meeting. He double-checked my cell-phone number and said he would be in touch soon. Miss Hathaway told him they had to start for Lucretia Pepper's office right away if they didn't want to be late."

"Go on," I said, though Felix so obviously didn't want to.

"Bobbo looked so sad," Felix said. "You would have pitied him, too. Anyway, he told us that he would give anything to have just one great idea for a Christmas reality-TV special, anything that would let his network survive and keep on producing programs for families. And that's when I said, well—"

I have loved Felix dearly for going on eighteen centuries, but sometimes he can be so exasperating.

"Great heavens, man, tell me what you said!" I urged. Though Layla later told me I did, I'm sure I didn't shout. I just sounded definite.

Felix grimaced. "What I said to Bobbo was, 'Well, it's Christmas. Maybe Santa Claus will bring you a wonderful reality-TV idea.' And all of a sudden his eyes lit up and he whooped out loud. Miss Hathaway jumped a foot, she was so startled. 'That might be it!' Bobbo shouted. He really yelled. People all around us were staring."

"Bobbo grabbed Felix and gave him a great big hug," Sarah added. "He said to Felix, 'You're a genius! Even if Lucretia Pepper doesn't like *Merry Monkey,* she's going to love my new plan for next Christmas!' Felix asked him, 'What plan is that?,' but Bobbo said he needed time to fine-tune the premise, whatever that means. He went racing off, dragging Miss Hathaway behind him. He called back to Felix that he'd be in touch soon, and that next Christmas FUN-TV would jump all the way back to the top of the ratings."

Layla and I exchanged glances. There was obviously the very real possibility of disaster here, though it was impossible to know what form it might take.

"Bobbo Butler didn't say anything else, Felix?" I asked. "Nothing more about Santa Claus and this reality-TV program he wants to produce for next Christmas?"

"No, not a word," Felix said, trying to sound hopeful. "He and Miss Hathaway disappeared into the crowd. Who knows? By now he might have forgotten whatever it is he thought of."

I hoped he had. We went ahead with all our preparations for Christmas Eve, and on the night of December 24 we recorded the FUN-TV special *Merry Monkey* while we were out circling the globe and delivering gifts to boys and girls everywhere. Of course, all of us were tired when we returned to the North Pole as dawn broke on Christmas Day, and so we went to bed. It wasn't until December 26 that we gathered in front of a widescreen television to watch Bobbo Butler's holiday program. To be honest, it wasn't very good. The monkey in the starring role kept eating the wrapping paper on his gifts instead of handing them through cage bars to the other animals in the Central Park Zoo.

But at the end of the program—which had, by the way, no commercials sponsored by LastLong Toys—Bobbo Butler himself appeared to speak directly to the audience. Even before his name flashed onscreen, I knew who he must be. Felix and Sarah had very accurately described his wild fringe of dark hair, otherwise bald head, and obvious eagerness to please.

"Folks, if you've stuck around to watch the conclusion of *Merry Monkey*, all of us at FUN-TV truly appreciate it," he said. "We know that every Christmas Eve you've got a wide variety of programs to choose from. That's why we're so proud to make this announcement a whole year in advance."

Bobbo took a deep breath. So did all of us watching at the North Pole. Then he continued:

"Next year, right here on FUN-TV, we will proudly join with Last-Long Toy Company to bring you the most wonderful holiday special ever, and perhaps the first reality-TV show that's really suitable for the whole family. You'll hear more details in the months ahead, but for now, plan to keep two hours on Christmas Eve reserved for the show that everyone will want to watch on December 24, the show everyone will talk about for years afterward. One year from tonight, folks, right here on FUN-TV, it will be . . ."

Bobbo paused for emphasis.

"It will be . . . *The Great Santa Search*!" And with that, FUN-TV signed off for the night.

All of us at the North Pole spent the rest of December 26 and all of December 27 wondering what *The Great Santa Search* might be about.

Then on December 28, Felix's cell phone rang. Heather Hathaway was calling. She said Bobbo Butler wanted to see him right away in New York City.

Like Heather Hathaway, this woman was tall; unlike Bobbo's personal assistant, she was wide as well, with the menacing heft of a rhinoceros that might at any moment decide to charge. Her short, stiffly coiffed hair was as hard as a helmet. Makeup was caked thick on her face; it was impossible to tell her age.

Four

 eather Hathaway was a striking woman for reasons other than her great height. In her early thirties, she had dark, expressive eyebrows that were in constant motion, sometimes knitted in deep thought and at other times arched in surprise. She kept her brown hair pulled back in a long ponytail that always had some strands escaping. Being quite a busy person, and constantly preoccupied with keeping the erratic Bobbo Butler on schedule, she rarely smiled. But when she did smile, her whole face lit up, as it did when she greeted Felix on December 29 as he arrived at the FUN-TV offices in New York City.

"Thanks so much for coming!" she said, taking Felix's overcoat and hanging it neatly in a closet. "Bobbo has been excited ever since he met you, and you gave him that wonderful idea for our next Christmas special!"

"What idea was that?" Felix asked. He was very nervous. When Bobbo had summoned him the day before, Felix begged not to go to the meeting alone. He wanted me to come, too, or at least Sarah. But the rest of us agreed Bobbo was more likely to reveal everything about this mysterious *Great Santa Search* if there were fewer people around. Felix was charged with finding out everything he could and then promptly reporting back to the rest of us at the North Pole.

"Oh, I'm going to let the chief tell you the details himself," Miss Hathaway replied. "Go right through that door. They're waiting for you." Before Felix had time to ask who *they* might be, she was whisking him into a paneled conference room where Bobbo and a gargantuan woman were seated at a heavy rectangular table. Like Heather Hathaway, this woman was tall; unlike Bobbo's personal assistant, she was wide as well, with the menacing heft of a rhinoceros that might at any moment decide to charge. Her short, stiffly coiffed hair was as hard as a helmet. Makeup was caked thick on her face; it was impossible to tell her age. She might have been forty or fifty or even a well-preserved sixty. After dismissing Heather Hathaway with a curt nod, she stood and extended a heavily jeweled hand for Felix to shake. He tried not to flinch.

"I am Lucretia Pepper, president of LastLong Toys," she announced in the same self-confident tone a queen might use to identify the country she ruled. "And you must be Felix, the genius my old friend Bobbo has been telling me about!" Though her words were warm and her smile was wide, her eyes remained cold, and her voice bothered Felix most of all. It was curiously high-pitched, even childlike, not at all in keeping with her hulking appearance.

"Pleased to meet you," Felix said, grimacing as her hand squeezed his hard. "Hello, Bobbo."

Bobbo waited until Lucretia Pepper had released Felix's hand and sat down again before he stood and shook hands, too. His grip seemed almost feathery compared to hers.

"It's a treat to see you again, Felix," Bobbo said. "I think you're going be impressed with what we've got to tell you, and we hope you'll want to be part of *The Great Santa Search* team."

"Well, I'd certainly like to hear more about it," Felix replied, and sat down himself. We had instructed him to speak as little as possible, which, for Felix, was always a challenge. But we hadn't factored in the presence of Lucretia Pepper.

"I'd first like to learn more about your own background, Felix," she said. "I'm sure you understand that Bobbo and I must know potential associates better before we share confidential plans with them." She looked pointedly at Bobbo, waiting until he nodded nervously before returning her gaze to Felix. Clearly, their partnership was not one between equals. "How did you become an expert in both toys and Christmas history?"

"I've always loved the holiday, and I tried to learn as much about it as I could," Felix said, struggling to keep his voice from shaking. Lucretia Pepper had fixed him with a steely stare, and it made my old friend even more nervous. "As far as toys, well, I've built more than my share."

"Really?" she asked, tilting her huge head forward. "What company did you build them for?"

"Oh, quite a few," Felix replied, keeping his response intentionally vague. "I've always preferred consulting to working in just one place. I've spent lots of time on the job in Europe and Asia Minor as well as in America. Really, I'd prefer to talk about this *Great Santa Search* idea. I'm sure it must be fascinating."

Just for a moment, Lucretia Pepper's smile faded. When she frowned, it was easy to imagine storm clouds puffing out of her ears and lightning shooting from her eyes. She was clearly used to controlling conversations. But then the massive woman rearranged her lips back into a smile.

"Of course, Felix," she said. "You're quite direct. I respect that. Bobbo, won't you enlighten our friend?"

Bobbo jumped to his feet. "It was what you said about Santa Claus bringing me a wonderful idea for a reality-TV show," he declared. "I immediately thought, 'Why not a Christmas Eve reality show with Santa Claus in it?' The problem, of course, is that Santa Claus *isn't* real."

"Many would disagree," Felix protested.

"Perhaps. Well, in the next instant I remembered that people watching reality TV like to suspend their disbelief. Especially on Christmas Eve, the night we always have our big FUN-TV holiday special, they might be willing to believe in Santa Claus again if we gave them a reason to." As he spoke, Bobbo was practically quivering with excitement; his enthusiasm for his plan had caused him to forget the forbidding presence of Lucretia Pepper. "Felix, now what do you suppose we could do to create a reality show involving Santa Claus that everyone in the country would want to watch?"

"I can't wait to hear," Felix replied honestly.

"The most popular reality shows let audiences vote. How's that for a clue?"

"You'll ask people to vote on whether they believe in Santa or not?"

"No, no," Bobbo scoffed, waving his hand in disdain. "We've got something much better than that. Reality-TV audiences want to see *competition*, Felix. They want to see a winner and, perhaps even more, lots of losers. Can't you guess? We're going to have a show where people vote for Santa!"

Felix rubbed his face and looked perplexed, which he was. "But how can they do that, Bobbo? There's only one Santa. What does voting have to do with it?"

Now Bobbo was actually hopping up and down with glee. "Wrong, Felix! Go to any city in America during November and December. There are Santa Clauses everywhere—posing for photos with children in malls, ringing bells on street corners, telling you to buy this product or that one on TV commercials. No two of them look or sound exactly alike. Why, we're a country *crammed* with Santas. And how do you suppose that makes people feel?"

"I'm sure you'll tell me, Bobbo."

"It makes everyone feel confused and frustrated. Parents don't know what to tell their children when the kids ask which one is the *real* Santa. Little boys and girls can't understand why there are so many. And teenagers may be the most frustrated of all. They're at an age to doubt almost everything, and Santa's one of the childhood beliefs it hurts them most to lose. But they're sharp enough to realize all these guys with fake beards and pillows stuffed down their fronts are frauds. There are too many impostors going around claiming they're Santa Claus. People of every age have had enough of it. As a culture, we've reached the point of Santa saturation."

Bobbo was echoing the same concerns we'd felt at the North Pole since James Edgar adapted J. W. Parkinson's original "Santa-in-the-store" plan back in Brockton in 1890. Felix couldn't help nodding in agreement. Bobbo's enthusiasm was infectious, and his point was irrefutable.

"So what we're going to do," Bobbo said, leaning forward confidentially and lowering his voice, "is settle this Santa thing once and for all."

"You mean you're going to have a show that reveals all the mall and street-corner Santas are pretenders in red robes?" Felix asked.

Lucretia Pepper snorted disdainfully. The force of the air exhaled through her sizable nose actually ruffled Felix's hair.

"Oh, tell him, Bobbo," she commanded. "Stop building up the suspense."

"Yes," Bobbo agreed, and although he didn't add "ma'am," the subservient word was still understood by all three in the room. It might be Bobbo's original plan, and his TV network, but Lucretia Pepper was in charge.

Bobbo collected himself for a moment, glanced nervously at Lucretia Pepper, then continued. As soon as he resumed talking, his enthusiasm once again overcame his obvious fear of the woman.

"It's just the best idea for reality TV anyone's ever had, Felix, if I say so myself. We are going to hold a Christmas Eve competition next year that lets a studio audience select the real Santa Claus! Now, what do you think of that?"

Felix thought a lot of things, many of them unfit to be spoken aloud.

Fortunately, Bobbo and Lucretia Pepper mistook his inability to immediately express himself as a sign that he was stunned by the ingenuity of
Bobbo's proposed program.

"Well—" Felix tried, but further words failed him. "But—" he began
again, then stuttered to a sudden halt. Finally, after several deep breaths,
he was able to gasp, "How are you going to get Santa Claus in your studio? He's rather busy on Christmas Eve!"

Lucretia Pepper howled with laughter, and Bobbo chuckled heartily.

"You see, Lucretia?" Bobbo asked. "Is this guy going to add authenticity to the show, or what? 'Santa's rather busy on Christmas Eve'!
We'll work that right in; it'll add to the tension. Those last couple of
segments, maybe we can have a clock superimposed onscreen showing
time running out for the Santa vote, so the winner can get his sleigh in
the air and start delivering those presents. It's magic, just *magic!*"

For the first time, there seemed to be a hint of genuine pleasure in Lucretia Pepper's otherwise gargoyle-like grin. "It's a splendid touch.
Bobbo, you've made your share of mistakes in recent years. That *Merry
Monkey* disaster you just put on the air is a good example. But I believe
that this time you've got the right program and the right man advising
you about it. Yes, be certain to show a ticking clock onscreen."

"Wait," Felix protested. "I don't understand this whole *voting* thing."

"Just amazing!" Bobbo said. "He still doesn't have the basic concept,
and yet he's already tossing out great ideas. Felix, it's like this. We're
going to send a scout to all the biggest shopping malls in the country,
because they hire the most authentic fake Santas anywhere. We'll pick,
oh, the ten best, and bring 'em to our New York studio on Christmas
Eve. We'll pack the audience with kids who still believe in Santa Claus.
The ten contestants will compete in different events, though I don't
know what they'll be yet. Reindeer-roping, maybe. Present-wrapping.
We'll think of them later. After each round, the kids in the studio vote
out one of the Santas until only two are left. Then for the grand finale—
oh, this is so good, you're going to *love* this—the two remaining Santas

each get, what, three minutes to speak directly to the audience and explain why *he* should be voted in as the real, actual, one-and-only Santa Claus. The kids vote, we get a winner, and right there on FUN-TV we present the official Santa, case closed. It can't miss. The ratings will go through the roof."

Felix thought sadly that Bobbo might just be right. "Are you certain you want to do this, Bobbo?" he asked. "What if, for instance, the Santa who's selected is really awful? Won't you be risking millions of children watching the program being so disappointed that their belief in Santa is damaged or even lost forever?"

"We're going to do our best to see that doesn't happen, Felix," Bobbo said. "We'll work hard to get ten contestants who've got the right look and voice and, I guess, attitude. These big malls hire only good ones, usually from companies that screen potential Santas to weed out anyone unsuitable. We'll end up with a fine Santa, I promise."

"Your concern does you credit, Felix," Lucretia Pepper added. "That's all the more reason for you to be part of *The Great Santa Search* team. You'll help shape the program format, work with Bobbo to design the various competitions, and even coach our ten Santa finalists on the real history of the holiday. Of course, the winner must be a Santa Claus children can believe in. LastLong Toys will settle for nothing less in its new national spokesman."

It took Felix a minute to process what he'd just heard. Finally, he managed to croak, "I beg your pardon?"

"It's nothing we have to talk about right now, Felix," Bobbo said quickly. "Just the business end of the show. Nothing you'll be involved with."

"That's entirely incorrect, Bobbo," Lucretia Pepper snapped. "As much as you've come up with a brilliant concept, there is still going to be a financial bottom line, and the more familiar with it everyone is, the better chance we have of all of us being happy when everything's over. And I *do* want to be happy, Bobbo. LastLong Toy Company is making a considerable investment in *The Great Santa Search*. We expect to get our money's worth, including the *right* Santa Claus as our spokesman."

"Santa Claus doesn't endorse specific toys," Felix protested. "I mean, at the North Pole he and his friends *make* them. Why would he be a spokesman for *yours?*"

Bobbo Butler grimaced, and hunched his shoulders as though to avoid a blow. Lucretia Pepper briefly seemed to consider swinging her hamlike fists, but instead burst into high-pitched laughter.

"He's just *astonishing*, Bobbo," she declared. "Listen to the resentment he's able to get into his voice when he pretends to believe in Santa Claus. I could almost think he does! If we can just bring that kind of apparent sincerity to *The Great Santa Search*, you'll have your ratings blockbuster and LastLong Toy Company will have an excellent return on our investment. And," she added, the girlish note in her voice suddenly absent, "I hope you both realize how *seriously* we take investments. Felix, do you know what my company is paying to be the exclusive sponsor of this program?"

Felix shrugged.

"On a Christmas-season special, networks with high ratings can charge as much as $500,000—yes, that's *half a million dollars*—to air one thirty-second commercial," the towering woman said. "Of course, FUN-TV has had terrible ratings, but Bobbo still charges $300,000 for thirty seconds. In each sixty minutes of airtime, perhaps forty-two minutes are actually part of a program, another five or so are used by networks to advertise other shows, and thirteen are set aside for commercials. Are you good at multiplying, Felix? For the commercials that would usually air during just one hour of *The Great Santa Search*, Bobbo expects $7,800,000. But *The Great Santa Search* is two hours long, so Bobbo is charging—and LastLong Toy Company is paying—$15.6 million. That's a great deal of money, don't you think?"

"Certainly," Felix admitted.

"As our corporate Christmas gift to the millions and millions of adults and children who are watching—they'd *better* be watching— LastLong Toy Company is going to pay for two hours' worth of commercials, but we're not going to actually put any on the air. *The Great Santa Search* will be almost two consecutive hours of uninterrupted entertainment. But at the end of the program, whoever's elected Santa will be presented to everyone watching as the new spokesman for LastLong Toys. Afterward he'll be featured in all our advertising and make personal appearances on behalf of our products. Didn't Bobbo tell me he met you at our Rockefeller Center skating show? Think what a greater sensation it would have been if we'd had Santa out there hawking our ice skates— the one and only, the *official* Santa Claus!"

It made painful sense to Felix. It was, he thought, the logical if disastrous culmination of what J. W. Parkinson had started so long ago.

"Bobbo, did you think of this . . . this . . . *scheme?*" he mumbled.

Bobbo hung his head. "I thought up *The Great Santa Search*, Felix, the voting and all. When I met with Lucretia to see if she'd buy commercial time on the program, she came up with the rest of it. Santa as the LastLong spokesman, I mean."

"And what a wonderful partnership we're going to have!" Lucretia Pepper announced, her voice once again high-pitched and sinisterly cheerful. "Bobbo, I must fly. As agreed, I'll have the first few million dollars deposited in the FUN-TV account. You'll be able to pay your overdue bills after all!"

Heather Hathaway was coming in through the conference-room door as Lucretia Pepper swooped out. They collided, and the younger woman bounced off the door frame. Lucretia Pepper didn't bother apologizing. Instead, she continued on her way through the outer office and then into the corridor, waving one meaty jeweled hand in impersonal farewell. Miss Hathaway rubbed her shoulder and glared after her.

"Are you all right?" Bobbo asked her, real concern in his voice. "I hope you're not bruised. Lucretia doesn't realize her own, well, *strength.*"

Miss Hathaway looked at her boss and blushed. Felix had no idea why. "I'm fine, Bobbo," she said. "I hope the meeting went well."

"I suppose it did," Bobbo said, and he looked and sounded ashamed again. "Felix, I hope you understand. *Merry Monkey* was just a ratings disaster. No one anywhere watched it."

"Some of my friends and I did," Felix said.

"Well, then, you were about the only ones. My own children didn't watch it. *The Great Santa Search* can change everything for our network, but no other potential sponsors besides LastLong have even been willing to meet with me because our ratings have been terrible for so long. Lucretia's gruff, I know, even rude sometimes, but she understood right away what size audience we'd be able to attract if we had enough money to produce the kind of quality program I was describing. So she offered me a deal. She'd sponsor the whole thing for $15.6 million, but afterward the Santa who was elected had to become the LastLong spokesman. Felix, I needed the money to produce the show and save my network."

"What about saving children's belief in Santa Claus?" Felix asked, trying hard not to sound angry. "No one's going to accept Santa Claus as a spokesman, a *shill,* for a company whose toys break the moment anyone starts to play with them."

"Actually, they might," Bobbo said, and, standing beside him and still rubbing her sore shoulder, Heather Hathaway nodded. "Lots of people rely on television to tell them what to believe. The old-fashioned idea of Santa and his helpers making the toys at the North Pole and then delivering them by whizzing around in a sleigh pulled by flying reindeer doesn't cut it these days. But Santa endorsing a certain brand of toys? That, kids might believe. They see all their other so-called heroes doing it. Why not him?"

"Because Santa Claus is *different,* Bobbo," Felix argued. "That's why he's been special to children for centuries. He represents love and sharing, not some company's products."

Bobbo sighed. "Look, Felix, I'm going to broadcast this show next

Christmas Eve. LastLong Toys is going to sponsor it. I'd like you to be my consultant, on everything from real Christmas history to picking the ten candidate Santas to planning all the actual details of the program. We can work out whatever salary you want—Miss Hathaway will handle that. I know you've got some misgivings, but look at it this way: as part of *The Great Santa Search* team, you can make this as authentic as possible—throw in bits of real Christmas history, and satisfy yourself that we've got some fine Santa candidates for the kids. What do you say?"

"I need to think about this, Bobbo," Felix said. "Can you give me a few days to make up my mind?"

Bobbo agreed. "Just don't take too long, Felix. We've got lots to do." They shook hands. As Miss Hathaway reached for Felix's arm to escort him from the office, Bobbo called after him, "Felix, wait. I want you to know this. I believed in Santa Claus for a long, long time. I wish I still did. But at least more children might keep on believing, if we make *The Great Santa Search* good enough. Help me make that happen, Felix."

As she helped Felix into his coat, Miss Hathaway leaned down and whispered, *"I* still believe."

Somehow, her words comforted Felix on his long trip back to the North Pole.

I'd rarely had to call a North Pole meeting for any emergency purpose. But Felix's report of Bobbo Butler's plan for *The Great Santa Search* certainly required immediate discussion. So, after breakfast . . . everyone drifted singly or in small groups to the conference room, and found places to sit around the long table.

CHAPTER

Five

n the morning of January 1, while many others in the world were celebrating the New Year, I convened a meeting of my oldest and dearest companions at the North Pole. We gathered in a large, well-lit conference room that had its walls covered with world maps and giant computer and radar screens. This was where, on Christmas Eve, Amelia Earhart would monitor weather conditions around the globe and radio to me in my sleigh if blizzards or thunderstorms necessitated changes in air routes. There was a long, wide conference table surrounded by comfortable chairs—each year we might gather a few times to talk over gift-giving ideas and test some of the new toys that Leonardo, Ben Franklin, and Willie Skokan were constantly inventing. I'd rarely had to call a North Pole meeting for any emergency purpose. But Felix's report of Bobbo Butler's plan for *The Great Santa Search* certainly required immediate discussion.

So, after breakfast—Lars's pecan waffles, cinnamon scones, and fresh-squeezed orange juice tasted delicious despite our collective concern—

everyone drifted singly or in small groups to the conference room, and found places to sit around the long table. Before I called our meeting to order, I looked around and marveled at my luck in forming such a colorful, unique fellowship. At the far end of the table, Attila the Hun lounged with his wife, Dorothea. The few outsiders who knew of us were always astonished that this legendary warrior had eventually dedicated himself to the gentler task of gift-giving, but the Attila I knew was warmhearted and sincerely remorseful for the havoc he once wreaked with his sword and spear. Attila and Dorothea chatted quietly with St. Francis of Assisi, who even before joining our fellowship had been devoted to encouraging Christmas joy through the establishment of holiday traditions. In the early 1200s, Francis wrote some of the earliest carols that were specific to Christmas, and he suggested the first "manger scenes" to remind everyone that Baby Jesus came into the world as a poor, rather than wealthy, child. To Francis's left sat Leonardo da Vinci and Willie Skokan, the great painter-inventor and equally great craftsman, respectively. The two were fast friends and seldom apart; on this occasion they had spread in front of them as usual bits of paper filled with sketches and designs for toys no one else but that pair could have ever imagined. Ben Franklin sat beside them, seeming distracted by some random thought that caused his brow to furrow. Ben always appeared to be thinking, as opposed to daydreaming. There is a great difference.

Along the other side of the table were Amelia Earhart, the finest aviator of the early twentieth century, and Theodore Roosevelt, surely the most colorful American president of any era. Bill Pickett, the great African-American cowboy, was leaning toward them, no doubt telling some rip-roaring tale about wrestling steers or riding bucking broncos. Sequoyah, the brilliant Cherokee who invented a whole new alphabet for his tribe, sat calmly beside Arthur, whose exploits as a war chief somehow expanded into legends of a king with a magical sword and great castle called Camelot. Felix and Sarah looked the most concerned of anyone, but they had reason to be—they'd actually met Bobbo Butler, and Felix, of course, had made the nerve-racking acquaintance of Lucretia Pepper. Finally, Layla sat on my immediate right, looking serious but not anxious. However our discussion might proceed, I knew my beloved wife would remain calm, always preferring common sense to wild conjecture.

Layla gently nudged my arm. "We should begin," she suggested. "There's so much to talk about, and we still have to finish preparations for Epiphany."

She was right, of course. On January 6, children in Italy expected gifts from an old woman named Befana, and we would never want to disappoint them. That meant on the night of January 5 we'd transport mountains of toys and countless tons of candy across the seas, where Layla in particular would take great delight in dressing as the legendary peasant woman and distributing treats to all the Italian boys and girls who believed.

"Please, let's come to order," I suggested, and the words I used sent an unmistakable message. We're generally quite informal at the North Pole. In the eyes and imaginations of most of the world, Santa Claus is a sort of genial ruler over all his other helpers, but that was—is—simply not true. Still, someone has to chair each meeting, if only to be certain everyone has a chance to express himself or herself. A few of our number—Teddy Roosevelt and Felix, especially—are fond of their own voices, while others like Willie Skokan, St. Francis, and Dorothea are unlikely to offer opinions unless specifically asked. So I used more formal language than usual to get everyone's attention. We had urgent business to discuss; *The Great Santa Search* threatened everything we had tried to accomplish for so many centuries.

"Two days ago, Felix returned from New York City and delivered his shocking news," I reminded them. "The idea of a studio audience supposedly voting for the real Santa Claus while countless American families watch is bad enough. That LastLong Toy Company intends to use the winner as its corporate spokesman is completely unacceptable. Today, we must try to come up with some sort of plan, because if we simply sit back and let events take their course, it's possible children in America will have to choose between believing in the LastLong Toy Santa or deciding no Santa Claus exists at all."

I was surprised to see Francis immediately raise his hand, and yielded the floor to him at once.

"Santa, it has been our traditional policy not to try in any way to affect events," he said, brushing his thin hair back from his forehead. "We have always referred to ourselves as *gift-givers*, not *history-makers*. If we attempt to intercede with *The Great Santa Search*, aren't we violating our own rule? If Americans choose to embrace the winner of some silly TV contest as the real Santa, isn't that their right, foolish though it might be? Perhaps we should do nothing but observe."

Arthur stood as Francis returned to his chair.

"In most cases, old friend, I would completely agree," he told Francis. "But there are rare moments when some sort of intervention is absolutely required. Surely all of us here remember how Layla came forward in England in 1647 to lead protesters when Parliament attempted to ban the celebration of Christmas forever. If she hadn't done that, it was possible, even probable, that the holiday would have been lost there forever, and never introduced in the English colonies in the so-called New World that became America. This *Great Santa Search* may be the greatest threat to Christmas since, not because it threatens celebrating the holiday, but because it thwarts the real purpose of the celebration. Our gifts have always been meant to enhance the special time when we all should offer thanks to God for his son. We give gifts to demonstrate to children that real happiness is derived from love and generosity. All of us here realize that some will consider Christmas as nothing more than a fine opportunity to collect presents from others. That's why the presence—not the *presents*—of Santa Claus is so important. By symbolizing the act of gift-giving, he reminds children it is always better to give than to receive. It's a lesson they carry with them into their adult lives, and hopefully pass on to their own children in turn. Any declaration of an 'official Santa' whose sole purpose is to help one greedy company sell even more of its terrible toys jeopardizes the message we have spent centuries attempting, mostly successfully, to communicate." Arthur paused to take a breath, and suddenly looked embarrassed. "I'm sorry. I intended to make a brief comment, not a speech. I feel strongly about this, as you can see."

"We all do, Arthur," Ben Franklin said soothingly. "I find myself wondering, though, if the threat is as great as we fear. Isn't it true that all the recent Christmas Eve specials on FUN-TV have hardly been watched by anyone?"

Leonardo looked up from the sketches he and Willie Skokan had been studying. He, not surprisingly, was the North Pole computer expert. If requested to do so, Leonardo could log on to the Internet and track down any bit of information required, no matter how obscure. Now he reached into a voluminous pocket and withdrew a handful of crumpled papers. For all his brilliance, Leonardo was not especially organized. The rest of us had to wait while he smoothed out the papers, then peered at each one as though seeing it for the first time. Some sheets he recrumpled and jammed back into his pocket. A few others were shuffled into some sort of order. Only then did Leonardo clear his throat, glance briefly around the table, and begin speaking.

"Just over a week ago, the *Merry Monkey* Christmas Eve special on FUN-TV drew a two-tenths of one percent market share," he announced. "*Share* means the percentage of households with televisions that are tuned in to a specific program while it is on the air. Roughly translated, this two-tenths of one percent indicates approximately 219,800 households watched *Merry Monkey*."

Bill Pickett whistled.

"More than 200,000 families! That's a whole lot of people, Leonardo."

Leonardo smiled.

"Bill, my good friend, consider this: there are some 110 *million* television households—families who watch television—in America. I'm afraid 219,800 of them is almost the tiniest market share possible."

"Then my point is well-taken," Ben Franklin said. "Why are we so worried? I admit that every child's belief in Santa is important, but at least where FUN-TV is concerned, the network's ability to damage children's beliefs appears to be quite limited."

Willie Skokan cleared his throat, and everyone else was startled. Willie *never* spoke during our meetings.

"We have to consider the *potential* viewership here," he blurted, and immediately sat down again.

Leonardo patted his best friend on the back. "Exactly, Willie. While FUN-TV currently attracts very few viewers, there is no reason the network can't reach a much wider audience the moment it has a program more people want to watch. From Felix's description, *The Great Santa Search* could attract widespread attention. If that's the case, there would be many millions of viewers instead of a few thousand."

Attila, the old Hun war chief, phrased his question in a military way.

"If this battle goes against us in the ratings, Leonardo, what's our worst-case scenario?"

Leonardo looked through the wrinkled papers on the table in front of him, frowned, dug back into his pocket, extracted the other papers he found there, peered at each, and finally exclaimed, "Ah!" as he found the one he was looking for.

"To date, Attila, the most-watched non-sports program in television history was aired in 1983. It was the final broadcast of a popular series called *M*A*S*H*, and it drew a share of just over 60 percent. About 50 million households tuned in to the show."

That figure impressed us. There were gasps all around the table.

"But remember," Leonardo cautioned, "there are many more households with televisions now than there were in 1983. Of course, they also have more programs to choose from. There was no real cable television then. These days, most people have hundreds of channels available at any given viewing moment. In recent years, no program has even approached a 60 percent market share. Bobbo Butler will have to work hard and spend a lot of money on advertising if he expects to match that, let alone set new viewing records with *The Great Santa Search*. It won't be easy."

"He has the money he needs, $15.6 million, remember?" Felix reminded us. "And though he's fallen on hard times of late, I'm convinced Bobbo knows the television industry inside out. He'll find ways to let everyone know about *The Great Santa Search*."

Theodore Roosevelt leaped to his feet. I'd been surprised he'd stayed silent this long.

"Enough of this mealymouthed discussion!" he declared. "Action is wanted here, not talk! Now, Santa Claus, have you considered the most obvious way of defusing this threat? By that I mean, going to this Bobbo person yourself and demanding he desist, at peril of being socked right in the snoot!"

"You know we never resort to violence, Theodore," Layla said calmly.

"Oh, I know, but snoot-socking can be very effective," Theodore replied, sounding sulky. "I just thought it ought to be mentioned. What I'd really recommend is this: Santa Claus, you've got a bully pulpit, perhaps the bulliest of them all. We're worried Bobbo Butler might get his silly program watched by millions of children who would then lose their faith in Santa Claus for one reason or another. Correct?"

"Yes, Theodore," I replied, wondering what was coming next.

"And Bobbo—what a silly nickname!—can do this because of modern media? Not only through his own network, but perhaps being featured on talk shows on other channels? And also articles in newspapers and online news sites and so forth?"

"Obviously," I said, hoping he'd get to the point. Theodore did love the sound of his own voice, and was never content to say something briefly and then sit down.

"Well, then, why not use your own bully pulpit and beat him to the punch, so to speak? If you, the real Santa Claus, contacted every media news outlet in the world and called a press conference to reveal yourself here at the North Pole before this so-called *Great Santa Search* ever got on the air next Christmas Eve, wouldn't that do the trick? With the one-and-only Santa already on every television screen, not to mention every magazine cover and newspaper front page, who would care about some reality program with ten fakers? No one! FUN-TV would get a zero market share, if such a thing is possible. Isn't this the simplest, most effective way of dealing with the problem?"

I heard several murmurs of assent. Theodore certainly had a point. If Bobbo was threatening us through the electronic medium of television, we could use the same means to thwart him. But that could only be done at a terrible, unacceptable cost.

"That's insightful, Theodore," I said, and the former American president nodded to acknowledge the compliment. "Unfortunately, what you suggest is the very thing we cannot do."

"Why is that?" Theodore asked.

"We must all remember why we live at the North Pole," I said. "Why have we chosen to live and work in an undetectable environment as far from civilization as remains possible in this widely traveled world? It's because privacy is important to us, and for two reasons. One is obvious. If our presence and location were common knowledge, we'd be overrun not just by the media, but by well-meaning, Christmas-loving tourists who would want to see our toy shops and feed the reindeer and pose for pictures with us and interrupt, however unintentionally, the vital non-stop work that is necessary if we're to effectively carry out our gift-giving mission. If I called a press conference to identify myself and explain what we do here, Theodore, why, afterward we'd never be left to work in peace."

"All right," Theodore grumbled. "You could leave out our exact location at the North Pole, then. But you could still announce yourself as the real Santa Claus. Fly in to the press conference on your sleigh pulled by the reindeer. That would do the trick."

"Now you touch on the second reason I can't do what you suggest," I said, making sure I sounded gentle so Theodore wouldn't feel I hadn't appreciated his comments. "We've all talked a great deal over the centuries about magic and illusion, how illusion can always be explained but magic simply *is*. Our fellowship, our mission, combines both. What some would call magic, we recognize as gifts from God—living without aging, being able to travel at speeds a hundred times faster than ordinary men and women. These are things that can't be explained, and of course they would greatly impress the public. But in trying to fit whatever Christmas expectations children might have, we've often turned to illusion, too, though only when absolutely necessary. After Clement Moore charmed American boys and girls with *A Visit from St. Nicholas*, for instance, Leonardo invented a way reindeer could *appear* to fly by rigging their harness and a sleigh with wings. When the reindeer run fast enough, air pushes under the wings and lifts the sleigh. It's the same principle that allows airplanes to fly. But the children believe it's the reindeer themselves who are soaring, and we let them believe it. If I *whooshed* down by sleigh to a press conference and some sharp-eyed reporter figured out how the reindeer really don't fly as such, that might cast doubt on the rest of our very legitimate magic and mission. In these cynical times, people look for reasons *not* to believe, Theodore. Trying to circumvent *The Great Santa Search* by calling my own press conference would, I think, end up doing more harm than good. It's best for everyone that the real Santa remains just mysterious enough. *Believing* in me is a far better thing than actually *seeing* me."

Layla waved her hand; she had something to add. Instantly, everyone gave her their complete attention.

"In the past we've taken extraordinary measures to keep our location and methods of gift-giving secret," she said. "Surely all of you remember the Roswell incident in 1947."

We certainly did. That year, Americans seemed even more fascinated than usual with the possibility that aliens—*spacemen*—might be visiting the earth, either in friendship or else to enslave the human race. In response, Leonardo had invented a very realistic "alien" doll whose oddly shaped head, size, and greenish color reflected the images suggested in the most popular novels, comic books, movies, and radio programs (a lot of people didn't have television then).

I don't fly in my sleigh only on Christmas Eve. The reindeer are spirited, energetic animals who not only enjoy but require frequent exercise. So several times each month from January through November, I climb onto the sleigh and take my eight wonderful horned-and-hoofed steeds out for long excursions through the night sky. Just as I was preparing to take off on a July evening in 1947, Leonardo bustled up and asked if I'd load some of his new alien dolls on the sleigh. He was worried their particular shapes and weight might upset the load balance necessary for stable flight on Christmas Eve, and wanted to see in advance if they would. So I helped him load a few dozen of them, and then took off. That night I thought it would be pleasant to fly out over the American Southwest, where the scent of desert sage often wafts high up into the air. My route took me into the skies of southeastern New Mexico. As Leonardo had feared, the alien dolls somehow never settled properly in the sleigh, and just north of the little town of Roswell most of them tipped out and fell to the ground. Unfortunately, a few people in the area saw the dolls land in the distance, and by the time I'd contacted the U.S. government to retrieve them—Harry Truman, the American president at that time, was our friend, though we were always careful not to identify ourselves to any heads of state who were not absolutely trustworthy—rumors were flying around Roswell that aliens had invaded. Soldiers from the military base in Roswell found the dolls before the curious townspeople did, and locked the "aliens" away in an airplane hangar until we could secretly come and retrieve them. Afterward, the army announced that a weather balloon had crashed outside Roswell, and all that had been collected from the area was balloon debris. If they'd told the truth—that Santa Claus had accidentally spilled some dolls out of his sleigh—our gift-giving mission might have been irreparably compromised.

Not everyone believed the weather-balloon story. Ever since, a considerable number of people have been certain the government covered up the crash of an alien spaceship. I never again wanted to experience such unfortunate confusion or risk having any of our North Pole secrets revealed.

Theodore sighed. "I'd forgotten about Roswell," he admitted. "But we can't just sit back and let this *Great Santa Search* go unchallenged. Surely we can do *something*."

For the next half-hour, we tried to think what that might be. Someone would suggest something, but someone else would offer a reason it wouldn't work. Amelia Earhart wondered if Leonardo couldn't invent an electronic signal that would jam the FUN-TV broadcast, but Bill Pickett reminded her that this was essentially sabotage, and therefore something morally wrong that we could not do. Dorothea thought Bobbo Butler might be persuaded to cancel his *Great Santa Search* plans if it was demonstrated to him that the *real* Santa Claus didn't want him to do it, but Sarah made a good case for not even bothering.

"He's desperate to save his television network," she said out loud. "That is what Bobbo cares about right now. He made it clear to Felix that he's not a believer himself, so what good would it do for Santa to approach him? Bobbo would think he was just another impostor."

"What about Lucretia Pepper?" Sequoyah wanted to know. "Could Santa perhaps persuade her to pull her money out of the project?"

Felix had the answer to that one. "There are always people who care only for themselves," he said. "They have no interest in whether things they do hurt others. At least Bobbo wants FUN-TV to stay in business so families can watch wholesome programs together. Lucretia Pepper only wants to add more money to an already-considerable fortune. If *The Great Santa Search* will help LastLong sell even more toys—and it will—then the risk of innocent children losing their belief in Santa Claus means absolutely nothing to her. She'd sneer in Santa's face."

I was just ready to suggest that we'd talked enough for one meeting, that perhaps it would be best if we all took a day to reflect before continuing to debate the best response to *The Great Santa Search*. But then I happened to catch Layla's eye. She was looking at me intently, and as our gazes locked it seemed to me I understood exactly what she was thinking. This is sometimes the case with couples who have been together for a great deal of time, and to my knowledge no marriage in the history of the world has lasted longer than ours. The right action to take was suddenly clear to me. Common sense was necessary in any response, and also the observing of our fellowship's moral beliefs, which included no violence or sabotage. But sometimes daring was called for, even risk, and this was one of those occasions.

"All right," I said, standing once again. "Here is what I think we need to do. Feel free to point out any errors in my judgment, anything I might be leaving out or forgetting. Leonardo, use the Internet to get all the information you can about Bobbo Butler and Lucretia Pepper. Don't hack into any restricted sites, of course. But we want everything that's public record. The more we know about these people, the better. Then, Felix must contact Bobbo tomorrow and tell him he's ready to join *The Great Santa Search* team. Afterward, we'll always have up-to-the-minute inside information about what is going on. I know that means Felix is technically spying for us, but I'm sure he'll be certain to offer Bobbo only helpful advice. When the program goes out on the air on Christmas Eve, it *will* be broadcast live, won't it, Felix?"

"Bobbo was very clear about that," Felix said. "He wants viewers to believe Santa has to hurry to his sleigh as soon as the program is over."

"And whoever is selected as the real Santa will end the program with a short speech?"

"That's what I understand."

"All right. What I'm getting at here is that we need information from Felix to be certain the right Santa Claus gets the most votes. Then that winning contestant can use his final featured moments on the program to talk about the right reasons to celebrate Christmas, not about LastLong Toys."

"You mean we'll fix the voting so that our favorite contestant wins?" Ben Franklin asked, sounding puzzled. "I thought we didn't believe in sabotage, Santa."

"We don't, Ben," I assured him. "The members of the studio audience must vote as they think best. We'll let their own eyes and ears and hearts help them make that decision in favor of one specific contestant."

"Who will that be, Santa?" Bill Pickett asked, and out of the corner of my eye I saw Layla smiling.

"Why, me, of course, Bill," I replied. "I'm going to compete on *The Great Santa Search*, and I'm going to win it!"

When it hit my stomach, it knocked me backward and quite took my wind away. I gasped for several seconds before I was able to ask Theodore to please not ever do that again.

Six

t's true we love nothing better than racing around the world leaving children gifts on the occasions of St. Nicholas Day, Christmas, and Epiphany. We derive great pleasure from those frantic nights, which test even our miraculous ability to travel faster than any other humans in history.

But it's also a fact that, by the time we return home, we're worn out. What we call "the mornings after" find us sleeping late, perhaps rising only in time for a tasty brunch prepared by Lars. On the mornings of December 6, December 25, and January 6, while children shriek with delight upon discovering their presents, those of us at the North Pole are probably enjoying well-earned rest.

This is what I was doing in the early morning of January 6. After our meeting where I decided I would enter and win *The Great Santa Search* competition, I put the whole thing out of my mind to prepare for Epiphany gift-giving. It is always quite complicated. As is also the case in the days leading up to St. Nicholas Day and Christmas, prior to

Epiphany we must finalize our lists of boys and girls and the gifts being
delivered to each, map out travel routes at the last minute to allow for
unexpected storms or high winds, load the sleigh carefully so that the
first gifts to be delivered are on top (no matter how carefully we plan,
some always end up on the bottom, and valuable time is lost rooting
through the entire load of gifts to reach them), and, just before takeoff,
check to see that all the reindeer's harnesses are secure. The reindeer and
sleigh whisk me from house to house only in America. They are not involved in the holiday gift-giving traditions of many other cultures, so on
St. Nicholas Day and Epiphany they are used to transport us and our
gifts from the North Pole to our destination countries. From there, our
fellowship often delivers gifts on foot, each toting a heavy sack of toys
and a list reminding us what is to be taken where. It's a challenge to get
everything delivered before daylight, when the children we love so
much wake up and rush to find their presents!

As always, it was exhilarating for all of us to speed around leaving
Epiphany gifts. We returned to the North Pole exhausted but happy
sometime after midnight. Following a snack of hot chocolate and Lars's
homemade chocolate-chip cookies, still warm from the oven, we all went
off to bed, planning to sleep much of the new day away. But it seemed I
had scarcely turned out the light and closed my eyes when there was an
insistent tapping on the door of the bedroom where Layla and I slept.

I squinted at my bedside clock—it was 6:00 a.m. Between early October and early March, we have to rely on clocks at the North Pole to
know what time of day it is. That's because, for all that time, the sun
never shines at all. It is always dark outside. The opposite is true from
late March through late September. Then, the sun never stops shining,
and we still need our clocks. There's no other way to tell morning from
night.

But in this case my clock confirmed that it was *very* early morning,
and right after one of our three long, tiring nights of holiday gift-giving,
too! I first felt annoyed, but then wondered if there might be some sort

of emergency. I stumbled up, pulled on my robe, and tried to tiptoe to the door without turning on my bedside lamp so I wouldn't wake Layla. I immediately stubbed my toe on the nightstand, and when I hopped in pain my elbow made contact with the lamp, which crashed to the floor. So I was not in the best of moods when I opened the door and found Theodore Roosevelt standing in the hall outside.

"Whatever is the matter, Theodore?" I asked. "Is there a problem of some sort?"

Theodore grinned, his large square teeth and eyeglasses glinting in the hallway light. "Nothing at all's the matter, Santa!" he boomed in a cheerful voice that was entirely inappropriate for such an early hour. "It's time for you to get up. You begin training this morning, you know!"

"No, I *don't* know, Theodore," I hissed. "It's six in the morning on Epiphany, and, if you don't mind, I'm going back to bed." I yawned, looked at him more carefully, and added, "Why are you dressed like that?"

Theodore wore a bright green New York Jets football jersey—he'd once been governor of New York and never lost his special affection for sports teams from that state—gray sweatpants, and a baseball cap with "*World's Greatest President*" emblazoned on the front. We'd given him the cap a few years earlier as a 150th birthday present. He'd since taken to wearing it everywhere. What I'd never seen him wearing until now was the silver whistle dangling from a cord around his neck.

"Don't joke, Santa Claus," Theodore said sternly. "You're planning to compete on *The Great Santa Search*, aren't you? There will be all sorts of contests, though we don't yet know what kind. But running and climbing will certainly be involved. You said we'd begin preparing right after Epiphany gift-giving. Well, that gift-giving's over. Now we've got to start getting you into decent physical shape. You're quite overweight, you know, and I can't remember the last time you had some real exercise."

I chose to ignore his reference to my weight—I'm rather big-boned and carry any extra pounds quite gracefully—and instead concentrated on his preposterous claim that I didn't exercise.

"I'm constantly getting exercise, Theodore," I argued. "All day I'm hurrying around our North Pole offices, seeing first to this and then to that. I often go hours without even sitting down."

"But when you do sit down, it's at a table," Theodore replied. "Chewing and swallowing don't count as exercise. When is the last time you did a chin-up or jogged a few miles?"

"Never," Layla called from under the warm covers of our bed. "Of course, I've only known him for sixteen centuries. He might have been a fiend for exercise before that."

"Please go back to sleep," I said to her, then returned my attention to Theodore. "Your point is well taken. I'll tell you what—come back at noon and perhaps we can take a walk."

Theodore shook his head. "This can't be put off, Santa. We're going to start every morning from now until the broadcast with hard, healthy exercise before breakfast. The combination of working up a good sweat and following a sensible diet for a change will soon have you feeling like a new man. Now, get dressed in comfortable clothes. Not good ones, mind you. Perspiration stains can be difficult to get out in the wash."

"I really don't think—" I began, but Layla, her voice still somewhat muffled by the covers, informed me I would find a sweatshirt and sweatpants in the middle drawer of our bureau. "Now, I know I don't own either of those items," I replied, and then realized what was going on. "Admit it," I demanded of the Layla-sized, covered lump swaddled so comfortably in bed while I was being rousted out by Theodore. "You two planned this. Layla, you got me workout clothes, didn't you?" Theodore, still standing in the doorway, tried and failed to look innocent. I think Layla chuckled, but her head was still hidden under the covers and she might have been snoring. She certainly didn't deny it.

Sighing, I put on the new workout clothes as well as a comfortable pair of athletic shoes that I often wear during long days at the North

Pole. I know most children and many parents expect me to always be shod in high black boots, and I do wear those when I'm making my holiday gift-giving rounds, along with bright red robes trimmed in white fur. At all other times, I must admit I prefer comfort to style, especially where shoes are concerned. After more than seventeen hundred years of faithful service, my feet have earned some pampering.

No sooner had I tied my shoelaces than Theodore was urging me out the door. "It's getting on quarter past six," he nagged. "Breakfast is at eight sharp. We have lots to do before then."

"We spent last night delivering gifts, Theodore," I reminded him. "No one will even be stirring until noon, when Lars will serve brunch."

"*You* are having breakfast at eight," Theodore said, and didn't explain further.

We hustled down the hallway at a faster pace than I found comfortable. Theodore's legs were shorter than mine, but he moved them at a very rapid rate. When I began to lag behind, he looked back over his shoulder and said, "Come on, come on!" I was in no hurry because I knew where he was taking me.

It is never warm or even comfortably cool outside at the North Pole. During winter, the temperature regularly drops as low as 35 degrees below zero and even in the so-called "summer months" it rarely gets warmer than 32 degrees above zero, which is still officially designated as "freezing." Even if we could spend much time outside, there is no actual *land* to look at or walk on. The Arctic ice cap is some ten feet deep, and usually covered with thick layers of snow. During the coldest months, it can expand to a size roughly equal to the continental United States. There are no trees or other sturdy shrubbery. Everything is pale and cold. This has its own certain barren beauty, especially when the gorgeous Northern Lights—electrons and protons from the sun colliding with atoms of oxygen and nitrogen, among other things, in the earth's upper atmosphere—suddenly blaze green, red, and blue across the inky sky. But anyone standing long in the icy air would suffer frostbite.

So in designing our North Pole home, which is a dazzling array of underground buildings connected by tunnels we have come to think of as "hallways," Leonardo added a cavernous indoor gymnasium that eventually included basketball and handball courts, gymnastics equipment, an Olympic-sized swimming pool, and a quarter-mile track. The gymnasium is open to all of our fellowship. Sometimes when the holidays draw near, many of my companions work late in the toy factory and relax afterward with a friendly game on the basketball court or perhaps a rowdy session of water polo in the pool. Willie Skokan is fond of the parallel bars in the gymnastics area, and after all these centuries he is still quite lithe. Sometimes, just for the fun of it, he spends the entire day walking around on his hands. Attila loves handball, but he competes so aggressively, shouting and throwing his body wildly into every shot, that no one really likes playing with him. Layla, Sarah, Dorothea, and Amelia Earhart meet in the evenings before dinner to jog together around the track, sometimes forgetting how many laps they've completed if the conversation proves especially interesting, which it often does.

I rarely visit the gym myself. I feel obligated to spend much of my spare time reading about new or changing holiday customs around the world, and if I do this seated in a comfortable chair in my den, and if I occasionally doze off while conducting my intense research, well, what is the harm of it? I certainly don't *mind* exercise, it's just that I have other priorities.

"Here we are, Santa," Theodore announced, throwing open the double doors that led into the gymnasium. All the lights were already on; still sleepy, I blinked in the sudden glare. When my eyes adjusted, I saw Theodore opening a locker along the near wall. He took out some sort of large, heavy ball, a stopwatch, and a jump rope.

"We'll start out with some simple stretching exercises to loosen up your muscles, Santa," he said briskly. "Now, spread your feet about shoulder-width apart and begin by touching your toes a dozen times. Do it the right way, please, returning to full standing position after each time you bend down."

"Is this really necessary?" I asked.

Theodore raised the silver whistle to his lips and blew hard. The resulting loud, ear-piercing sound made my head ache.

"It's time to *exercise*, Santa!" he barked, and I suddenly understood how army recruits must feel when a grumpy drill sergeant organizes calisthenics. Glumly, I moved my feet apart as ordered and bent down to touch my toes. Unfortunately, Theodore noticed that my fingertips hovered a good dozen inches above my feet unless I bent my knees, which he immediately made clear was not allowed.

"I said to do it the right way, Santa," he commanded, and there was a certain steely note in his voice that must have harkened back to his days in the White House, when he issued orders to everyone and expected to be obeyed. "Keep your legs straight! Suck in your stomach! Get those fingers down to your toes!" I wanted badly to oblige him, if only to stop him shouting in my ear, but the lower my fingertips were able to go, the more a series of alarming crackling sounds issued from my already-aching back. I huffed and crackled and bent and strained for what seemed like a very long time before I finally made fleeting contact between fingertips and toes. Theodore blew his whistle again, and informed me I would be expected to do better tomorrow.

"By the time I'm done with you, you'll be able to touch your toes a hundred times in a row," he said. "You're going to be amazed how much progress you'll make."

"I'll be amazed if I even survive until breakfast," I replied. "Really, Theodore, my back is hurting. Haven't we done enough for the first day?"

Theodore polished his glasses on his New York Jets jersey, held them up to the gymnasium lights to check for remaining specks of dust, put them back on, and peered at me.

"I hope you're joking, Santa Claus," he said. "I've put a great deal of time into developing a workout routine for you."

"Thank you, Theodore," I told him. "What torture have you planned for me next?"

"We're going to tighten up that stomach of yours," he said ominously. "Have you ever worked out with a medicine ball before? No? Well, here is how it's done. I'll stand a few feet away, and then bounce the ball off your belly like *this*. Say, why is your face turning red? That was a *very* soft toss!"

The ball was so heavy that I suspected it had some sort of cast-iron core. When it hit my stomach, it knocked me backward and quite took my wind away. I gasped for several seconds before I was able to ask Theodore to please not ever do that again.

"But it's good for you, Santa!" he protested. "In my college days when I was on the boxing team, we worked out with medicine balls all the time. It's quite a bully exercise!"

"I doubt boxing will be one of the competitions on *The Great Santa Search,* Theodore," I said. "If it is, we'll find a way to disguise you as me and you can get in the ring."

I was being sarcastic, but Theodore didn't realize it. "Really, Santa?" he cried. "Could I? Do you promise? Boxing is such fun."

"You have my solemn oath, Theodore," I said. "Meanwhile, please put the medicine ball away. I notice a jump rope there by your feet. I'm sure that sort of exercise will be quite good for me, and pleasant, too. For centuries I've seen children skipping rope, and I always wanted to try it myself. May I?"

Theodore handed me the jump rope. I took one handle in each hand and pulled it up in an arc over my head, trying at the same time to hop off the floor so there would be room for the rope to pass under my feet. Perhaps I twirled the rope too fast, or didn't jump high enough. In any event, the rope somehow snagged around my ankles and I went toppling off-balance into Theodore, who staggered, tripped over the medicine ball, and tumbled onto his back. He immediately jumped up, placed the whistle between his lips, and blasted out a particularly harsh, ear-splitting note.

"Concentrate, Santa Claus!" he barked. "Jumping rope is not intended to be a contact sport!"

"I'm sure it won't happen again," I assured him. I untangled the jump rope from my ankles and tried again, and again. The results were no better. Every time I twirled the rope quickly and tried to jump, it hit my ankles or got snarled at my shins. If I swung it very slowly, I could take only a ponderous hop that concluded with me thumping hard back on the floor while the rope sagged behind me. Theodore impatiently snatched the jump rope from me and demonstrated how it was supposed to be done. He immediately fell into a brisk, graceful rhythm, with the rope slapping pleasantly against the floor each time it passed beneath his feet. All the jumping made the whistle on the cord around his neck flap madly up and down. After a minute he stopped and handed the jump rope back to me.

"Any little girl in the world can do this, Santa," he remarked. "Surely you can, too."

But I couldn't. It was much harder than it looked. Theodore looked more and more exasperated. Finally he waved at me to stop.

"You can't touch your toes, catch a medicine ball, or jump rope," he said. "This is going to be tougher than I thought."

"If it's too much trouble, just say so, and I'll go back to bed," I informed him. "It's not as though *I'm* having a good time, either."

Theodore immediately looked stricken. "Oh, I'm sorry, Santa," he said. "It's just that I know how important it is for you to win this *Great Santa Search*, and you really do need to be in better physical shape for it, just in case. What sort of events did Bobbo Butler mention to Felix? Stocking-stuffing was one, I think. Another was reindeer-roping. How can you lasso a reindeer if you can't even use a jump rope? Please let me help you with all this. I promise to be more patient."

I could hardly be angry with my dear old friend. He meant so well, and he was certainly right in suggesting I ought to get myself into better physical condition.

"That's fine, Theodore," I said. "All right. Obviously that's enough jump-roping, or jump-*tripping*, for one day. What do you want me to do next?"

Theodore consulted a list he drew from his pocket. "It's time to run, Santa. Well, not actually *run*. *Jog* is a more appropriate term. I don't expect you to get on the track and run for miles, at least not yet. Each time around is a quarter mile. Do you think you could go around twice? I've got a stopwatch here. Maybe you could jog two laps in, oh, five or six minutes? That would be an excellent start."

He led me to the track, and offered several suggestions about how to jog. I was to *shuffle* my feet rather than lift them up high as I went along. I should try to breathe through my nose rather than my mouth. My arms should pump gently back and forth at the same rate as my legs. These things, he promised, would improve my stamina.

"Just do your best," Theodore said as he held up the stopwatch and signaled for me to start. He sounded mournful, as though he already knew I wouldn't be able to jog even a hundred yards without stopping, let alone half a mile.

But in his excitement at designing a training regimen for me, Theodore had apparently forgotten that one of the powers granted to all of our gift-giving fellowship is the ability to move faster than is possible for normal people. In the evenings at the North Pole gymnasium when Layla and the others jogged around the track, they did not bother to run as fast as they could. The deliberately slow pace allowed them time to unwind from their workdays and chat with each other about inconsequential things. On any given St. Nicholas Day, Christmas, or Epiphany, I moved at speeds the fastest Olympic athlete could never match. So when Theodore asked me to do my best as I ran around the track, it didn't take me five or six minutes to complete two laps. I was done in five or six seconds.

"Well, *that* was easy!" I announced with a certain sense of satisfaction. Theodore looked shocked, then grinned as he realized there was one area of athletic endeavor, at least, in which I already excelled.

"I hope one of the contests on *The Great Santa Search* is a foot race," he said. "I suppose I can cross running off your daily workout list."

"Just so long as you don't cross off breakfast," I replied. "Now that I've been working out a while, I feel terribly hungry. Exercise certainly helps work up an appetite. What do you say?"

"I say, let's be off to the kitchen!" Theodore agreed. He handed me a towel to wipe off my face—I had actually gotten a bit sweaty—and we left the gym through another hallway that led to our dining area.

We eat cafeteria-style at the North Pole. The dining hall itself is filled with long tables where we sit and serve ourselves at mealtimes from great heaping platters of food prepared in a spacious, adjacent kitchen by Lars and his staff, which includes a grizzled old railroad chef named Worth who prepares some of the best fried chicken anyone has ever tasted. Now, I hardly expected fried chicken at this early morning hour, but I still had visions of fluffy scrambled eggs, thick slices of ham, and perhaps a jelly doughnut or two washed down with several tall glasses of freshly squeezed orange juice.

But when we arrived in the dining hall, there was no one there. Theodore reminded me that everyone else at the North Pole was sleeping in, even Lars.

"So I'll be preparing your breakfast myself, Santa," he announced proudly. "I like fixing a meal now and then. I used to do it all the time at the White House. Everyone loved my special pancakes with swirls of strawberry preserves."

"Now, that sounds delicious, Theodore," I replied enthusiastically. "Will you be making those pancakes for me this morning?"

"Not exactly, Santa," Theodore said. "Why don't you make yourself comfortable at that table over there, and I'll just go into the kitchen and get things going. It won't take long."

"I hope not," I called after him. "I'm starving."

I expected Theodore to be gone ten minutes at least, and more likely twenty. Cooking fine meals takes a while. But it seemed like no time at all before the swinging doors to the kitchen bumped open, and Theodore emerged carrying a tray covered by a green cloth.

"Here you are, Santa!" he said cheerfully, placing the tray on the table in front of me. "Dig in!"

Smiling with anticipation, I pulled the cloth off the tray and was puzzled to find beneath it only a medium-sized bowl of steaming oatmeal.

"Is this the first course, Theodore?" I inquired. "I believe you forgot to put butter and brown sugar on the tray. That's what I always like to put on my oatmeal."

"No butter or brown sugar for you, Santa," he said. "Too many calories. This oatmeal is your first course this morning, and also your last. Don't look so unhappy. For lunch, you'll get a nice fruit salad with yogurt dressing."

"I can't eat oatmeal without butter and brown sugar, Theodore," I protested.

"That's your decision," he said, "but it's a long time until lunch. If you're as hungry right now as you say you are, you probably want to eat that oatmeal just the way it is."

So I did, one plain, boring spoonful at a time.

"Why aren't *you* eating, Theodore?" I asked. "Aren't you hungry, too?" He was sitting at the table watching me eat and chatting ominously about push-ups and sit-ups and getting the hang of jumping rope.

"I'm going to wait until noon, Santa," Theodore said. "Lars has promised brunch will include smoked salmon and freshly baked blueberry muffins. It's going to be a memorable meal."

"When will I be allowed to enjoy blueberry muffins again?" I inquired. The thought of Lars's delectable baked goods made the oatmeal taste that much worse.

"Why, just as soon as you've won *The Great Santa Search*!" Theodore said cheerfully. "Finish every bit of that oatmeal, Santa. You need to keep up your strength! Children all over the world are depending on you!"

"I hope next Christmas Eve some of them leave out blueberry muffins for me," I mumbled. But I did eat all of the oatmeal, because it was hours until lunch and my fruit salad with yogurt dressing.

"Young Mr. Butler's picture was included with the newspaper article—slide, Willie—and you can see he was a very cheerful-looking boy. He asked the reporter to identify him as 'Bobbo' in the story because he thought that was a good name— this is a direct quote—'for a show-business impresario.'"

Seven

 he next day, Felix called Bobbo Butler at the FUN-TV office in New York City to say he would accept a position on *The Great Santa Search* staff. Bobbo was predictably effusive, promising Felix that afterward he'd be bragging about being part of the most famous broadcast in television history. When Felix repeated this to the rest of us, some wondered why Bobbo remained so certain the program would attract unprecedented public interest. Though he'd mentioned *The Great Santa Search* on Christmas Eve at the conclusion of *Merry Monkey,* there hadn't been any speculation about the show in the news media. Of course, very few people had watched *Merry Monkey.* I felt sure Bobbo had all sorts of marketing plans in mind and was glad Felix would be finding out about them.

Bobbo informed Felix his title would be "senior consultant," and that he should come to New York in another two weeks for the program's first planning meeting. Bobbo himself would be producer, but Felix also needed to meet the show's director and set designer and several other important members of "the team."

That agreed upon, Bobbo then informed Felix he was handing the phone over to Heather Hathaway, who would discuss salary with him. She astonished Felix by telling him he would be paid several hundred thousand dollars, broken down into monthly increments. She asked for a home address where the paychecks could be sent, and Felix supplied her with a post-office box number in Boston, where Bobbo Butler assumed he and Sarah lived. We had post-office boxes in a number of major cities all over the world, so on the rare occasions when we needed to communicate with outsiders we wouldn't have to reveal our North Pole location. Certain government officials and special friends had our North Pole e-mail addresses, but we did not include Bobbo Butler or Heather Hathaway in this exclusive group.

"Well, my new salary means that's one less toy patent we'll have to sell this year," Felix told me proudly. Our North Pole toy-manufacturing operation is both extensive *and* expensive; we pay for raw materials like wood and paint and plastic by licensing some of the inventions of Leonardo, Ben, and Willie Skokan to carefully selected toy companies who pledge to produce only the highest-quality products for children. We never do business with manufacturers who don't adhere to the most rigorous standards—LastLong Toys, for example, was not and would never be our partner. Some of the income is also used to defray other expenses like food for humans and feed for reindeer; upkeep of our electric, heating, and plumbing systems; clothes; and assorted costs of travel. We are exceptionally fortunate not to need health-care benefits. Everyone who lives and works at the North Pole is blessed with apparently endless good health. And, of course, there's no need for North Pole salaries. Everything any of us might want is supplied, and no one is afflicted by the terrible disease of greed. Felix's considerable *Great Santa Search* salary would be contributed to the general North Pole account, to be used as needed.

We were glad there was a little time before Felix had to go to New York to meet with Bobbo, because Leonardo was working hard to find out all he could about him, and about Lucretia Pepper, too. A few times, Leonardo asked me if he might not be allowed to hack into certain government files to see if there might be any information in them about the two that might prove useful to us. It was something my friend the famous painter-inventor could have accomplished; there was no password he couldn't guess or firewall he couldn't crack. But at the North Pole, as it should be everywhere, we respect each individual's right to privacy. Anything that was a matter of public record about Bobbo Butler and Lucretia Pepper we could and would study, but even if we were working against them regarding *The Great Santa Search* we would still observe appropriate limits.

Just before Felix was supposed to return to New York, Leonardo announced he'd completed his Internet investigations and wanted to report on what he'd discovered. It was a welcome distraction for me. Every morning at 6:00 a.m., Theodore knocked on my bedroom door to escort me to the gymnasium. There he would direct me through an increasingly difficult series of exercises that left me feeling sweaty and quite sore, often with muscles aching in body areas where I had not previously realized I even had muscles. Afterward he would escort me to the dining hall, where I would have to swallow down oatmeal or plain, tasteless cold cereal while all around me everyone else enjoyed omelets and French toast and English muffins. At lunchtime, I interrupted my workday for salad of some sort. Dinner, always a highlight of everyone's North Pole day, found me settling for broiled chicken breast or vegetable soup while the rest of our fellowship dined splendidly on pot roast or shrimp-stuffed crab cakes or the unmatchable enchiladas and tamales Lars likes to cook while wearing a massive Mexican sombrero. At times each day my stomach rumbled so loudly that anyone standing near me thought they were hearing thunder. Feeling sore and hungry at the same time is a particularly depressing combination. Theodore assured me that, after a month when I weighed myself and saw how many pounds I had lost, it would all seem worth it. I wasn't as positive. Once or twice—all right, nearly every night—I attempted to sneak out after midnight to raid the six-foot-high refrigerator in the kitchen, but my annoyingly alert wife always woke up and ordered me back to bed. I know I mentioned earlier that no one is anyone else's boss at the North Pole, but Layla has a certain air of command that makes disagreement with her difficult, if not impossible.

When we all gathered in the main conference room to listen to Leonardo's report, several in our fellowship had to muffle giggles because my stomach was rumbling at a particularly concussive rate. It was not my stomach's fault. Leonardo had chosen to call us together in mid-afternoon, and the garden salad I'd consumed just a few hours earlier hadn't come close to satisfying my appetite. Four slices of tomato, a half-dozen leaves of lettuce, a bit of radish, and some cucumber slices, plus a small pear for dessert, simply do not constitute a full meal.

Then Leonardo came in, laden with what appeared to be a dozen manila file folders that were each crammed with documents. Willie Skokan trailed after him, also carrying a pile of folders. Leonardo directed him to drop them on the long table, and, after Willie did, dropped his own folders on top. The resulting mountain of material rose nearly to Leonardo's chest, and then he had to find his reading glasses, fumbling though various pockets and becoming increasingly confused until someone told him the glasses were perched on the top of his head. Leonardo put his glasses on and then had to spend several more minutes shuffling the file folders until he had them in the right order. Finally, he cleared his throat and we all leaned forward to listen.

"We are dealing with two very interesting people," he began. "I'll begin with Bob O. Butler, who has referred to himself as 'Bobbo' ever since the fifth grade, when he was asked to produce a school Christmas play. Willie, the first picture, please." Willie Skokan pushed a button; the room darkened and a photograph of a school flashed on the screen that covered one wall. "Milligan Elementary School in Ward, Ohio, in 1961. This is where Bob O. Butler staged what was apparently a spectacular program; the local newspaper did a story afterward. Every child in the school participated. There were production numbers where dozens of children danced while all the teachers played kazoos. Young Mr. Butler's picture was included with the newspaper article—slide, Willie—and you can see he was a very cheerful-looking boy. He asked the reporter to identify him as 'Bobbo' in the story because he thought that was a good name—this is a direct quote—'for a show-business impresario.' We can see that Bobbo Butler knew early in life what he really wanted to do. In looking through his subsequent school yearbooks, it seems that every year he always organized some sort of holiday extravaganza. As a senior at Dewberry High in Ward, he gave an interview to his school news-paper and said—do we have that photo, Willie? Good—that he would always try to help everyone especially enjoy Christmas because—this is another direct quote—'Santa Claus is very real to me.'"

"What a lovely sentiment, Leonardo," Layla commented. "Tell me, what kind of record of Bobbo Butler's childhood do we have in our own North Pole archives?"

"Lights, Willie," Leonardo requested. He adjusted his glasses and fumbled with the pile of file folders on the table in front of him, picking up and discarding each in turn until he found the one he wanted. "Bobbo Butler of Ward, Ohio, was one of our most exemplary children, a maxi-mum true believer."

Leonardo's description of young Bobbo Butler as a *maximum true be-liever* told us a great deal. It was one of several categories we used at the North Pole to record when and under what circumstances we no longer delivered Christmas gifts to individual children. This was and will al-ways be a critical moment in any young person's life, and we take it very seriously.

Even Santa Claus can't do *everything*. Each Christmas, our fellowship is taxed to its physical limits by endeavoring to bring presents to every deserving, believing boy and girl. Every year, naturally, there are new children who expect and must receive our presents, so they will learn through this wonderful, traditional process how important it is to celebrate each holiday season with acts of love and generosity. But because North Pole resources, though immense, still have their limits, this also means that each Christmas a certain percentage of children must for the first time do without a gift from Santa, though hopefully this will not in any way lessen their enjoyment of the holiday.

From the moment we became organized enough to establish toy factories in certain cities, and afterward when we consolidated our operations at the North Pole, one of our greatest challenges has been to keep careful track of all the world's children who believed in and hoped for gifts on St. Nicholas Day, Christmas, and Epiphany. There were always homes where we were not welcome. In some cases, this was because the families there were not of the Christian faith. We respect all beliefs. Because our mission is intended to spread ideals of universal goodwill, we do hope our holiday gift-giving also benefits those who don't participate in "Santa" traditions.

But we're still welcome, or, I should say, *expected*, in millions of other households with children who can't wait for the one morning each year when gifts from the North Pole ought to be waiting for them. Before the advent of computers, we had to maintain thick ledgers listing the names and addresses of each deserving boy and girl. It was extremely difficult, but necessary. Much of the months of November and December were taken up just planning proper delivery routes, because the list of places where we had to stop changed each year as we added and subtracted names.

I know certain popular holiday carols (and, sometimes, exasperated parents) suggest otherwise, but we never eliminate children from our gift-giving because of bad behavior. No child is perfect; reasonable discipline from responsible adults is necessary in the life of any young person. Gift-giving is a gentler form of lesson, and one all of us at the North Pole believe is just as effective.

We stop bringing children gifts under certain specific sets of circumstances, and, over the years, we have developed code words for these. Now that the North Pole is equipped with state-of-the-art computers (usually Leonardo, Ben Franklin, and Willie Skokan are the masterminds of technological breakthroughs), we are able to enter raw data on each child as it arrives in the form of reports from parents, teachers, clergy, and so forth. As in the cases of Bobbo Butler and Lucretia Pepper, this means Leonardo can call up a report on anyone's childhood gift-giving history at the touch of a keyboard.

Some children are classified as *believers*. During their early years, they believe in Santa. They're thrilled by the thought I'll visit their homes and leave them a gift. But at some point, at age six or seven, perhaps, they stop believing. Often it's because an older sibling mocks their belief. Sometimes they're so disappointed by "department store" Santas that they decide there can't be a real one. They might have stayed up on Christmas Eve to try to see me, only to see instead their parents putting gifts under the tree. (They wouldn't realize I arrive much later, after even parents are in bed and fast asleep.) In any event, they no longer expect me in their homes. Now, this doesn't mean they no longer get Christmas gifts, but all of these will now come from parents and other caring relatives and friends. Believers don't have to lose their love of the holiday or necessarily fail to understand and practice the love and generosity exemplified by the season. When they grow up, they even tell their own children about Santa, because they think they're entertaining with stories about someone mythical. That's all right.

True believers are children who retain their faith in me much longer. They know in their hearts that I exist, and because of that, they also gradually realize even Santa can deliver only so many gifts on one night. So each of these generous boys and girls at some point—usually around the age of ten, or eleven, or twelve—makes it clear he or she no longer expects gifts from Santa, which allows me a bit more precious time on Christmas Eve to visit the home of a younger child instead. It's such a natural, generous gesture. True believers always grow up to be warmhearted, admirable adults who encourage their own children to believe in me because they know that belief offers rewards far beyond a gift to open on Christmas morning. The majority of children are true believers.

Then there are the rare, wonderful *maximum true believers*. These boys and girls reach the moment when they voluntarily give up my gifts so that others might receive them, and their love for me never wavers. Besides welcoming me into their homes forever, they find ways to personally spread Christmas generosity into their communities, often by organizing efforts to make certain the neediest children enjoy happy holidays. They become in the finest sense my most valuable companions, every bit as important to what I do as anyone at the North Pole. I have often thought that maximum true believers are God's special Christmas gift to me, and I am grateful for them.

It's almost unheard-of for a child who was a maximum true believer to reach a point in adult life where he or she no longer believes in Santa Claus. Bobbo Butler had told Felix he didn't. My curiosity was aroused.

"Leonardo, does your research give any indication when and why Bobbo stopped believing in me?" I asked.

Leonardo shuffled some papers. "I think we can tell. I've got some reports here. Now, after he grew up Bobbo always held Christmas in his heart. When FUN-TV was dominating television, he was often quoted as saying his network's annual holiday broadcast was his favorite show of the year. He wanted everyone everywhere to love Christmas and Santa Claus as much as he did. I suppose here at the North Pole we didn't take as much notice was we should have because we seldom watch television at all. But Bobbo certainly still believed, right up until five years ago."

"What happened then?" I wondered.

"I have some of this from media reports and more from two other children's files that I'll come to in a moment. When reality TV began to snatch high ratings at the expense of more wholesome, family-oriented programming, the FUN-TV network got into terrible financial trouble. Fewer companies wanted to buy commercial time on their programs. Bobbo wanted to save his company, naturally, and so he began to put in twice as many hours on the job as he had before. Soon he was working all day and then sleeping on a cot in his office. He rarely went home to be with his wife and children."

"I think I know what happened next," Layla interjected. "Mrs. Butler became unhappy."

"That's what court documents indicate," Leonardo agreed. "Four years ago, Lily Chin Butler sued her husband for divorce. She claimed he no longer spent time with her or their two daughters, Cynthia and Diana. Apparently she had asked him to change his ways, and he promised he would, but his concern for his network overwhelmed him and he didn't shape up. So the Butlers divorced."

"This is a sad story, but not an unusual one," I noted. "How did this divorce cause Bobbo to stop believing in me?"

"We learn *that* from our North Pole records for Cynthia and Diana Butler," Leonardo replied. "Cynthia is now ten and Diana is eight. According to our files, until four years ago both girls seemed destined for classification as maximum true believers. They believed in Santa Claus with all their hearts, and it wasn't surprising, given how their father loved you and Christmas so much. But after the divorce, the girls blamed all the hours Bobbo would put in on his annual holiday specials for the breakup of their parents' marriage. Since then they have hated Christmas and—I'm sorry—they apparently despise even the idea of you. Diana more so than Cynthia. Since the divorce, they have refused to allow their mother to put up a Christmas tree. They won't accept Christmas gifts from anyone. Apparently they are so bitter that they don't like to see or even talk to their father during the month of December. Bobbo realizes, of course, that the divorce was his fault. He put business before family, as too many grownups unfortunately do. He still loves Christmas, but resents the holiday at the same time because of his daughters' attitudes. That's why he says he doesn't believe in you anymore. And, having lost his daughters in part because of his devotion to the holiday, he's determined not to lose his network. Exploiting Christmas and Santa Claus might make him feel guilty deep down inside, but he's still willing to do it. At least, that's how it seems to me."

"You're undoubtedly right, Leonardo," I said. There were murmurs of agreement all around the table. "Felix, as you spend time with Bobbo, you might try to learn more about this. Since he was a maximum true believer, it might be possible that sufficient urging could persuade him to begin believing again. And now, Leonardo, what about Lucretia Pepper?"

"This fifty-year-old woman is fascinating in many unfortunate ways," Leonardo replied. "I honored your instructions not to break into any secret files. I'll tell you, though, that there are many of them for Lucretia Pepper. I suspect by the identity of the organizations that have gathered confidential information on her—the Justice Department, the U.S. Attorney General's office, and practically every Better Business Bureau in the country—that she is suspected of all sorts of questionable behavior."

"Has she ever been taken to trial on any charges?" Ben Franklin wanted to know.

Leonardo shook his head. "Lucretia Pepper retains the services of the best lawyers in the world," he said. "Once or twice, according to news reports, it was rumored she was in legal difficulty, but apparently her lawyers always got her out of trouble. We'll have to be *very* careful in dealing with her. She has sued countless individuals for slander, usually when they've complained publicly about the quality of LastLong Toys. One mother whose son's toy train broke an hour after he received it for his birthday made the mistake of complaining about it at a school gath-

ering. Someone reported her remarks to Lucretia Pepper, and she successfully sued the woman for $100,000, claiming LastLong products
were being unfairly defamed in public. This is a very dangerous lady."

"What is her personal background, Leonardo?" Amelia Earhart
asked.

"She is the daughter of Delbert Pepper, founder of LastLong Toy
Company," Leonardo said. "The Pepper family lived in Scarsdale, New
York. As a child, young Lucretia attended the finest private schools. She
had no brothers or sisters. From birth, her father trained her to succeed
him as head of the family business. He is the one who taught her to
spend as little as possible on raw materials, and to build toys that broke
quickly so new ones would have to be purchased to replace them. She
obviously learned that lesson well. She received an undergraduate business degree from Yale"—this elicited a snort from Theodore, a proud
alumnus of Harvard—"and a graduate degree from Wharton. Lucretia
made fine grades, all A's except in Business Ethics, which she failed several times before finally passing. I note from an article in a school newspaper that, after she finally passed, she was accused of hiring a stand-in to
take the Business Ethics final exam for her. But her family's lawyers
squelched that. I understand the professor making the accusation was
eventually fired. Hmm. In any event, Delbert Pepper passed away ten
years ago, and, as planned, his daughter succeeded him as president of
LastLong Toys. Every year since, the company's profits have increased
dramatically."

"To some, I'm sure her life is considered a success story," Arthur observed. "There are many people who believe making money to be the ultimate reason for living."

"She makes it, but except to invest it in ways that bring her even more
riches, she doesn't spend it," Leonardo said. "There are no records what-
soever of any charitable gifts, either by her or by LastLong Toys. While
she's willing to spend millions for product publicity, she won't give one
cent to help the poor."

Layla wanted to know if Lucretia Pepper had a husband and children. Leonardo said she had no family at all. She'd never married, and her parents were both deceased. There was no record anywhere of her having friends or pets or hobbies.

"Well, there's at least one more source of information, Leonardo," I said. "What is Lucretia Pepper's status in the North Pole gift-giving archives?"

Leonardo nervously cleared his throat in the way people do when they're about to say something unpleasant. "Santa Claus, Lucretia Pepper was a never."

"Ah," I muttered. "I suppose I shouldn't be surprised."

Sadly, every so often we encounter children who cannot and will not accept even the possibility that Santa Claus exists. In our files, they are designated as *nevers* because they never have believed—not in Santa Claus and not in the generosity of spirit that characterizes the holiday season itself. From the time they learn to talk, they mock other children who believe in me. They do their best to embarrass others into abandoning their beliefs. At Christmas they want lots of gifts for themselves and resent anyone else receiving even a single present. Afterward, they never believe they have gotten enough. There are not many of them. I'm glad, and not because they consider me an annoying myth. Never children are inevitably unhappy and usually grow up to be adults like Lucretia Pepper who are obsessed with building their own massive fortunes and couldn't care less about anyone else. I reluctantly accept that they don't believe in me—this is their right. But I do mind that they disparage and try to ruin the beliefs of others.

"Since she's a never, I expect we can't hope Lucretia Pepper might change her mind about this *Great Santa Search*," Bill Pickett drawled. "You better keep on getting in shape, Santa Claus. You'll need to be, come December. Theodore tells me you might have to rope a reindeer or two, so sometime I expect I'll be joining you two in the gym. Ever use a lasso before?"

"I can't say that I have, Bill," I replied. "You're right. Based on what Leonardo has told us, it appears we're dealing with two people with very different reasons for trying to use Christmas for their own ends. Felix, pay careful attention to everything Bobbo says when you attend your meeting with him in New York the day after tomorrow. In fact, take notes."

"I can't read my own handwriting," Felix admitted. "Could I bring Sarah with me this time? She learned to take wonderful notes when she was writing her travel books about colonial America. I'll tell Bobbo that I always work with my wife. Perhaps he won't mind."

Sarah was willing, so it was agreed she should go to New York, too. We filed out of the conference room, talking in subdued voices about Bobbo's unhappy loss of Christmas faith and about Lucretia Pepper being a never. Everyone else returned to their places in the toy factory or in offices where they checked shipments of raw materials or maintained our correspondence with certain companies and governments. I limped back to the private quarters I shared with Layla. My back ached from Theodore's rigorous schedule of early-morning exercises, and I badly needed to soak in a hot tub. It was still a long way to December and *The Great Santa Search,* but not nearly long enough.

This time, Bobbo introduced four people—sound engineer Ken Perkins, costume designer Eri Mizobe, set designer Robert Fernandez, and Mary Rogers, whom Bobbo introduced as "the best director anywhere in television, and she's going to prove it with *The Great Santa Search*."

Eight

arah and Felix had a great deal to report when they returned from New York City. What they had thought would be one short visit with Bobbo Butler stretched into several meetings spread out over three days. There was much more involved in planning a holiday television special than those of us at the North Pole had realized.

My friends arrived in Bobbo's office as requested at 10:00 a.m. on a Monday morning. Heather Hathaway welcomed them warmly, then escorted them to the same conference room where Felix had met earlier with Bobbo and Lucretia Pepper. This time, Bobbo introduced four people—sound engineer Ken Perkins, costume designer Eri Mizobe, set designer Robert Fernandez, and Mary Rogers, whom Bobbo introduced as "the best director anywhere in television, and she's going to prove it with *The Great Santa Search.*"

"How are you folks?" Mary asked, and Sarah and Felix couldn't help but grin at the Texas twang in her voice. "Felix, Bobbo has bragged on you no end. And this lady is Sarah, your wife? I always like to see couples working on a show together. That's how I met three of my own husbands."

"I hope you don't mind that I brought Sarah," Felix said. "She's a great source of ideas, and has been involved in some of my previous projects."

"Of course Sarah is welcome," Bobbo replied genially. "Miss Hathaway, I think if you'll bring coffee for everyone and then sit over there to take notes, we can get started."

When Heather came back and passed around coffee, Sarah gasped when she saw the mugs. They were red and white; the handles were painted to look like candy canes. Each had "*The Great Santa Search*" stamped on one side in lovely, flowing script.

"Where did you get these, Bobbo?" she asked.

"I know a manufacturer in New Jersey," Bobbo said. "Do you like them? We've had a thousand made up, and in another month or so when we really start promoting the program we're going to send one of these mugs to everyone who writes about television. Journalists love free gifts. Every time one of them drinks coffee from that mug, he'll think of *The Great Santa Search*. Of course, that's just the tip of our promotional iceberg. I'm sure you and Felix will think of even better gimmicks. For a change, we've got a big enough budget to pay for anything within reason. Just don't tell me we need to give away flying reindeer."

"We'd never suggest that," Felix said. "After all, there are only eight."

Felix hadn't meant to be funny, but everyone around the table except Sarah and Heather Hathaway began to laugh.

"And their names are Donder and Rudolph and Prancer and what else?" Ken Perkins asked, chuckling.

"Actually, Rudolph isn't one of Santa's eight flying reindeer," Felix said. "He was originally created as part of a sales promotion for Montgomery Ward. The idea of a red-nosed reindeer is wonderful, but that's just something made up. There's never been a red-nosed reindeer at the North Pole."

"See?" Bobbo said proudly. "We've got a real Christmas expert here. Felix, you pay close attention to everything we discuss. If something doesn't match up to official holiday history, say so right away. We want to be as authentic as possible."

"Speaking of which, let's get back to what we were talking about before Sarah and Felix arrived," Mary said. "We've got to figure out how to find these ten men who'll be on the show competin' to become the real Santa. Does everybody still think we just need to search the malls?"

"The Santas hired by the biggest malls are usually the most authentic-looking," Robert Fernandez said. "They have the best costumes and most of the time their beards are real. That could be *very* important if some of the competitions on the show involve sudden movements. We wouldn't want beards flying off into the crowd. That would just *kill* us with the critics."

"The mall idea makes sense, but it also presents a problem," Eri Mizobe interjected. She was a slender, serious-looking young woman. "If we get the media coverage we want, some reporter is sure to ask how we can be certain one of our ten contestants is the *real* Santa. If it comes out in the press that we're getting contestants only from the mega-malls, we'll be accused of not making the competition open to anyone who claims he's Santa."

"So what do you suggest?" Mary asked. "We can't have five hundred fat men in red suits on our program."

"At some point we need to have an open audition, one that the media can come and cover," Eri said. "Maybe we can use the same theater where we'll hold the actual program. We'll invite anyone who wants to be voted the real Santa to come and audition. We'll have them go through some kind of interview process, and in the end probably one or two of them would be good enough to be among the ten who compete on the show."

"But one of the mall Santas will win," Ken Perkins predicted. "The companies that provide them actually train their Santas how to act before they send them out in public."

Bobbo thought the Santa open audition ought to be announced in March and then held during the late spring, perhaps May. He said that was television's "sweeps" month when every network tried especially hard to dominate ratings.

"If we generate media buzz with the auditions in May, that'll keep momentum building right into the fall," he said. "By the time Halloween rolls around, kids all over the country will be too obsessed with finding out who the real Santa is to even think about trick-or-treating."

The Monday morning meeting continued for another two hours. Ken Perkins wanted to know if one of the events on the show might require the would-be Santas to sing Christmas carols; if so, he'd have to install extra microphones and either bring in a studio orchestra or prepare tapes of background music.

"I like the carol-singing," Mary said. "Gives it that *American Idol* feeling. Good reality-TV tradition there, besides Christmas history."

"I don't know that singing is something the real Santa Claus would necessarily be good at," Felix warned, and with good reason. He'd been listening to me warble off-key for centuries. "You wouldn't want to have some otherwise perfect Santa be eliminated because he couldn't carry a tune."

"Ah, if a few of 'em are awful singers, that'll just be comic relief," Mary replied. "We'll need some laughs. You wouldn't want this to get too serious."

By noon, when Bobbo suggested it was time for lunch, Felix and Sarah were certain everything possible had been discussed. But Heather Hathaway was sent out for sandwiches, and it took the whole afternoon for Bobbo and his non–North Pole associates to decide which theater to rent for *The Great Santa Search* (Manhattan's Ed Sullivan Theater was the eventual choice) and whether all the competing Santas had to wear traditional red-and-white costumes.

"I'm imagining more of a rainbow effect," mused Robert Fernandez, the set designer. "That whole North Pole motif is so *stark*. Let's brighten up the background—some aqua and lemon shadow effects, maybe—and Eri can put our Santas into robes of contrasting colors."

"I could do that, but I believe it would detract from the sense of authenticity we're trying to achieve," Eri said. "Felix, you're the history expert. What do you think?"

"The Santas definitely need to stick to red and white," Felix said firmly. Robert looked unhappy for a moment, but then smiled widely.

"Well, at least those red robes will look good in the dance routines," he said. "Mary, have we hired the choreographer?"

"Wait a minute," Sarah interrupted. "*Dance* routines? The ten Santas are going to *dance?*" She sounded almost as horrified as I must have looked when she and Felix informed me of this later.

"Oh, we've gotta have dancing," Mary Rogers said firmly. "Singing and dancing—it sells that spirit of entertaining competition to the audience. Haven't you ever watched a Miss America pageant?"

Before Felix or Sarah could reply, Bobbo looked at his watch and announced everyone would have to return to the conference room at ten the next morning.

"It's almost six now, and I'm supposed to pick up my daughters for dinner at seven," he explained. "They live with their mother up in Scarsdale. I'm going to take them to a restaurant there. I've got to leave now if I'm going to be on time." Bobbo shook hands with everyone and rushed out.

Felix and Sarah needed to find a hotel, and Heather Hathaway volunteered to help. She and Sarah consulted a list of hotels that Bobbo kept in the office, and soon they made a reservation at one a few blocks from the FUN-TV offices. They arranged to stay for two nights. Heather told them there were still many preliminary details of *The Great Santa Search* to talk about.

"Do you have dinner plans, Heather?" Sarah asked. "Felix and I are going to find some nice little restaurant. Perhaps you could suggest one."

Heather mentioned a place that was convenient and not too expensive—"On my salary, I can't afford fancy places," she laughed. "But the food is very good. Once in a while when we've been working late, Bobbo and I have eaten there. I think he likes it a lot, though he's never said so." These last words were spoken quite wistfully, and Sarah shot Felix a quick look that puzzled him.

Over dinner—delicious Italian lasagna with spicy tomato sauce, warm garlic bread, and spumoni for dessert—Felix and Sarah became great friends with Heather. She was a native of Langdon, North Dakota, near the Canadian border. Her family owned and operated a farm there.

"Langdon is wonderful if you like small-town life," Heather explained. "I had nothing against it, but when I was in high school I was Helen Keller in our production of *The Miracle Worker.* As you probably know, as a child Helen Keller couldn't see, speak, or hear, but because of a wonderful teacher named Annie Sullivan she learned to communicate. Afterward, I had two new ambitions. I thought sign language and lip-reading were fascinating, so I learned how to do both, and well enough to win some national competitions. I also discovered I loved being on stage in front of an audience. From then on, my dream was to live in New York so I could become a famous actress on Broadway. I moved to the city right after I graduated from college."

Heather shared some amusing stories about her early years in New York, when she auditioned for every on- and off-Broadway production but kept losing out on roles because she was always taller than the leading men.

"But I loved everything about show business," she explained, waving a lasagna-laden fork. "The creativity involved in thinking of a play or program, then doing all the things necessary to make it happen in front of an audience, is just magical to me. I really believe in magic, don't you?"

"We think there's magic in every life and certainly in both of ours," Sarah replied.

"When I was twenty-six, and after living in New York for almost five years, I finally realized I wasn't ever going to become a famous actress," Heather continued. "There were two choices. I could give up completely and go back home to help run the family farm, or I could find some other way to stay in New York and show business. About the same time, I saw an ad in a magazine for an executive assistant to the president of FUN-TV. I'd watched some of that network's shows when I was much younger and remembered how sweet they always were. I interviewed with Bobbo and he hired me. I take notes during his meetings, I'm the one who's sent out to get coffee, and three or four times a week I have to help him look for his wallet or his reading glasses, which he's constantly misplacing. He doesn't pay me much because he can't. Until we got this *Great Santa Search* deal with LastLong Toys, every month we couldn't be sure we'd have enough to pay the office rent. But I keep things running as smoothly as possible, and once in a while Bobbo will ask me if I have any ideas for shows he's producing. Sometimes he even lets me write a scene or two."

"It sounds like you're a young woman with great potential," Felix said. "Have you thought about changing jobs and perhaps moving on to a bigger, better network than FUN-TV?"

Heather shook her head vigorously.

"Bobbo needs someone who really understands him," she said. "If I weren't there I don't know what might happen to him. He's such a good, decent guy, though you've probably noticed he doesn't have a lot of common sense. But when he thinks he has a good idea, he gets as excited as a little boy at, well, *Christmas,* and that's what I lo—"

Heather stopped in the middle of a word. Felix, spooning up his spumoni, waited for her to finish the sentence, but she didn't. Instead, she blushed and looked down at her plate.

After a few moments of uncomfortable silence, Sarah said, "Bobbo mentioned he had to leave to have dinner with his daughters and that they live with their mother. I assume he's divorced and can only see the girls at certain designated times."

"That's right," Heather confirmed. "Cynthia is ten. Diana is almost nine. Bobbo adores both of them. He and their mother divorced not long after I came to work at FUN-TV. Bobbo was miserable because he missed the girls so much. He's allowed to see them only once a week, though he can call them every day if he wants to, which he always does. He says the divorce was completely his fault because he got too wrapped up with work. Tonight he'll take them out to dinner and ask them to tell him all about what their week was like, and then he'll drop them off at home and drive back to his apartment in the city, already counting the days until he can see them again. Even so, that's much better than last month, when they didn't want to see him at all. Bobbo says he used to love Christmas, but now he dreads December."

The final factor in the breakup of Bobbo's marriage, Heather believed, was the inordinate amount of time he would devote each year to producing FUN-TV's annual Christmas Eve special. From the day after Thanksgiving to long after Cynthia and Diana had fallen asleep on the night of December 24, it wasn't unusual for Bobbo to never get home to Scarsdale at all. Instead, he'd work late and then nap for a few hours on a couch in his Manhattan office.

"After the divorce, I believe it was Diana who told Bobbo that she hated Santa Claus and Christmas because they'd taken her daddy away from her," Heather said. "She was just four. Now the girls usually won't even let their father come visit them during the whole month of December. I keep hoping they'll change their minds and realize how very much he loves them. No parent is perfect. But since the divorce, Christmas has been ruined for Cynthia and Diana, and for their father, too. That's why

I'm so pleased to see him excited about *The Great Santa Search*. Deep in his heart, he knew *Merry Monkey* wasn't very good, but because he's always so sad now during the holidays, he just couldn't think of anything better. Maybe if *The Great Santa Search* is as wonderful as we think it's going to be, Bobbo will learn to love Santa Claus and Christmas again."

In their hotel room that night, Felix asked Sarah why she thought someone as capable as Heather stayed in her low-paying job at floundering FUN-TV.

"It's simple," Sarah said. "She's in love with Bobbo, and she hopes if she stays with him long enough, he'll fall in love with her."

"If he hasn't after four years, I'd guess he never will," Felix replied.

"Four years is nothing," Sarah remarked, rolling her eyes. "How long did we know each other before you realized you loved me?"

"It was only a matter of minutes," Felix assured her. "If I waited a century or two to tell you, it was only so you'd have enough time to learn to adore me completely."

"Do you really expect me to believe that?" Sarah asked sarcastically, but she gave her husband a warm hug and kiss and fell asleep hoping Heather Hathaway's romantic dreams came true, too.

Much of Tuesday's discussion at FUN-TV was focused on events in which *The Great Santa Search* contestants would compete. Mary Rogers was adamant: carol-singing would have to be included.

"The real fun here could be that the Santas won't know in advance what song they'll have to sing," she suggested. "We'll put titles on slips of paper, toss 'em in one of those funny red Santa hats, and make the competitors each pull one out. That'll keep 'em from gettin' any chance to rehearse. Plus, we won't know which ones can carry a tune and which can't. Some of 'em are bound to be horrible. That'll be funny, and it'll make the whole thing seem that much more spontaneous."

Robert and Ken liked the idea of a dance number with all ten Santas to start the show; that kind of onscreen action would encourage audiences to sit down and pay close attention, especially if not all the Santas were light on their feet.

"If one of them trips and the audience starts howling with laughter, that'll be even better," Ken said.

"I'm sure one of them will," Felix predicted gloomily.

Bobbo said that pace was important. Scenes with lots of action needed to alternate with calmer ones. All sorts of talents needed to be tested. This would give everyone watching a way to pick his or her favorite. He also wanted all the competitions—"challenges"—to have some connection with Santa's traditional Christmas Eve duties.

"No sense having them run the hundred-yard dash or anything like that," Bobbo remarked. "We need challenges that play out on a set designed to look like a living room on Christmas Eve—you know, with a fireplace that has stockings hung in front of it."

That inspired eventual agreement on two challenges, chimney-sliding and stocking-stuffing. Santa contestants would race against the clock to see who could slip down a fake chimney fastest while hauling along a heavy bag of toys. In another segment, contestants would race the clock by vying to fill the most stockings with toys within a specified time, perhaps sixty seconds.

"Lucretia Pepper will like that one," Eri Mizobe said. "We can use LastLong Toys." Bobbo told Heather Hathaway to make a note of that and to remind him to call Lucretia Pepper later with the news.

Robert Fernandez wanted to know why there would be two "speed challenges" if the studio audience was supposed to be voting Santas out of the contest after each individual competition. Mary said it would be best to have both "clock" and "vote" challenges, so if those in the studio quickly arrived at a consensus favorite, the winner wouldn't be a foregone conclusion early in the two-hour broadcast.

"We've got to keep the viewers wonderin' who'll win," she reminded everyone.

Even without commercial breaks on behalf of LastLong Toys, it soon became clear there couldn't be more than six challenges. The first few would take longest, because there would be more competitors then. Bobbo had already decided that the final event would have the two surviving Santas each delivering a short, heartfelt speech explaining why he alone should be voted the "official" Santa Claus. Along with carol-singing, chimney-sliding, and stocking-stuffing, that made four, so two more were needed. Bobbo then remembered he'd originally considered reindeer-roping, and Mary immediately agreed. That would involve lots of *action,* she explained.

"People are used to watchin' shows where everything and everybody gets blown to smithereens," she said. "On *The Great Santa Search* we won't have that going for us. If we can't have bullets flyin', we can at least get some lassos in the air. I guess we can rent some reindeer from the Central Park Zoo."

Robert Fernandez cleared his throat and said, "I don't like to be a party pooper, but, well, *poop.* This is live television, and I doubt those reindeer from the zoo will be potty-trained."

"Okay, we'll go to a taxidermist and buy some stuffed reindeer," Ken suggested.

"That will alienate animal-rights activists," Eri argued. "We should use models of reindeer that obviously aren't real. They can look cute, with big eyes and goofy antlers. Put them on some sort of conveyor belt so they move from one side of the stage to the other while the Santas take turns trying to rope them. That would work—and no poop involved."

"That's five," Mary said. "We need one more."

It took a while to come up with the sixth challenge. Bobbo insisted that, whatever it was, it had to be something historically associated with Santa. Present-wrapping was discussed, then discarded. Ken said Santa's helpers probably did that for him. Mary thought the finalist Santas might arm-wrestle, but Sarah quickly pointed out that arm wrestling was rather violent, and Santa Claus never resorted to violence. Eri said hopefully that the Santas might participate in a Christmas quiz, having to answer questions about real events in holiday history. Felix enthusiastically endorsed that one, since it would give me a tremendous advantage. After all, I'd been present for most of it.

But Heather Hathaway, offering her opinion for once, said the quiz was a bad idea. Viewers who didn't know the answers themselves might feel they were somehow being mocked. That would make them change channels.

"We can't have that," Bobbo said emphatically. "All right, then, Felix, I think we're going to put this one on you. You're the Christmas expert here. We need one more challenge that involves Santa tradition and won't offend animal-rights advocates or viewers who don't know holiday history. What's it going to be?"

Now, here I must give my beloved old friend Felix a great deal of credit. He came up with something brilliant.

"Cookie-eating," Felix announced. "It's got everything we need. Kids always leave cookies out for Santa. We set trays of them in front of the competitors, and they each try to eat the most in, let's say, sixty or ninety seconds."

"I like it!" Mary declared. "Those fat men jammin' cookies into their mouths, and crumbs spillin' over their red coats. Clock in one corner of the screen countin' down the seconds. We can put big glasses of milk by the cookie trays so they can wash down the snacks. Bobbo, I think you need to give Felix a bonus for that one!"

"Oh, no bonus is necessary," Felix said. "I just feel certain the real Santa loves cookies, so this will be his favorite challenge on the whole show."

It took another day of meetings before preliminary planning was complete. The longest discussion involved who would make up the live studio audience. Bobbo had originally envisioned an entire crowd of children who were still young enough to all believe in Santa Claus. Ken, who had a son and daughter of his own, said it was very unlikely parents of kids that age would let them go sit in the Ed Sullivan Theater all by themselves. Eri thought it would be a good idea to have children come with their parents "so we keep that whole family theme working." Everyone liked that, and then Heather Hathaway, speaking up for the second time, suggested that grandparents be added to the mix.

"We want three generations of viewers, don't we?" she asked. "So we'll have three generations in the audience."

By late Wednesday afternoon, everyone was anxious to go home. Bobbo said he'd be in touch soon, because the first steps in the long *Great Santa Search* publicity campaign were about to begin. Sarah and Felix asked him to explain more about that, but Bobbo said he knew all of them were worn out and, besides, publicity would be handled by Last-Long Toy Company's marketing department.

"We'll meet back here in April," he concluded. "I hope you'll each take some time to rest, because from April on we'll be working nonstop until Christmas Eve."

That didn't worry Sarah and Felix. They were used to that schedule, only without a few months off. What did concern them on their trip back to the North Pole was how I would react when I learned I would have to sing and dance as well as rope reindeer, slide down a chimney, eat cookies, and explain to an audience of untold millions why I should be chosen for a wonderful job that already was mine to begin with.

But when they returned, I was already in a grumpy mood. Their news only added to the gloom I'd felt since the day before, when I learned my new regimen of diet and exercise might not bring the results I had every right to expect.

Theodore swore my initial weight would remain a secret between us. I would have been too embarrassed for anyone else to know. But now, dressed in a T-shirt and gym shorts, I proudly stepped back on the scale. Everyone leaned forward to stare at the screen that would announce my new, vastly reduced weight.

Nine

or weeks, everyone at the North Pole had been telling me how wonderful I was about to look and feel. The combination of lots of exercise and a healthy diet would result in a trimmer, more energetic Santa, they promised, often as they wolfed down Lars's fabulous desserts while I made do with bran cereal or perhaps a tiny dollop of cottage cheese. I always responded that we'd have to see, wouldn't we? But deep inside I felt rather hopeful myself. After centuries of knowing I weighed a few pounds—all right, many pounds—more than I should, it would have been immensely satisfying to inform Layla I needed trousers with smaller waistlines.

Theodore had suggested that I not weigh myself during the early portion of my *Great Santa Search* training.

"Give it two weeks, or, even better, three," he'd urged. "Then you can climb on the gymnasium scale and feel thrilled at all the pounds that are gone. It will be a bully moment for you, Santa. We'll invite everyone else to come and share in the excitement."

So every morning I got up and ran and jumped and bent and stretched and sweated. Mealtimes found me eating sensibly; Lars complained that he'd have to start stocking twice as much lettuce, broccoli, and other vegetables. I even stopped trying to sneak out of my room to raid the refrigerator in the middle of the night.

The day before Felix and Sarah returned from New York, I exercised as usual, took a refreshing shower, and then returned to the gym instead of going into the dining hall for breakfast. Everyone else was gathered in the gym beside a scale placed between the rows of lockers. In all the time we'd lived at the North Pole, I had stepped on that scale only once before. Theodore had insisted I do so just as we started my training, so we'd know what I weighed when we began. The scale had an electronic screen that flashed the weight of whoever stood on it. Theodore swore my initial weight would remain a secret between us. I would have been too embarrassed for anyone else to know. But now, dressed in a T-shirt and gym shorts, I proudly stepped back on the scale. Everyone leaned forward to stare at the screen that would announce my new, vastly reduced weight. The night before, relaxing after dinner, we'd all speculated how much I would prove to have lost. The consensus was at least twenty-five pounds. I was privately hoping for thirty.

So we all stared at the little screen, and after what seemed to be an eternity, a number popped up. A very disappointing number. The same number, in fact, that had appeared when I'd first weighed myself several weeks earlier.

"This is impossible," Theodore muttered. "Santa, I'm sure there's something wrong with the scale. Step off it for a moment." I did, and Theodore reached down, shook the scale a bit, and then stepped back and gave it a firm kick. "There," he said. "Try again."

I did. Everyone leaned forward. My weight was the same.

"Will someone tell me why I haven't lost an ounce?" I asked plaintively. My wife and friends all looked as distressed as I felt. They came over to gently pat me on the back and offer words of encouragement.

They meant well, but I didn't feel better. After all that exercise and all that delicious food I'd given up, I was still as stout as ever.

"Perhaps we haven't worked *hard* enough, Santa," Theodore said. "It's my fault entirely. You've done all that I asked. Tomorrow we'll start at 5:00 a.m. instead of 6:00, and then—"

"That won't help," Leonardo da Vinci interrupted. "Where his weight is concerned, it will make no difference what time Santa starts to exercise, or how long he exercises, or what he does or doesn't eat, for that matter."

I got off the scale. "Whatever do you mean, Leonardo?" I asked.

"It's unfortunately obvious," he replied. "Now, Santa, of course you're aware that through the magic of your mission, you've stopped aging. In effect, every part of your body—your heart, your brain, your muscles and bones and nerves and digestive system—is apparently invulnerable. They stay healthy and strong."

I nodded. "Please go on."

"Well," Leonardo said, "the same is true for—please forgive me, I'm just being honest—all your, well, *fat cells*. These are impervious to being lost through exercise or diet. They are, like you, timeless, perhaps eternal. You can do nothing to get rid of them. They are part of you, and always will be."

My friends had said of me over the centuries that I was somewhat self-conscious about my weight, and they were right. No one really *likes* being heavy. Until Theodore began my training regimen, though, I'd never really dedicated myself to doing anything about it. I had my gift-giving mission to occupy most of my attention, and, besides, there was so much food that tasted good. So it was hard to accept that when I'd finally tried to get thinner, it was impossible.

My disappointment was so profound that I might easily have given up exercising and following a more sensible diet, but Layla, as always, knew exactly what to say to me.

"It's too bad about not being able to lose weight, Santa, but that wasn't the real reason you've been working so hard with Theodore," she reminded me. "The goal has been to get you into the best physical shape possible to compete in *The Great Santa Search*. Benefits from regular exercise include healthier heart rate, more physical endurance, and a greater sense of self-esteem. Tell the truth: haven't you begun to feel better? Don't you have more energy than you did before?"

Over her shoulder, I saw Theodore. He looked regretful, and my heart went out to him.

"You're right, Layla," I replied. "Theodore, my waistline might remain the same, but my determination to benefit from your expert advice is stronger than ever. Keep helping me, old friend. I may not be the slimmest Santa Claus in this television competition, but I'll surely be the best-prepared! At least until *The Great Santa Search*, I'll remain on the diet and exercise programs you developed for me." Then we all went off to breakfast, where everyone else dined on Lars's savory *huevos rancheros* with *chorizo* (a spicy egg dish accompanied by sausage) while I gulped down my usual oatmeal without butter or brown sugar.

Of course, I couldn't help feeling privately disappointed about the impossibility of my ever losing weight. That is why, when Felix and Sarah returned the next day with their news about my having to sing and dance as part of the competition, I was already not in the best of moods.

"Surely you can convince Bobbo and this program staff of his that Santa Claus doesn't have to sing and dance," I protested. But they told me about producer Mary Rogers and ratings and choreography, and I reluctantly concluded that singing and dancing were in my future.

"There's probably nothing we can do about your voice," Layla said firmly. "Don't look so offended. We've all heard you try to sing. But dancing might be different. I've never actually seen you dance. Perhaps that's one of your talents you've never told me about?"

I shook my head. "Though there were village celebrations I attended that included dancing, I never danced myself when I was a bishop in the early Christian church," I explained. "It would have been considered undignified. And I haven't danced in all the centuries since. There has never been any opportunity."

"Dancing was and remains part of many countries' holiday traditions," St. Francis of Assisi noted. "I wrote some of the first Christmas carols in the early 1200s just so people would have special holiday music to dance to. Perhaps you're a natural dancer, Santa. Let's find out right now!"

Before I could protest, Francis, Felix, Sarah, Ben Franklin, and Willie Skokan all started singing "Jingle Bells" and clapping their hands to establish a solid rhythm. Layla took my arm and pulled me out into the center of the floor.

"This isn't the kind of dancing you'll have to do on *The Great Santa Search*, but at least we can discover if you've got natural rhythm," she said. "Put your left hand in mine, right hand on my waist—one and two and *go*," and away we whirled.

Despite what some suggested afterward, I really did try my best. Layla moved her feet nimbly, and I tried to do the same. Somehow, her instep got between the floor and my foot. She grimaced with pain but gamely kept dancing.

"Sorry," I whispered.

"Concentrate!" she hissed back.

Then I stepped on her other foot—the crunching noise almost drowned out our friends singing "Jingle Bells." Layla dropped my hand and leaned down to massage her bruised toes. I bent down to assure her I was very, very sorry for injuring her twice in succession, and somehow our heads collided. Layla straightened with some difficulty and announced we'd danced enough for the first lesson.

"Francis, can you be responsible for teaching Santa to dance?" she groaned, hobbling a bit more than I thought absolutely necessary. "I'm not sure I'll be healed in time to do it myself."

He looked at me doubtfully. "I'll try my best, Layla."

My friends' news about the other competitions—*challenges*—on *The*

Great Santa Search was much more welcome. Chimney-sliding would not, we all believed, present much of a problem. I had far more experience doing this than anyone else in history. Stocking-stuffing was another sure victory. If I could fill them fast enough to please every hopeful child on Christmas Eve, I could surely speed through that competition as though the other contestants were moving in slow motion.

"Perhaps I'd better train hard in the area of cookie-eating," I suggested. "Wonderful work, Felix, in suggesting that one. I won't disappoint you, I promise." But Theodore reminded me that cookies were not included on my current diet.

"I'm sure when the time comes, you'll excel in this area," he assured me.

That left reindeer-roping. In all my time at the North Pole, and at the Cooperstown farm before that, I'd never roped one of the flying reindeer because I'd never had to. Intelligent, perceptive animals, they simply came when called. Sarah explained how *The Great Santa Search* would involve make-believe targets rather than real reindeer. She added that I was sure to win the roping challenge because I had the best possible instructor. She was right.

In his day, Bill Pickett was perhaps the most famous and talented of all rodeo performers. He could ride any bucking bronco, wrestle any snorting bull to the ground, and rope whatever target was set in front of him. He did all this in a time in America when black men and women were too often considered inferior and not allowed the same rights as white citizens. It was a tribute to Bill's skills, and his character, that he was able to overcome such crippling prejudice and become a national hero to people of all races. Since he had joined our fellowship in 1932, we always found him to be among our most valuable companions. Besides assisting with the development and crafting of toys, he was always ready to help out with the reindeer. We had a full-time handler whose job it was to feed, groom, and exercise them, but Bill had a special touch with all hoofed creatures. While I made a point of taking all eight rein-

deer and the sleigh out for regular training flights, Bill liked to place a hal-
ter on them individually to give extra exercise to whichever reindeer
needed it. Comet and Blitzen especially liked additional runs out along
the North Pole's ice and snow.

So it was natural for Bill to join Theodore and me when roping became part of our training regimen. I was surprised to see him leading
one of the reindeer into the gym on the first morning I was to try my
hand at tossing a lasso.

"Vixen here had a restless night," Bill explained. "She hasn't had a
good run in a week or more, so she's got all that pent-up energy. I talked
to her and she's proud to help you with your roping practice, Santa." As
Bill spoke, Vixen watched him with wide, bright eyes. It was easy to believe she understood every word that was being spoken.

"So what we'll do is, Vixen will stand about ten feet away to start
with," Bill continued. "Now, later on you can practice lassoing a reindeer on the run—Felix told me that on *The Great Santa Search* they'll
have those models moving around the stage somehow—but for now
you can use a stationary target. Get on over there, Vixen." She obediently trotted to the designated spot, her hooves clicking smartly on
the wooden gymnasium floor. "Here's the rope, Santa. Have you ever
used one before?"

I hadn't, so Bill explained the basics. One end of the braided rope was
passed through a metal ring, called a *honda*, attached to the other end. A
noose or loop about six feet in diameter was formed, with the rest of the
rope coiled and held in the left hand. The right hand grasped the loop,
with a little extra rope gathered as well. Keeping the right wrist loose,
the loop was to be gently swung from right to left overhead. When
enough momentum had been established and the swinging hand reached
a point at the front of the right shoulder, the right arm stretched to full
length, a step was taken forward, the right arm was brought down level
with the shoulder, and the loop was released, with the right side of the
loop a bit lower than the left.

"It's not as complicated as it sounds," Bill assured me. "Watch while I do it." He gathered up the rope, shook out a good-sized loop, whirled the loop over his head, and with a smooth, quick motion tossed it at Vixen. The loop settled around her thickly muscled neck like a loose-fitting collar. Bill walked over, took the rope from around the reindeer's neck, gave her a quick hug, and came back to where Theodore and I stood. "Now you try," he instructed.

I had some trouble at first. I couldn't make the loop the right size, and then I didn't twirl the rope fast enough and the loop slipped down over my head instead of flying smoothly to where Vixen patiently waited. Bill untangled me, and Theodore was nice enough not to laugh. The first few times I actually managed to toss the loop, it seemed to go in every direction but toward Vixen. But Bill was a patient teacher. He kept encouraging me, and on perhaps my tenth toss the loop actually did float properly through the air. It still flew several feet from where Vixen stood, but the thoughtful reindeer moved over quickly and stretched out her neck so the loop settled over it. Bill whooped, Theodore clapped, and even Vixen seemed to be smiling. After that I had more confidence and did much better. By the end of an hour, my shoulder was sore from rope-twirling and tossing, but I was consistently able to get the loop loosely around Vixen's neck from all sorts of angles and distances.

"Well done, Santa!" Bill exclaimed. "We'll practice with a stationary target for a few more days, then move up to lassoing reindeer on the run. By the time you're on that TV show, you might just be one of the best ropers in the world!"

"I just have to be the best roper among the ten would-be Santas," I replied. "But thank you, Bill—and thank you, too, Vixen. I know you're only supposed to get sugar cubes on special occasions, but I hope you'll accept some from me now." Vixen's muzzle tickled my palm as she gently ate the treats from my hand.

For the first time in North Pole history, we began keeping careful track of television news programs and many print publications. In Feb-

ruary, Bobbo Butler and the LastLong Toy Company marketing department started the publicity campaign for *The Great Santa Search*. They
began with occasional items on programs and in articles about the television business. Commentators and reporters mentioned in passing that
the FUN-TV network was planning a holiday blockbuster. Though
Bobbo had mentioned *The Great Santa Search* at the conclusion of *Merry
Monkey*, very few people had actually been watching. These new remarks were on shows and in publications that reached much larger audiences. We wondered why until Amelia Earhart pointed out that they
were inevitably programs sponsored by LastLong Toys. Lucretia Pepper was spending a lot of money to make certain *The Great Santa Search*
got sufficient publicity.

By early March, there was speculation in some popular magazines
about what form *The Great Santa Search* might take. Did FUN-TV network president Bobbo Butler mean that the *real* Santa Claus might host
his own holiday special? Commentators were doubtful. From CNN to
the Fox Network, it was widely suggested that Santa had many other
things to do on Christmas Eve. But the "buzz," as Bobbo called it, kept
growing stronger. Then, during the third week in March, Bobbo held a
press conference at the Ed Sullivan Theater in New York City. Every
major television network and cable channel sent reporters and camera
crews; so did all the important newspapers and magazines from around
the country. A few days earlier, Bobbo had revealed to Felix and Sarah
and the rest of *The Great Santa Search* team what he planned to say, so all
of us at the North Pole knew what was coming. Still, we wanted to see
the press conference for ourselves. Because the press conference was
carried live on television, we gathered around one of our big-screen
TVs to watch. Bobbo walked out on stage. If anything, the fringe of hair
around his bald head bristled even more wildly than Sarah and Felix had
described.

"I want to thank all our friends from the media for coming today,"
Bobbo began. "I know it's barely spring, but already there's a sense of

Christmas in the air—or there will be, anyway, when you learn more about *The Great Santa Search.*"

For more than 150 years, Bobbo explained, children in America had met a bewildering series of pretenders who insisted they were Santa Claus. He told about J. W. Parkinson and James Edgar and the Salvation Army—as consultants, Felix and Sarah had provided Bobbo with volumes of information about Christmas history. The result, Bobbo said, was that too many children weren't at all certain whether Santa Claus even existed. But *The Great Santa Search* would change all that.

"From 8:00 to 10:00 p.m. on Christmas Eve, right here in this very theater, FUN-TV will bring together the ten most outstanding Santas in the country," Bobbo said. "One of them will be the *real* Santa Claus. How will we know which one? Because all ten will compete in a series of challenges, with some winners established by beating the clock and others through a vote by our studio audience—an audience, incidentally, made up of three generations gathered together in the wholesome holiday spirit that typifies the best tradition of America and Christmas!"

At the end of the program, Bobbo promised, the audience—"who will represent all of you out there who love Christmas"—would select "the one, the only, the *official* Santa Claus!"

There was an excited murmur from his audience in the theater. Even jaded journalists can become enthusiastic if they think they've come upon a particularly interesting story.

"Where will you find these Santas, Bobbo?" someone cried out.

Bobbo leaned into the microphone and grinned. "Mostly, we're going to keep that part of it a secret. I can tell you that we've hired a team of experts who know exactly where to look for Santa."

"What if Santa isn't that easy to find, Bobbo?" another reporter wanted to know. "Maybe your experts won't look in the right place."

Bobbo's grin widened. "We've thought of that, and it brings me to our next announcement. We don't want to overlook anyone who might turn out to be the bona fide Santa we all want to meet so much. So on

March 31, one week from today, FUN-TV invites anyone who claims to be Santa to come right here to the Ed Sullivan Theater in New York, where we'll hold open auditions for *The Great Santa Search* from noon to 6:00 p.m. We'll set up an interview process that will eliminate all but the most persuasive, and then they can meet with a panel of judges who will decide which of them, if any, should be included among the ten finalists on *The Great Santa Search* itself."

"Can we come to cover the audition, Bobbo?" one particularly famous TV newswoman wanted to know. She didn't so much ask a question as state the obvious. Everyone in the media knew exactly what Bobbo was up to—extensive coverage of the open audition would practically guarantee high ratings for *The Great Santa Search*.

"Come in red suits and white beards and audition yourselves, if you want to!" Bobbo replied.

After a few more questions—someone wanted to know what the challenges would be (Bobbo said that would be announced closer to the program itself) and someone else asked why such an important competition would take only two hours (Santa would have present delivering business to attend to, Bobbo explained—it would be Christmas Eve, after all)—Bobbo thanked everyone for coming. Ben Franklin, looking thoughtful, reached over and switched off our television.

"There was no mention of LastLong Toys or how the winning Santa is supposed to become the company's spokesman," he said. "I wonder why there wasn't."

"Those are the kind of details that will be made public later," I said. "For now, they want to build excitement, and I think they've succeeded. Felix, Sarah, have you heard from Bobbo about any further plans for the open audition next week?"

"He called just before the press conference began," Felix replied. "There wasn't time to tell you before it started. Bobbo wants Sarah and me to fly down to New York; I'm to be one of the judges, along with Bobbo and Heather Hathaway and the rest of the program staff. Some recent college graduates who are working as FUN-TV interns will do the initial screening of whoever shows up. Bobbo thinks we might have fifty or even a hundred people claiming to be Santa. The more who audition, the more interest there is in *The Great Santa Search,* he believes."

"We already know one person who'll be showing up," I said. "We've been talking about what I must do to become one of the ten finalists on Christmas Eve. Of course, I could get hired as a Santa at some big mall; when you go around the country evaluating mall Santas you could pick me then, Felix. But we've agreed I'll go to this Ed Sullivan Theater in New York, answer the interns' questions, do whatever I have to in front of the judges, and I don't see how I won't be an obvious choice as a finalist. I mean, I'm *Santa.* How hard could this be?"

I waved goodbye to him as he rode off, then turned to go inside. But one
of the guards gently but firmly placed his hand on my chest and said,
"Where do you think you're going, pal?"

Ten

hen the weather cooperates—cool breeze, bright sunshine, no awkward puddles to avoid—there are few experiences more exhilarating than strolling about New York City. The Ed Sullivan Theater is located on Broadway, one of the most famous avenues in New York. Times Square is about a dozen blocks further south; to the north is Central Park and Lincoln Center, an elegant hodgepodge of venues where symphonies and ballets are often performed. At any time of the day or night, Broadway is busy, its sidewalks thick with pedestrians and the street itself jammed bumper-to-bumper with buses, private cars, and taxis. But all the commotion is usually quite exciting. There's a definite special energy involved. On those occasions when I visit New York, I always like to take a long walk along Broadway, starting at the lower end of Central Park with its golden monument to those who fought in the Spanish-American War and concluding amid the garish neon signs that cover whole huge walls in Times Square.

So I knew exactly how to find the Ed Sullivan Theater from my hotel across from Lincoln Center on West Sixty-third Street and Broadway. I was pleased to take my usual enjoyable stroll. It was a magnificent spring day, with bright sunshine and temperatures in the very comfortable mid-seventies.

I wore a dark blue sports coat, open-necked white shirt, and charcoal gray slacks. There appeared to be no reason to wear my so-called "Santa suit" of red coat and pants with white fur trim. It seemed clear from Bobbo's comments at the previous week's press conference that costumes were not required, only the ability to convince first some FUN-TV interns and then the final panel of judges that I was well qualified to be Santa Claus. But, to be on the safe side, I brought along my "Santa" clothes in a valise. It never hurts to be prepared, I reminded myself.

As I mentioned, Broadway is always crowded. But as I neared Columbus Circle, it seemed that there were even more pedestrians than usual, all hurrying in the same direction as me. Every car on the avenue was stopped dead in place; horns were blaring. It was just after 11:00 a.m., and Bobbo had said the open audition for *The Great Santa Search* would begin at noon. Under ordinary circumstances, even walking at normal "people" pace it would have taken about fifteen minutes to walk from my hotel to the Ed Sullivan Theater, but now I began to worry that I might not make it on time. It was impossible to walk any faster—people were shoulder-to-shoulder across the sidewalks on both sides of Broadway. I couldn't flag down a cab, because none of the cars on the street were moving.

A policeman trotted by on horseback. I called out to him, "What's causing all this congestion?"

He reined in his steed, leaned down from his saddle, and replied, "There's a mob out in front of the old Sullivan Theater. Haven't you heard about that Santa Claus show? They're having auditions for it today, and at least a thousand people are trying to get inside. If I were you, I'd take a detour around Broadway."

"But I can't," I said. "I'm trying to get to the theater myself. It's very important that I do."

The policeman looked at me, taking in, I suppose, my white beard and wide waistline.

"I'll bet you want to try out to be Santa Claus!" he said, smiling. "I guess you do look a little like him. I think Santa's taller, though."

"I'm tall enough," I answered. "Please, could you help me get to the theater? I'd appreciate it very much."

"You may be too short to be Santa, but at least you're polite," the policeman replied. "Here, I'll pull you up behind me. Hang on tight!" With that, he reached down, took my hand, and hauled me up on the horse, which I'm sure didn't appreciate the extra burden but did not snort or buck in protest. As soon as I was settled, he nudged the horse's sides lightly with his heels, and off we trotted. It was an awkward ride. I had to hold on to my valise and the policeman's waist at the same time, and once or twice I came perilously close to falling off. But I managed to remain generally upright, and people on the sidewalk gaped and pointed at us as we passed.

The policeman pulled his mount up in front of the Ed Sullivan Theater. The name of the venue was emblazoned in yellow letters on a dark blue sign. Guards in uniform were stationed in front of the theater; my friend the policeman called to one, "I brought Santa Claus for you," as he helped me slide down from the back of the horse to the sidewalk. I waved goodbye to him as he rode off, then turned to go inside. But one of the guards gently but firmly placed his hand on my chest and said, "Where do you think you're going, pal?"

"I'm going to go in and convince the judges that I'm Santa Claus," I replied in equally friendly fashion. "Isn't there an audition here today?"

The guard rolled his eyes. "You got that right, buddy, but it's not as easy as you seem to think. There's you and about a thousand others. Take a look around."

I did. All around me, for a hundred yards down the sidewalk in both directions and even across Broadway, people who obviously planned to audition for *The Great Santa Search* were waiting. They comprised a colorful lot. Many were older and more than half had beards, but those beards were every possible hue, from snow white like mine to all sorts of bright, dyed colors. There were stout men, certainly, but some thin ones, too. Many wore variations of "Santa suits," and more than a few were in full holiday regalia, including shiny black boots. One man led on a leash a Great Dane with fake antlers dangling from its head. A sign hanging around the dog's neck read "*Dasher.*"

There were men of every race—and a few women, too. One carried a sign suggesting that the Santa Claus tradition was sexist. It made me smile, because she had obviously never met Layla. And weaving their way through the mob were cameramen from every TV network, recording the crazy scene for their evening newscasts. *That* would thrill Bobbo Butler, I knew.

"How do I get inside?" I asked the guard, who gestured toward the front theater doors with his thumb.

"The people in charge are going to send out assistants and have all of you form a line," he said. "You're lucky that cop brought you right up front. My best advice is to hold your ground. It's going to get even more nuts than it already is."

Exactly at noon, a number of young men and women emerged from the theater. I guessed they were FUN-TV's interns. One had a battery-powered megaphone. She shouted into it that everyone who wanted to audition needed to form a single line. That announcement resulted in further chaos rather than order. All the would-be Santas surged toward the theater, elbowing each other in very unseemly fashion. The guard I'd been speaking to winked, then yanked me right to the head of the line.

"Just be sure to bring me something special on Christmas Eve," he chuckled. I looked carefully at the name badge on his coat.

"I certainly will, Gary Elders," I promised. "Don't I remember that, as a boy, you especially liked baseball equipment from Santa? This year, you'll receive the finest catcher's mitt you've ever owned." And it would be, too: Jackie Robinson, who was the first black athlete to play in the major leagues, is now one of my North Pole helpers. He designs all of the sports equipment we distribute on Christmas Eve.

The guard stared at me, muttered, "Yeah, well, good luck," and moved away to help control the other Santa hopefuls trying to shove their way into line. I wish I could have seen his face on Christmas morning. Every so often, Santa Claus *does* bring gifts to special grown-ups.

I regretted the chaos. So many would-be Santas behaving badly didn't set a good example for children. But that was beyond my control. At least I was at the head of the line. It would be a simple thing, now, to get through the first round of questions and then go before the panel of judges. Felix didn't think they would ask me to sing or dance. I might have to talk a bit about life at the North Pole or something similar, he'd predicted. Mostly, Bobbo and the others would just want to get the open audition over with so they could concentrate on mall Santas, since they remained certain their eventual winner would come from that relatively small, select group.

One of the interns, a trim young woman dressed in a stylish business suit, motioned me over. She held a pen in one hand and a clipboard in the other.

"You're the first one in," she announced. "Follow me."

Now, *this* was more like it! She guided me through the theater lobby and past the entrance to the main auditorium. The doors to the auditorium were open, and I glanced in as we passed. The stage looked very small, and so did the tiers of seats. I remembered Felix telling me the Ed Sullivan Theater had an audience capacity of 461. A long table was set on the stage, and sitting behind it, chatting idly, were Felix and Bobbo Butler. I didn't know any of the others with them, but I guessed the very tall woman was Heather Hathaway and the other four must be director

Mary Rogers, sound engineer Ken Perkins, set designer Robert Fernandez, and costume designer Eri Mizobe. It would be interesting to meet them in person, as I felt certain I would after my initial interview.

The FUN-TV intern and I proceeded along a lengthy corridor and then up a flight of stairs. We entered a wide room that contained perhaps a dozen square tables, with folding chairs set up by each. The young woman walked to the table farthest from the door, sat down, and motioned to me to take the seat across from her. She put her clipboard down on the table and studied it for a moment. Behind us, other interns led more Santa candidates into the room. They seated themselves at the adjacent tables. When each table was taken by an intern and a would-be Santa, the door was shut.

"My name is Emily Vance," the young woman informed me as she looked up from her clipboard. Her blond hair was pulled back in a severe bun, and her expression was properly businesslike. But there was still a sense of softness, a not-quite-disguised sweetness and even lingering childish innocence, about her. Like many young people in their early twenties, Emily was still in the process of transitioning from youth to adulthood. It can be a difficult, even frustrating, time. "I'm going to ask you some questions from a list we're supposed to use, and I want you to answer them as completely and persuasively as you can," she said. "Got it?"

"That seems simple enough," I replied. "I'm ready to begin."

She picked up her pen. "Name, please."

"Santa Claus."

Emily rolled her eyes. "You have to take this seriously."

"I am. My name is Santa Claus."

The young woman sighed, rolled her eyes again, and then suddenly nodded. "Oh, I get it. You're doing this completely in character. That's pretty good." She made several notes on the paper attached to the clipboard. "I guess you'll tell me next that your hometown is the North Pole."

"Exactly," I said. "I've lived there since 1913. Before that, I lived on an isolated farm near Cooperstown, New York."

Emily looked up from her clipboard. "If you don't mind my saying, try not to add too many unnecessary details. Stick to the real Santa story. You're from the North Pole, period."

"I just thought you might want to know," I said. "All right, I'm from the North Pole."

"What's in your bag?" Emily wanted to know.

"I didn't know if I would need my red-and-white clothes," I told her. "I brought them just in case. Would you like to see them?" When she nodded, I opened the valise and took out my red coat with fur trim and red trousers. I hadn't brought my hat or boots.

Emily rubbed one of the coat's sleeves between her fingertips.

"Gee, real wool!" she exclaimed. "Where'd you buy this? It must have cost a fortune."

"I like wool," I replied. "It keeps me quite warm, and that's important when I'm flying my sleigh through freezing winter snowstorms."

"That's not bad," Emily said approvingly. "The part about keeping warm while flying through snowstorms is a nice little detail. You were smart to think of it." She consulted the list of questions again. "Okay, when and why did you first give presents?"

"Oh, that goes back a very long way," I told her. "In 292 AD I was twelve years old and living in the little town of Patara in the country of Lycia, which is known today as Turkey. A merchant named Shem had three daughters who wanted to get married, but their father had lost his fortune and could not provide them with dowries. I quietly went into their home one night and left coins for each in stockings they had hung to dry by the fire." I smiled at this very happy early memory, but Emily was not equally pleased. In fact, she seemed irritated.

"I told you, stick to the real Santa story."

"I am," I protested.

Emily sighed again. She had very expressive sighs. This one clearly indicated she was quickly losing patience with a foolish old man who was wasting her valuable time.

"Look," she said, "At first I had some hopes for you. You've got the right look, you know? Fat, but not too fat. Old, but not decrepit. I think that beard is real, isn't it? And actually white, not just dyed that color? But you've got to do better with these answers. Think about it. Santa Claus is American, and you're telling me you're an Arab."

"I have no specific nationality because Santa Claus loves all children and nations," I explained. "By birth, I suppose I am Turkish, which, by the way, is not the same thing as an Arab, which itself is a catchall term for natives of a vast region."

"Oh, please," Emily scoffed. "On *The Great Santa Search*, nobody's going to vote for you if you're not American. Are you trying to make me eliminate you? You seem like a nice man. I'd like you to do well—it'll look good on my résumé if I'm the one who processes the guy who wins. But you've got to work with me."

"How do I do that?" I inquired politely.

"By sticking to the actual facts about Santa Claus."

"And what are those?"

Emily put the clipboard down on the table and looked around the room, probably feeling jealous because all the other interns appeared to be flying through the interviews with *their* Santas.

"It's really simple," she said. "Santa Claus is American. He lives at the North Pole. He started giving his presents, I think, after the Revolutionary War when we won our freedom from the British. He gives toys as gifts, not money to girls who want to get married. Are you with me so far?"

"The North Pole isn't in America," I pointed out. "If I live there, how can I be an American?"

Emily's shoulders shook with the force of her latest sigh.

"The North Pole is American if we want it to be. Are you going to argue about everything?"

"Not at all," I assured her. "Technically, I suppose you're right that

Santa Claus is American, because that is the name by which I'm known to American children. Of course, in Britain I'm Father Christmas, in France I'm Père Noel, in—"

Emily waved her hand to cut me off in mid-sentence. She made several notes, looked at me doubtfully, and said, "Enough about that. Let's keep going. Tell me about the North Pole."

"That would be a pleasure," I replied. "I live in a large self-contained environment with some dear friends who help me in every phase of my gift-giving mission. These very special men and women—"

Emily waved her hand again. "Don't say men and women. Say *elves*."

"Why would I say that?"

"Because Santa Claus lives at the North Pole with his elves. Everybody knows that."

Now it was my turn to sigh.

"Thomas Nast, why did you ever have to draw those cartoons?" I muttered.

"What?" Emily asked. "Thomas who?"

"Thomas Nast was a cartoonist for *Harper's Weekly* and other publications during and after the Civil War," I said. "He was very talented, and his drawings encouraged belief in Santa Claus, which I appreciated. But what I didn't appreciate was him drawing me as an elf and surrounding me with elf helpers. That's where this whole silly elf business comes from. My friends who work with me are real human beings, not mythical creatures."

"Legolas the elf is my very favorite character in *Lord of the Rings*," Emily snapped. "Don't make fun of elves."

"I didn't mean to offend you," I assured her. "All three books in the *Lord of the Rings* trilogy are wonderful."

"Are they books, too?" Emily asked. "I thought they were just movies. The guy who played Legolas was really cute. Anyway, let's get back to my questions. I don't think we need much more. Now: why do you want to be Santa Claus?"

"I already *am* Santa Claus. Perhaps you should ask why I love *being* Santa."

Emily looked around again. Already, most of the other interns were shaking hands with their first Santa candidates, ushering them out the door, and sitting down with their next round of applicants.

"Okay, whatever. Why do you love being Santa?"

"It is a privilege to help children learn the true meaning of Christmas, which is gratitude to God for sending us his son Jesus, and gaining from that gratitude a sense of love and generosity of spirit toward others," I said. "It is always my goal for Santa Claus to be part of the holiday celebration, but never mistaken for the reason for the holiday itself."

Emily put down the clipboard and pen.

"I think that's all I need to hear. Mister, you can't bring God and Jesus into a Christmas Eve TV special. Do you know how many viewers would change channels? Do you have any idea what would happen to *The Great Santa Search* ratings? The last thing people want to think about on Christmas Eve is something *serious*. Santa Claus isn't about Jesus. He's about toys under the tree on Christmas morning. Jeez, don't you know *anything* about Christmas?" She stood up and extended her hand. "Thanks for coming in. You can go out through that door; somebody will escort you back to the street."

"Are you eliminating me from the audition?"

"You're just not Santa Claus material," Emily declared. "All that Arab stuff, and the North Pole isn't America, and no elves. And then bringing Jesus into it. You need to learn your Christmas history better. Next!"

I stood up and shook hands.

"You did believe in Santa Claus once, didn't you?" I asked gently.

Something briefly flashed in Emily's eyes—surprise at my question, certainly, but also the joy of some childhood Christmas memory, and finally regret for innocence lost.

"I guess," she said. "But then I grew up."

Another young intern guided me back down the corridor and toward the theater lobby. As I passed the open door leading into the main auditorium, I could see Felix and the other judges down on the stage. They were talking with the first few candidates who'd passed the initial interview process. One was the man with the Great Dane.

I was startled to see a large framed photograph of Santa Claus on one wall—startled because I had difficulty believing it wasn't me. This actor—he looked so genuine, it seemed rude to think of him as an *impostor*—had a fine white beard, genial smile, and husky physique.

Eleven

t least we didn't choose the man with the Great Dane as a *Great Santa Search* finalist," Felix said soothingly. "Almost nine hundred Santas tried out at the open audition, and we ended up picking just two of them. It's no disgrace that you didn't get through the first round."

Felix and all my other friends were trying hard to lift my spirits, but without much success. I'd been so sure I would go to New York, sail through the audition, be chosen as a finalist, and then not have to worry anymore about getting the opportunity to compete on the Christmas Eve program. There, of course, I'd win easily and then thwart Lucretia Pepper's plan to have the "official" Santa serve as spokesman for Last-Long Toy Company. Now, nothing seemed certain. What if I never had the chance to be on *The Great Santa Search* at all?

But when I expressed my concern to everyone at the North Pole on the day after my disastrous trip to New York, they took turns telling me not to worry.

"After all, only two places out of ten are taken so far," Amelia Earhart noted. "You'll get one of the other eight. Remember, Felix is one of the people who'll be making those selections. Just get a job as Santa at a big mall. It's not going to be that hard."

"That's what I thought about the open audition, and I was wrong," I reminded her.

"But becoming a mall Santa is entirely different," Leonardo said. He and Willie Skokan had barged through the door to my den, carrying more of their manila file folders. "There's a specific process to be followed, Santa Claus. May I tell you about it?"

I was sitting in my favorite easy chair, a pot of steaming chamomile tea on a small table in front of me. I waved Leonardo and Willie to seats on the other side of the table, and poured them each a cup. Layla, Felix, Sarah, Amelia, Bill Pickett, and Teddy Roosevelt were already in the room. I have a rather large den.

"I thought I'd have to simply fly the sleigh to some city or other, go to its largest mall, find the mall's employment office, and apply for its holiday position of Santa," I said. "I hope I'll do better with some mall personnel manager than I did with young Emily, the FUN-TV intern. I'm afraid she found me to be quite unqualified."

Leonardo shook his head, which made his long white beard waggle. He and Willie dropped their folders on the table.

"It no longer works that way, at least at most of the larger, more popular malls," Leonardo told me. "Mall management considers it crucial to have highly believable Santas working during the Christmas season. Someone like J. W. Parkinson's silly Kris Kringle would never be hired today. Willie and I have done considerable research on this. The malls work with what I suppose you might call 'Santa search firms,' companies that hire and train prospective Santas before they ever interact with trusting children. These companies provide Santas to the malls, guaranteeing their ability to help boys and girls enjoy the holidays without endangering their belief in, well, *you*. So what we must do is select one of these companies, have you hired by it, and then placed in some prominent mall where Felix can 'discover' you and recommend you as a finalist on *The Great Santa Search*."

I sipped my tea and nodded. "I'm pleased that there's some procedure in place to ensure competent Santa imitators. Still, Leonardo, you seem to take it for granted that one or another of these Santa companies will hire me. It simply isn't enough to be the *real* Santa. If it was, I'd already have been picked as a finalist in yesterday's audition."

"You have to consider the circumstances," Layla said in the slightly sharp tone she sometimes used when she felt I was missing an obvious point. "Bobbo Butler allowed interns to ask superficial questions and make their own snap judgments. While I'm sure those young people did their best, if Emily is an example then they clearly knew very little real Santa history, or even cared about it. If these search firms are as committed to high Santa quality as Leonardo obviously believes, then they will recognize how qualified you are. Until you're given reason to think otherwise, give them the benefit of the doubt."

I finished my tea and set down the cup. Leonardo immediately pushed a dozen sheets of paper into my hand.

"I contacted one of the search companies and asked them to send an application," he explained. "The Noel Program is based in Golden, Colorado. They provide Santas to malls around the country every holiday season. They really want to hire only the most qualified people, Santa. You can tell from the questions they require applicants to answer."

There was a letter stapled to the application form. I adjusted my glasses and read it out loud:

"*Dear Santa,*" it began. "*Thank you so much for your interest in The Noel Program. We are delighted you have contacted us!*"

"Already, they're friendlier than Emily!" Layla observed. "Please keep reading, Santa."

"*We serve more than 175 malls nationwide,*" the letter continued. "*Our Santa Team always welcomes cheery and enthusiastic gentlemen with natural white beards to perform the role of the lovable character Santa Claus during the holiday season."*

"Ah, I see that they realize I'm lovable," I said to Layla.

"Some of the time," she replied. "Go on with the letter."

So I did. It requested that I completely fill out the application forms provided, then send them on to the company office in Colorado. When they were received, I would be contacted by telephone. If I was considered a prospective Santa candidate, a personal interview would be arranged.

"I suppose I ought to get this application filled out," I suggested. "Does anyone have a pen?"

Amelia lent me hers, and I turned to the first page of the application form. The first request was for basic personal information—name, address, and employment background.

"I suppose I can't put down my name as 'Santa Claus,'" I said. "Like Emily at yesterday's audition, they'd think I was joking."

"Well, you can certainly say your first name is Nicholas," Sarah reminded me. "But a last name is necessary, too. Have you ever had one?"

Actually, I hadn't. When I was born in 280 AD, people were generally known only by one name. I was simply called "Nicholas" then. So Theodore suggested it might be great fun to think up a new last name for me, and the suggestions flew—"North," from Amelia, alluding to my home at the North Pole, and "Priest," from Sarah, since that had been my original profession. Layla thought "Grinch" might be a delightful possibility—we all loved that fanciful Christmas story written by Dr. Seuss.

But it was quiet Willie Skokan who came up with the best one.

"Why not call yourself 'Nicholas Holiday'?" he asked. "It's in keeping with the spirit of the Christmas season, and 'Holiday' is quite a common last name."

Everyone agreed, and that was the name I wrote at the top of the application.

I next had to supply a home address, social security number, and telephone number. That part was easy. Leonardo's wizardry with computers and electronic data systems allows us to create satisfactory personal backgrounds when necessary. Felix and Sarah, for instance, had to supply an address and other data to FUN-TV before officially becoming employed there. I used one of our North Pole cell phones as my contact number.

"Employment history" was a bit more difficult. I almost put "bishop," which was factual but liable to result in additional scrutiny by the Noel Program staff. I did not want to mislead anyone, though—after some discussion we finally settled on "self-employed toy consultant," adding Willie Skokan's name and North Pole cell phone number if Noel decided to check references.

"I'll only tell them good things about you, Santa," Willie assured me.

Next came something labeled "Data Sheet." The questions were quite curious—Did I have a natural beard? ("Yes.") Did I have my own black Santa boots? ("Of course.") Did I have my own tiny round gold Santa glasses? ("Actually, they have silver frames.")

"These Noel people are very thorough," Bill Pickett observed. "Are you sure you shouldn't just get some gold-framed glasses?"

"I will if they insist," I said. "But I don't see why it would make any difference."

I noted on the Data Sheet that I hoped for full-time holiday employment and that I was willing to travel from my home (which we'd said was in Half Moon Bay, California, an hour's drive south of San Francisco; Layla and I were particularly fond of a seafood restaurant there called the Fish Trap, and it just seemed like a nice town to be from) to any mall in the country where I might be assigned.

A section called "Special Notes" asked if I spoke any languages other than English. Now, *there* I felt certain I would surpass any of Noel's other prospective Santas. I'd been born and grew up in Lycia, where I learned to speak Turkish, Greek, Latin, and Aramaic. In the centuries since, I'd spent considerable time in Spain, Italy, France, and Germany; I spoke those countries' languages perfectly. I proudly listed them all.

Then came the final page: "Frequently Asked Questions for Santa Claus." I was instructed to write down the answers I would give if children happened to ask me such things as how I knew the name of every boy and girl; how I was able to leave presents for every child in the world in just one night; how I prepared for my Christmas Eve flight; what I liked to do on the day after Christmas; and why I chose to live at the North Pole.

"I think I should answer them all truthfully," I said. "For instance, I believe it should be explained to children that Santa *doesn't* deliver gifts to every child in the world on Christmas Eve. There's St. Nicholas Day and Epiphany, too."

"Perhaps you should only give the answers they expect," Amelia Earhart cautioned. "All these malls are in America, after all, and American children care only about Santa Claus and Christmas Eve."

"I just don't think that's correct," I replied. "That is, I believe children are naturally curious and like to learn new things. If they hear about holiday customs in other parts of the world, it will enrich their enjoyment of the season. Differences in cultures should be interesting rather than threatening, Amelia."

When every question was answered on the application form, I posed for the snapshot Noel required. I wore my full Christmas Eve costume. It felt odd to be wearing those clothes in April. I sealed the application form and photo in an envelope, added sufficient stamps for delivery, and then hopped in the sleigh and flew to Half Moon Bay. We had to mail the application from there so the postmark on the envelope would be from the appropriate place. Layla came along, and we enjoyed dinner afterward—seafood at the Fish Trap. I had my fish grilled rather than fried. Theodore had me in the habit of eating healthier food, though I assured

Layla I would allow myself occasional treats once *The Great Santa Search* competition was over.

"For instance, I'll enjoy Lars's delicious desserts perhaps one night each week," I predicted.

"I'll believe it when I see it," she replied. After sixteen centuries, Layla knew me all too well.

Then I spent several increasingly anxious weeks back at the North Pole, training with Theodore in the mornings, going about my usual planning process for the next cycle of holiday gift-giving in the afternoons, and worrying every waking minute whether the Noel Program would hire me as a mall Santa or not. If they didn't, how would Felix ever be able to include me as one of the ten *Great Santa Search* finalists? Layla insisted there was no cause for concern. If the company really sought out only the best possible Santas, it was certain to hire me, she said. But as the days passed and April turned into May, the cell phone I kept in my pocket remained silent.

Then one afternoon as I was testing some new remote-controlled toy race cars with Bill Pickett and Ben Franklin, the cell phone buzzed. It took me a moment to realize what was happening, but then my heart leaped. Only the Noel Program had that number. They were finally contacting me!

Motioning for my friends to stop racing the cars around the room—they made loud noises when they crashed into the walls—I snapped the phone open and said hello.

"May I speak to Mr. Nicholas Holiday?" a woman inquired.

I almost blurted, "Who?" before remembering that was the name I'd used on the application.

"This is Nicholas Holiday," I replied, trying to sound calmer than I felt.

"Mr. Holiday, my name is Stephanie Owen and I'm a vice-president of the Noel Program," she said. "Thank you for your application. It's one of the most interesting we've received so far this year. And from your photograph, you certainly look the part. The beard in particular is just lovely, almost too perfect to be real."

"It's real, I promise," I told her, feeling more hopeful by the second. "And please call me Nicholas." She laughed, said I should call her Stephanie, and asked a few more questions—Did I really speak all those languages? Had I lived in many other countries before settling in California?—before confirming what I'd hoped.

"We'd like to arrange a meeting with you," Stephanie said. "Could you come to our offices in Colorado?"

I said I'd be glad to do so. Stephanie said I should arrive at the Noel offices the following Monday at 10:00 a.m. She added that her company would reimburse me for my travel costs, but I said that would not be necessary.

"They wouldn't ask you to meet with them if they didn't plan to hire you," Theodore said after I'd gathered everyone together to announce the good news. "You're as good as on *The Great Santa Search*. Bully!" (This was Theodore's favorite word to express great pleasure.)

I arrived for my appointment promptly at ten, wearing the same sport coat, dress shirt, and slacks I had worn to the FUN-TV audition. After dropping me off a block or two from the Noel Program office, Bill Pickett took the delighted reindeer for a long, energetic flight. He promised to come back and pick me up in about two hours. I didn't think my meeting at Noel would last longer than that. If it did, Bill and the reindeer would gladly log additional flying time until I was ready to return to the North Pole.

Stephanie Owen was a pleasant-looking woman with very broad shoulders and straw-blond hair. She greeted me with a handshake and escorted me into a comfortable office. I was startled to see a large framed photograph of Santa Claus on one wall—startled because I had difficulty believing it wasn't me. This actor—he looked so genuine it seemed rude to think of him as an *impostor*—had a fine white beard, genial smile, and husky physique. The white trim on the cuffs of his red suit was spot-less. His arms were wrapped around a quintet of beaming children, who gazed up at him adoringly. If anything, I thought, he looked more like me than I did.

Stephanie saw me staring at the photo.

"That's Jimmy Lee from Leeds, Alabama, and he's perhaps the greatest Santa in the entire history of mall Christmases," she explained. "From the moment fifteen years ago when he first sat down and invited a child to sit on his lap, he *was* Santa Claus. He knows all about the history of the season. He loves the children just as much as they love him. We feel it's an honor to be associated with Jimmy Lee. Every year, the managers of all the biggest malls in the country beg us to assign him to theirs. Why, a few have even offered us bribes!"

"How do you decide which mall will be blessed with Jimmy Lee's presence?" I asked carefully. I admit I was just a bit annoyed by Stephanie's claim this fellow was such a superior Santa. Though, I had to admit ruefully to myself, he certainly *looked* perfect.

"He likes to be somewhere different each year," Stephanie said. "So we pick a region—the northwest, perhaps, or maybe mid-America, and put the names of all our mall clients in that area in a hat. Jimmy Lee comes here to our office in October—that's when our Santas get their assignments—and draws the winning name. It's very exciting. Last year he was in Seattle, the year before in Houston, and so on. After he's been a mall's Santa for one Christmas, he doesn't go back to that mall again. When a Santa's as special as Jimmy Lee, as many malls as possible should have the opportunity to be his holiday headquarters. Someone so wonderful has to be shared."

"That's very generous of you and Jimmy Lee," I said.

Stephanie gazed fondly at the photograph.

"This Christmas we think we'll *really* have to share him," she said. "You've heard about *The Great Santa Search* competition on Christmas Eve, of course. Someone from FUN-TV has already contacted us to say they'll be visiting all the big malls where our Santas work. It's a foregone conclusion, to us at least, that Jimmy Lee will win. Who else?"

"Why, *I* might," I suggested.

Stephanie chuckled. "Nicholas Holiday, I like a Santa who is optimistic! Now, why don't you sit down and we'll have a chat. We've talked enough about Jimmy Lee. I'd like to know more about *you.*"

For the next half-hour, Stephanie asked me all sorts of questions. As much as possible, I told her the absolute truth. I was born in Turkey, lived all over the world, and had loved the holiday season for as long as I could remember. She wanted to know how I had become a "self-employed toy consultant," and I replied that I very much enjoyed tinkering with toys and discovering ways they could be improved.

"Why, at this point in your life, do you want to work as Santa Claus?" she inquired.

"Because nothing is better than being Santa," I replied. "I believe that with all my heart."

"We were particularly intrigued by one of your responses on the application," Stephanie continued. "You wrote that if children asked how you took presents to every boy and girl in the world on the same night, you'd tell them you actually do your gift-giving on three nights. None of our other Santas have ever mentioned St. Nicholas Day and Epiphany on their applications. Why do you think American children should know about those celebrations?"

"Children have far more sense than most grown-ups give them credit for," I replied. "It's a fact that many boys and girls who don't live in America expect to receive their holiday gifts on December 6 or January 6. In telling them this, I'm respecting rather than insulting their intelligence. And there's another reason for sharing this information. May I tell you what it is?"

"Please," Stephanie said.

"The more we understand the holiday traditions of other cultures, the more we can share in a universal spirit of goodwill," I replied.

"That's true for people of all ages. I believe that the more everyone knows about the real history of Christmas, the more they will love it. And, after all, Santa Claus should be part of the Christmas celebration without being mistaken as the reason for it. I would hope people love Santa because of what my gifts truly represent—reminders of the greatest gift ever given."

Stephanie sat back and rubbed her chin.

"Well," she said. She seemed deep in thought.

"Have I offended you?" I asked, remembering how young Emily from FUN-TV chastised me for bringing religion into Christmas.

"Not at all," Stephanie replied. "You expressed yourself beautifully. While we ask our Santas not to bring up personal religious faith—it's for parents to discuss such things with their children, we believe—we never think it's wrong for a Santa to reinforce the inspiration for Christmas *if* the child mentions it first."

"I feel quite relieved," I told her, and it was true. "If I may, I'd like to ask about something else. You may think it's unimportant, but it has troubled me ever since I first read your application form."

Stephanie looked concerned.

"Please, ask whatever you'd like."

"Well," I said, "it has to do with spectacles, or glasses, if you prefer. You asked whether I had 'tiny round gold Santa glasses,' and mine, as you can see"—I took them from my coat pocket—"actually have silver frames. Do you require gold frames, and, if so, why?"

Stephanie opened a desk drawer and took out several dozen small photographs. Each was of a mall Santa, who had smiled at the camera. Each wore an identical pair of small, round, gold-framed spectacles.

"Many boys and girls visit more than one mall and speak to more than one of our Santas during the same Christmas season," she explained. "Now, our Santas don't look exactly alike, but we try to have them appear as similar as possible so young children in particular aren't confused. We'll gladly furnish you a pair of gold-rimmed glasses so you can match all the others. We don't consider even the smallest detail to be unimportant, and we do expect outstanding performances by our Santas. I hope, this Christmas, you'll be one of them."

"Are you offering me a job?" I asked.

Stephanie laughed.

"Yes, I am," she said. "I can tell you're going to be a fine Santa. Maybe you'll even be another Jimmy Lee. Now, let's discuss some details. First, I'm sure, you'll want to know about salary."

"Actually, the salary doesn't matter," I said. "I'll accept whatever you think is fair."

"You really *are* unique," Stephanie declared. She explained that her company paid their Santas based on a combination of experience and performance. Since I'd never worked as a mall Santa before, I would have to start at minimum pay, but if I did good work, there would be merit raises. I would be assigned to a specific mall, Stephanie continued, and would work there full-time for about forty-five days beginning in early November and up through Christmas Eve. I would be notified of my mall assignment sometime in October.

"If you prefer a specific region we'll try to accommodate you," she added. "And if you do have to temporarily move somewhere, we help with travel costs and rent."

"I have friends in most major cities," I informed her. "I'm sure I'll be able to stay with them. Assign me wherever you like." Actually, I could commute by sleigh from the North Pole to any city in America. I'd sleep in my own bed every night no matter where I was assigned.

Stephanie had me fill out a few more forms. I remembered to say I was sixty-three, my age back in the year 343 AD, when I gave up being a priest and embarked on a full-time gift-giving mission. I hadn't grown physically older since.

"By the way," I said, "you mentioned I'd work through Christmas Eve. But if I happen to be selected for *The Great Santa Search*, I would have to be in a New York City theater that night."

"You *are* optimistic," Stephanie said. "We've already decided that if any of our Santas become *Great Santa Search* finalists, and we expect several will, then we'll send substitute Santas to replace them in their malls on Christmas Eve. We always have some 'floaters,' as we call them, available in case a Santa becomes ill or can't report to work for some reason."

"You do seem to think of everything," I told her. I was thinking of something, too—specifically, how much I was going to enjoy proving to Jimmy Lee that he wasn't the best Santa anywhere. It wasn't the nicest thought, but no one is perfect, the real Santa Claus included. Now that I was going to be a mall Santa I was once again certain I would compete on *The Great Santa Search*, where I would win. I had to. The possibility of a false Santa Claus acting as the spokesman for LastLong Toy Company was absolutely unacceptable.

I opened the valise and pulled out the red coat and trousers and hat, all with white fur trim. Mr. Sneed yanked them from my hands and inspected them, turning the garments over in his hands to check, I suppose, for worn places.

Twelve

he months seemed to rush by. I practiced roping with Bill Pickett until we wore out all the lariats at the North Pole. Every day, Theodore directed me through a series of increasingly difficult exercises. At mealtimes, I dined sensibly. Sometime in August, I realized I hadn't consumed any sugar since the beginning of my training on the morning of January 6, Epiphany. Though I hadn't lost a pound, I'd gained considerable energy. In all my seventeen centuries, I could not recall feeling better.

During these same months, *The Great Santa Search* became one of the most talked-about topics in America. Just as Bobbo Butler predicted, his Christmas Eve competition had captured the ongoing attention of the media. As a result, it was virtually impossible for anyone to read a magazine, listen to the radio, or watch television without some daily reminder of FUN-TV's holiday special on December 24. Most of the coverage resulted from the unceasing efforts of publicists hired by the LastLong Toy Company, but not all of it. A supermarket tabloid revealed that Rick Press, one of the two open-audition winners, was actually wanted by police in Florida for selling "prime beachfront property" to unsuspecting senior citizens. Only after giving him all their money did these unfortunate people discover they owned swampland instead. Immediately, every major television network and print publication began covering "the Santa scandal." After Press was arrested, Bobbo announced that he could only compete on *The Great Santa Search* if he was innocent of all criminal charges against him. Instead, Press loudly declared his guilt, adding he had hoped to be voted the "real" Santa on Christmas Eve so he could spend the rest of his life atoning for his crimes by inspiring children to love the holidays. He was then kicked off *The Great Santa Search*, but within a week signed a publishing contract for a tell-all book, and not long afterward a major network paid him millions for the right to produce a made-for-television movie about his life: *From Sinner to Santa*. That undoubtedly made the three years he was sentenced to spend in prison easier to endure.

"At least there are nine places available on *The Great Santa Search* now instead of eight," Felix reminded me. "That improves your chances of getting selected."

"I hope you're joking, Felix," I said. "Now that I'm going to work as a mall Santa, you're going to see to it that I'm picked for the program. We're agreed on that, aren't we?"

"I haven't seen you working in a mall yet," he joked. At least, I hoped he was joking. "If I come to observe and you're not doing a good job, I might have to leave you off my list. We want only the very best for *The Great Santa Search*, you know!"

"I'm going to be the best," I assured him. "I really am Santa, after all. I just wish Stephanie Owen would call and tell me where I'm going to work. It's nearly October."

All the publicity for *The Great Santa Search* made me especially anxious to get started. Media commentators were speculating endlessly on where the program competitors might be found. Already, most of them assumed malls would be logical locations. Several veteran mall Santas were tracked down and interviewed about their interest in competing. All of them were, and each promised he would be the winner.

Whole weeks of media coverage focused on who would serve as *The Great Santa Search*'s master of ceremonies. The names of three ex-presidents were mentioned, as well as the star of a late-night TV talk show, a comedian who regularly hosted the Academy Awards broadcast, the reigning Miss America, and several famous athletes. One columnist made headlines by suggesting the Easter Bunny be selected "in the spirit of crossover holiday collaboration, and proof to all Americans that spokespersons for opposing groups or causes can still work together for the common good." Just as speculation reached fever pitch, Bobbo announced *he* would be the host. Heather Hathaway privately told Sarah and Felix that Bobbo had intended to be master of ceremonies all along.

"He couldn't stand not being on the program that makes FUN-TV one of the major networks again," Heather said. "I think, sometimes, that Bobbo forgets the star of the show is going to be the winning Santa."

"Heather is an exceptionally perceptive woman," Sarah told Felix later. "Have you noticed? She studies people carefully and seems to have considerable insight into their motives. It's so sad Bobbo Butler doesn't appreciate her properly."

"He's told us she's the best executive assistant in the television business," Felix reminded her.

"That's just it—he thinks of her as an *assistant*."

Eventually, Lucretia Pepper was interviewed on a weekly television prime-time news program after reports surfaced that LastLong Toy Company would be the sole sponsor of *The Great Santa Search*. She refused to confirm that the winning Santa would become her company's year-round spokesman, saying only that various possibilities were under consideration. She did say that LastLong toys were the most popular choice for Christmas gifts, and announced that there would be a brand-new set of action figures based on the various *Great Santa Search* challenges available in stores right after the program aired.

"But won't that be too late to sell toys associated with Santa?" she was asked by one of the most famous TV reporters of all. "On December 26, Christmas will be over for another year."

Lucretia Pepper looked directly at the camera and smiled.

"After watching *The Great Santa Search*, children in America will be obsessed with Santa Claus all year long," she predicted. "They'll be asking for Christmas presents, especially the new LastLong Santa action figure, from January through December. The simplest way to say it is that Christmas presents won't just be for Christmas anymore."

"Won't that make December 25 itself much less special?" the reporter wanted to know. "That would be terrible."

"But as a result, LastLong Toy Company will create more than one thousand new jobs to meet increased demand for our products," she replied. "We're not hurting Christmas, we're helping the American economy. I certainly hope you're not questioning our patriotic motives or our corporate love for the holiday."

On several occasions, Felix and Sarah were summoned to New York for meetings with Bobbo and the rest of *The Great Santa Search* staff. There were discussions about how the stage sets should look, and how tall the chimneys for the sliding competition should be, and how Bobbo, as host, should dress. It was finally agreed that he would wear a special red tuxedo with white fur cuffs and collar trim.

Sarah and Felix said that the attention to smallest details was incredible. The appropriate length of the antlers on fake reindeer took hours to determine. A *Great Santa Search* theme song had been commissioned, and everyone had to listen to every possible variation of it, from waltz to rap. Motown-style, with a good beat for the audience to clap along with, was the eventual choice. Newly hired choreographer Lauren Devoe cast the deciding vote.

"She says we'll need a strong beat to disguise the simple steps for the dance routine she's developing," Felix reported. "She feels the ten Santas may be limited in their dancing ability."

At the end of the first week in October, there was still no word about my mall assignment. I fretted that perhaps Stephanie Owen had forgotten me, but on October 10 my cell phone vibrated and she was finally in touch.

"I have some wonderful news for you, Nicholas Holiday!" she began. "Usually our first-time Santas start out in smaller towns and malls, but we've decided you're right for one of the biggest and best. You're assigned to the Galaxy Mall in Cleveland, Ohio! Have you ever been to it?"

"I've certainly been to Cleveland," I said. "I don't believe I've gone to a mall there."

"Well, this one is absolutely fabulous," Stephanie assured me. "There are four stories and over five hundred shops, many of them quite up-scale. Your Santa set is going to be one of the most spectacular anywhere. I don't want to describe it ahead of time. You'll see for yourself. Now, you'll officially start work on the second Saturday in November, but we're asking that you actually visit the mall one or two days before that, so you can meet the Galaxy manager, make sure its Santa suit fits, and get settled in."

"I have my own Santa suit," I replied. "It fits perfectly. I'll bring it with me."

"We're really committed to our Santas wearing authentic-looking suits," Stephanie cautioned.

"I give you my word that no Santa suit is more authentic than mine," I promised.

Stephanie provided additional information. The manager of Galaxy Mall was named Lester Sneed. She warned me that he was rather gruff. But his mall attracted some of the largest crowds of Christmas shoppers in the entire country.

"In fact, Jimmy Lee was the Galaxy Mall Santa four Christmases ago," Stephanie added. "You know we wouldn't let Jimmy Lee go to a mall that wasn't one of the very best!"

"And where will Jimmy Lee be spending this particular Christmas?" I inquired. It is always good to keep track of the competition.

"We just drew his location this morning," she said. "He'll be right there in New York City! Isn't that just *perfect* for *The Great Santa Search*?"

"How convenient," I replied. "Well, I hope the program talent scouts find their way to Cleveland, too."

"I'm sure they will," Stephanie agreed. "Meanwhile, can we help at all with Cleveland logistics? Housing, transportation, that sort of thing?"

I told her I'd be able to make my own arrangements, and thanked her for the call.

"I'll try to live up to your expectations," I said. "Should I get in touch with Lester Sneed, the Galaxy Mall manager, right away?"

"We've sent him your file," Stephanie said. "I think if you call in a few weeks and make an appointment to see him just before you officially go to work, that would be fine. Good luck!"

But I couldn't wait to see the mall where I was to work. Within the hour, Layla, Willie Skokan, Arthur, and I were in the sleigh and speeding through the cool fall skies to Cleveland. We found the Galaxy Mall close to the shores of Lake Erie. Arthur was particularly excited because the Rock and Roll Hall of Fame was not far away.

"I might just visit there while the rest of you inspect the mall," he said. "Do you think the Hall of Fame might have a Beach Boys exhibit?" Arthur was quite fond of the Beach Boys, and would make his way about the North Pole humming "Help Me, Rhonda" or "I Get Around" at any hour of the day or night. Over the years, all of us had developed unfathomable attachments to various musical groups, books, or films. Theodore couldn't get enough of travel books written by Bill Bryson. Amelia Earhart joked that any movie was wonderful if Sean Connery was in it. I, myself, have never succumbed to fandom of any sort, though I will admit to a limited, sensible fondness for SpongeBob. Besides sports and occasional news programs, we had never watched television until *The Great Santa Search* forced it on us. Now, we had to pry Lars from in front of the widescreen set every night when it was time for him to begin preparing dinner. If he'd had his way, he would have watched the Food Network every waking minute. He'd already sent off several fan letters to Rachael Ray and Emeril Lagasse.

We assured Arthur that the Beach Boys would be well-represented in the Hall, and when I discreetly set the sleigh down near Galaxy Mall he hurried off. After instructing the reindeer to hover out of sight until we returned, Willie Skokan, Layla, and I made our way to the mall. There was no chance we'd be unable to locate it. Galaxy Mall was a massive structure that dwarfed every other building around it. The parking lot alone seemed to exceed the size of America's smaller states. When we stepped inside we were overwhelmed by the sheer immensity of the place. Glass elevators delivered shoppers to each of four levels; the pungent aroma of curry and barbecue and pizza wafted from the food court. The array of shops was bewildering. Every hundred feet or so there was a giant map indicating what was where, and each had a helpful arrow accompanied by the assurance "*YOU ARE HERE.*"

"This is amazing!" Layla observed. "How can anyone know where to go or what to do? There's just too much of everything!"

But a flood of other mall visitors felt otherwise. Men, women, and children of all ages poured into and out of stores, jostling one another and shouting to companions and, in more cases than I could count, chattering into cell phones. Above the din came regular announcements over some massive public-address system—there was a ten-minute sale in *this* store, a half-day "shopper's special" in *that* one. Willie Skokan, Layla, and I were swept up in the irresistible flow of humanity. We tried frantically to hang on to one another. Finally we found ourselves stumbling past the food court where, with considerable effort, we separated ourselves from the rampaging herd and caught our breaths.

"It can't be like this all the time," I said hopefully.

"I think it can," Willie Skokan replied. "Leonardo and I have done some research, and we found that—"

Layla and I never heard what they had found, because another blaring announcement was being made on the mall's public-address system:

"Remember, customers, that in only three weeks, that's twenty-one days, Santa Claus arrives at Galaxy Mall! We're busily building our own Santa Land on the first floor of the west wing. Be on hand for our traditional welcoming ceremony there at 4:00 p.m. on Santa Saturday, and then bring the children often so they can sit on Santa's lap and tell the jolly old elf everything they want for Christmas! Of course, anything made by Santa and his helpers will be on sale in our shops! We've already got the holiday spirit at Galaxy Mall!"

"Let's go see what this Santa Land is going to be like," Layla suggested. We inched our way back into the mob. It took us almost half an hour to finally arrive on the first floor of the mall's west wing, where it was instantly clear we'd come for nothing. Huge plywood barriers had been erected around an area fully ten thousand feet square, with a massive plywood sheet fixed over the top to thwart anyone from ascending two or three stories to try to peek from above. The protective barrier only added to the mystery of the sounds coming from within. Hammers pounded, chainsaws buzzed, and the muffled shouts of workers combined in a tantalizing cacophony.

"Obviously, this mall takes Santa seriously," I said. "It will be interesting to see what they've done when I officially arrive in three weeks. Meanwhile, let's collect the reindeer and Arthur and get back to the North Pole, where it's quieter."

The three of us who'd been to the mall were mostly silent on the sleigh ride home. Arthur sang "Good Vibrations" until we asked him, please, to stop, and then he hummed the tune to himself all the rest of the way.

I returned to the Galaxy Mall on the day before "Santa Saturday." I was dressed in a gray business suit, and I had my Santa costume with me in the same valise I'd brought to the audition in New York City. The mall was still crowded, but this time I knew what to expect. A woman at an information kiosk gave me directions to the mall manager's office, which was on the second level, tucked behind the men's and women's restrooms. The office was surprisingly small; I later learned that, in malls, prime floor space is always reserved for stores and crowd-attracting exhibits. The manager's office is built wherever it can be wedged in.

There was barely room in Lester Sneed's office for a tiny desk, two uncomfortable chairs, a phone, and the man himself. He did not stand up to greet me, instead shoving out his hand and briefly clasping mine.

"Lester Sneed," he growled.

"I'm Nicholas Holiday. Please call me Nicholas."

He didn't invite me to call him Lester.

"I don't like a Santa without experience," he declared, and I was taken aback. There was no welcome in his voice, only exasperation. "For what we pay those Noel people, I expect the best Santa they've got. Instead they send me a rookie. What's going on?"

"I don't consider myself a rookie," I replied, trying to remain polite. "It's true I've never worked as a mall Santa before, but I know what's required and I'm perfectly qualified."

"I decide that, pal, not you." Mr. Sneed leaned back in his chair as far as he could. It wasn't far, because the back of his chair immediately bumped against the wall. He silently started at me for several long moments. Not knowing what else to do, I stared back, using the time to study him. Lester Sneed was a gray-haired, sour-faced man of perhaps fifty. His gray beard was scraggly and grew thicker in some places on his chin and cheeks than others. He wore a rumpled blue suit and white shirt with a faded maroon tie. There was about him the air of a man who found little to enjoy in life. There were no photos of family or friends on his desk, only piles of paper with "Priority" stamped on almost every sheet. As he sat, he drummed his long, thin fingers on the top of his desk.

"Okay," he said suddenly. "You're here. Show me the Santa suit."

I opened the valise and pulled out the red coat and trousers and hat, all with white fur trim. Mr. Sneed yanked them from my hands and inspected them, turning the garments over in his hands to check, I suppose, for worn places.

"Looks okay," he announced, and tossed the garments back to me. "Custom-made? I didn't see any brand labels."

"I have a fine tailor," I said. "This suit was made exclusively for me."

"With what you people charge me, I guess you can afford it," Mr. Sneed snapped. "Okay. Let's go look at the Santa Land set."

"You say 'okay' a lot, don't you?" I asked, trying to make friendly conversation. I wanted to get along with Mr. Sneed, who was, after all, my boss. I hadn't ever really had one of those before.

"What's it to you, buddy?"

"I meant no offense," I told him. "And, please, call me Nicholas."

"Let's get moving, buddy."

Mr. Sneed did not say another word to me as we made our way from his office to Santa Land. Helped by long experience, he expertly weaved his way through the crowds. I did my best to keep up.

The plywood barriers still blocked every view of Santa Land, but there was a door cut in one wall, and Mr. Sneed and I went through it. As I stepped inside, I gasped. I couldn't help it.

The boundary of Santa Land was circled by a miniature railroad track, and a lovely little steam engine with a dozen open cars attached stood ready to offer a merry ride. A wrought-iron bridge rose over one section of the track—this, obviously, was where visitors would enter Santa Land. The bridge was bedecked with holly that had to be plastic but certainly looked quite real. And in the center of Santa Land was an incredible structure. Red-and-white candy canes fully twenty feet high supported a rotunda of sparkling icicles. I realized the candy canes were plaster and the icicles were plastic, but they were so skillfully crafted that they in no sense seemed artificial. Underneath the rotunda was nothing less than a throne, a high-backed seat seemingly made from toy blocks, with a ten-foot-tall Raggedy Ann doll on one side and an equally giant wooden soldier standing at attention on the other. A series of brightly colored steps led to the throne, and along the steps plastic-limbed Christmas trees gleamed with thousands of colored lights.

"This is astonishing," I said to Mr. Sneed.

"Expensive, is what it is," he replied. "Okay. Sit in your seat. Got to make sure you fit. You're pretty broad across the beam."

I gingerly went up the steps and settled myself on the throne. Though it appeared to be constructed of wood blocks, in fact the portion on which I sat was cushioned. It was very comfortable, and I told Mr. Sneed so.

"Okay, then, got some people for you to meet," he said, and waved over a group I hadn't previously noticed, since I'd been so overwhelmed by Santa Land itself. Four young men and three young women walked up.

"These are the helpers," barked Mr. Sneed. "Dave, Scott, Xander, Seiler, and Yelena are your elves. Jill's the photographer; most parents'll pay extra to have their kids' pictures taken on your lap. Ralphie's her assistant. Okay with all that?"

"I actually don't have elves," I protested, more out of habit than any hope someone would believe me. "My North Pole friends are real people."

"You're Santa, but I'm the boss," Mr. Sneed said. "I want elves, so you get elves. Okay?"

"Okay," I replied.

"I got things to do, so you people get acquainted. Santa, Holiday, whatever your name is, these people did the same jobs here last year, so they know what they're doing, even if maybe you don't. Jill, make sure this new guy knows where the dressing room is. I want all of you in costume and ready to go tomorrow at 3:00 p.m. Opening arrival ceremony's at four. I want it to be perfect. Okay?"

"Okay," the others chorused. That seemed to be the response Mr. Sneed preferred. He nodded, though he didn't smile, and walked off without another word, leaving me with seven strangers in the middle of Santa Land.

"How do you like Old O.K.?" the helper named Dave asked me.

"Who?" I asked.

"Old O.K. You know, Mr. Sneed. That's what we call him. Friendly guy, eh?"

"Don't get started, Dave," Jill the photographer said. "Your name is Nicholas, isn't it? We're all pleased to meet you. Let's go over to the dressing room and we'll fill you in on everything else."

All seven proved to be delightful people. They each loved Christmas and told me they derived great pleasure from helping children enjoy it. With the exceptions of Jill and Ralphie, who were both professional photographers, the others went to college in the area and worked at Galaxy Mall over the holidays to earn extra money. They asked about my background, and I told them the usual story of being a freelance toy consultant who had decided, at age sixty-three, to spend more time with the children who played with toys.

"The main thing to remember is, smile and be jolly no matter what the kids on your lap do or say," Jill cautioned me. "I know you probably think they'll all act fine, but you're going to be surprised at some of the things that happen. Two years ago, a little girl yanked part of Santa's beard off, and it wasn't a fake beard."

"Really," I mumbled, instinctively placing a protective hand over my own whiskers.

"Do you have lots of pairs of those gold-framed little glasses?" Jill continued. "Toddlers especially like to grab at those, and I've seen Santas lose a half dozen in one day. Most kids will want a hug, but every so often one may throw a punch, especially if you don't promise to bring whatever present you've just been asked for. That's another thing: lots of times you need to be vague when they ask what you're bringing them. Tell them their parents will help make that decision."

"That's actually the way it works," I said. "With input from teachers, ministers, and other caring adult friends, of course."

"My," said Jill, "you really do get into the role, don't you?"

She next explained the jobs each of the seven played in what was termed "the production." Seiler and Yelena were "greeters." They met adults and children at the bottom of the bridge and escorted them into line, chatting in friendly fashion and trying to make them feel comfortable. Xander and Dave served as "hosts." They brought children from the head of the line to where Santa sat, even as they quietly conferred with parents to get some idea of what should and shouldn't be promised to boys and girls in the way of Christmas gifts. Scott was cashier. If parents asked Jill and Ralphie to photograph their children with me, they were charged for the snapshot. When Scott had extra time, he picked up litter so Santa Land remained sparkling clean. Jill herself was "production coordinator" in addition to taking photos. As such, she was the senior member of the group and could give special instructions to any of the others.

While the rest of the crew was occupied checking their costumes in the dressing room (Ralphie inspected the cameras), Jill also mentioned that Mr. Sneed had a special reason for being so grouchy.

"Up until four years ago, he was the mall's Santa himself," she said. "Then the owners decided they wanted to use a Santa search company instead. Mr. Sneed loved playing Santa. That's when he grew his silly-looking beard. The kids seemed to like him. But then they brought in an outside Santa, and he was just better at it than Mr. Sneed. Everything about him was perfect."

"Jimmy Lee," I mumbled.

"Yes, Jimmy Lee. He was such a hit that we've used the Noel Program to supply our Santas ever since, and Mr. Sneed has never been allowed to do it again. So don't take it personally if he's unfriendly to you. He actually loves Christmas and wants all the children who come to

Galaxy Mall to have a great time with Santa. He just wishes that he was the one in the red suit."

After I'd hung my own red suit on a hook in the dressing room, Jill reminded me to be in costume the next day no later than 3:00 p.m.

"Mr. Sneed will want to inspect us before we go out," she said. "Don't be nervous. You're going to have a wonderful time."

"I think I will," I replied. I felt very excited. After long months of planning and preparation, tomorrow I would actually start working in a mall!

"Can I tell you what I want you to bring me?" Harper asked. "Please do," I replied, and actually felt a sense of anticipation. After all the gifts I'd given to so many children for so many centuries, this would be the first time I'd ever received a direct request from a child in person. What fun!

Thirteen

he next afternoon I waited anxiously in the dressing room. Outside the plywood walls of the dressing room I could hear the muffled sounds of thousands of excited voices and shuffling feet. The children of Cleveland were ready to greet Santa Claus!

"Okay, then," Mr. Sneed barked. "It's 4:00 p.m. Time to get rolling. All of you remember, this is a special experience for these kids! Make it perfect for them. Smile no matter what. Greeters, get 'em in as fast as you can. Get 'em on Santa's lap, push the parents to buy the pictures, thank 'em for coming, and always keep the line moving. Nothing worse than frustrated parents who have to wait two hours for their kid to meet Santa. Think they'll stay and shop in our mall afterward? Okay, let's— wait a minute. Ralphie, where are your elf ears? What's the matter with you, buddy?"

Ralphie, who already looked rather silly—grown men shouldn't wear candy-striped leotards—hung his head and reached in his pocket.

He extracted two flesh-colored, plastic points, which he stuck on the tops of his ears. The other six helpers already had theirs on.

"All elves have pointed ears," Mr. Sneed lectured. "I don't want to have to remind anybody of that again. Okay, let's go."

Mr. Sneed reached for a cordless microphone resting on the dressing-room table. Motioning for the rest of us to remain completely silent, he flipped a switch on the microphone and declared in a surprisingly deep, dramatic voice, "*Ladies and gentlemen, and children of all ages. Everyone who loves Christmas, welcome to Santa Land in Galaxy Mall. Our favorite holiday friend has arrived from the North Pole. But first, let's greet Santa's elves!*"

Jill, Ralphie, Yelena, Xander, Seiler, Scott, and Dave hurried out the door. There was loud applause and cheering. The atmosphere was simply electric.

Mr. Sneed looked at me quite sternly, then spoke into the microphone again.

"*And now, direct from the North Pole, here's the star of the season—Santa Claus!*"

As I'd been instructed earlier, I walked slowly from the dressing room. Children and parents were packed tight on all four levels of the mall, leaning forward and straining to see me. The cheers were deafening. Boys and girls and more than a few grown men and women were shouting, "Santa! Santa!" and I was somewhat blinded by what seemed to be thousands of cameras flashing. I raised my white-gloved hand in greeting, and the din grew more intense. I couldn't stop smiling. How wonderful to be among so many Christmas-loving people! Yes, I'd spent centuries bringing gifts to millions like them, but that was always in the dark of night when they were asleep. This was my first opportunity to be in direct, wide-awake contact with any of them while wearing my traditional Santa costume, and if they were excited, I was thrilled. I paused in my walk to the wooden block throne and waved energetically with both hands, turning around slowly so that I would be able to at least momentarily face everyone. I have rarely experienced a more gratifying moment.

Then I approached the throne and, after one final wave, took my seat. As I did, Seiler and Yelena ushered the first breathless children and their parents across the wrought-iron bridge into Santa Land. Xander and Dave went forward to meet this initial group, taking charge of them while the two young women returned to the bridge to guide in the next contingent. Jill and Ralphie readied their cameras, and Scott took his place by the photo-table cash register.

A bright-eyed little boy, followed by his beaming mother and father, was first in line. Just before the child was brought up to me, Xander leaned forward and briefly whispered with the parents. Then Xander looked at me and nodded discreetly. This was the agreed-upon signal that the present the youngster was about to request from Santa would, in fact, be under his tree on Christmas morning. I did feel a qualm about making what would be a very brief visit with this child all about some toy or other he hoped to receive from me. What a joy it would have been to regale him and every child in line with stories about the joy of Christmas gift-*giving* rather than *getting*. But I nodded back at Xander, and he gently led the child up to me on my wooden block throne. I reached down, picked him up, and settled him on my knee, noting to myself that he was a fine, healthy-looking youngster with thick hair and sparkling eyes.

"Merry Christmas!" I told him. "And how are you today?"

He grinned, and replied, "Hi, Santa. My name is Harper Cummings. I'm seven."

While I'm able to remember the names of many children present and past, I can't recall every one. But Harper's enthusiasm assured me that he was at least a believer, and perhaps a true believer. What fun to actually talk to a Santa-loving child!

"It's a pleasure to meet you, Harper," I said, and meant every word. "What shall we talk about?"

Harper giggled. "My little sister Andrea flushed her doll down the toilet."

"I'm sure it was an accident," I said. "Where is Andrea this afternoon?"

Harper wrinkled his brow. "She's over at her friend Marcia's house. She's coming to see you next weekend."

"I'll look forward to that," I replied. Looking over Harper's head, I could see Xander and Paul already gesturing for me to hurry. I couldn't blame them—there were *lots* of other children waiting in line.

"Can I tell you what I want you to bring me?" Harper asked.

"Please do," I replied, and actually felt a sense of anticipation. After all the gifts I'd given to so many children for so many centuries, this would be the first time I'd ever received a direct request from a child in person. What fun! Perhaps Harper would want a toy truck. I knew Willie Skokan had just crafted some wonderful ones with horns that really honked. Or maybe he'd ask for a basketball. We'd recently manufactured several thousand of them, and they all bounced beautifully.

Harper ducked his head as though telling me a secret. "Here's what I want," he whispered.

"What?" I whispered back.

"I want a PS3 with its Blu-ray disk drive and Cell processor chip."

"I beg your pardon?" I had no idea what Harper was talking about.

"You know, Santa. PlayStation 3. The Cell processor runs at 3.2 gigahertz, and that whole system will have two teraflops of overall performance."

"Teraflops," I said hesitantly.

"Yep," Harper agreed, looking happy at the prospect. "My friend Charles has the PS2 and thinks it's really cool, but wait 'til you bring me the PS3. Hey, you're not going to bring him one, too, are you?"

"Who knows?" I muttered.

Xander walked up and carefully began to lift Harper off my lap.

"More kids are waiting, Santa," he reminded me.

Harper hopped down, but whirled around as Xander began leading him away.

"You *are* bringing my PS3 and everything, aren't you?" he called back anxiously.

"With teraflops," I promised. After all, I'd received the signal from Xander that Harper's parents intended to give him the gift he wanted.

"Thanks, Santa. You're the greatest!" Harper called, and scooted back to where his parents were waiting. They handed money over to Scott. Apparently, Jill or Ralphie had snapped a photograph of Harper sitting on my lap.

I hissed to Xander, "What's a teraflop?" but he was busy bringing twin girls over to me, again nodding to indicate their parents wanted me to tell them they'd be getting whatever it was they were about to ask me for.

Nora and Carol were nine. I could tell they both were teetering on the edge of Christmas disbelief. Probably some of their friends at school were telling them Santa really didn't exist. But they still seemed to be believers, at least marginally.

Unlike Harper, they didn't volunteer their names and ages. I had to ask. But they were ready, in fact eager, to tell what they wanted from me for Christmas.

"CD burners!" they said in unison.

Now, I did know that things called CDs, an abbreviation for compact discs, had replaced vinyl record albums. I was not entirely ignorant of current technology. But I certainly did not think it was appropriate for children to burn them.

"Are you certain?" I asked. The twins nodded their heads vigorously.

"Excuse me for a moment," I said. I had one twin sitting on each leg, so I gently set them down. Then I walked over to where their parents were waiting. They were a pleasant-looking couple, and I knew they would be appalled to learn what their daughters had just requested from Santa.

"I think there's a problem," I whispered.

The girls' mother stamped her foot.

"I *told* them they're too young for tattoos!" she exclaimed. "When they said they each wanted one for Christmas, I said absolutely not. Didn't I, Harold?"

"You bet, Susie," her husband agreed. "That's exactly what you told them."

"I was actually more concerned about pyromania," I said. The parents looked puzzled. "Burning things," I added. "Apparently, compact discs."

Now Susie laughed.

"Oh, *that's* all right," she told me. "They're each getting a CD burner from us. Or we can say they're from you, if you want."

"Certainly not!" I replied. "Santa Claus would never condone something so potentially dangerous!"

Susie and Harold looked at me incredulously, as though I were the one saying something foolish.

"Where'd you people get this Santa?" Susie asked Xander. He shrugged, and seemed embarrassed.

"CD burners don't set fire to anything, dude," Xander whispered to me harshly. "They copy CDs, that's all. Burning's just a term. Don't you know anything?"

"Apparently not," I said. Modern technology has, for the most part, passed me by because I usually don't need to know much about it. Leonardo is in charge of our North Pole operations concerned with computer programs and video games and the like. Though we develop prototypes for computers themselves, we license these to outside manufacturers and use the proceeds to underwrite all our operational expenses. Reindeer feed isn't cheap.

My own manufacturing involvement is usually limited to the traditional sorts of toys I've given as gifts down through the centuries—dolls and wagons and balls and other simple yet pleasure-giving things. You could say, as Layla often does, that I'm deliberately old-fashioned. I don't disagree. I have no quarrel with technological breakthroughs that have resulted in more complex playthings. But I could tell just from these first few youngsters I'd met at Galaxy Mall that I had a great deal of catching up to do.

From that moment on, so long as their parents approved, I told children I would bring them the gifts they wanted whether I knew what those gifts were or not. I went back to the building-block throne and informed Nora and Carol that they could look forward to many happy hours of CD-burning. They hugged me while Jill, beaming, stepped forward to snap a picture.

After that, things seemed to happen in a blur. As soon as one child jumped off my lap, another hopped up onto it. Almost all of them were quite specific about what they wanted me to bring them for Christmas.

Barry wanted a chemistry set so he could mix up a potion that would turn his teacher's teeth "a really sick green."

"I don't think that's a good idea," I said.

"That's only 'cause you don't know my teacher," he replied.

Alison asked for a tennis racquet, which was fine. But she also wanted me to give her the ability to win her school's tennis championship.

"If you practice hard enough, perhaps you'll become good enough to be champion," I suggested.

"If I have to practice, I'll get all sweaty."

"Well, I'll bring you the racquet, but you'll have to provide the sweat."

There were occasional youngsters who became so excited about meeting Santa that they forgot completely whatever gifts they meant to ask me for. Six-year-old Byron sat tongue-tied on my lap for several minutes while his mother urged him to "tell Santa what you want! Hurry up! Other kids are waiting!"

"Ummm," Byron said.

"Would you like a toy truck, Byron?" I asked, trying to be helpful. I was also suggesting a truck because we'd made thousands at the North Pole and no child had asked for one yet.

"Hmmm," said Byron.

"Perhaps a basketball?" I inquired. We had plenty of those at the North Pole, too.

"He wants a PS3," his mother said sharply. "Don't you, Byron?" Byron managed to nod.

"With a Blu-ray disk drive and Cell processor chip?" I added, remembering Harper Cummings's request.

"Yeah!" Byron blurted.

"It will give you two teraflops of overall performance," I assured him. I still didn't know what that meant, but it seemed like the right thing to say.

From the mall's standpoint, I suppose, my first day as Santa was an acceptable one. At the end of my six-hour shift, 4:00 p.m. until 10:00 p.m., when Galaxy Mall closed for the night, I had visited with just over eight hundred children. I say "children" in a general sense. Most of my lap-sitters were between three and ten years old. Some parents had brought infants for me to hold, and I enjoyed that. I also was pleased by visits from grown men and women who, to judge by the delighted smiles on their faces, remained maximum true believers. A few teenagers waited in line to see me for the sole purpose of saying unkind things about Santa Claus being make-believe, and stupid besides. I wasn't angry. I felt sorry for them. They had to be very sad themselves, I knew, to make such an effort to hurt the feelings of someone else. I wished them a Merry Christmas anyway, and meant it.

My frustration came from a different source. I was asked many more times for presents I knew nothing about. Besides PS3s and Xboxes and Blu-ray disk drives and teraflops, there were multiple requests for things called MP3 players and iPods. Other children asked for extravagant things I knew about, but could never bring—ponies and designer clothes and visits from famous rock musicians or professional athletes or movie stars.

There were times each Christmas Eve—and St. Nicholas Day, and

Epiphany—that whatever simple gift we would bring from the North Pole for a boy or girl might be the only gift that child received. More often, whatever present we left would be one among several or even dozens of others from the child's family and friends. Extravagant items were beyond our ability to provide.

"Sometime, somewhere, too many people got the wrong idea about Santa Claus and his gifts," I said to Layla and several of my other longtime companions after I'd made my weary way back to the North Pole that night. "The greed of some of these boys and girls is troubling. We work hard to give presents that enhance holiday celebrations for children, but we could never bring anyone a pony, for goodness' sake. When I told one boy named Robert that I couldn't promise to bring him a fire-engine-red Mustang convertible, he actually jumped off my lap and kicked my shin. I think he might have been eight."

"But most of the children weren't like that, were they?" Amelia Earhart wanted to know.

"No, of course not," I assured her. "Hundreds gave me warm hugs, and I couldn't begin to tell you how many said they loved me and would leave out cookies and milk on Christmas Eve."

"Well, then, you have to decide whether to become discouraged by the actions of a few or encouraged by the responses of many," said Layla in her no-nonsense way. "If part of your problem is not being familiar with newer sorts of toys and gadgets, we can fix that. Perhaps Leonardo could prepare a few study sheets."

"I'd be glad to," Leonardo said.

"Please remember to include something called teraflops," I requested. "And now, if you'll all excuse me, I must go to bed. It's been quite a tiring day, and I have to be back at the mall at eleven tomorrow morning. Santa Land is open from noon until 10:00 p.m. on Sundays."

It took the better part of a month, but I gradually grew more comfortable in my mall Santa role. Leonardo coached me in modern toy terminology. (A "teraflop" is a way of measuring the speed at which a computer or computer game operates; a single teraflop can represent *one trillion* numbers being processed, which is apparently something a modern-day seven-year-old might know but someone born in 280 AD like me wouldn't.) I learned about digital music players and the difference between DVD-R and DVD+R. And when an eleven-year-old boy requested a Blackberry for Christmas, I even knew he wasn't asking me for fruit.

I mastered the art of giving each child on my lap my full attention without forgetting how many more children were waiting for their turns with Santa. I happily answered thousands of questions about what it was like living at the North Pole and how I could visit the home of every child in just one night ("Three nights, not one!") and whether the reindeer *liked* pulling my sleigh. I even began to enjoy the challenge of responding to children who, for one reason or another, were hostile. The more unpleasant they acted, the harder I tried to make them feel welcome. It didn't always work, but sometimes their frowns would turn to smiles. Above all, I was warmed by the sense of how many people, children and grown-ups alike, truly loved Christmas.

"You're just the most fantastic Santa ever," Jill enthused one early December evening as we prepared to shut down Santa Land for the night. Most of my "elves" were helping Scott clear away scattered trash, while I waved goodbye to several children and their parents who were obviously reluctant to bid Santa Claus farewell.

"It's great fun for me," I replied. "Look at that little girl just crossing the bridge. She gave me the most wonderful hug, and told me if my sleigh got too crowded I should bring presents for her brothers but not her. Well, I won't forget young Christina Weeks on Christmas Eve, I can promise you that!"

"You sound like you plan to personally bring her a present!" Jill exclaimed.

"I just might; after all, I'm Santa Claus," I said. In fact, I was already imagining the doll I'd leave for little Christina to discover on Christmas morning. That was what she had asked for.

"I just wish Mr. Sneed didn't look so unhappy," Jill continued, gesturing toward the top floor of the mall. Mr. Sneed was slumped against the rail, watching forlornly as Christina and her parents and the other lingerers who hated leaving Santa finally made their ways out into the parking lot. I wasn't surprised to see him there. Often, each day, I glimpsed him watching enviously as children paraded one after another to sit on my lap and whisper their requests into my ear.

"Did he really love playing Santa so much?" I asked.

"I remember that when he played Santa, he never took a dinner break," Jill said. "He told me that he didn't want even one child to miss seeing Santa because Santa had gone off duty for a while. But I can understand why the mall owners decided to hire an outside Santa. Mr. Sneed's gray beard was too scraggly. He wasn't fat enough to be Santa, and he wouldn't put a cushion under his costume because he said the children might notice it was fake instead of a real belly. When I first saw Jimmy Lee looking perfect in his Santa costume, I realized Mr. Sneed just couldn't compare to him."

I hadn't thought of Jimmy Lee for a while. I'd been having too much fun.

"I guess no Santa could compare to Jimmy Lee," I said.

"You might," Jill replied, which surprised and pleased me. "He always says just the right thing. He looks like everyone imagines Santa ought to look. But you, well, you're sort of *real*. Say, I heard something interesting this morning. I was in Mr. Sneed's office, reminding him we need replacement lights for some of the trees in Santa Land. His phone rang. It was somebody from that *Great Santa Search* program that's going to be on FUN-TV. They're going to come here to the mall next week to check you out. I think they might pick you to be on their program! Wouldn't that be something?"

"It certainly would," I said. Jill hadn't surprised me. Felix already mentioned a few days earlier that he would be coming to Galaxy Mall soon to observe me in action. Already, another half-dozen Santas from malls around the country had been selected as *Great Santa Search* finalists. They didn't know themselves that they'd been picked. Bobbo Butler wanted to keep the names of the finalists secret at least until mid-December, to reduce the chances of nosy members of the media writing about them too far in advance of the program itself. About a week before Christmas Eve, Felix said, all ten finalists would be notified and brought to the FUN-TV offices for a briefing on the show. I was eager to compete against them. My experiences at Galaxy Mall had reinforced my belief that being Santa Claus was an honor—and a responsibility I took very seriously. It was unacceptable that some false "Santa" would use my name and image to promote the shoddy products of LastLong Toy Company.

"Do you want to be on *The Great Santa Search?*" Jill asked.

"Oh, yes," I confirmed. "Definitely."

He gestured toward the little girls. "Now, then, remind me of your names." "I'm Cynthia," said one. When her younger sister didn't speak up, Cyn added, "That's Diana. She says she doesn't believe in you, but sometimes I still do."

Fourteen

hile I was perfecting my skills as a mall Santa, program-planning continued at the FUN-TV offices in New York City. On the same day that Jill the photographer told me about someone from *The Great Santa Search* coming to the Galaxy Mall, Bobbo Butler convened a meeting.

"Eight Santa finalists down, two to go," he reminded Felix, Sarah, and Heather Hathaway. The four of them were in the FUN-TV conference room. It was late afternoon, and they'd spent the last several hours deciding how to distribute tickets for *The Great Santa Search,* which was now only two weeks away. The Ed Sullivan Theater had 461 seats. Eleven of these would go to hand-picked members of the media, men and women who represented the very biggest newspapers and television programs. (Oprah Winfrey, Katie Couric, Jon Stewart, and David Letterman were among those whose attendance was already confirmed.) Another 150 were promised to executives of LastLong Toy Company and their families. That left only three hundred for the general public.

Bobbo originally suggested that these simply be made available on the morning of December 24 "on a first-come, first-served basis; they'll be lining up for 'em a week in advance, and that line will stretch all the way from the box office back to Central Park. That story will headline every TV news program for days. What a lead-in to the broadcast itself! Ratings magic, I tell you!"

But Heather tactfully reminded her boss that they hoped the audience would include small children and grandparents. It would be very cold in New York City during the week before Christmas; there probably would be snow. It would look like FUN-TV didn't mind that very young and very old people lined up for *Great Santa Search* tickets were suffering from the winter weather, she suggested. That sort of bad publicity might hurt the show's ratings rather than boost them.

"You're right, Miss Hathaway," Bobbo reluctantly agreed. "Can you think of something better?"

"What about an online ticket giveaway, chief?" Heather asked. "Our www.thegreatsantasearch.com website is averaging more than two hundred thousand hits an hour. We could put out a press release tomorrow morning that, say, this Saturday we'll make the tickets available for free. Anyone interested can log on and apply. The FUN-TV computer system can pick 150 winners of two tickets each at random. They'll be notified electronically, and those who live out of town will have enough time to make travel arrangements to New York."

Bobbo thought the idea was wonderful, and Felix and Sarah liked it, too. Bobbo instructed Heather to write and send out the press release the next morning, though he added that three hundred wasn't the actual number of tickets that would be available to the public. Everyone on the program staff would each receive two, he said. Felix asked if he and Sarah could have a few more for special friends, but Bobbo said all the rest had to be distributed in the online lottery.

"You and Sarah are going to be backstage anyway," he said. "So you'll have four to give away, and I'll even let you bring one of your friends backstage with you during the program. Will that do?"

Felix thought it was quite generous, and told Bobbo so. Heather did some quick mental arithmetic and said that meant 288 tickets would be available to the public.

"Not quite," Bobbo said, a wide smile splitting his face. "I need two myself. Diana and Cynthia are coming to the program!"

"I thought your daughters weren't fond of Christmas anymore," Sarah said.

Bobbo's grin grew even wider.

"All these months, I've been telling them about *The Great Santa Search,* and promising that when it made Daddy's network successful again I would have more time to spend with them," he explained. "The girls have really been warming up to me lately. It's just wonderful. In fact, their mother is letting them have dinner with me in the city tonight, as long as I get them home by ten since it's a school night. Say, Sarah and Felix, why don't you join us? And you, too, Miss Hathaway."

Felix, Sarah, and Heather said they had too much work to do to go out to dinner—they planned to stay at the FUN-TV office and order in pizza.

"Then after I've taken the girls to dinner, I'll bring them here," Bobbo said. "I'm planning a special treat for them after we eat, and I'd like the three of you to be part of it. And by the way, Miss Hathaway, make sure you use our network credit card to pay for the pizza. Order all the extra toppings you want. Thanks to *The Great Santa Search,* it's good times again for FUN-TV!"

After Bobbo had left, Heather, Felix, and Sarah poured themselves cups of coffee and settled back in the conference room's comfortable chairs. It had been a hectic day. During the morning, Lauren Devoe had gone over the opening dance routine, Ken had talked about sound checks, and Eri had final sketches of costumes for everyone to look at.

Mary discussed how long each show segment would take. Everything had to be calculated down to split seconds. Then the afternoon found Felix, Sarah, Bobbo, and Heather having to plan for ticket distribution. With December 24 looming, there was a real sense of urgency to *The Great Santa Search* meetings now.

"I don't think many people realize how complicated it is to put together a television program," Felix said, slouching down in his chair until it almost appeared he was sitting on his neck. "Heather, I don't see how you and Bobbo can do this all the time."

"We really don't," Heather admitted. "In the last few years when FUN-TV ratings were so bad, sometimes Bobbo hardly put any planning into shows at all because he was so discouraged. I've never seen him work as hard as he has for *The Great Santa Search*. Of course, we're all working hard. You're flying to Cleveland tomorrow, aren't you, Felix? You think you're going to find our ninth Santa finalist there."

"I've heard good things about the Santa at Cleveland's Galaxy Mall," Felix said carefully. "His name is Nicholas. We've actually got a great regional mix of finalists among the eight we have so far. There's Luis from a mall in Miami, and Buck from Kansas City, and Andy from Chicago. We have some Santas from smaller cities and malls, too. Brian from Missoula, Dillard from College Station in Texas, and Zonk from Rutland, Vermont. Wesley wasn't a mall Santa at all; he was starring as Santa in a Christmas play in St. Paul. And Joe is the finalist who made it through that open audition. I think he's from Bloomington, Indiana."

"If the Cleveland Santa is picked, that makes nine finalists," Sarah said. "There's not much time left. Where will you find the tenth?"

Felix sighed.

"Right from the beginning, there was one name that everyone kept mentioning," he said. "He's Jimmy Lee, and this Christmas he's working right here in New York at the Manhattan Mega-Mall just east of Central Park. The people from the Noel Program told us he's the inevitable *Great Santa Search* winner because there's no mall Santa, or any other kind of Santa, who's half as good. It's odd—I was already going to go see him sometime this week, but Bobbo mentioned him to me today, too. I wonder how Bobbo heard about him."

"I can tell you," Heather said. "He got a call this morning from Lucretia Pepper. She told him some LastLong Toy people had been to Manhattan Mega-Mall and saw Jimmy Lee there. They thought he was wonderful, and she insists that he ought to be a finalist."

"How did they find out his name?" Sarah asked.

"I have no idea," Heather replied. "But Lucretia Pepper knew it. If he's any good at all, Felix, please pick him as a finalist. We want to keep our sponsor happy."

Around 7:00 p.m., the pizza arrived. By mutual consent, they decided to talk about anything but *The Great Santa Search* while they ate.

"Have you and Felix done all your Christmas shopping, Sarah?" Heather asked as she carefully raised a drippy slice of double-cheese-and-Italian-sausage pizza to her mouth.

"No, but we usually wait until the last minute," Sarah said. "Late on Christmas Eve, in fact."

"Really?" Heather replied. "Where do you find a good store open then?"

"We're lucky; where we live, there's a wonderful place that has all the presents anyone reasonable could want," Sarah laughed. "What about you, Heather? Is your shopping done?"

Heather said she'd purchased gifts for her parents and mailed them to North Dakota almost a month earlier.

"And I found some nice bracelets for Diana and Cynthia," she added. "Bobbo's so excited about *The Great Santa Search* that I'm afraid he might forget to buy them Christmas presents. That would be terrible, especially since the girls seem to be getting along better with him. Wait— I think I hear them coming in."

Bobbo bustled into the conference room accompanied by two young girls. Ten-year-old Cynthia seemed quite gentle and very funny. Her eight-year-old sister Diana was rather outspoken. She informed her father that he had to get them back home to Scarsdale by ten.

"Mom says to keep reminding you it's a school night, because you're going to forget," she said. "Last time we had dinner with you on a school night we didn't get home until after midnight, and Cyn fell asleep the next day in class. Her teacher got *real* mad."

"But I had a nice dream," Cynthia said cheerfully. "There was a spaceship in it. Maybe I was flying to the moon."

"Or possibly the North Pole," Heather suggested. "Your father is so excited you'll both be coming to the studio for his Christmas Eve show. You'll help pick the real Santa Claus, and maybe afterward he'll take both of you to the North Pole for a visit. Wouldn't that be fun?"

Cynthia thought it would be, but Diana said Heather was being silly.

"There's no Santa Claus, and Christmas stinks, anyway," she declared. "People talk about time for families and being together for the holiday, but all they really care about are their stupid *jobs*." She glared at Bobbo as she said this.

Her father looked guilty, and reminded Diana that just as soon as *The Great Santa Search* was over, he'd start spending more time with his daughters.

Diana sneered.

"You always say you're going to spend more time with us, but then you never do."

"I really mean it this time," Bobbo promised.

"That would be nice, Daddy," Cynthia said. "Are we really going to pick Santa Claus on your show?"

"Definitely," Bobbo said. "There are going to be all sorts of contests for the ten finalists. They're going to sing and rope reindeer—not real ones—and climb down chimneys and put toys in stockings and even eat cookies. It will be great. The audience is going to vote twice during the program for their favorites, and the other times we'll eliminate Santas

who finish last in the competitions. You and Diana might cast the deciding votes!"

"There's no Santa Claus, and you're just going to make people pick
from a bunch of actors," Diana said, managing to sound bored and hostile at the same time. "Cyn and I don't believe in Santa Claus anymore,
Daddy. Why do you keep acting like we do?"

"I sort of believe in him," Cynthia said. "I remember he brought me
a bicycle when I was seven."

"Mom and Daddy got you that," Diana declared. "They just told you
Santa brought it."

"Well, maybe he did," Cynthia muttered.

For several very long moments, no one at the table spoke. Then
Heather said cheerfully, "We ordered too much pizza and there's a lot
left over. Cyn, Diana, would you like some?" Cyn did. Diana said
grumpily that she was full already, and maybe it was time for Daddy to
bring them home. But Heather praised the nice earrings Diana was
wearing and asked her questions about school until the little girl relaxed
and began chattering comfortably. She even ate two slices of pizza while
Heather turned the conversation back to *The Great Santa Search*, em-
phasizing how pleased Bobbo was that his daughters would be in the
audience.

"Why does she keep mentioning that?" Felix whispered to his wife.

"Heather knows it would break Bobbo's heart if Cynthia and Diana
decided not to be there," Sarah whispered back. "At the same time, she's
reminding the girls how much their father loves them. Heather just has
an amazing ability to understand how people think."

So while the last slices of pizza were eaten, the Butler girls heard
about Eri Mizobe's plan for Santa costumes—all the finalists would be
dressed in gorgeous red velvet robes with snow-white fur trim—and
how Robert Fernandez's crew was building a whole herd of wooden
reindeer for the roping competition.

Then Felix talked about the eight *Great Santa Search* finalists he'd found so far. He mentioned flying to Cleveland the next day to scout a promising candidate. That was when Bobbo announced his surprise.

"It's not much after eight, so there's a little time before I have to take the girls back to Scarsdale," he said. "Somebody told me today about a great Santa at the Manhattan Mega-Mall. What do you say that we all pile in my car and go over there to take a look at him? From everything I hear, he ought to be one of our finalists, Felix."

Diana didn't want to go to the mall. She said she had homework and was tired. But Cynthia wanted to, and Felix said he had to go see this Jimmy Lee sometime. Heather and Sarah coaxed Diana until she finally said fine, she'd come, but nobody had better ask her to sit on some phony Santa's lap. Cynthia said she'd sit on Santa's lap for both of them.

Bobbo drove an SUV, so there was plenty of room in it for all six people. They soon reached the high-rise parking garage for Manhattan Mega-Mall, and then took an elevator and two escalators to enter the mall itself. They set out to find Jimmy Lee, and it wasn't hard.

Felix told me later that Santa Land at Galaxy Mall in Cleveland was impressive, but didn't remotely compare to "Clausville" at Manhattan Mega-Mall. To begin with, at my mall I had seven "elf" helpers; Clausville boasted forty. A whole army of men and women in leotards and fake pointed ears bustled around a roped-off area easily three or four times as large as Galaxy Mall's Santa Land. Besides photographers selling pictures, Clausville had booths offering Christmas candy and cookies, holiday-themed books, bright sweaters and T-shirts decorated with Christmas sayings and symbols, and literally mountains of toys, many of which, Felix and Sarah noted, were shoddy LastLong products.

In the middle of Clausville, high on a raised platform, was a gleaming throne apparently made from giant candy canes. Seated on that throne was a red-robed, white-bearded fellow who simply glowed with happy holiday spirit. His charming smile was mirrored on the faces of hundreds of children and adults lined up waiting to briefly meet him. Everything about Clausville was spectacular, but the Santa in the center of it all effortlessly held everyone's attention.

"Wow," Felix breathed. He couldn't help himself. Then he looked at the others standing beside him. They appeared equally impressed. Even Diana Butler's eyes were wide with astonishment.

"Now, *that's* a Santa," Bobbo Butler declared, and Felix, even though he knew I was the real one and not Jimmy Lee, found himself nodding in agreement.

Heather suggested that they all join "the Santa line" so Felix could see and hear Jimmy Lee in action. It took almost twenty minutes just to maneuver themselves down to the lowest mall level and then fight through the crowds to the entrance of Clausville, where two lovely young women in elf costumes informed them there would be about a sixty-minute wait in line.

"That's too long, Daddy," Diana insisted. "Remember Cyn and I have school tomorrow."

Bobbo reluctantly agreed.

"I bet he's perfect, though," he said. "Felix, make sure you get this guy for the show. I mean, maybe he *is* Santa Claus."

"Told you there might really be one," Cynthia whispered to Diana.

They turned to leave, but as they reached the Clausville entrance they were stopped by a medium-sized, balding man.

"Are you Mr. Butler?" he inquired. "Mr. Bobbo Butler of *The Great Santa Search*?"

"Why, yes, I am," Bobbo replied, beaming. He was always happy when he was recognized, and the advance publicity for *The Great Santa Search* had kept his face on the news and his picture in the papers for months.

"Well, it's an honor to have you visiting Clausville, sir," the bald man assured him. "I'm Mr. Fuquay, the mall manager, and it's such a pleasure to meet you. My whole family is going to be watching your program on Christmas Eve—my wife, our four children, and our seventeen grandchildren!"

"Imagine that," Bobbo said. "Why, your family alone is a bigger audience than we drew last year with *Merry Monkey.*"

Mr. Fuquay looked confused. He was quite good at it. His forehead rippled with sudden, deep furrows, and his eyebrows knitted together.

"I'm afraid I don't know about any *Merry Monkey* program, sir," he said.

"You and the rest of America," Bobbo laughed. "Well, I'm glad this time we've got a show you want to watch. We hoped to meet your mall Santa tonight, but unfortunately we can't stand in line for an hour. My girls need to get home to Scarsdale. It's a school night." He looked over at Diana. "See? I remembered."

Mr. Fuquay's expression changed from concern to joy.

"Please, Mr. Butler, you don't have to worry about standing in line! A celebrity like you, sir, well—would these lovely girls be your daughters?" He gestured toward Cynthia, Diana, and, unfortunately, Heather, who shook her head emphatically.

"I'm Mr. Butler's executive assistant," she said.

"I do beg your pardon," said Mr. Fuquay. "Well, then, these two young ladies certainly want to meet Santa Claus!"

Cynthia nodded so hard that her bangs flopped up and down. Diana made a face, but she didn't disagree.

"All right," Mr. Fuquay announced. "I expect all the grown-ups want to meet him, too. Follow me, please." He guided the four adults and two girls past the winding line. The people in front, who'd been waiting a long time for their turns with Santa, grumbled when they saw newcomers being escorted in front of them, but Mr. Fuquay explained that this was Mr. Butler's party, Mr. Butler of *The Great Santa Search* that everyone in America would be watching on Christmas Eve.

"You've got to have Mega-Mall's Santa on your show, Mr. Butler," a father being displaced at the front of the line told Bobbo. "I've brought my boy here eight straight nights to see him. He's the best Santa ever!" His son, a strapping six-year-old, shouted "Yeah!" in agreement.

"Watch *The Great Santa Search* on Christmas Eve and see," Bobbo suggested.

Mr. Fuquay led the way up steep stairs to the candy-cane throne, and there the group was greeted with a hearty "Merry Christmas!" by a man whose beaming face was framed by the most perfect of snow-white beards. Genuine pleasure emanated in his pleasantly deep voice. Blue eyes twinkled behind his gold-rimmed spectacles, and when he stood his belly protruded just the right amount from his spotless, shining red suit.

"Santa Claus, may I present Mr. Bobbo Butler," Mr. Fuquay announced. "Mr. Bobbo Butler of *The Great Santa Search*, you know."

Mega-Mall Santa laughed.

"Of course!" he exclaimed. "Mr. Butler of *my* show! I'm glad to meet you and your friends"—he nodded to Felix, Sarah, and Heather—"but I'm especially pleased to see these two wonderful people." He gestured toward the little girls. "Now, then, remind me of your names."

"I'm Cynthia," said one. When her younger sister didn't speak up, Cyn added, "That's Diana. She says she doesn't believe in you, but sometimes I still do."

"Really?" Mega-Mall Santa inquired. Felix knew the man's real name was Jimmy Lee, but somehow it was hard to think of him as anyone other than Santa Claus. "Well, that's too bad. Perhaps you'll believe in me again," he said to Diana, who didn't say anything, but at least didn't make a face.

"My daughters are going to be in the studio audience on Christmas Eve, Santa Claus," Bobbo said. "So they'll see you again there. If, of course, you're one of our finalists," he added, glancing meaningfully at Felix.

"Just let me know soon; I already have a lot to do on Christmas Eve!" he replied. "Now, Cynthia and Diana, get a good night's sleep so you'll do well in school tomorrow. Try to believe in me again. I have some very special gifts to leave under your tree this year!"

"I wonder if he'll bring me an MP3 player," Cynthia mused as they made their way back to the parking garage. "Diana, you should have told him what you wanted, too." Diana didn't reply, but she also didn't say anything more about Santa being stupid or not existing.

Bobbo dropped Heather, Sarah, and Felix back at the FUN-TV offices before returning his daughters to Scarsdale.

"That fellow was amazing," he whispered to them, keeping his voice low so the girls wouldn't hear. "Felix, I think we've found our winner."

"We'll find out on Christmas Eve," Felix replied. "Well, I'll go to Galaxy Mall in Cleveland tomorrow. If I select the Santa there, and then if I pick Jimmy Lee—"

"Of *course* you're picking Jimmy Lee," Bobbo interrupted.

"Well, that will make up our ten finalists," Felix said. "I'll see you when I get back from Cleveland, Bobbo."

While they got ready for bed in their New York City hotel room, Felix and Sarah discussed Jimmy Lee.

"If I hadn't known the real one for so long, I could certainly believe he was Santa Claus," Sarah admitted. "His voice, and his smile, and, well, everything about him is just right. Even little Diana was impressed by him."

"True, but do you remember what he said to the girls?" Felix asked. "He told them he hoped they'd believe in him again, but right afterward he promised them special presents. That's bribery. The *real* Santa would never stoop to that."

"I wonder if he was good at playing Santa from the beginning, or if he really had to work hard at it," Sarah said, ignoring her husband's criticism of Jimmy Lee. "You can tell he's someone who's loved Christmas all his life. I'm sure he's at least a true believer, or even a maximum true believer. Has Leonardo checked into his background at all?"

"No, but he certainly should," Felix replied. He picked up his cell

phone and called the North Pole. This late in December, in the time between St. Nicholas Day and Christmas, he knew everyone would be up
working very late. When he was connected with Leonardo, he asked him
to do a background check on Jimmy Lee.

"I have to fly to Cleveland tomorrow to see the real Santa at Galaxy
Mall," Felix told Leonardo. "So could you run your check before you go
to bed tonight, then call me early in the morning before I leave for the
airport if there's anything you find out that I should know?"

Leonardo agreed. Felix soon was asleep. The next morning he was in
a taxi heading to LaGuardia Airport in New York when his cell phone
rang. It was Leonardo.

"The Jimmy Lee you're asking about is from Leeds, Alabama, correct?" he asked. "Not the Jimmy Lee from Birmingham or the one from
Tuscaloosa?"

"I'm sure the real Santa said this Jimmy Lee is from Leeds."

"Well, then," Leonardo said, "I have interesting news. This man is
supposed to be a great mall Santa?"

"I have to admit, he *is* great."

"Odd," Leonardo mumbled.

"What's odd about it?" Felix demanded.

"Jimmy Lee from Leeds, Alabama, is a never."

I followed her inside and was greeted by a quite stunning sight. The nine
individuals seated around a long table composed one of the most
amazing groups of human beings I'd ever encountered.

Fifteen

t was clear Mr. Sneed was not pleased by the possibility I would be selected for *The Great Santa Search*. That added to his other concerns. With eight days left until Christmas, the crowds of shoppers had swelled to the point that there was sometimes an hour wait just to be admitted to the mall parking lot. The crush made Mr. Sneed especially nervous. He fretted about small children becoming separated from their parents in crowds, and the mall food court running out of French fries. Now he also had *The Great Santa Search* to worry about.

"Okay, some guy from that program's coming today," Mr. Sneed informed me when I arrived in the Santa Land dressing room. "Even if he asks you to be on it, you don't have to say yes. We're going to have mobs of kids all the way up through Christmas Eve. You've done okay for a beginner. If you're on that show, your company might send me a real loser to fill in for you."

"If I'm picked, perhaps you could step in as Galaxy Mall Santa," I suggested. "Jill has told me you're very good at it."

For a single fleeting second, it seemed that Mr. Sneed might smile. But he fought the impulse, and his lips remained in their usual pursed position.

"Ah, that was a while ago," he muttered. "I really haven't got the beard for it, I guess, or the belly." He ran his fingers through his scraggly whiskers. "Guys like you with the white beards and the big bellies are better. Well, the *Great Santa Search* guy wants to meet me in my office right at ten. You just do everything like usual with the kids. No showing off, okay? Remember, this is all about them having a great time with Santa, not you getting to be on some TV show. The kids here at the mall come first. Promise?"

I promised, and then, dressed in my Santa costume, I made my way out into Santa Land, where an agreeably long line of children and their parents was already stretched from my wooden block throne to the wrought-iron bridge. By the time Mr. Sneed and Felix appeared a half-hour later, I'd already greeted some forty-five children. Their gift requests had ranged from an electric race-car set to a donkey. The girl who wanted the donkey said she'd always thought they looked interesting. I assured her they were, but added that they rarely made good house pets.

"Could you bring me a PS2, then?" she wanted to know.

"A PS3 might be better," I suggested. "Two teraflops of performance, you know." I was beginning to love all this new toy- and game-related jargon.

From the corner of my eye, I saw Felix and Mr. Sneed maneuvering so they could clearly see and hear me. Felix looked distinguished in a pinstripe suit. Sarah had bought him a whole new wardrobe in New York City stores. It was hard to believe this was my same old dear friend who'd been dressed in a filthy tunic when I'd first met him in a Roman alley nearly seventeen centuries earlier.

As he and Mr. Sneed watched closely, I pulled a lovely little boy with curly golden hair up onto my lap and asked him his name.

"I'm Nathan!" he crowed. "I'm going to be six!"

"That's a wonderful age, Nathan," I replied. "My name is Santa Claus."

Nathan giggled.

"I know. Mommy says you might bring me a toy truck if I'm good."

I glanced over at Nathan's parents, who stood with Xander. Xander was nodding.

"I'm sure you will be good, and I think there might be a fine toy truck at the North Pole for me to bring you," I said. "And please, Nathan, always remember that Christmas is about more than you getting a present from Santa."

"I know that, too. Daddy wants it to be about you bringing him a bowling ball, but Mommy says you're going to bring him a new lawn mower, and he better use it."

I noticed Nathan's father did not look particularly cheerful.

"Well, please tell your daddy that Santa loves him even if he does happen to receive a lawn mower instead of a bowling ball," I said. "We don't always get every Christmas present we want, but the thought behind the gift is what's most important. In this case, that thought might involve a nice-looking lawn. Merry Christmas, Nathan. I can't wait to come to your home on Christmas Eve."

"I'll leave out milk and cookies, Santa," he promised, and gave me a big hug as Jill and Ralphie snapped their photographs.

"Okay, Santa, I've got somebody here who wants to meet you," Mr. Sneed called around noon as I prepared to take my forty-five-minute break for lunch. "Guy's name is Felix, uh—guess I forgot his last name."

"Felix *North*," said my old friend, grinning and extending his hand. "And your name is Nicholas Holiday, I think. It's a pleasure to meet you."

"Likewise," I said, enjoying the chance to pretend we hadn't been greeting each other on a regular basis for almost seventeen centuries. "I understand you're an executive with *The Great Santa Search.*"

"I am," Felix replied, "and based on my observation of you this morning, I'd like to invite you to compete as one of ten finalists on our Christmas Eve broadcast. I guess you know about the program, what's going to happen at the end and so forth."

"Someone will be elected as the official Santa Claus," I said. "It sounds very exciting. I'd like to participate, if that's all right with Mr. Sneed. I'm under contract to work for him right up through Christmas Eve, and, of course, Santa Claus never breaks his word."

"I'm *sure* Mr. Sneed won't mind," Felix said, though he didn't really sound sure. Obviously, his conversation with Mr. Sneed had indicated my boss wasn't the most agreeable of employers. "Can Nicholas Holiday, here, be excused on Christmas Eve to compete on *The Great Santa Search?*"

"That might be tough," Mr. Sneed suggested. "The mall owners pay this guy's placement agency a ton of money, and they sure wouldn't like it if that Santa Land seat of his got filled by some replacement on one of our biggest holiday-shopping nights. I'm going to have to think about this."

Felix looked at me over Mr. Sneed's shoulder, and rolled his eyes.

"The Santa placement agency you use is the Noel Program, correct?" he asked. "Well, I've been in touch with Ms. Stephanie Owen there, and she assures me Noel will provide substitute Santas as needed for any of their employees who are selected for *The Great Santa Search*. You'll have a satisfactory white-bearded man in a red suit here on Christmas Eve, I promise."

Mr. Sneed rubbed his face with his hand.

"Well, that sounds okay, but maybe the bozo they send for that night won't be any good," he said. "This guy here has done okay with the kids. I don't want any of 'em disappointed by a second-rate Santa. We couldn't have that."

"There's a simple solution, Mr. Sneed," I said. "I'm told that you make an excellent Santa Claus. I'd consider it a personal favor if you would step in to be Santa in my place on Christmas Eve. The children will love you."

Now Mr. Sneed did grin. He couldn't help himself.

"That's nice of you," he said. "But I really shouldn't."

"Why not?" I asked.

"Like I said before, I don't have the beard for it. Or the belly. Look at you, that big gut, and it's all real. I hate using pillows. They're too fake. The kids catch on."

"Now, Mr. Sneed," I said. "We both know that Santa is more than his beard and a few extra pounds. Please agree to take my place on Christmas Eve. I'm asking for my own sake as well as the children's. I'll be a better competitor on *The Great Santa Search* if I don't have to worry about the boys and girls back at the Galaxy Mall suffering with an unsuitable Santa."

Mr. Sneed pretended to think it over.

"Okay, buddy, I guess I can do it. For you, that is. I'll get my red-and-white outfit over to the dry cleaners today and tell 'em it's a rush job, 'cause I'll need it on Christmas Eve."

"Actually, you'll need it sooner than that," Felix noted. "Tomorrow we want to get all ten *Great Santa Search* finalists together at the FUN-TV offices in New York, so we can go over the program schedule with them, fit them for their costumes, and so on. That means you'll need to substitute for Nicholas Holiday tomorrow and on Christmas Eve both, Mr. Sneed. I hope that won't be a problem."

Mr. Sneed had a dreamy look on his face. I could tell he was already imagining himself in full Santa regalia, perched on the wooden block throne and helping hundreds of children enjoy the happiest of holidays.

"We'll manage," he said. "Okay, buddy, good luck to you. I hope you win this thing. Mr. North, by any chance is a guy named Jimmy Lee one of your other finalists?"

"We're not supposed to say anything about that," Felix replied. "But if you'll keep it to yourself, Mr. Sneed, then, yes, he is."

"Ah, well, second place is no disgrace," Mr. Sneed told me. He clapped me on the back and hurried off to fetch his Santa suit and take it to the dry cleaners.

Felix flew back to New York that afternoon, and I took the sleigh to the North Pole when my day's work at Galaxy Mall was complete. I felt quite excited. For months I'd thought about competing on *The Great Santa Search,* and now it was certain I would. The next day, I would meet the other nine would-be Santas, including Jimmy Lee. Then Sarah, who was back at the North Pole, too, told me about him being a never. This was shocking news.

"But you say he seems so right in the Santa role," I told her. "How can he possibly appear to love Christmas so much if he doesn't personally believe in me or the spirit of the holiday at all?"

"He's obviously a talented performer," Sarah replied. "Leonardo insists that there's no mistake. Jimmy Lee never believed in Santa Claus. He was raised by parents who mocked the whole history of the holiday, Santa included. He learned from their unfortunate example. Worse, he never outgrew his disdain for Christmas. But he never disdained money. He's spent his whole life involved in all sorts of get-rich-quick schemes, though none ever worked out as he'd hoped. It's unfortunate that he found a way to use the holiday he otherwise hates as a means of filling his bank account."

"Go on," I said.

"Jimmy Lee is fifty-five now," Leonardo continued. "When he was forty, he applied to the Noel Program and was an instant success as a mall Santa. They pay based on both experience and excellence, you know. According to their company records—we hope you don't mind that Leonardo hacked into their files—Jimmy Lee earns almost $75,000 each year just during November and December when he's Santa in a mall."

"That's awful," said Theodore Roosevelt, who'd been eavesdropping. "This fellow hates Christmas and loathes the concept of Santa Claus, but he'll pretend to be him anyway because he makes so much doing it. I'd be wary of him during this broadcast, Santa. If Jimmy Lee makes $75,000 now as one among many mall Santas, can you imagine the fortune he could wring out of being the one and only *official* Santa Claus from *The Great Santa Search*?"

"Well, it's not going to come to that," I promised. "I admit, though, that I'm curious to meet him. And I will tomorrow, at the FUN-TV office. It may be that he's not as bad as you imagine, Theodore. Anyone who makes fun of the beliefs of others is obviously unhappy himself. Who knows? During the course of the competition, the true spirit of Christmas might touch even Jimmy Lee!"

The next morning, I hitched up the reindeer and flew to New York City. I landed the sleigh in a discreet corner of Central Park, used hand signals to instruct the reindeer to hover out of sight until I returned, and then took a pleasant stroll to the FUN-TV meeting at Rockefeller Center. The December air was bitingly cold, but I wore a warm coat. Besides, compared to weather conditions at the North Pole, New York City seemed tropical.

I recognized Heather Hathaway right away, as much for the warm smile that Felix and Sarah had described as her great height. She greeted me in formal though friendly fashion, informing me I was the last of the ten finalists to arrive and that everyone else was waiting in the conference room. I followed her inside and was greeted by a quite stunning sight. The nine individuals seated around a long table composed one of the most amazing groups of human beings I'd ever encountered.

All but two had beards of varying lengths and shades, mostly to mid-chest and white, though one had dark brown whiskers. Collectively, they defined the possible degrees of *stout*, running the gamut from a slightly bulging tummy to a fellow whose belly actually protruded so far forward that the front of it rested on the conference table. No two wore the same sort of clothing. There were blue jeans and expensive, tapered slacks, flannel shirts, and plush cashmere sweaters. One man had a cowboy hat jammed on his head, even though he was indoors.

Though it was difficult to tear my eyes away, I glanced at the others in the room. Felix was at one end of the table, and Sarah was on his right. On Felix's left was Bobbo Butler—I recognized the bristly rim of hair around his otherwise bald scalp from watching him so often on TV. The rest of the *Great Santa Search* staff was present—Mary the director, Ken the sound engineer, Eri the costume designer, Robert the set designer, and the woman in the black leotard had to be Lauren the choreographer.

Then there was a large, formidable-looking woman with makeup caked thick on her sharp-featured face—Lucretia Pepper, of course. I wondered why the LastLong Toy Company president found it necessary to attend.

"Well, now we're all here," Bobbo Butler announced. "Welcome, everyone. I hope you realize you're part of television history, and part of Christmas history, too. Exactly one week from tonight, we're going to work together and give America the official Santa Claus that it deserves. Think of it!"

After a moment, Heather Hathaway clapped. Then everyone else did, too. Bobbo nodded to acknowledge the applause.

"Everybody needs to know everybody else, so let me get it started. I'm Bobbo Butler, president of the FUN-TV network. The tall woman over there is my assistant, Heather Hathaway. Does anybody want her to bring coffee? No? Well, I'm sure we'll want some later. Stay to take notes for now, Miss Hathaway. Here to my left is Mary Rogers, who'll be our director next week, and Ken Perkins, the sound engineer who'll make you all sound perfect, and Eri Mizobe, who you'll get to know *very* well in a bit when she measures you for the Santa costumes you'll wear on the show. Robert Fernandez has designed the sets, and they're gorgeous. Lauren Devoe is our choreographer—yes, you're going to dance and do lots of other things. We'll be getting to that. On my right, this is

Sarah North, who's an assistant to her husband, Felix North. All of you know Felix. He's the one who picked you. I think he's the greatest Christmas historian in America. Any questions you have about Christmas history, just ask him."

Bobbo paused to clear his throat.

"Last but not least, this lady beside me is Lucretia Pepper, who has generously taken time away from her job as owner and chief operating officer of LastLong Toy Company to be with us today. LastLong is the sole sponsor of *The Great Santa Search*. She has made this broadcast possible. I know we'd all like her to say a few words."

Lucretia Pepper uncoiled and coolly fixed each of us finalists with a brief, penetrating stare.

"What an honor to be among so many potential Santas," she said. "I'm sure any of you would make an outstanding spokesman for my company's equally outstanding toys. I hope you are already aware that the winner of *The Great Santa Search* will be obligated to spend the next full year exclusively representing LastLong Toy products, and we will have a company option binding you to us for an additional five years if we choose to exercise it. Please us and we will. My attorneys have drawn up contracts for the winner to sign immediately following the program. You might like to know that there is a generous salary involved. One million dollars per year, to be specific. Is one of you ready to become rich as well as famous?"

There was a chorus of "Yesses" and "You bets" from most of the finalists. The man in the cowboy hat whistled shrilly. I said nothing. I saw Lucretia Pepper's eyes briefly dart in my direction; she had noticed my lack of enthusiasm for her announcement.

"I think, Bobbo, that it would be appropriate now to learn the names of our ten finalists," she suggested.

"Of course, Lucretia," Bobbo replied. "Felix, you're the one who made the selections. Will you do the honors?"

Felix stood up and fiddled nervously with his tie.

"Right from the beginning, let's be sure you all understand some things," he said. "We want to keep an air of mystery about you. The less the public knows in advance, the more their curiosity will make them watch *The Great Santa Search*. As the first condition of you becoming our official finalists, you each must agree that you will not speak or communicate in any way with the media between now and the program on Christmas Eve. That means granting no interviews, making no phone or e-mail contact with reporters, or anything like that. Got it?"

We did.

"For now, we're going to identify each of you by your first name and the city where we found you," Felix continued. "On the program itself, you'll each be identified by number—Santa 1, Santa 2, and so on. We don't want children watching our program to wonder how Santa got some other name. When I picked you, I told each of you that you were not to tell even your family or closest friends. If any of you just couldn't resist—and I'm sure some of you couldn't—then make sure they know they're under the same rule not to talk to the media as you are."

Felix hadn't told *me* this in Cleveland, but of course he didn't have to. My wife and friends knew everything about *The Great Santa Search* and its selection process already.

"But there's no reason the ten of you can't get to know one another a little better," Felix said. "I'm going to introduce each of you. Remember that on Christmas Eve we want to project a spirit of friendly competition. We believe you are the best Santas in America. Act like it. Now, here we go. This is Andy from Chicago." Andy was one of the two beardless finalists. "Luis from Miami." He was the most slender among us. "Dillard from College Station." This was the fellow wearing the cowboy hat. "Brian from Missoula." He had the dark brown beard. "Zonk from Rutland." Zonk was the other beardless competitor, and, by the looks of him, the oldest—except for me, of course. "Nicholas from Cleveland." It felt odd being described as from Cleveland rather than the North Pole. "Wesley from St. Paul." I knew he had been in some sort of Christmas play there, rather than working as Santa in a mall. "Joe from Bloomington." He had the huge belly. "Buck from Kansas City." I liked his warm smile. "Jimmy Lee from right here in New York City."

Jimmy Lee appeared very much at ease. He wore tailored slacks and a baby-blue cashmere sweater. When Felix called his name, he waved languidly in response. His snow-white locks curled in an engaging way around his ears and the nape of his neck. His equally snow-white beard rested in fluffy splendor on his chest. The rest of the finalists, I felt, seemed somewhat ill at ease. The pressure of knowing they would soon appear on a television program watched by millions was affecting them, as it would almost anyone. But Jimmy Lee showed no signs of nervousness. His relaxed posture reflected an attitude of complete self-confidence bordering on arrogance. He did nothing blatantly offensive, but there was no mistaking that he believed, and expected everyone else to believe, that the actual *Great Santa Search* competition was a formality. Lucretia Pepper certainly seemed to agree. When the other nine of us were introduced, she stared hard. But when Felix announced Jimmy Lee's name, she looked at the man from Leeds, Alabama, and actually smiled.

"Thank you, Felix," Bobbo Butler said. "Now I'm going to tell you about what you'll be doing on the program—keep it all in confidence, remember. We're letting you know ahead of time so you can practice some things a little, if you want. After I do that, we'll need you to go with Eri Mizobe for your costume fittings. You are not to bring your own Santa suits to the Ed Sullivan Theater on Christmas Eve. Everybody wears the same things. We don't want to give any of you an unfair advantage over the others. Miss Hathaway, do you have the list of challenges?"

"Right here, chief," Heather said, handing a printed sheet of paper to her boss. Bobbo fumbled in his shirt pocket for his reading glasses, couldn't find them there, poked around in all his other pockets, still couldn't find them, and finally looked up to see Heather holding them out to him. He put them on and pretended to study the sheet for a moment. Ever the showman, Bobbo did this to build tension; obviously, he'd memorized the six challenges long ago.

"All right, then," Bobbo finally said. "You heard we're going to have a dance number to begin the show. It starts at 8:00 p.m., and we're going to ask you to be in the studio at three that afternoon. Don't worry, Lauren is keeping things simple for you. After you get measured for your Santa costumes today, she's going to go over the basics of the dance routine with you. Now, on *The Great Santa Search* the challenges will follow the opening dance in roughly the same order that Santa would probably follow on Christmas Eve. First is reindeer-roping, though we won't be using real reindeer. Wooden reindeer will be pulled across the back of the stage by conveyor belt. I guess you Western boys from Montana and Texas might have an advantage there. The two Santas who rope the fewest in—what, Miss Hathaway, forty-five seconds?—those two are eliminated. So we've got eight of you left for the second challenge, which will be Christmas carol–singing. There's going to be a big surprise then. Don't ask, because we're not going to tell you what it is. After you all sing, the audience votes. One Santa is eliminated."

"To vote, the audience'll use little devices mounted on their armrests of their seats," Mary Rogers interjected. "They'll push buttons marked one through ten for their favorite. Whoever gets the fewest votes is out."

"Exactly," Bobbo agreed. "Miss Hathway, could you bring me some coffee? Next comes chimney-sliding with seven Santas left competing. You'll have to get up on the roof of a fake house and slide down the chimney, and do it while carrying a big sack of toys. The two slowest are eliminated. Now there'll be five left."

Bobbo paused as Heather handed him a steaming cup of coffee. He took a slow, deliberate sip.

"Then the set will switch to a living room decorated for Christmas," he said. "You know—Christmas tree, mistletoe, stockings hung by the chimney with care. The five remaining Santas each get sixty seconds to fill as many stockings with toys as possible. The three Santas who can cram toys into the most stockings get to go on."

Lucretia Pepper had something to add.

"I think that only stockings full of *unbroken* toys should count," she said. "If finalists place any damaged toys in stockings, then those stockings would not be included in the final total. After all, on Christmas Eve Santa doesn't leave broken toys for children."

Bobbo seemed puzzled.

"Well, fine, Lucretia," he said. "You're paying for the program, so you can certainly suggest a rule. We'll do it that way. Now, after stocking-stuffing comes a fun challenge, cookie-eating. Simple as it sounds. Cookies get eaten. The Santa who eats—and that means chewing up and completely swallowing—the fewest cookies in sixty seconds is gone from the competition. That leaves two."

Bobbo paused again, milking the moment. All around the table, would-be Santas leaned forward, hanging on his every word, except for Jimmy Lee, who slouched comfortably in his seat, and me, because Felix and I had discussed all these details many times before.

"Now, the last two Santas have to appeal directly to the studio audience," he finally explained. "Each one has to tell why he and not the other one deserves to be elected America's official Santa. They'll both have three minutes to do it in. The audience votes, and we've got our winner."

Lucretia Pepper cleared her throat.

"The winner is then presented as the spokesman for LastLong Toy Company, and for the duration of his contract with us cannot work for anyone else," she declared. "I don't want anyone to forget that."

"We won't, Lucretia," Bobbo promised.

For the first time, Jimmy Lee sat up straight.

"It would be an honor," he said. "An *exceptional* honor."

No one else seemed to have anything to say, so we finalists trooped off to be measured for our *Great Santa Search* costumes. I couldn't help noticing how magnificent Jimmy Lee looked in his.

"Well, we can see them, and we're far enough away that they shouldn't notice us," Sarah said. "But we can't hear what they're saying, and that's what we need to do." Heather didn't reply. Her eyes were locked on the far table where Jimmy Lee and Lucretia Pepper sat with their heads close together, talking.

Sixteen

n December 20, four days before *The Great Santa Search* broadcast, Sarah and Heather Hathaway decided to go out for lunch. The ten finalists had been chosen. All the tickets were distributed. The day of the show itself would be tremendously hectic, but until then there was a little time for the staff to rest. After lunch, Sarah and Heather thought, they might even find something else relaxing and interesting to do, and perhaps not go back to the office at all. They'd become good friends over the past months, and had promised to stay in touch after the program was over.

Over a meal of miso soup and sushi, though, they found themselves talking about the show. Heather predicted *The Great Santa Search* would achieve record ratings, and FUN-TV would be saved. She disliked Lucretia Pepper and couldn't bring herself to think well of Jimmy Lee, saying there was something about him that bothered her even though she was certain he'd win.

"I guess mostly I'm happy for Bobbo," she added. "I wish he could have found a different sponsor. I know he feels terrible about what Lucretia Pepper is going to do. But the FUN-TV ratings have been so bad, Sarah, and nobody else would even consider buying advertising time with us. It was Lucretia Pepper or no *Great Santa Search*. Please don't hate Bobbo for selling out to LastLong Toys. He was only doing what he had to."

Sarah finished her soup and pushed the bowl away.

"I certainly don't hate Bobbo," she said. "I think that in his desperation to save his television network, he's chosen to risk the belief millions of children have in Santa Claus. That belief is precious. Much more than gifts, Santa Claus represents generosity of spirit, something Lucretia Pepper obviously lacks."

"Bobbo has a generous spirit and he's special," Heather said wistfully. "I just wish he'd, well, I guess you know."

"I do," Sarah assured her. "Someday he's going to understand just how special you are, too. But in the meantime, you can't focus your whole life on him. Maybe if you weren't always right there for Bobbo, available at his every beck and call, he'd realize he really needs and cares for you."

Heather sighed. "As far as he's concerned, I'm just the assistant who works for him."

"Well, you're not going to work for him this afternoon," Sarah said briskly. "I'm told there's a wonderful new exhibit at the American Museum of Natural History. Would you like to come with me to see it?"

"I love that museum," Heather said enthusiastically. "Did you know Theodore Roosevelt was one of its greatest supporters? There's even a statue of him in front of it."

"You don't say," Sarah replied. Up at the North Pole, Theodore constantly bragged about "his" museum.

"I'll just call Bobbo and tell him I won't be back today," Heather said. She took her cell phone from her purse. When she reached Bobbo, he said it was fine for her to take a few hours off, but then he had questions about some minor things and Heather ended up spending almost ten minutes talking to him.

Sarah didn't want to appear to be eavesdropping on their conversation, so she idly looked around the congested streets. Her eye was suddenly caught by a bulky man making his way through the crowd. He had a floppy hat pulled low on his head, and a muffler obscured the lower portion of his face. But there was something about his eyes and the way he moved, languidly yet deliberately, that seemed familiar. Then a gust of wind blew off his hat, which skittered along the sidewalk, and the man stalked over to where it lay. As he bent down to retrieve it, the muffler briefly fell away from his face.

It was Jimmy Lee.

At first, Sarah simply wondered why he wasn't at Manhattan Mega-Mall, dressed as Santa and greeting adoring children. All the *Great Santa Search* finalists were back at their mall jobs, except for Wesley from St. Paul, and he was in Minnesota starring in his holiday play. None of them were supposed to deviate from their previous routines, for fear someone in the media might notice and publicly identify a competitor in advance of the program.

Yet here was Jimmy Lee, swaddled in so many winter clothes that he was virtually unrecognizable. Sarah found this odd, but then the situation became odder still, for Jimmy Lee raised an arm and waved briefly to catch the eye of someone walking toward him. It was Lucretia Pepper. She stalked up to Jimmy Lee, whispered in his ear, and accompanied him down the sidewalk.

Sarah tugged at the sleeve of Heather's coat.

"Look at that!" she hissed.

Heather was still talking to Bobbo. She waved impatiently at Sarah and said into her cell phone, "I'm sure your wallet is somewhere on your desk. Just move some of the papers around. You'll see it."

"*Heather*," Sarah whispered urgently. "Get off the phone." Jimmy Lee and Lucretia Pepper were about to disappear into the crowd. When

Heather didn't conclude her call, Sarah simply yanked her along as she hurried after them.

"Just look on your desk, please, Bobbo," Heather pleaded, and snapped her cell phone shut. "Sarah, why are you dragging me like this? What's your problem?"

"Jimmy Lee has met Lucretia Pepper, and they're walking right ahead of us," Sarah explained. "Don't you think that's odd?"

Heather stared.

"Maybe they just bumped into each other by accident," she said.

"Hardly," Sarah replied. "I saw him wave at her. She went right to him, even though he had most of his face covered by a hat and muffler. She was expecting him. They had an appointment."

"I wonder why they'd do that," Heather mused. She and Sarah had to maintain a brisk pace. A few dozen yards ahead of them, Lucretia Pepper and Jimmy Lee were scuttling along rapidly. The sidewalks were crowded, but they made good progress because Lucretia Pepper simply lowered her shoulder and knocked aside anyone in her path. It was difficult to keep up with them.

"I don't know, but it can't be anything good," Sarah said. "We need to see where they're going."

"It's not against the law for people to meet," Heather pointed out. "Do we have the right to spy on them?"

"Heather, this is Lucretia Pepper and Jimmy Lee," Sarah retorted. "*The Great Santa Search* is in four days. The Christmas beliefs of millions of children are at stake, and these two are having some sort of secret meeting. Look at how he's got his face covered up, and how fast she's making them walk. They don't want anyone to know what they're doing. If it was innocent, they could talk at the FUN-TV offices or at the theater on Christmas Eve. No, they're up to something."

"You're right," Heather said. "Come on, we've got to cross the street before the light changes. We can't let them get away!"

Jimmy Lee and Lucretia Pepper hurried down Madison Avenue past

Grand Central Terminal and the Pierpont Morgan Library. Just beyond Madison Square Park and the Flatiron building, they ducked into a coffee shop.

"They certainly wanted to get as far away as they could from Manhattan Mega-Mall and the LastLong Toy Company offices," Sarah remarked, puffing. She and Heather were out of breath from their frantic, lengthy walk. "That coffee shop is fairly large. Let's see if we can go in and sit down without them noticing us."

The shop was teeming with customers, who were packed around dozens of small tables. The buzz of general conversation was quite loud. When Heather and Sarah went in, they soon spotted Lucretia Pepper and Jimmy Lee huddled together at a table toward the rear. None of the other tables around them was vacant; the only place for the two women to sit was a table on the far side of the room.

"Well, we can see them, and we're far enough away that they shouldn't notice us," Sarah said. "But we can't hear what they're saying, and that's what we need to do."

Heather didn't reply. Her eyes were locked on the far table where Jimmy Lee and Lucretia Pepper sat with their heads close together, talking.

"Heather?" Sarah queried. "Heather, did you hear me? Because we can't hear *them*."

"Maybe we can't hear them, but we can still know what they're talking about," Heather muttered. "Give me a minute, Sarah. I'm trying to concentrate."

"What do you mean?"

"I can read lips, remember?" Heather replied. "Quiet, please. She's asking him—oh! How awful!"

Sarah couldn't help herself.

"What? What are they saying?"

Without taking her eyes off the pair, Heather muttered, "I'll tell you if you'll just keep quiet."

"I will," Sarah promised.

"All right. She just asked if he really understood what he was supposed to do during the show. He said he did. He said he knows he's supposed to mention LastLong Toys any time he can, and especially during his speech in the final challenge. But he's worried the stupid audience might vote against him earlier so he won't make it to the final challenge."

"It's awful that he's going to talk about LastLong Toys during the program," Sarah declared.

"No, what's really horrible is that he's calling the audience stupid. In television, we have to respect our audiences, even when it's hard. Hush, Sarah. She's telling him something about—what's she saying?—oh, all right. She said he doesn't have to worry about the audience vote. He's so much better than all the others that everyone will vote for him, and besides, there are 150 seats reserved for LastLong executives and their families. They've been told they all have to vote for Jimmy Lee or they'll be fired immediately. So he's got 150 solid votes to start with. Only about three hundred other people will be in the theater and voting. With that kind of built-in advantage, he's bound to win."

"What cheaters!" Sarah blurted. "Sorry, Heather. I'll keep quiet."

"Now they're talking about the challenges that don't have audience votes. She says he shouldn't have trouble with the reindeer-roping because she hired the world-champion rodeo cowboy to give him lessons. He says he quit at the Manhattan Mega-Mall so he'd have time for the lessons, and he's gotten pretty good. Carol-singing won't be a problem, he says. He's got a great voice. Modest, isn't he? I don't know what she just said. She had her coffee cup in front of her mouth. Now they're talking about stocking-stuffing. She's reminding him only unbroken toys will count. She's going to be backstage to make sure when it's his turn, he gets the right kind of well-manufactured toys. All the other Santas will get regular LastLong toys, and most of them break the moment anyone touches them, let alone tries to shove them in a stocking. So that's why she made up that rule the other day during our meeting with the finalists. This is all so *evil*! And she says don't worry, she'll take care of the cookie-eating contest. *Oh!* That—that—*witch*!"

"What? What?" Sarah demanded.

"She says Bobbo will probably ask that ugly, gawky girl Heather to get the cookies, but Jimmy Lee shouldn't worry. She'll fix things. Lucretia Pepper's got some nerve calling *me* ugly! Has she looked in a mirror lately?"

"Perhaps you should pay attention to what else they're saying," Sarah suggested gently.

"Fine. So far as the final speech goes, he doesn't care which of the other Santas is left. Jimmy Lee says he personally will sound sincere and look wonderful, and he'll fool the studio audience just like he's fooled kids for fifteen years since he started playing Santa in malls. He says she shouldn't worry. He may hate Christmas, but he loves the money he's going to win."

Now Lucretia Pepper set down her coffee cup, stared intently into Jimmy Lee's eyes, and shook her finger at him as she spoke.

"She's telling him to remember the bottom line. For that million dollars, it's his job to make children all over America believe that Santa will bring them only LastLong toys," Heather reported. "She says if he doesn't do that, she'll make him regret it for the rest of his life. He says she can count on him."

Lucretia Pepper and Jimmy Lee stood up and left the coffee shop. Heather and Sarah ducked their heads as they passed, then got up themselves and followed the conniving pair outside.

Jimmy Lee pulled his hat down over his forehead and wrapped his muffler around his face. He shook hands with Lucretia Pepper and disappeared into the crowd. She turned and began walking north, to the LastLong Toy Company office.

"Well, that was just horrifying," Heather said. "I guess we have to go back to FUN-TV now and tell Bobbo. It's going to break his heart. *The Great Santa Search* was going to save his network, and now it's not going to happen after all."

"Why not?" Sarah asked.

"We just found out the sponsor and one of the contestants are planning to cheat," Heather said. "They've packed the audience with Jimmy Lee voters, and they're going to fix the stocking-stuffing and cookie-eating challenges so he's sure to win them. It's not going to be an honest contest. Bobbo will have to call it off."

"And what would happen then?" inquired Sarah.

"We'll have to broadcast some other program in place of *The Great Santa Search*," Heather predicted with a sigh. "Maybe it'll be a rerun of *Merry Monkey*. Everybody will switch channels. The media will tear Bobbo apart. He could explain about Lucretia Pepper and her cheating, but she'd be sure to sue him and without the LastLong money Bobbo can't afford to pay office rent, let alone a lawyer. So he'll be ruined and FUN-TV will shut down. I'll lose my job. Probably I'll have to go home to North Dakota and live on the farm again. And instead I'd hoped that Bobbo and I—well, I guess it doesn't matter anymore what I hoped."

"Don't give up on those hopes just yet," Sarah said. "In fact, I don't think you should tell Bobbo about any of this. You know what people say about the best-laid plans often going wrong. That's also true for evil schemes. Let me deal with this, Heather. The best thing you can do is wait. On Christmas Eve, I may need your help. But for now, try to go on as you usually would."

"What are you going to do?" Heather asked.

Sarah couldn't tell her friend about how she and Felix had been providing inside information about *The Great Santa Search* to me long before the LastLong Toy Company president had even known Jimmy Lee existed. She certainly couldn't tell Heather how some of the smartest individuals in human history would soon gather together at the North Pole and come up with ways to ruin Lucretia Pepper's plot.

"I don't know, yet," Sarah answered honestly. "But I promise to think of something. Say, you're going to have to go on to the museum without me. I just remembered an appointment."

She waited until Heather was out of sight before taking out her own cell phone and calling me at Galaxy Mall in Cleveland.

As I pulled on the red trousers, Emily reappeared with my dressing-room partner.
Being an old-fashioned, modest sort of fellow, I tried to hide behind a chair, but I
tripped and nearly went sprawling, though I still managed to hold up my pants.

Seventeen

left Galaxy Mall in Cleveland for the last time on December 23. Even though Santa Land was scheduled to be open until 10:00 p.m., my personal work shift ended at noon, when we closed for an hour so Santa could eat lunch and rest his lap. I was able to leave early because Lester Sneed, the mall manager, was so eager to fill in for me.

"Okay, glad to do it," he said enthusiastically when I asked if he would take my place after lunch. We'd already arranged for me to be gone the next day, of course—I was due at the Ed Sullivan Theater in New York City at 3:00 p.m. on Christmas Eve. But I had some errands to run before then, and I needed extra time. Mr. Sneed had apparently substituted for me quite adequately when I'd made my one-day trip to New York for the *Great Santa Search* finalists meeting almost a week earlier. Jill the photographer told me she couldn't tell who was having more fun, "Santa" Sneed or the children clamoring to tell him what they wanted for Christmas. Even Xander agreed that "Old O.K." did well.

"Will you need to go home to get your costume?" I asked.

"Nope," Mr. Sneed replied. "Got it right in my office. Hey, if you've got a lot of errands, I could step in for you all day, okay? Be a pleasure."

"I think it would be fine if you just took over for me after lunch," I assured him. Privately, I was somewhat concerned. Though Mr. Sneed had the best of intentions, it was also true his gray beard was rather scraggly and his waistline was not of full Clausian proportions. Children who'd waited in line to see a completely authentic-looking Santa—and I believed I fit that description—might feel let down to see a less-convincing version take over for the afternoon and evening.

But it had to be that way. I had important things to do. Ever since Sarah contacted me with the news of Lucretia Pepper and Jimmy Lee plotting to fix *The Great Santa Search* competition, all of us from the North Pole had been devising ways to thwart them. Many possibilities had been considered and for a while it seemed we would ask Leonardo to come up with some sort of electronic device to divert audience votes from Jimmy Lee to me. Leonardo is such a genius that he would surely have developed an invention to do just that. But Layla eventually pointed out that this ploy would never work. The moment Lucretia Pepper saw that her "rock solid" 150 LastLong employee votes weren't being credited to Jimmy Lee as intended, she'd assume the vote controls on the studio seats were somehow faulty and demand on the spot that some other means of voting—perhaps raising hands—be used instead.

"Anyway, you have to beat Jimmy Lee without lowering yourself to his level," my wife insisted. "So what if he gets 150 fixed votes? That's still not a majority. You just have to convince all the honest voters to pick you."

But the two nonvoting challenges that Lucretia Pepper and Jimmy Lee planned to win through cheating were another matter entirely. Stocking-stuffing and cookie-eating were events that I intended to win decisively. We felt we had come up with ways to do just that—and one of them required me to abandon my Galaxy Mall Santa duties earlier than scheduled on December 23.

After I changed into everyday clothes in the dressing room and carefully packed my Santa regalia in a suitcase, which I then took with me, I made my way to a large toy store on the second level of the mall. There, I spent several hours selecting and purchasing a considerable number of small LastLong toys—plastic action figures, sports cars, dolls with jointed limbs, and so forth. The clerk recognized me as the mall Santa and joked, "You going to load up your sleigh with these tomorrow night?" I assured him Santa Claus delivered only North Pole–manufactured toys on Christmas Eve.

As I left the store, I happened to look down at Santa Land below me. There was, as usual, a long line of children waiting for their turns with Santa. I was struck by how excited they all seemed—their smiles were visible and their happy laughter quite audible, even though I was certainly fifty or more yards away. What I noticed most, though, was the obvious joy apparent in both parties when each boy or girl joined the bearded man wearing the red suit and sitting on the wooden block throne. I could tell from Mr. Sneed's every gesture that he loved the experience of greeting them and that his pleasure was completely reciprocated. The children hopped eagerly up on his lap, and when they left, almost all of them offered him warm farewell hugs. I wasn't jealous. It was a wonderful sight.

Then I took my hefty sack of LastLong toys outside to the remote corner of the mall parking lot where I knew the reindeer hovered overhead. It took the briefest of moments for Dasher and the other seven to swoop down, pause while I loaded the toy sack and valise in the sleigh, took up my seat in front, picked up the reins, and gave the signal to swoop into the sky. Any normal human beings in the lot would not have noticed anything except, possibly, an infinitesimal flicker of movement out of the corners of their eyes. In two minutes, we were sailing above the clouds far beyond Cleveland, and in another half hour I was guiding the sleigh in for a North Pole landing.

Willie Skokan and Leonardo da Vinci were waiting in the barn. While I unharnessed the reindeer and fed them some extra treats, my two friends lifted the sack of LastLong toys from the sleigh and hurried off with it to their workshop.

"It won't take them long to do what they have to," I observed to Layla when she joined me in my study. "It did feel quite odd to fly *back* to the North Pole with toys loaded in the sleigh. It has always been the other way around."

"Well, tomorrow is going to be a Christmas Eve unlike any other," she reminded me. "While Willie and Leonardo are working, there's really nothing more for you to do. Why not take a nap? You'll need all your energy for the competitions."

"I'm not a bit tired," I informed her. "I think I'll just spend the afternoon studying Amelia Earhart's tentative flight plan for tomorrow night. After I win *The Great Santa Search*, I'll still have my full Christmas Eve delivery schedule to complete."

"Study away," Layla said cheerfully, and left me alone with Amelia's voluminous charts and maps. I must have remained awake reading them at least thirty seconds after my wife had gone.

After dinner that evening—Lars prepared his delicious *pollo de Portugal*, a chicken dish with red and green peppers that Francis discovered centuries earlier while traveling in that country—we gathered to review our plans for the next night. Everyone had something important to do, but not all of these tasks were related to *The Great Santa Search*. Christmas Eve is, of course, one of our three busiest nights of the year. Even as I was onstage, routine last-minute preparations for global gift-giving would be underway at the North Pole and most of our beloved companions would have to be occupied with these. Felix and Sarah were not at this meeting, because they were in New York City fulfilling their own last-minute obligations as part of *The Great Santa Search* staff; they would, of course, remain there until the program was over. Layla, Arthur, St. Francis, and Bill Pickett would use the four "friends" tickets granted by Bobbo Butler to Sarah and Felix. Willie Skokan would be the additional friend they were allowed to bring backstage during the show. His presence there would be critical. All my other gift-giving associates would remain at the North Pole, keeping our Christmas Eve operation there in full, effective swing.

A few were particularly unhappy to miss *The Great Santa Search* events. I explained to Amelia Earhart that she must be on hand at our headquarters to monitor the weather; changes in flying conditions are a constant on Christmas Eve, and if, after I was done with television and back in my sleigh, I encountered an unexpected snowstorm, the delay might result in children somewhere not receiving their well-deserved gifts from Santa. She reluctantly agreed.

Theodore Roosevelt was harder to convince. He loved New York City—he had once lived there and later served as police commissioner, after all—and argued that, as former president and commander in chief, it was important for him to be "where the action is. What will you do, for instance, if fisticuffs are required?"

"They won't be, Theodore," I assured him. "Brute force is not the most effective way to defeat evil."

"But sometimes a good poke in the belly comes in handy, Santa Claus," he argued. "I've trained you in lifting weights and jumping rope and so forth, but never in boxing."

I finally persuaded my enthusiastic friend to remain behind because, if he appeared at the Ed Sullivan Theater, too many people might recognize him.

"Yours is one of the most familiar faces in American history, Theodore," I explained. "Your presence might very well cause considerable speculation."

Theodore always liked the fact he had been and remained quite famous.

"Well, perhaps you're right," he agreed. "All right, I'll stay behind. But do you promise to throw a manly punch or two if the situation calls for it?"

"I'm sure that won't be necessary," I said hopefully.

The morning of December 24 came as it always does at the North Pole—in complete darkness and with freezing winds whipping over the ice and accumulated drifts of snow. I dressed in warm street clothes and spent most of the morning visiting all the North Pole workshops, making certain all was in readiness for that night's gift-giving. This is always a day of particular excitement for us, and my imminent participation on *The Great Santa Search* only added to everyone's high-spirited mood.

By lunchtime, I admit I had begun feeling nervous. It was an unusual sensation for me. My life's work is devoted to service to others and spiritual faith; these things enrich and calm rather than disturb the mind. I didn't doubt I was going to win *The Great Santa Search*. We knew exactly what Lucretia Pepper and Jimmy Lee were up to and had planned accordingly. And, despite anything they might attempt, I had one insurmountable advantage—I really *was* Santa Claus.

Still, I was a bit jumpy, and Layla suggested I lie down for a bit before we had to get in the sleigh and fly to New York City. Instead, I sat quietly in my study, remembering all the challenges of the past centuries and how things had somehow always worked out for the best. In particular, I remembered myself as a boy back in the long-forgotten country of Lycia, when I yearned to give gifts and survived a rough beginning to eventually be honored by centuries of doing exactly what I loved best. I was—I am—so lucky, so blessed. And realizing this, my nerves were calmed, and by the time Layla knocked gently on the door to inform me it was time to leave I was eager to experience what I knew would be a memorable evening.

Layla, Bill, Francis, Arthur, Willie, and Attila all climbed in the sleigh with me. Attila was coming because someone had to fly the reindeer back to the North Pole after the rest of us had been dropped off in New

York City. Once it had been returned to our snowy headquarters, the sleigh would be carefully loaded with just the right amount of toys. Then, at the appropriate time, Attila would fly it back to an alley behind the Ed Sullivan Theater. The moment that *The Great Santa Search* was over, I would hurry out to the alley, greet my beloved reindeer, and instruct them to whirl me up into the winter sky so my Christmas Eve gift-giving could begin. Attila would join my other friends as they returned to the North Pole via train and, eventually, dogsled.

We landed in the alley behind the theater just before 3:00 p.m. Felix was waiting for us there. He informed Bill, Layla, Arthur, and Francis that they would find their tickets at the box office around 7:00 p.m. Those four all wished me luck, then trooped off to enjoy a few hours of strolling amid the colorful sights and sounds of New York City on Christmas Eve. Felix told me I was expected in the theater lobby and instructed Willie to come with him through a backstage door. Willie did, carrying with him the big sack of LastLong toys I'd purchased at Galaxy Mall the day before.

I went around to the front of the theater and was greeted by the same security guard I'd met on the day of *The Great Santa Search* open audition. Gary Elders didn't recognize me, but a yelping crowd of reporters and cameramen did. Apparently they'd been outside the theater all day, waiting for the finalists to arrive. My white beard and impressive waistline clearly identified me; there were shouts of "Look at the cameras!" and "Where are you from?" and "Are you the real Santa?"

"Hurry up inside," Gary urged me, and he called back, "You'll have to watch the program to see if he's the one," to the media mob.

Several FUN-TV interns were in the lobby, ready to escort finalists to wherever we were supposed to go next. It was too perfect: the young woman greeting me was the same one who'd dismissed me from the open audition.

"Hello, Emily Vance," I remarked.

She looked startled.

"How did you know my name? Oh, you must have read it on my badge. Which one are you?" Clearly, all Santas looked alike to young Emily.

"Nicholas Holiday, from the Galaxy Mall in Cleveland."

Emily consulted a list.

"Fine, you're in Dressing Room D. Follow me."

I was surprised by how cramped it was behind the main theater stage. There was a virtual warren of small, square dressing rooms. Mine was quite plain. There was a table with a mirror, a small bathroom, two chairs, and a clothes rack that had a half-dozen empty wire hangers dangling from it. On two more hangers were dazzling red velvet Santa costumes. Accessories—white gloves, black boots, the famous red "Santa hats" with white fur trim and pom-pom—were stacked on the chairs.

"You're in here with Zonk from Green Mountain Mall in Rutland, Vermont," Emily said. "There's a meeting about the opening dance routine in ten minutes on the main stage. You're supposed to be in full costume but not makeup. I'll be back for you."

"Makeup?" I asked, horrified. But Emily was already out the door. She seemed to be a young person who was always in a hurry.

Sighing, I took off my street clothes. The Santa suits were tagged *"Cleveland"* and *"Rutland,"* so I knew which was mine. As I pulled on the red trousers, Emily reappeared with my dressing-room partner. Being an old-fashioned, modest sort of fellow, I tried to hide behind a chair, but I tripped and nearly went sprawling, though I still managed to hold up my pants. Emily left without comment, but Zonk made one.

"Jeez, how can you dance if you can't even get your pants on without falling over?" he asked, laughing. But his tone and laughter were quite good-natured, and I knew he was being friendly, not insulting.

"I'm really not sure," I replied, clambering up. "We don't dance too much at the North Pole."

"Nah, 'cause we're too busy tripping over penguins," Zonk said. I considered telling him penguins lived at the South rather than the North

Pole, but thought better of it. Instead, as we dressed we chatted about Christmas and our experiences with children while serving as mall Santas. Zonk did most of the talking. He was quite an outgoing, gregarious sort. I learned that he first began dressing up as Santa to delight his small grandchildren on Christmas Eve and had been so good at it that friends of the family began asking if they could bring their little ones over to meet "Santa," too. Then the Santa working at the Rutland mall quit unexpectedly, and Zonk was asked to fill in until a new one was sent by the Noel Program. But he was so popular that Noel's Stephanie Owen asked if he'd like to keep the job himself. That had been six years ago; ever since, he was the mall's Santa. Stephanie had offered to send him to more prestigious malls in bigger cities, but Zonk was perfectly happy to stay in Rutland.

He kept up a constant stream of chatter even when Emily returned to take us to the dance session. I learned Zonk had once been in the Navy, and that he got his nickname from the sound he made when he tackled rival players in high school football games.

"There was this loud *zonk!*" he claimed. "Nobody else's tackles sounded like that. I've always been real unusual. Like, I've got ageusia."

That stopped me short: "What?"

"Ay-GOO-see-uh. I can't taste things. Which is good, considering my wife's cooking."

Lauren Devoe was waiting onstage. The other Santa finalists came trailing in. Everyone was in proper costume. Brian from Missoula looked a little odd with his dark beard. Zonk and Andy from Chicago had no beards at all. False whiskers, I presumed, would be provided to them later. We all milled around for a moment, shaking hands and wishing one another luck. Jimmy Lee stood apart from the rest of us. He clearly was not interested in being sociable.

"Everybody gather 'round," Lauren instructed. "We tried some basic dance moves back when we met at FUN-TV. I know it didn't go very well, but like I told you then, don't worry about being great dancers.

You don't have to be. And we've already taped the vocals with a hired choir, so you won't have to sing. You'll be doing that later in one of the challenges anyway. In this first number, concentrate on getting the steps right. Show some energy. Act like you're having fun, even if you aren't. The idea is, this dance will give the audience at home and in the studio a chance to see all of you. It lasts only two minutes, and then you're off-stage while Bobbo Butler talks and things get set up behind the curtain for the first challenge. Now, we're going to hear the theme song." She gestured toward the control booth and recorded music began to play:

> *Searching for Santa, searching for Santa,*
> *We must find the bringer of toys.*
> *Searching for Santa, searching for Santa,*
> *A magical evening for all girls and boys!*
> *And so we're searching for Santa, searching for Santa,*
> *What better way to spend Christmas Eve?*
> *We'll all just glow by the end of the show*
> *Because we'll finally know who Santa is and all can believe!*
> *We hope that you know Santa loves you too*
> *You make his days seem merry and bright.*
> *So by your leave on Christmas Eve*
> *We'll be searching for Santa tonight!*

Lauren demonstrated the various dance steps she'd tried to teach us at the FUN-TV offices—step-step-*slide*-step-pirouette-turn-*slide*-step.

"Just remember to move to the beat," she added. "We decided it would be better not to run through the dance before the actual show. Let's just be, well, natural." I emitted a quiet snort. Dancing, I knew, was anything but natural for me.

Then show director Mary Rogers bustled up, explaining it was past 5:00 p.m. and there was still a lot of stage setup to be done.

"These Santas need to get back to their dressing rooms for makeup," she added.

"All right," Lauren said cheerfully. "This is supposed to be entertainment tonight, not ballet. Just do your best. From what I remember at FUN-TV, you two"—she gestured to Joe and Jimmy Lee—"need to be in the middle of the front row. You'll line up in two rows of five tonight. If you fall down while you're dancing, anybody, just grin, get up, and keep going. It's live TV. We're going to give them something amazing to look at, one way or the other."

Emily and the other FUN-TV interns led us back to our dressing rooms. While we were gone, someone had placed boxed meals on the tables. There was a chicken-salad sandwich in each, along with an apple, a chocolate-chip cookie, and an eight-ounce plastic bottle of water. Zonk and I sat down to eat.

Just after 6:30 p.m., a man and woman knocked on our dressing-room door and said they had come to "make us up." This involved rouge and powder and eyeliner. The process was rather embarrassing.

"Now, you don't want all those wrinkles around your eyes to show on camera, do you?" the makeup man coaxed.

"I earned every one of those wrinkles," I responded. "I have no problem with them being visible."

But the makeup couple did. Zonk's makeup process was even more excruciating. They had brought with them a fake white beard, which they attached strand by strand to his cheeks and chin. It did look quite real, and they warned Zonk it would be necessary to let the adhesive wear off gradually.

"Don't try to pull the beard off," he was informed. "You'll take skin with it."

At 7:00 p.m. we could hear rumblings from the theater itself; the audience was beginning to be seated. Members of the backstage crew scurried frantically about. The tension made Zonk even chattier. I learned the names and ages of his grandchildren and the location of every birth-mark on his body. Just as he was beginning to describe his recent root-canal surgery, our dressing-room door opened and Felix came in.

"It's time to pick your numbers," he said rather formally, and I knew he was being careful not to acknowledge me in any special way. "Take turns reaching in this box; take out one slip of paper. There will be a number on it from one to ten. That's how you'll be identified during the program—no other names at all, remember. It will be Santa 1, Santa 2, and so forth."

Zonk went first, and picked number 8. I took my turn, and became Santa 6.

At 7:45 all the finalists were gathered just offstage. We could hear the audience but couldn't see it. The curtains were drawn. But behind the curtains was a spectacular stage set, with cutouts of snowy mountaintops and towering fir trees glowing with colorful Christmas lights. Lauren showed us where we were to take our places in the two lines of five, and then Mary Rogers came down from the control booth to wish us all luck.

"Just remember, this is live television," she reminded us. "No matter what happens, keep goin'. And remember to smile."

Then a larger group approached us. I could see Sarah, and also Robert the set designer and Eri the costume designer and Ken the sound engineer and nasty Lucretia Pepper and, lingering just behind everyone else, Willie Skokan, who grinned at me and furtively offered the "thumbs up" sign that all was well. Bobbo Butler stepped up in front of us, with Heather Hathway standing to his right.

"This is it," Bobbo said, sounding nervous and excited, certainly an understandable combination for a network president who was about to gamble his company's future on a live television program. "Do your best. If you're eliminated, act like a good sport. Each challenge has a time limit. Don't dawdle. Get on- and offstage promptly when it's your turn. You may be wondering how we're going to handle some of the challenges—what order you'll go in and so forth. We deliberately haven't told you. We want to keep as much spontaneity as possible. That's what reality TV is all about. Last questions?"

No one had any.

Bobbo glanced at his watch.

"All right, then," he said. "Seven fifty-nine." He was dressed in his red velvet tuxedo with white trim on the cuffs of his coat and pants. Perhaps it should have looked ridiculous, but somehow it seemed impressive. So did Bobbo. His fringe of hair was neatly combed for once, and he looked alert but not frantic.

He looked at his watch again. I could see Mary Rogers in the control booth; it had large glass windows. She said something into a microphone on the console in front of her. A stagehand standing just to the side of the curtains waved at Bobbo.

"This is it," Bobbo said. He pushed past the curtains and walked onstage.

The Great Santa Search was on the air.

Critics wrote later that the resulting carnage was among the most entertaining moments ever broadcast on television. Perhaps it was. One of the main goals of so-called "reality" TV is to let audiences observe people looking foolish, and in this instance that goal was served well.

Eighteen

ost ballyhooed television holiday specials kick off with flashy production numbers, which include loud music and lots of action to capture the audience's attention. But Felix had told me Bobbo Butler wanted something simpler and far more dramatic.

So instead of drumrolls or trumpet fanfares, *The Great Santa Search* got underway with Bobbo walking out onstage. Those of us backstage were able to watch on monitors. The theater was dark; he was illuminated by a single spotlight. The crowd applauded enthusiastically, and Bobbo gestured for silence.

"We're here to make television and Christmas history," he said solemnly. "We're going to have fun, but there's serious business involved, too. My name is Robert O. Butler. Call me Bobbo. I have the privilege of being president of the FUN-TV network. Backstage we have ten men in red-and-white suits. Each claims he's Santa Claus. But there's only one. Tonight, this studio audience will help decide who that really is. If you'll look at that clock on the studio wall, it reads 8:01 p.m. Eastern Standard Time. By 10:00 p.m., the one and only Santa will have been identified. We'll have seen him, heard him, and none of us will ever again have to wonder, 'Is there really a Santa Claus?' That's what *The Great Santa Search* is all about."

Bobbo paused, and the audience applauded again, heartily but briefly. They, and certainly the millions of others watching at home, were anxious to hear more.

"During the next two hours, I'll occasionally come onstage to visit with you," Bobbo continued. "After all, this is live television, and we'll need to change some sets and let our Santas get in place for some of the competitions that will help decide which one of them is who he claims to be. But there will be no commercial breaks. Thanks to our generous sponsor, the LastLong Toy Company, this program will run uninterrupted, and that's a good thing, too. Because there's a lot we have to do before 10:00 p.m. Remember, we can't run late: it's Christmas Eve, and Santa's going to be a busy man after we're off the air!"

Bobbo paused again; backstage, Lauren and other crew members pulled the ten Santa finalists into two lines of five. As she'd instructed, Joe from Bloomington and Jimmy Lee were in the center of the front row. I was on the far right in the second row.

"Are you ready to select Santa?" Bobbo asked the studio audience.

"Yes!" they chorused.

Bobbo looked concerned.

"That didn't sound very enthusiastic," he chided. "Are you ready?"

"*Yes!*"

"The real Santa Claus is backstage. Let's make sure he hears you. Are you ready?"

"*YES!!!*"

Bobbo spread his arms theatrically and shouted, "Ladies and gentlemen, children of all ages, meet—*our Santas!*" The curtains opened incredibly quickly. *The Great Santa Search* theme blared out:

Searching for Santa, searching for Santa,
We must find the bringer of toys! . . .

And we ten finalists were dancing.

For a very few seconds, it seemed that something miraculous was happening. We stepped and slid in something very close to unison. Brian from Missoula, whose dark beard was now thickly colored to look pure white, was next to me in line. His eyes were squinched tight with concentration. In front of me was Wesley from St. Paul. The back of his neck was a brighter red than his costume. I noted these small things with a sense of wonder, because my feet seemed to be operating without any direct connection to my brain. My boots stepped and shuffled exactly as they were supposed to be doing. The same seemed true for everyone. Then we had to pirouette.

Critics wrote later that the resulting carnage was among the most entertaining moments ever broadcast on television. Perhaps it was. One of the main goals of so-called "reality" TV is to let audiences observe people looking foolish, and in this instance that goal was served well. I believe the main culprit was my new friend Zonk, who spun out of control on the end of the front line and smacked into Buck from Kansas City, who was directly behind him. At least that's what Buck claimed two weeks later, when he sold his *"Great Santa Search* inside story" to a publication called the *National Enquirer*. No matter who was originally at fault, Buck lurched sideways into Luis from Miami, who went sprawling and tripped Dillard from College Station, and I staggered when Dillard caromed into me, and we all ended up falling. The only two finalists who remained on their feet were Joe from Bloomington, whose bulk was impervious to flailing bodies, and Jimmy Lee, who coolly stepped to one side and continued making minimal movements to the theme music.

From the side of the stage, I thought I heard someone, probably Lauren, hissing, *"Keep going!"* and that was what we did. We picked ourselves up and tried to form some semblance of the original two lines.

The song was up to "*We hope that you know Santa loves you too, You make his days seem merry and bright*" by the time all ten of us were back on our feet, and it was hard to hear the final lines because the audience, too, was standing, applauding and cheering and laughing at such a concussive level that it seemed our dance number had been a great success. The music ended, we stood panting and nursing various injuries, and the crowd kept roaring. Bobbo came back onstage, laughing as he, too, clapped heartily.

"Maybe they can't dance, but next we're going to find out whether they can rope some reindeer!" he announced. "Our Santas are going to head backstage to put Band-Aids on their bruises"—the audience chuckled as one—"but before they do, we're going to very briefly let them say hi." He pulled Andy from Chicago to his side. "Here's Santa 1!"

No one had mentioned being introduced. Andy, his Santa hat drooping over his eyes after various dance collisions, stood mutely by Bobbo, perhaps trying to think of what to say.

"Hi," he finally muttered. Santa 2 (Dillard) could only manage, "Hello." But Jimmy Lee was No. 3.

He strolled comfortably up to Bobbo, looked out at the audience, waved genially, and declared, "Merry Christmas, and may your holiday joy LastLong!" I found this unsubtle mention of the program sponsor quite offensive, but Sarah told me later that Lucretia Pepper, standing backstage, beamed with ill-concealed satisfaction.

Santas 4 and 5 (Luis and Buck) awkwardly mumbled greetings. Then it was my turn, and I smiled and said simply, "Hello. I'm Santa Claus." Now, *that* elicited audience reaction, mostly cheers and whoops. From the corner of my eye, it seemed that Jimmy Lee was glowering, but I might have imagined it.

Santa 7 (Brian) tried saying exactly the same thing, but I'd said it first so the audience reaction was far less enthusiastic for him. Besides, his nose was bleeding. When we all fell over one another, someone's elbow or knee had apparently smashed into his face during the melee. Earlier, the makeup experts must have put some sort of coloring on his beard to make it white instead of dark brown, but now his whiskers appeared to be spattered with crimson polka dots.

"Better get that nose taken care of, Santa 7," Bobbo quipped. "Your suit is supposed to be red and white, not your beard. But say, folks, aren't all of our Santas great sports? Let's give them another hand."

As Santa 8, I thought Zonk made a fine impression by casually saying, "Hey, there," as though he was greeting old, familiar friends. Santa 9 (Wesley), having had time to think about it, launched into a lovely speech about how everyone watching was certain to have a Merry Christmas if they voted for him. He might have said more, but Bobbo cut him off.

"It's Christmas Eve, Santa 9," he cautioned. "Not much time, and lots yet to do."

Santa 10 (massive Joe) contented himself with a quick "Merry Christmas," and then we finalists were ushered offstage while the curtains closed behind Bobbo.

"First challenge in two minutes, at 8:12," one of the stagehands announced. Behind the closed curtains and to my right, I could see the crew frantically hauling what appeared to be hundreds of coiled ropes to one side. Part of the floor toward the rear of the stage was lowered, and new flooring hydraulically replaced it. Placed on that new flooring was a conveyor belt stretched out in perhaps a thirty-foot oval. On this belt were a dozen wooden full-body reindeer silhouettes, the animals apparently frozen in graceful mid-leap. Their forelegs extended, and their antlers were tall and majestic, much more elaborate than the lovely stubs on the heads of my real reindeer.

"One at a time, you'll be called onstage," said Felix, who had walked up while I was looking at the stage set. We finalists gave him our full attention. It was one thing to fail as dancers; those who performed worst in the challenges would be eliminated from the competition.

"You'll each have forty-five seconds to rope as many reindeer as you

can," Felix continued. "You'll see a mark on the stage where you're supposed to stand. Don't worry if you step over it just a little. You won't be
disqualified for that. If you rope one of the reindeer—I mean, *when* you
do—drop your end of the rope and let it just be pulled along with the
wooden reindeer on the conveyor. Pick up a new rope and keep going.
The two Santas who rope the fewest get eliminated. In case of a tie, audience applause level decides who stays and who goes. Got it?"

We did. Onstage, Bobbo Butler was telling the studio and television
audiences much the same things. In the extra half-minute between Felix
concluding his instructions and the curtains opening again, I listened as
Bobbo went on to explain how the evening's challenges would roughly
simulate the order of Santa's usual activities on Christmas Eve.

"In this first event, our Santas will be racing the clock," Bobbo said.
"In the next event, plus one other, we're going to ask our studio audience to determine the results by their votes. More on that later. Right
now, we begin our series of challenges the same way Santa begins his
Christmas Eve—by roping the reindeer!"

Of course, I never had to rope the reindeer. None of us at the North
Pole did. They came when we called them. Reality TV, I mused, actually
had very little real about it. But there was no time for further philoso-
phizing. The curtains opened, and the audience *oohed* and *aahed* to see
the wooden reindeer whirling on the conveyor belt. They were quite attractive reindeer models, I had to admit. We Santas were sent out in a
line determined in order by number—Santa 1 was first, and so on. As
Santa 6, I was comfortably in the middle. Just in front of me, I heard
Buck, as Santa 5, mutter, "Am I supposed to be Santa or a cowboy?" The
answer, evidently, was "both."

Bobbo welcomed us back. He reminded everyone that time was flying, and soon, so would Santa and his reindeer, "but you've got to catch
them first, and there's forty-five seconds for each of our Santas to do it
in." The studio audience was encouraged to keep an eye on the clock; at

home, viewers were informed, they should keep track of two small clocks superimposed on opposite corners of their television screens. The one on the left would keep track of the time left in each Santa's individual attempt; the one on the right indicated how much time was left before the conclusion of *The Great Santa Search* and "the beginning of the real Santa's long night's work!"

Forty-five seconds can seem very long if you just sit still or if you're listening to or watching something boring. But when that's the time you have to accomplish something quite complicated in front of an audience of millions, forty-five seconds seem to expire in a single short instant. Santa 1, Andy from Chicago, was called forward by Bobbo. He picked up a rope from the pile on the floor, took his place at the line marked on the stage, and Bobbo shouted, "Go!"

Santa 1 frantically made a loop, spun it briefly over his head, and threw it in the general direction of the circling wooden reindeer. The loop plopped perhaps a yard in front of him—the reindeer spun unroped another dozen feet away. The audience hooted. Andy tried again. He was inadvertently offering a lesson in how not to use a lasso: you *cast* rather than *throw* it, as Bill Pickett had constantly reminded me at the North Pole. *Casting* allows the loop to retain its shape as it floats through the air. It goes farther and can then drop over its target. It took Santa 1 quite a bit to figure this out, and just before a buzzer blared to note the passage of forty-five seconds, one of his casts managed to snare a single reindeer antler. Bobbo solemnly announced, "One reindeer for Santa 1. I hope if he's the real Santa, he starts trying to catch the reindeer *very* early in the morning of December 24. Otherwise, poor old Dasher will have a tough time pulling the sleigh all by himself!"

Santa 1 shuffled offstage, and Santa 2, who was Dillard, took his place by the pile of lassos. I had thought he would probably do well, being from Texas, but it quickly became obvious that not every Texan knows how to use a rope. Dillard didn't snare a single wooden reindeer.

Jimmy Lee was Santa 3. He'd had, as Sarah and Heather learned, private lessons from a champion rodeo cowboy who was paid by Lucretia Pepper to instruct him. He calmly shook out a nice loop, twirled it properly, cast it perfectly, and smiled as it settled neatly around a wooden reindeer neck. There was applause from the audience, which obviously appreciated not only the roping success but the elegance with which it was accomplished. Never seeming to hurry, Jimmy Lee made eight more casts in his forty-five seconds, succeeding with seven. The eighth looked just as perfect, but somehow the loop slipped off the reindeer's head. Jimmy Lee shrugged gracefully, and the buzzer sounded.

"That's eight reindeer for Santa 3," Bobbo bellowed. "Why, he roped the whole herd!"

There was some grumbling among the other finalists who had yet to try.

"That Number 3 is going to blow us away," somebody muttered. Jimmy Lee walked offstage without acknowledging the rest of us.

But there is some advantage in watching others try before you have to, and Santa 4, Luis, had obviously benefited from Jimmy Lee's example. He cast rather than threw, and though his results were not as impressive he still managed to rope three reindeer before his time was up. Santa 5, Buck, also roped three.

Then it was my turn. The seating area of the theater was darkened so I couldn't actually see him, but I was certain that somewhere in the studio audience Bill Pickett was leaning forward, hoping I would remember everything he'd spent so many months trying to teach me. And I did.

With a minimum of fuss, I cast at and lassoed eight reindeer in a row. Unlike Jimmy Lee, I didn't even have any near-misses. I just imagined I was back in the North Pole gym, with Theodore and Bill by my side and lovely little Vixen volunteering as my target. I could have made many more than eight casts in the allotted forty-five seconds, but I saw no reason to use my special power to move faster than normal humans. It was clear eight would be more than enough to ensure my continuing in the competition.

"Amazing," Bobbo declared. "We've got another Santa who's caught the whole herd!"

I wished I could have seen Bill's expression, but I still knew he was pleased.

Santa 7, Brian, seemed intimidated by my performance. On his first try, the rope slipped out of his hand and went flying offstage far from the wooden reindeer. There was much audience laughter. He never succeeded in snagging a single target.

Zonk, Santa 8, roped four. I noticed that on every cast he moved a little farther in front of the clearly marked line. Whether he did this on purpose or by accident I don't know.

Santa 9, Wesley, roped two, and massive Joe, Santa 10, managed only one. But that was still enough.

"Santas 2 and 7 roped zero reindeer, and they are eliminated," Bobbo announced. "Say goodbye, 2 and 7!" Dillard and Brian waved at the audience, which responded with a friendly cheer, and then were whisked away.

Bobbo talked about the inspiration for *The Great Santa Search*, how he and his assistant had been watching a skating exhibition at Rockefeller Center "sponsored by our wonderful friends at the LastLong Toy Company, who are also the generous sponsors of this program," and how the crisp winter air and the sight of so many people enjoying the massive Christmas tree there made him think of how fine it would be for Santa Claus, the real Santa Claus, to suddenly appear and make the whole moment absolutely perfect. He didn't mention meeting Sarah and Felix, or how Felix's chance remark actually initiated the whole *Great Santa Search* business.

At that moment, Emily the FUN-TV intern instructed me to join the other finalists gathered backstage with Felix.

"Carol-singing is the next competition," he said. "When it's your turn, you'll walk out onstage, take a slip of paper from the big drum on a table on Bobbo's right, and hand the slip to Bobbo. He'll read it and announce the Christmas carol you'll sing. We've got taped instrumental accompaniment. When the music begins, start singing. Some of the songs are longer than others. That's why, after Bobbo reads the slip you draw, he'll take the correct lyrics sheet from the table on his left and hand it to you. If you don't know the words to your carol, there they'll be. But sing only the verses on the sheet. We're trying to limit each singer to ninety seconds."

"What are the names of the songs in the drum?" asked Santa 9, Wesley from St. Paul.

"I can't tell you that," Felix said. It was true. He didn't know which carols they were himself. He knew which they *weren't*—Bobbo had explicitly instructed Heather Hathaway to research famous songs that were not under current copyright, so he and FUN-TV could avoid paying performance royalties to their owners. Even with the money from Last-Long Toy Company in the bank, Bobbo couldn't break many of the penurious habits he'd developed during FUN-TV's recent tough financial times.

"Do we have to stand around while the other Santas are singing?" my pal Zonk asked. "I have to go to the Little Santa's room, if you know what I mean." There were murmurs of agreement from the rest of us.

"If you hurry," Felix said. "Now, we drew the singing order at random. It'll be Santa 4 first, then 8, 6, 3, 5, 1, 10, and 9. It's posted right over there on that blackboard if you forget."

Backstage, there was a sudden flurry of activity as stagehands hauled out a long table and three immense padded chairs.

"What are those for?" one of the Santas asked.

"Never mind," Felix said quickly. "It's the surprise Bobbo's been promising since he first announced *The Great Santa Search*. None of us knew what it was until a minute ago. You'll find out soon enough." I knew my old friend very well, and could sense a certain apologetic tone.

"Just remember this is *reality* TV," he added, and hurried away without elaborating further.

"One minute to the first singing Santa," a stagehand said, and Luis from Miami began frantically clearing his throat. I was scheduled to be third. Zonk had hurried off to our dressing room, so I knew the bathroom there would be in use. Besides, I was curious to see how the other Santas performed, so I stayed just offstage to watch. I had little hope my own singing would be much more than adequate. This challenge would, I thought, be my closest call.

Onstage, Bobbo was explaining the rules of the singing challenge, and how audience members would vote.

"You'll find a small console built into the right armrest of your seat," he said. "For this challenge, and for the last one when you'll also vote, these consoles will be activated and a small light will appear up at the top. See it?" Apparently they did. "Now, there are ten clearly numbered buttons on the console. As Santas are eliminated, their individual buttons are deactivated. Right now, you can no longer vote for Santa 2 or Santa 7, because they're already out. After our eight remaining Santas have sung the carols that they will select completely at random, we'll ask each member of the studio audience to vote in support of one Santa by pressing his numbered button on their consoles. Just push *one* button for the Santa whose performance you think was best. Then, if the folks in the studio will watch the monitors on their right, and everyone at home watches the bottom on their television screens, the vote totals will appear in seconds. The Santa with the fewest votes is eliminated. The other seven go on. Got it?"

They did; there was a burst of applause.

"And now, just before our first singing Santa comes out, we've got a big surprise," Bobbo announced. "You're going to be amazed at what's happening next."

Based on the audience's reaction, he wasn't exaggerating.

As I sang, I acted out the sleigh's overturning, and when I hit some particularly
unpleasant notes I rolled my eyes to indicate to the audience that
I was fully aware of my abysmal vocalizing.

Nineteen

adies and gentlemen, boys and girls, our next competition requires expert analysis," Bobbo announced. "Please say hello to three very special friends, pioneers of reality television who've come to spend Christmas Eve with us!" The curtains parted, revealing the long table and three chairs, and from the left three people—two men and a woman—walked briskly to Bobbo's side, waving and smiling. The audience gasped and cheered.

"*Yes!*" Bobbo shouted. "Our Santas are going to sing. And if they are, who better to critique their performances for you than, straight from *American Idol*, none other than Randy Jackson, Paula Abdul, and Simon Cowell!"

I'd heard of *American Idol*, though I'd never actually watched the program. I knew it involved young would-be singing stars who performed popular songs and were periodically eliminated by viewer vote until one winner remained.

Bobbo traded a few quips with his guests. Randy, a rangy fellow wearing glasses and a diamond stud in one earlobe, said he couldn't wait "to hear Santa gettin' down, 'cause he's gonna be da bomb!" I had no idea what that meant. Paula, who I felt had a lovely smile, remarked that when she was a little girl, she couldn't wait to get up on Christmas morning to see what Santa had brought her.

"And I still can't," she added breathlessly. "Maybe this year, he'll bring me a doll!" She was obviously a true believer, at the very least.

I was puzzled by the audience's reaction when Simon, who seemed pleasant enough, commented that "Santa will get a fair chance to prove himself. I'm prepared to be convinced—or not." They booed, and I thought some of the booing sounded less than good-natured.

"If you'll take your seats," Bobbo suggested, and they sat behind the table. Randy was on the left, Paula in the middle, and Simon on the right.

Bobbo quickly reiterated how audience members should vote.

"Please wait to select the best singing Santa until *all* our finalists have performed," he stressed. "And I should note that all eight songs have been selected at random from among the most popular Christmas tunes of all time."

Backstage, Santa 1—Andy from Chicago—tugged at Felix's sleeve.

"What *key* will the backing tapes be in?" he asked. "Can you at least give us some idea of *tempo?*"

"Bobbo wants spontaneity," Felix replied. "All I can tell you is, just do your best."

I was, frankly, nervous. I have never been able to sing very well, always trying to compensate in volume and spirit for whatever I might lack in talent. At least most of the other finalists seemed equally worried. Jimmy Lee, still standing somewhat apart, was the only one who appeared unconcerned.

"Let's go," Bobbo commanded. "Again, our finalists are performing in the order determined by a backstage draw. Here's Santa 4!" Luis from Miami walked onstage. Small tables had been set on either side of where Bobbo stood. Luis reached into a colorful drum resting on the first one and took out a slip of paper, which he handed to Bobbo, who then picked up a lyric sheet from the other table and handed it to Luis.

"Santa 4 will sing 'Up On the Housetop'!" Bobbo announced. He walked quickly offstage. Behind the table, the three *American Idol* judges leaned forward.

The moment Bobbo was offstage, recorded music began to play. Taking a deep, desperate breath, Luis started singing, his eyes frantically darting across the lyric sheet clutched in his hand:

> *"Up on the housetop reindeer pause, out jumps good old Santa Claus,*
> *Down through the chimney with lots of toys,*
> *All for the little ones' Christmas joys.*
> *Ho, ho, ho, who wouldn't go*
> *Ho, ho, ho, who wouldn't go*
> *Up on the housetop, click, click, click,*
> *Down through the chimney with good Saint Nick?"*

Halfway through his song, Luis managed to tear his eyes away from the lyric sheet. He looked out at the audience and began to move awkwardly to the music, and as he did Paula Abdul jumped up from her chair and began to dance, too. As she did, the audience began to clap, and Luis, who was staring out at them and didn't see Paula, assumed the applause was for him. He began singing much louder, and when he finished the second verse the music abruptly cut off. Luis bowed and grinned.

Bobbo came back onstage.

"*American Idol* judges, what did you think?" he asked.

Randy went first.

"Well, Mr. Claus Number 4 sure was *feeling* the music," he remarked. "Gotta give the ol' guy that. But it's one thing to move and another to dance, you know? Props more for effort than performance."

"I think Santa 4 sounded very genuine and sweet," Paula enthused. "Bravo."

Then Simon cleared his throat.

"That was absolutely awful," he declared. "The reindeer would have done better."

Luis looked shocked.

"Thank you, Santa 4," Bobbo said hastily. "And now, Santa 8."

Zonk walked onstage as Luis was walking off. He plucked a slip of paper from the drum and handed it to Bobbo.

"Santa 8 is singing 'Deck the Halls,'" Bobbo said. He tried to hand Zonk a lyric sheet, but my dressing-room friend waved it off.

"We sing this all the time at the North Pole," he explained, and the comment earned him considerable applause from the audience.

When the music started, Zonk began singing:

"Deck the halls with boughs of holly
Fa-la-la-la-la, la-la-la-la
'Tis the season to be jolly
Fa-la-la-la-la, la-la-la-la"

I thought he sang quite well. His enthusiasm was obvious. When he was through, Randy pronounced him "a little pitchy, but still *alllll* right." Paula said he deserved a hug, and scampered over to give him one. Simon grumbled that "it was nothing special, but still a vast improvement over that first incompetent."

Then it was my turn. I took a slip of paper from the drum and handed it to Bobbo. He glanced at it, grinned, and said, "Santa 6 is going to sing one of the most traditional holiday favorites—'Jingle Bells'!" He handed me a lyric sheet.

I felt slightly better. At least this was a carol I knew by heart. I moved to the center of the stage. A single hot spotlight shone on me. The music began.

Then I forgot the words.

That in itself was no cause for panic. After all, I had the lyric sheet in my hand. But as I tried to read it, the spotlight was directly in my eyes and I couldn't. So the music blared out and not one sound came from me. I frantically tried to shade my eyes so I could read the lyrics. I sensed as much as heard concerned murmuring from the audience. It was an awful moment.

"Wait," Bobbo Butler snapped. "Can we dim that spotlight a little? It's blinding Santa 6." The light switched off. After a moment, my eyes could focus again. "This is what happens on live television, folks," Bobbo explained. "Is it all right if we start Santa 6's music again and give him another chance?" There were scattered shouts of agreement. I looked at the lyrics, and they were instantly familiar.

The music began to play for the second time, and I was ready:

"Dashing through the snow
In a one-horse open sleigh,
Over the fields we go
Laughing all the way;
Bells on bobtail ring,
Making spirits bright,
What fun it is to ride and sing
A sleighing song tonight!
Oh, jingle bells, jingle bells,
Jingle all the way!
Oh, what fun it is to ride
In a one-horse open sleigh!"

Now the problem was that I was singing spectacularly off-key, and knew it. For centuries all my dear North Pole companions routinely suggested I *hum* rather than sing whenever we gathered by the fire to enjoy performing Christmas carols. But that wasn't an option on the Ed Sullivan Theater stage. The harder I tried to sing well, the worse I sounded.

I thought about simply quitting in mid-song, but then I would have been disqualified. So I sang the second verse about the sleigh driver and Miss Fanny Bright getting dumped in a snowbank, and even though they "got all sot," or wet, they still were singing "Jingle Bells" at the top of their lungs, and so was I. As I sang, I acted out the sleigh's over-turning, and when I hit some particularly unpleasant notes I rolled my eyes to indicate to the audience that I was fully aware of my abysmal vocalizing.

After what seemed like hours, I finished the second chorus and the music stopped. The audience applauded—a lovely gesture, I felt, after what they'd just had to listen to. I tried to smile, but I felt certain I had just eliminated myself from the competition.

"*American Idol* judges?" Bobbo inquired.

Randy looked at me, his lips pursed sympathetically.

"It takes some guts to keep on going," he mused. "Good for you, dawg. But if Santa's gotta sing well, we all know you're not him. Maybe you got other more important talents. Just don't ever sing again when I gotta listen, okay?"

Paula blew me a kiss.

"I don't care if he was on-key or not," she told the audience. "It was like listening to your grandpa or favorite uncle when the whole family is gathered 'round the tree. Everybody knows he can't sing on-key and no-body cares. Santa 6, you can sing Christmas carols to me anytime."

Then it was Simon's turn.

"That was totally pathetic," he declared. "The horrible off-key yowl-ing aside, I didn't even detect any genuine Christmas spirit. In no way did you convince me that you might be Santa Claus. The bloody Easter Bunny could have done better." He waved his hand dismissively.

The audience began to boo—at Simon, I felt, not at me. He, in turn, grinned and informed them, "I'm just being honest."

I was still looking at Simon when I was bumped from behind.

"Out of my way," Jimmy Lee hissed as he brushed by me. His nasty tone was in direct contrast to the wide smile on his face, which he had turned toward the audience. I made my slow, sad way offstage, where Zonk clapped me on the shoulder and several of my other fellow competitors muttered encouraging things. I could tell, though, that they were also relieved after my awful showing. It seemed obvious which Santa finalist would soon be eliminated.

Jimmy Lee drew his slip, handed it to Bobbo, and beamed when informed he would sing "O Christmas Tree." Strolling confidently to center stage, he placed a hand over his heart and sang in an undeniably wonderful baritone voice:

"O Christmas tree, O Christmas tree,
How steadfast are your branches!
Your boughs are green in summer's clime,
And through the snows of wintertime.
O Christmas tree, O Christmas tree,
How steadfast are your branches!"

It wasn't just that Jimmy Lee sang perfectly on-key. His voice throbbed with great emotion. He made it clear he unapologetically *loved* his Christmas tree. I knew all the bad things about him, and still his singing moved me deeply.

And then, beginning the second verse, Jimmy Lee did something unexpected. He switched from English to German:

"O Tannenbaum, O Tannenbaum,
Wie treu sind deine blätter!
Du grünst nicht nur zur Sommerzeit,
Nein auch im winter, wenn es schneit.
O Tannenbaum, O Tannenbaum,
Wie treu sind deine blätter!"

The music stopped. Jimmy Lee was no longer singing, but Bobbo seemed spellbound. So did the audience. It was Jimmy Lee himself who finally broke the silence.

"I repeated the first verse in German rather than singing the second in English," he explained. "I hope that was all right. I especially wanted all the little ones to remember that Christmas is a holiday celebrated all over the world, not just in America. 'O Christmas Tree' was originally written and sung in German. So I tried to pay tribute to that."

Everyone seated in the theater rose as one. Their applause and cheers were deafening.

The *American Idol* judges were on their feet, too.

"That's it, get the sleigh and let the Big Dawg ride!" Randy shouted. "We got international Santa excellence here!"

Paula appeared to be wiping tears from her eyes.

"You took my breath away," she gushed. "Wow. That's all I can say. Wow."

As for Simon, he dashed across the stage to shake Jimmy Lee's hand.

"You are the one to beat in this contest," he declared. "You made me believe every word you sang, and I swear you made me believe in *you*."

Jimmy Lee was the picture of modesty as he smiled, waved to the audience, and walked offstage. He brushed past the rest of us finalists. Lucretia Pepper, not even feigning neutrality, hurried over to embrace him.

"Wonderful," she cooed. "Just *wonderful*!"

"Somebody get me some water," Jimmy Lee demanded, and a half dozen different stagehands scampered off to do his bidding. When the first one returned with a frosty plastic bottle, Jimmy Lee took a huge swig and handed the bottle back without a word of thanks. Then he marched off toward his dressing room, Lucretia Pepper at his side.

Onstage, Santa 5—Buck from Kansas City—was performing a credible rendition of "The Holly and the Ivy," but the audience's attention seemed listless at best. The *American Idol* judges tried to act enthusiastic with him and the other remaining contestants. But they, too, clearly believed they'd already heard the best performance. Standing offstage, I was extremely discouraged and expected the upcoming vote to go against me.

I felt a light tap on my shoulder and turned to see Felix.

"He was something, wasn't he?" my old friend remarked.

"It's bad enough I'm about to be eliminated, but it's worse that Jimmy Lee was so good," I replied. "The audience loves him. After this, who else has a chance to win?"

"The next three events don't involve voting," Felix reminded me. "They're skill competitions. Maybe he'll be terrible at chimney-sliding or stocking-stuffing or cookie-eating and eliminate himself."

"Remember, he and Lucretia Pepper are going to cheat in stocking-stuffing and cookie-eating," I reminded him.

Felix grinned.

"Maybe they think they are, but we're going to stop them," he said. "Willie Skokan and Heather Hathaway are ready to go. Say, those two have become instant friends. It turns out Heather likes to build and repair things. They have a lot in common."

Meanwhile, Santa 1, Andy from Chicago, sang "We Wish You a Merry Christmas." Santa 10, Joe from Bloomington, his bulging belly vibrating visibly, charmed everyone with "Jolly Old St. Nicholas." If Jimmy Lee's performance hadn't been so spectacular, Santa 10 might have earned a standing ovation.

"That does it," I muttered to Felix. "Nobody will sing as badly as me. I'm gone."

"We haven't heard the last Santa yet," Felix cautioned. "He might be worse than you."

"Hardly," I grumbled. "It's Santa 9, Wesley from St. Paul. You found him in a play there, remember? He probably sings as well as Jimmy Lee."

Santa 9 practically bounded out onstage. He clapped his hands when Bobbo said he'd be singing "The Twelve Days of Christmas"—"but only the first five days, actually! It's already almost nine o'clock!"

Clearly, this Santa finalist's experience in theater was helping him avoid the stage fright that the rest of us, except for Jimmy Lee, were suffering. The music began. Santa 9 sang.

"On the first day of Christmas my true love sent to me,
A partridge in a pear tree.
On the second day of Christmas my true love sent to me,
Two turtle doves,
And a partridge in a pear tree."

I have never actually heard fingernails being scraped across a chalkboard. But I am willing to wager that Santa 9's singing ranked high among the most noxious, horrible sounds ever emitted in human history. Members of the audience cringed and covered their ears. From his place at the *American Idol* judges' table, Simon Cowell yelped, "Stop! Please! I'll pay anything!" But Santa 9 seemed oblivious. He kept right on, putting special, if ear-splitting, emphasis on the drawn-out *"Five . . . golden . . . riiiiiiings!"*

When he was finally finished, all Randy had to say was, "Huh." Paula seemed lost in thought, apparently trying to come up with any sort of positive comment. She settled for, "I'll remember that as long as I live." Simon commented, "You have just made Santa what's-his-name, Santa 6, seem tuneful by comparison."

Bobbo called all eight remaining finalists back onstage. The applause was loudest by far for Jimmy Lee. The audience was reminded how to vote, pushing just one button whose number corresponded with the number of their favorite singing Santa. The results were almost instantly flashed on monitors all around the theater. Those of us onstage could see the totals clearly. There were 461 possible votes, since there were that many seats in the theater. Jimmy Lee, Santa 3, got 410. Joe, Santa 10, was second with twenty-seven. Santas 4, 8, 5, and 1 each had five. I received four—not coincidentally, the number of North Pole friends I had in the audience—and Wesley, Santa 9, got none. He was eliminated.

"Did you know he was such a terrible singer?" I asked Felix as Bobbo called Wesley back for a farewell bow. The same audience whose vote had just eliminated him responded with a rousing ovation. "Was that why you picked him?"

"Not really," my old friend replied. "Look, the play he was in wasn't a musical. How was I supposed to know he was a worse singer than you? Although, I guess there had to be one somewhere."

I had my doubts, and would have pressed Felix further, but he loudly announced to everyone backstage that it was time to get ready for the chimney-sliding challenge. With *The Great Santa Search* almost half over, I still had a chance to keep the name Santa Claus from becoming synonymous with "terrible toys." Jimmy Lee and Lucretia Pepper hadn't won yet!

I had a brief, distorted glimpse of the theater audience through the Plexiglas; then my boots thumped comfortably down on the floor of the fireplace. I stepped out onto the living-room set with the toy sack in perfect position on my shoulder and my long tassled cap perched at a jaunty angle on my head.

Twenty

ary Rogers sent someone down from the control booth to tell the remaining Santa finalists there would be approximately a five-minute break before the next challenge commenced. That much time would be needed to prepare the elaborate chimney-sliding set. We could go back to our dressing rooms for a brief bathroom break or just to sit down and catch our breaths. The FUN-TV interns would fetch us when we were needed.

As I made my way toward the dressing room I shared with Zonk, I passed Willie Skokan and tall, serious-looking Heather Hathaway. They were bent over a large canvas sack full of toys—a sack, I knew, that contained all the LastLong products I'd purchased the day before at the Galaxy Mall in Cleveland. It rested among six other sacks that looked exactly the same.

"We're making sure you get the right one," Willie whispered. "After the chimney-sliding, you'll keep the same sack for stocking-stuffing." Beside him, Heather looked momentarily puzzled.

Jeff Guinn

"I still don't understand why Santa 6 needs *this* sack," she said to Willie.

He smiled at her, and I wondered why I'd never realized for so many centuries that Willie Skokan was, in his sweet, simple way, a rather good-looking fellow.

"I'll explain after the program is over," he replied. "For now, trust me."

Heather smiled back. Before, I'd thought she looked pleasant enough. But now it seemed to me that she was quite pretty.

"For some reason, I do," she assured Willie. As I continued toward my dressing room I wondered if the pressure of competing on *The Great Santa Search* was somehow causing me to find everyone attractive, but then I passed Lucretia Pepper and knew that wasn't the case. The expression on her broad, blunt-featured face was ferocious. I had the impression of a particularly savage lioness about to devour her prey.

As I walked into our dressing room, Zonk was in the process of eating my unfinished chicken-salad sandwich.

"You don't mind, do you?" he mumbled, his mouth full. "All this competing business made me hungry."

"Maybe you ought to remain hungry," I suggested. "We've got that cookie-eating challenge coming up."

Zonk shrugged and took another huge bite of sandwich.

"Nah, I'm one of those people who can eat all day," he said. "It's crazy, I know, especially since I can't taste anything."

It seemed it hadn't even been a few moments, let alone five minutes, before we were summoned by Emily the intern. Bobbo had filled the time needed for changing the set by introducing various celebrities in the audience—Oprah Winfrey got the most applause, which seemed to annoy David Letterman—and reminding everyone about the generous decision by sponsor LastLong Toys to let the program be broadcast without commercial interruption.

We remaining Santa candidates clustered around Felix. He an-

268

nounced the random order in which the seven remaining finalists would participate in the chimney-sliding challenge: 5, 3, 10, 8, 4, 6, 1. Jimmy Lee would be second, and I would be sixth.

"You can see how it's all set up behind the curtain," Felix said. "The idea is to simulate actually getting out of the sleigh, carrying a sack of toys across a rooftop, then holding the sack as you slide down the chimney. So, each in turn, you'll take a sack of toys—they're right over there—and climb that ladder up to where the sleigh is suspended. Put the sack of toys in the back of the sleigh and climb on the seat in front. You won't be on camera until you're actually in the sleigh, which will then seem to float onstage to the roof of the set. As the sleigh reaches the roof, get off and take the sack of toys. Walk across the roof—you can see it's just going to be a few feet—and, making sure to hang on to the toy sack, position yourself in the chimney and slide down. Don't worry about falling straight down and hurting yourself. We've got the inside of the chimney curved, like the slide on a playground. The clock will start timing you as soon as the sleigh appears by the roof. You're done when you come out of the chimney into the part of the set that looks like a living room. The side of the chimney facing the studio audience is Plexiglas, so they can see you the whole way down. So will the TV audience. When you're done, come offstage with your toy sack. You'll need it for the next challenge, which is stocking-stuffing. The two slowest Santas in chimney-sliding will be eliminated. Questions?"

There weren't any. Santa 5, Buck from Kansas City, went first. Someone took him over to where the seven canvas sacks of toys had been piled. Heather Hathaway stood over my special one, while Willie Skokan helpfully picked up a different sack and handed it to him. I noticed that Lucretia Pepper had placed herself by the toy sacks, too. Just as Willie and Heather were making sure I got the right one, she was there to see Jimmy Lee took possession of his special sack.

"All right, on to our third challenge," Bobbo announced. "We've told you this competition is designed to roughly parallel Santa's actual schedule on Christmas Eve. So far he's roped the reindeer and sung some carols. Now it's time for him to get down to work. Santa's loaded his sleigh, and he's flying through the cold winter sky, all ready to land on that first roof and slide down its chimney. Why, I think he's coming now!"

The curtains parted, and the crowd gasped. Their reaction was appropriate, because they were looking at one of the most dazzling sets ever created. The high roof looked absolutely real, extending two-thirds of the way from one side of the stage to the other. Its chimney was high and wide. Beneath was a wonderful living room, where the mouth of the fireplace stretched fully six feet. The Plexiglas chimney wall extended above to the rooftop. Empty stockings dangled in front of the fireplace. On one side of the room was a large green Christmas tree festooned with colorful lights. It was all quite lovely.

High above the left-hand side of the stage, a golden sleigh with sparkling side panels was hydraulically pulled to the roof.

"It's Santa 5," Bobbo announced, and monitors began to record passing seconds as Buck from Kansas City gingerly eased himself off the front seat. I couldn't blame him for feeling uncomfortable. Even faux roofs can seem very high if you're trying to balance on them.

As the audience cheered, Santa 5 carefully inched to the back of the sleigh, where he picked up the sack of toys. He tried slinging the sack over his shoulder, but the sudden weight shift made him wobble. For a moment it looked like he might tumble off the roof completely— Robert, the set designer, had placed thick, pillowy cushions all around in case of just such an accident—but then regained his balance. Moving very deliberately, he tiptoed to the chimney and laboriously settled himself over the opening. He then made the mistake of lowering the toy sack ahead of him as he slid. As a result, the sack hit the bottom of the fireplace first, followed by Santa 5's seat smacking squarely onto the sack, crushing most of the toys in it. The sound of cracking plastic echoed through the theater.

"Santa 5's time in the chimney-slide is one minute, forty-eight seconds," Bobbo announced. Santa 5 got to his feet and remembered to take the sack of smashed toys with him as he limped off the set.

While Santa 5 had been sliding and smashing, the sleigh had been hydraulically pulled back offstage. Jimmy Lee walked over to the toy sacks. Lucretia Pepper pointed to one, which he picked up. Then he climbed the ladder, carefully placed the sack in the sleigh, and took his seat in front just as Santa 5 made his shamefaced way backstage.

"It's Santa 3," Bobbo shouted, and as Jimmy Lee came into view there was prolonged cheering. This time, though, he was competent rather than memorable. He got out of the sleigh, picked up his sack of toys, eased his cautious but steady way across the roof, made certain to hold the toy sack over his head as he slid, and recorded a time of 1:25. The only flaw in his performance involved his hat, which had been jarred slightly during his chimney descent and flopped comically over his left eye. Jimmy Lee impatiently straightened it, smiling all the while.

Things did not go as smoothly for Santa 10. Joe from Bloomington was severely overweight. He had trouble just climbing the backstage ladder to the sleigh, and when he took his seat in the front his bulk caused the conveyance to tip precariously forward. When the sleigh creaked into view, its front end pointed almost directly down, many of the audience members began to laugh.

Santa 10 had trouble just extricating himself from the front seat. When he finally did, he successfully retrieved his sack of toys, but had tremendous difficulty balancing as he tried to cross the roof to the chimney. When he settled his bulk over the opening of the chimney, his legs and seat slid down but the rest of him didn't. I knew what had happened. He was stuck. He wriggled frantically as perhaps thirty seconds passed, and then finally threw up his hands in surrender.

"Santa 10 is, I think, resigning from the competition," Bobbo announced. "Let's go ahead and close the curtain for a moment so we can help Santa 10 out of the chimney." The curtains shut, and while Bobbo reminded viewers that live television will have its unexpected moments, members of the stage crew tugged until Santa 10 was unwedged. He stumbled down the ladder and went directly to his dressing room.

My friend Zonk was next. He was a theatrical chimney-slider, to the point of pausing on the edge of the chimney, facing the TV cameras, and deliberately placing his finger beside his nose before sliding down. It was a slight mistake; in my old friend Clement Moore's epic poem, St. Nicholas placed his finger beside his nose before soaring back *up* the chimney after delivering his gifts. But Zonk's intended tribute to the epic Christmas poem was clear, and there was considerable applause when Bobbo announced that Santa 8's time was 1:19, the best so far.

It was certainly better than Santa 4 could do. Luis from Miami was able to climb out of the sleigh and take up his sack of toys without much trouble, but when he approached the chimney he circled it, examining it from all possible angles, while the clock ticked away. His overall time was two minutes exactly.

"Why were you moving so slowly?" Zonk demanded when Luis came backstage.

"I'm from Florida," he replied. "We don't have chimneys there."

Now it was my turn.

I walked over to the pair of remaining toy sacks. Willie Skokan gestured toward one and winked. I picked up the sack Willie had indicated and went to the ladder. Some of the other finalists had trouble climbing the ladder while holding on to their sacks of toys, but I didn't. Once I reached the top, I put the sack in the back of the sleigh. Despite its glittering gold side panels, the sleigh would not have impressed Leonardo. He would have pointed out that the bed of the sleigh was too wide (bad aerodynamics), the runners underneath were too short (insufficient traction), and the front bench had no seat belt (Santa never flies without his seat belt being securely fastened). But I climbed on the front bench and immediately there was a slight lurch as the hydraulic system was engaged to pull the sleigh over to the roof. I blinked in the sudden harsh light; once over the stage, the spotlights held me in their beam.

Below me Bobbo said, "And now, here's Santa 6." There was a reasonably warm crowd response. Though they all clapped for every finalist, the majority clearly reserved their highest regard for Jimmy Lee. A moment later the sled bumped onto the false roof. Without hesitation I hopped out. I knew exactly how to keep my balance. In one sure, confident motion I pulled the toy sack from the sleigh, hoisted it over my shoulder, and turned. From there it took only three quick steps to reach the chimney. Shifting the toy sack higher on my back, I swung my legs over the side of the chimney, made certain to bring my heels together so my feet wouldn't separate and slow my progress (a typical mistake by novices), and slid down smoothly. I had a brief, distorted glimpse of the theater audience through the Plexiglas; then my boots thumped comfortably down on the floor of the fireplace. I stepped out onto the living-room set with the toy sack in perfect position on my shoulder and my long tassled cap perched at a jaunty angle on my head. I couldn't help peeking offstage. Jimmy Lee was staring intently. I allowed myself a slight nod in his direction, then waved to the cheering audience.

"And Santa 6 is down the chimney in twenty-four seconds!" Bobbo enthused. "If there was a previous world record, I believe Santa 6 may have broken it!"

Layla later suggested that I strutted as I left the stage. I'm sure I didn't, but I admit it felt uplifting to have performed so well. Of course, I had an advantage the other six finalists didn't. I'd been sliding down chimneys since they were first invented almost five hundred years earlier.

Emily the intern greeted me backstage.

"That was totally awesome," she declared. "You can put your toy sack over there until the next challenge."

"Thank you, but I think I'll just hold on to it," I replied. I noticed that Jimmy Lee was also carefully clutching his bag, which Lucretia Pepper had undoubtedly made certain was full of sturdily constructed toys. He glared at me. I smiled in return.

While Santa 1, Andy from Chicago, took the last turn in the chimney-sliding challenge, I noticed Felix, Buck from Kansas City, and Lucretia Pepper engaged in a hushed but heated debate. I edged over to listen.

"Santa 5 has to keep his chimney-sliding sack of toys for use in the stocking-stuffing competition," Lucretia Pepper snapped. "Those are the rules."

"But a lot of them broke when I sat on them coming down the chimney," Buck protested. "Broken toys will count against me in stocking-stuffing. Unless I substitute unbroken ones for these, I'm going to lose."

"Surely it won't hurt to let him use unbroken toys," Felix said. "That's only fair."

"Following the rules is fair," Lucretia Pepper replied. "It's too bad Santa 5 broke some of his toys. But he's going to follow the rules. If he loses in stocking-stuffing because of a mistake in chimney-sliding, that's the way the Christmas cookie crumbles. I'm sorry." She didn't sound sorry at all.

Santa 1 completed his chimney-sliding in 1:41. Bobbo declared that Santa 4 and Santa 10 had been eliminated, and asked them to come back out onstage for a final bow. Santa 4, Luis, did, but rotund Santa 10 never emerged from backstage. Joe had changed clothes and left immediately for Bloomington, and I never saw him again. I regretted that, because he seemed to love Christmas very much, and he sang "Jolly Old St. Nicholas" quite well.

"We're down to our last five Santas," Bobbo announced. "Let's ask them to all come back out onstage." We trooped out, each carrying a toy sack. "The real Mr. Claus is either Santa 1, Santa 3"—there was another ovation for Jimmy Lee, but not quite as enthusiastic as before—"Santa 5, Santa 6"—there was another chorus of cheers, which thrilled me; the cheers weren't quite as loud as Jimmy Lee's, but I was certainly making up ground in popularity with the voters in the theater—"and Santa 8."

Bobbo looked meaningfully at the clock on the theater wall.

"It's now ten minutes after nine, so we have less than an hour to identify the real Santa Claus and send him on his Christmas Eve way. Fortunately, we can start our next challenge almost immediately. Can you guess what it is? Santa's come down the chimney, and now he's got to fill stockings in a hurry so he can move on to the next house. So, remaining Santa finalists, get ready. It's time for . . . *stocking-stuffing!*"

Heather's question had been posed in a very conversational tone. When Jimmy Lee looked puzzled, she continued matter-of-factly, "If somebody smart wins *The Great Santa Search*, a million dollars from LastLong Toys would be nothing, compared to what he could have made. But I guess you've thought of that."

Twenty-one

espite Bobbo's statement, the stocking-stuffing challenge couldn't really begin right after chimney-sliding. Stage-hands dressed as elves came onstage to hang a dozen foot-long, empty stockings across the front of the wide chimney. As they did, Bobbo explained the rules of the challenge. Again in random order—Santas 1, 8, 5, 3, and 6 this time—we finalists would have sixty seconds to fill as many of the stockings with toys as we could. To be considered full, there would have to be enough toys in a stocking to peep out over the top.

"There's one more catch," Bobbo said. "If any stocking contains a broken toy, it will not count toward that Santa's final total. Even one broken item disqualifies its stocking. So our Santas need to be very careful. At the conclusion of each finalist's turn, the toys in his filled stockings will be examined by none other than . . . the president of LastLong Toy Company herself, Lucretia Pepper!" That large, unpleasant woman made her way onstage.

"I'll keep everything absolutely fair and square, Bobbo," she promised, and I reflected how liars frequently claim they are doing one thing while doing exactly the opposite. With Lucretia Pepper as judge, Jimmy Lee didn't have to worry about succeeding in this fourth challenge.

He knew that, of course. As Santa 1, Andy from Chicago, carried his toy sack onstage and waited for Bobbo's signal to begin, Jimmy Lee actually sidled up to where I stood watching in the wings.

"You're a pretty good chimney slider," he remarked. In group meetings and onstage, his voice had been clear and unaccented. But I noticed that, with no audience other than me, he had a pronounced southern drawl. "Not bad on the reindeer-roping, either. It's a real shame you can't sing."

"At least I managed well enough so that I wasn't eliminated," I replied, watching as Bobbo snapped out a command to start the clock and Santa 1 began frantically pulling LastLong toys out of his sack and stuffing them in the first stocking. It was difficult if not impossible to keep them from breaking. The toys in the sack were comprised of tiny LastLong dolls and so-called "action figures." As was typical with that company's products, their spindly arms and legs were not securely joined to their bodies. The slightest pressure could detach plastic limbs in much the same way the dried wishbone of a roast chicken or turkey can be snapped with very little effort.

"You heard how much louder my applause was than yours," Jimmy Lee continued. "Even if you're the other one left at the end, no way you're going to get more votes than me."

I shook my head slightly, not in response to his comment but in sympathy for the onstage plight of Santa 1. Try as he might, it was proving impossible to stuff more than a few LastLong items in a stocking without breaking part of one off. Every time that happened, he had to extract the broken toy from the stocking and replace it with another. The clock on the theater wall included a prominent second hand, and as the end of his sixty-second turn approached, the audience began to chant, *"Ten—*

nine—eight—seven—" which only ratcheted the tension higher. When Santa 1's time was up, loud jingle-bell chimes sounded.

"Thank you, Santa 1," Bobbo cried. "Lucretia Pepper of LastLong Toys, please take a close look and tell us Santa 1's stocking total."

While Santa 1 looked on unhappily, she removed and inspected in turn each of the stockings in which he had placed toys.

"Santa 1's total is three stockings, Bobbo," she announced. "No, wait. There's a leg missing from a doll in this one. Santa 1 was clumsy. His final total is two."

"Who knows, Santa 1? That might be good enough to win," Bobbo said cheerfully. "All right, then. You wait offstage. It's time for Santa 8."

My dressing-room friend Zonk was one of those husky men who is actually quite nimble. I consider myself much the same. In any event, he literally bounded onstage with his sack of toys and waited for Bobbo to give the signal to start.

"This guy's a showman," Jimmy Lee observed as Bobbo barked out the command to begin and Zonk hustled over to where the stockings were hung by the false fireplace. "If he didn't have to go up against me, he might convince the voters *he* was Santa. But that's not going to happen."

"You have your reasons for feeling so confident," I responded, and Jimmy Lee's eyes narrowed. I could tell he was wondering what I meant by that. "But don't underestimate Santa 8."

Santa 1 had broken too many flimsy LastLong toys by cramming them in the stockings as fast as he could. Zonk had watched and learned. His stocking-stuffing pace was much more deliberate. He extracted one small doll or action figure at a time from his sack of toys, and inserted them very gently until a stocking was just full enough to be counted.

"I'll go faster than that," Jimmy Lee boasted. "None of my toys will break, either. Don't get your hopes up, pal. That million dollars from LastLong Toys is going to be mine."

"You're really going to settle for just a million dollars?" someone asked, and Jimmy Lee and I, both startled, whirled around to see Heather Hathaway standing beside us, with Willie Skokan just behind her. I'd been so preoccupied with watching Zonk, and Jimmy Lee had been so intent on trying to intimidate me, that we hadn't noticed them.

Heather's question had been posed in a very conversational tone. When Jimmy Lee looked puzzled, she continued matter-of-factly, "If somebody smart wins *The Great Santa Search*, a million dollars from LastLong Toys would be nothing, compared to what he could have made. But I guess you've thought of that."

"What are you talking about?" Jimmy Lee demanded.

Heather shrugged.

"Oh, I just meant that for a million dollars, LastLong Toys would be getting the winner cheap," she said. "That Lucretia Pepper is sure to insist on a contract that doesn't let him appear as Santa Claus for anyone else. He'll be stuck doing commercials and appearances for her company. Too bad."

"Stuck?" Jimmy Lee asked. "What do you mean, 'stuck'?"

Onstage, the seconds ticked down and the audience shouted, "Ten— nine—eight—seven" as Zonk placed toys in a final stocking. The jingle-bell chimes sounded, Bobbo called in Lucretia Pepper to inspect Zonk's work, and Jimmy Lee was oblivious to anything other than his conversation with Heather. She, in turn, seemed quite fascinated by everything onstage, and Jimmy Lee had to ask several more times what she meant by "stuck" before she turned her attention back to him.

"It's just that there would be so many other opportunities to make a lot more than a million dollars," Heather said. "Whoever wins here is going to instantly be one of the most famous people in America. *Everybody's* going to want to hire him to make appearances and give speeches. He could even count on a movie deal."

"*Movies?*" Jimmy Lee gasped. "There could be movies?"

"Sure," Heather replied. "Oh, look! They say Santa 8 filled five stockings! That's great!"

"What about the movies?" Jimmy Lee persisted, but Heather now seemed occupied with whispering encouraging things to Santa 5, Buck from Kansas City, as he prepared to take his turn.

"Just concentrate on not breaking the toys, and don't think about anything else!" she advised. Santa 5 nodded nervously and went onstage just as Zonk, Santa 8, hustled off. Heather patted his shoulder and told him he'd done wonderfully well. Jimmy Lee twitched impatiently.

"Get back to the movies," he insisted.

"Isn't it obvious?" Heather said. "Don't you think a hundred producers are watching *The Great Santa Search* right now and telling themselves that whoever wins needs to star in a movie about Santa's life? Wouldn't that be natural? And they'd have to pay the winner a *ton* of money to do it, because he could just tell all of them to start bidding at two million dollars, or five million, or ten million, who knows? That is, he could tell them that if he wasn't already under contract to appear as Santa exclusively for LastLong Toys. I don't think Lucretia Pepper is someone who likes to share, do you?"

"No, she wouldn't share," Jimmy Lee said thoughtfully. "Ten million dollars to star in a movie, you say?"

"Oh, at least," Heather replied carelessly. "And that might be only the beginning. Eventually there could be a TV series. Look! Poor Santa 5's toys are all broken even before he's putting them in the stockings!"

Sadly, this was true. Santa 5 had squashed most of his toys when he sat on his sack during the chimney-sliding. He had no chance to stuff even one stocking full of unbroken items. The crowd counted down, and in the end Lucretia Pepper declared that Santa 5's total was none at all.

"But you've been a great competitor and we wish you all the best, Santa 5," Bobbo assured him as he made his sorrowful way offstage. "With two more finalists to go, Santa 8's five stuffed stockings is the total to beat, and Santa 1 hopes his total of two is good enough to squeak through. We'll have to see. And now, here's Santa 3!"

The rest of us shifted aside so Jimmy Lee could have an unobstructed path onstage, but he didn't move. He seemed lost in thought. After a few moments, Bobbo repeated, "Santa 3 is the next finalist. Let's go, Santa 3!"

"They're calling you," I whispered, and nudged Jimmy Lee in the ribs with perhaps a bit more emphasis than necessary. He blinked, looked out at Bobbo, snatched his bag of toys, and waved at the audience as he walked out.

I looked at Heather Hathaway, whose expression was one of exaggerated innocence.

"Those were some very interesting comments," I said. "I wonder how you thought of them."

Heather smiled.

"I've negotiated with lots of performers while I've worked for Bobbo," she said. "I just thought Santa 3 might want to consider a few things."

"He certainly seemed to be considering them," I said, and thought Sarah and Felix were exactly right—Heather Hathaway was an extremely intelligent, capable young woman.

Onstage, Jimmy Lee's sixty-second time limit had commenced. As he began to fill his first stocking, I saw that he had a different advantage than we'd suspected. It had been our belief that Lucretia Pepper would provide Jimmy Lee with dolls and action figures whose limbs were much more securely attached than those of typical LastLong toys. That would keep them from breaking as he stuffed them in the stockings at the fastest rate he could manage.

Instead, the toys Jimmy Lee extracted from his sack were larger, one-piece items—plastic cars and flutes and shovels. Not only were they virtually unbreakable, they were bulky as well. Three or four could and did easily fill a single stocking. Jimmy Lee sailed down the line of stockings along the fireplace mantel, and by the time the crowd counted down, Bobbo called a halt, and Lucretia Pepper inspected, Santa 3's final total was eleven.

"We had only twelve stockings available," Bobbo observed. "If Santa 3 had a few more seconds, we would have had to bring out another dozen! Now we know how Santa can fill all the stockings in the world in just one night!"

Felix walked up. He told me not to be nervous, but that wasn't necessary. I wasn't nervous at all.

Jimmy Lee came offstage and immediately looked for Heather, who was nowhere to be seen. I knew she had gone with Willie Skokan to fetch the cookies to be used in the next competition.

"Where did that tall woman go?" Jimmy Lee asked me.

"I'm not sure," I replied. "And, if you'll excuse me, I think they want me onstage."

"Santa 3 was a stocking-stuffing machine," Bobbo said by way of greeting. "Do you think you can even come close to what he did, Santa 6?"

"I hope so, Bobbo," I replied. "Of course, I've had many more centuries of practice than Santa 3." This accurate comment earned cheers from the audience.

"Then let's see what you can do, Santa 6," Bobbo said. "Ready . . . set . . . *go!*"

There was never any question that in sixty seconds I could fill more stockings than Jimmy Lee or anyone else. As I'd learned seventeen centuries earlier, time was different for me than normal humans. Jimmy Lee had filled eleven stockings in one minute. If necessary I could have filled eleven *hundred* in the same period.

But that wasn't necessary on *The Great Santa Search*. Since two of the five remaining finalists would be eliminated, and the low totals so far were Santa 1 with two filled stockings and Santa 5 with none, all I had to do in my own minute was fill three with unbroken toys, or twelve if I wanted to win the challenge outright. The fragility of LastLong toys didn't have to be factored in. Back at the North Pole, Willie Skokan and Leonardo had taken the items I'd bought at Galaxy Mall and secured every leg, arm, and head tightly to plastic bodies. That was why Willie and Heather Hathaway had been instructed to see I took the right bag of toys onstage.

So my real challenge in stocking-stuffing was to make a statement strong enough to impress the theater audience members who'd be voting soon, without demonstrating so much of my special power that they and the vast television audience would realize real magic was on display. I'd thought carefully about how to proceed and had a plan.

To all those watching in the theater or in their homes, it must have seemed that I rushed to the stockings. I actually had to remind myself to keep my usual Christmas Eve speed almost completely in check. As I'd done untold millions of times over the centuries, I opened my bag, took an empty stocking in my left hand, reached down and pulled out a toy, and then in one smooth motion eased it down into the very bottom of the stocking. I repeated this action five more times—you can fit a lot more into any Christmas stocking if you put in only one thing at a time—until the first stocking was stuffed. I returned it to its hook over the fireplace and took down the second. I filled it in turn, replaced it, did the same with the third, and kept going until all twelve were overflowing with toys and hung back in place. Then I turned to Bobbo, smiled, and gestured to indicate there were no stockings left to be filled.

"I'm sure your special judge won't find any broken toys in these," I said helpfully.

The crowd in the theater just went wild. Bobbo pointed to the clock.

"That took you only thirty seconds, Santa 6!" he announced. "Stupendous! Mind-boggling!"

"I haven't inspected the stockings yet," Lucretia Pepper snapped, and she stalked over to the fireplace, favoring me with an especially nasty glare on the way. I nodded pleasantly in return and strolled over to stand by Bobbo as she frantically pawed through the dozen stockings, looking for any reason to reduce my final total. I believe she might even have stooped to trying sneakily to break a toy or two in each, but the TV cameras were recording her every move and she couldn't.

"Twelve stockings," she finally acknowledged. More cheering erupted.

"Fantastic, Santa 6," Bobbo enthused. "Can we have all our finalists back onstage? Here they come. Well, we have to say goodbye to two more of you, and with no filled stockings and two, respectively, Santas 1 and 5 are eliminated. We've enjoyed meeting you, friends, and Merry Christmas."

Zonk, Jimmy Lee, and I were left standing there. Zonk leaned over and whacked me on the back.

"Great job!" he said. There were microphones placed everywhere, so his compliment was audible to the theater audience and the TV viewers. The crowd in the theater responded with applause because Zonk was being such a good sport. Jimmy Lee, mindful of the pending vote after the final challenge, had no choice but to congratulate me too.

"Well done," he remarked, and his voice was warm even though his expression wasn't.

"How about that?" Bobbo asked. "Our Santas are not only intense competitors, but friendly ones, too! Now, *that's* the real Christmas spirit!" There was more applause. I suspected everyone in the Ed Sullivan Theater would wake up on Christmas morning to find their palms sore and swollen from so much clapping.

"It's twenty-five minutes after nine, and time is flying," Bobbo continued. "We've got to hurry if the real Santa is going to have time to climb in his sleigh and get his Christmas Eve rounds completed tonight. Santas 3, 6, and 8 square off next in a contest that the true Mr. Claus is bound to love. Gentlemen, if you'll just wait offstage for a moment, we'll get set up for the fifth and next-to-last challenge."

The three of us made our way to the wings. Behind him, Bobbo left the curtains open so everyone could see the elf-costumed stagehands hauling three comfortable overstuffed chairs and a trio of long, low coffee tables out in front of the fireplace. As they did, Bobbo began explaining that Santa had roped his reindeer, sung his carols, slid down chimneys, and stuffed every available stocking. Now, his night's work mostly complete, it was time to relax and enjoy a snack. Well, not *relax,* especially, because countless children left out cookies for Santa and he didn't want to hurt any feelings by leaving even a crumb behind anywhere.

I didn't hear the rest of what Bobbo said. I was distracted because Willie Skokan and Heather Hathaway were approaching me with bewildered expressions, and I could tell instantly that something had gone very, very wrong in our plans to keep Lucretia Pepper and Jimmy Lee from cheating in the cookie-eating competition.

My first bite of cookie was almost my last. Lucretia Pepper had planned well. The combination of crushed dill and onion powder burned my tongue and made my eyes water. I wanted to spit the nasty cookie out—and almost did.

Twenty-two

 e had thought it would be simple to thwart any attempt by Lucretia Pepper to somehow cheat in the cookie-eating contest so Jimmy Lee would win. On the morning of December 24, Heather Hathaway went to a bakery near Central Park and bought ten dozen round sugar cookies decorated with bright red sparkles. No one on *The Great Santa Search* staff thought it would be possible for anyone to gulp down more than thirty or so in the allotted sixty seconds, so 120 were plenty. Forty would be placed on each of three trays, and the trio of Santa finalists remaining would be served their mountains of cookies onstage.

The way Lucretia Pepper would try to cheat, we were certain, was to somehow get her hands on the cookies backstage before the competition and sprinkle something bad-tasting on those to be eaten by the two finalists matched against Jimmy Lee. So during the program, Willie Skokan kept a careful eye on the cookie trays. Lucretia Pepper never came near them.

While the stocking-stuffing competition wrapped up, Heather and Willie gathered the three trays of round sugar cookies and started taking them behind the curtain where three easy chairs had been set up by stagehands. There were low tables in front of the chairs, and resting on the tables were three tall glasses of delicious cold milk. But before my friends could place their trays of cookies on the tables, Lucretia Pepper ordered them to stop.

"Those cookies are just too drab to use on this wonderful program," she announced. "We'll use *these* instead." She gestured behind her, where three stagehands stood holding heaping trays of much bigger cookies festooned with a rainbow of colored sprinkles and cut into holiday-themed shapes—Christmas trees and bells and leaping reindeer. Truth-fully, they were considerably more eye-catching than those Heather and Willie carried.

"But we already have these other ones," Heather argued. "It's all arranged."

Lucretia Pepper glowered.

"I am the sole sponsor of this program," she said. "You'll use the cookies I tell you to, and you'll do it without arguing."

"Well, I *will* argue," Heather replied, but just then Mary Rogers came bustling down from her director's booth.

"What's the holdup with the cookies?" she demanded. "The last Santa's stuffing the stockings. We've got to keep moving back here."

"This young woman is causing a commotion," Lucretia Pepper said smoothly. "We have these lovely, very attractive cookies to put on the ta-bles and she is selfishly insisting we use plain ones just because she brought them."

Mary looked at both sets of trays.

"We're usin' the pretty ones," she said briskly. Heather started to ob-ject, but Mary waved her hand and added, "Look, I've got to get back to the booth. Put Lucretia's cookies on the tables. That's it."

It was at that moment that Zonk, Jimmy Lee, and I came offstage. We were immediately instructed to follow the stagehands to the chairs and tables set up behind the curtain. Lucretia Pepper held back Jimmy Lee and one of the stagehands, who didn't put his cookie tray down on the table in front of Jimmy Lee until Zonk and I were already seated with the other two trays in front of us. Short of shoving Jimmy Lee out of his chair so I could eat cookies from the tray on the table in front of him, there was nothing to be done. Something was going to be very wrong with the cookies Zonk and I were about to try to eat.

Perhaps if I'd had more time I could have come up with something, but on the other side of the curtain Bobbo Butler was addressing the audience.

"What I have to say almost defies belief," Bobbo declared. "Some ninety minutes ago I promised you that tonight we would be creating television history. That was guaranteed, of course, by the purpose of *The Great Santa Search*—identifying once and for all the real Santa Claus. And we're having fun doing that here at the Ed Sullivan Theater, aren't we? But something else just as amazing is happening all across America. Families in every city and town, in every neighborhood and on every block and street, have gathered together to spend their Christmas Eve watching *The Great Santa Search*—so many that we can announce this. There are approximately 110 million families in America watching television at this moment. Of those, eighty-five million are tuned in to *The Great Santa Search*. The biggest previous audience for any single program was just over fifty million. On behalf of FUN-TV and everyone associated with *The Great Santa Search*, I thank you for setting a new viewing record that may last as long as the television industry itself! Now, how's *that* for Christmas cheer?"

Behind the curtain, I settled in my chair and mournfully contemplated the plate of cookies in front of me. Zonk, sitting in the middle of the three chairs, turned to me, winked, and whispered, "Hope you worked up an appetite. Me, I'm starving!" I looked past Zonk and saw that Jimmy Lee seemed lost in thought.

"Okay, folks," Bobbo continued on the other side of the curtain. "Here comes our next-to-last challenge. We're close to identifying the real Santa Claus. Now, at this point in his night, he's filled all the stockings and it's time for a snack. Kids in America love to leave out cookies and milk for Santa to enjoy. So be it!"

The curtains opened, and there we three Santa finalists were in our chairs, with trays of cookies and glasses of milk on the tables before us.

"This is going to be very simple," Bobbo said. "You can see each of our finalists—from left to right they're Santa 3, Santa 8, and Santa 6— has a heaping tray of delicious cookies to enjoy. We're going to ask three elves to take their places behind the chairs."

Stagehands in elf regalia stood behind us. Each held a large electronic sign.

"The two Santas who eat the most cookies in sixty seconds will advance to the finals," Bobbo explained. "By eat, I mean chew up and completely swallow. The Santa who eats the fewest cookies is eliminated. There are forty cookies on each tray. The elves will keep track of how many cookies each Santa has eaten. At the end of sixty seconds, they'll enter the amounts on their electronic signs and hold them up one at a time until we see who was eliminated. Santas 3, 8, and 6, are you ready?"

Jimmy Lee jerked his head up. He'd been thinking hard about something. He waved at Bobbo to indicate he was ready. I nodded resignedly. I thought I would be able to choke down a few more bad-tasting cookies than poor, unsuspecting Zonk, but I wasn't looking forward to the experience.

Zonk picked up a cookie and brandished it toward the cameras.

"They look great!" he enthused. "I know it won't count, but I can't wait. I've got to eat one now!" And he crammed the cookie in his mouth.

Afterward, when we'd brought a few back to the North Pole for testing, Leonardo reported that the cookies placed in front of Zonk and me had been dusted by Lucretia Pepper with a nasty combination of crushed dill seed and onion powder. The colorful candy sprinkles on top effectively hid the vicious mixture.

I thought, as Lucretia Pepper and Jimmy Lee must have, that Zonk would immediately grimace and spit out the cookie. But he didn't. Instead, he swallowed, grinned, and smacked his lips.

"Let's start eating!" he suggested.

Then I remembered—Zonk had ageusia. He couldn't taste anything, so he wasn't able to tell that the cookies were supposed to be too horrible to eat. He and Jimmy Lee could both munch away happily, while I had to suffer through every foul bite.

"Keep a close eye on your favorite Santa finalist, folks," Bobbo commanded. "All right, then. Ready . . . set . . . *eat!*"

Jimmy Lee ate his untainted cookies at a steady, calculated pace. You could tell he'd studied how to consume the most in a limited time. He took big but not gigantic bites, chewing just thoroughly enough so that he wouldn't choke when he swallowed.

Zonk was more erratic. His plan, if he had one at all, was to quickly stuff cookies in his mouth until there wasn't room for one more crumb, somehow chew up and swallow it all, and repeat the pattern until time was up. So he got off to a good start, but within fifteen seconds he already had to stop and take several swallows of milk to wash down his massive mouthful. At least he didn't taste what he was eating.

My first bite of cookie was almost my last. Lucretia Pepper had planned well. The combination of crushed dill and onion powder burned my tongue and made my eyes water. I wanted to spit the nasty cookie out—and almost did. But then two things happened.

First, I remembered the millions of children who had left out cookies for me over the centuries. In many cases they'd baked the cookies themselves, and sometimes the results were not exactly delicious. But I ate those cookies anyway, because they had been prepared with love, and knowing that helped me ignore the less-than-pleasant taste. (One boy named Wilson loved licorice so much he actually put that in the cookies he prepared and left for me. Have you ever tasted baked licorice? Oh, I hope not!) So, in the past, I had been able to consume cookies regardless of how terrible they might taste.

Second, I'd just spent a whole year on the first diet of my life. For several centuries before that, I hadn't gone a day without cookies. I loved eating them. The batch of cookies in front of me might taste horrible, but they were still *cookies*. They had that wonderful, comforting cookie consistency that feels so right in your mouth when your teeth crunch everything up. Every dessertless day of my diet, I'd dreamed of the moment when I could once again enjoy all the cookies I wanted. Now it had arrived.

So I swallowed that first bite of cookie and took another, then another. Gradually the terrible taste seemed less important than the act of eating itself; it seemed I could almost hear my stomach joyfully shouting, "Finally! Cookies!" And the next thing I knew the jingle bells had sounded to end the sixty-second challenge, and the tray in front of me was quite empty. Jimmy Lee and Zonk each had cookies left on theirs.

For a moment, there was complete silence. Then Bobbo said in a voice filled with wonder, "Wow, Santa 6, you sure can eat a lot of cookies."

There were a few crumbs on my beard, so I brushed them off. I wasn't quite sure how to respond, and finally settled for, "Thank you."

Zonk was laughing, but Jimmy Lee's eyes bulged with shock. Somewhere offstage, I knew Lucretia Pepper was stunned, too.

"Well, we know Santa 6 goes on to the final challenge," Bobbo said. "Let's ask the elves standing behind the other two Santas to take turns showing us the total number of cookies eaten by each of them. Let's hear from the elf behind Santa 3."

Jimmy Lee's "elf" punched some buttons on his sign, then held it up. The number on the screen was *29*.

"Twenty-nine cookies in sixty seconds is quite impressive, Santa 3," Bobbo said. "I wonder if Santa 8 did better?"

Jimmy Lee never even glanced back at the electronic screen behind his chair. He'd obviously kept careful track of his cookie count, and knew it was twenty-nine. He'd expected Zonk and me not to be able to manage more than a few of the tainted cookies, so twenty-nine should have won easily.

But I'd polished off all forty of mine, and Zonk had certainly crammed down a considerable number of his. How fine it would be, I thought, if his total surpassed Jimmy Lee's, preventing the cheater from even advancing to the final challenge.

"Now, the total for Santa 8," Bobbo commanded, and Zonk's elf pushed buttons and held up his sign:

28.

"By one cookie, Santa 8 is eliminated," Bobbo announced, and the audience in the Ed Sullivan Theater gave my new friend a warm ovation as he waved, took one more cookie off his tray, stuffed it in his mouth, and walked offstage.

The most-watched program in all of television history had fifteen minutes left to go. The camera crews moved in for close-ups of Jimmy Lee and me.

Bobbo lowered his voice dramatically.

"And now, the final challenge," he said. "For the children of all ages in America who love and believe in him, you in our studio audience are about to choose the real Santa Claus."

He turned to Jimmy Lee and me.

"Santas 3 and 6, you can step offstage for just a moment. But don't go far. We'll be hearing from each of you very soon."

As soon as I was safely off-camera, Heather and Willie greeted me enthusiastically.

"How did you *do* that?" Heather wanted to know.

Willie answered for me.

"Santa Claus can do almost anything," he told her.

A few yards away, Lucretia Pepper and Jimmy Lee stood together, and it was obvious things weren't right between them. He said something and she shook her head emphatically while pointing her finger in his face. Whatever she said next made him angry, because his back straightened and his own finger shot out to point at her. Just then, she glanced in our direction and saw me watching. She said something else briefly to Jimmy Lee. He nodded and moved away, watching intently as she walked over to me.

"Well done, Santa 6," Lucretia Pepper said. "You certainly surprised me."

"The cookies you provided were quite interesting," I replied, trying to match her overly sincere tone. "Of course, I know you prepared them from your own special recipe."

She blinked, and I realized this woman was not used to anyone standing up to her. Her forcefulness, or, perhaps I should say, her nastiness, had intimidated everyone she dealt with—until now.

"You're not going to win," she declared. "Let's not pretend. I've seen to that. Jimmy Lee already has the votes. Be a good sport when you lose, don't mention anything that might embarrass either of us, and there'll be something in it for you afterward. I have deep pockets."

"Let's wait and see what happens," I suggested. "Perhaps in the next few minutes, you might learn something about the true spirit of Christmas. That's always possible, even for nevers."

"Nevers?" Lucretia Pepper responded. "What do you mean by *nevers?*" I smiled at her.

"That's one of the things I'm going to talk about," I said. "And because I'll have to rush off after we're done here, I'll say this now in case I don't have the opportunity later: Merry Christmas, Lucretia Pepper. It's my sincere wish that somehow, some day, the joy of Christmas touches your heart."

Before she could reply, Felix tugged at my sleeve.

"It's time, Santa 6," he said. "Bobbo Butler is explaining the final challenge."

I stood onstage. Perhaps I should have felt nervous. I didn't. Thanks to
Lucretia Pepper's duplicity, Jimmy Lee already had 150 votes
out of a possible 461. But he wasn't Santa Claus. I was.

Twenty-three

t's quarter of ten," Bobbo Butler reminded the 461 people in the Ed Sullivan Theater and the eighty-five million families watching *The Great Santa Search* at home. "Very soon, the one and only real, official Santa Claus will climb in his sleigh and fly through the Christmas Eve sky to bring presents to good boys and girls everywhere. But who *is* the real, official Santa? We've spent 105 minutes so far trying to find out. Christmas experts from *The Great Santa Search* staff spent months combing the country, and through their efforts we've presented ten Santa finalists to you tonight. Now it's down to the last two. Through reindeer-roping and carol-singing, from chimney-sliding to stocking-stuffing and just minutes ago during cookie-eating, these two individuals have proven they have all the necessary skills to be the undisputed Santa. But which one truly deserves your trust, your belief— I'll even say, your love? To know that, we have to know *them*, and this brings us to the final challenge of *The Great Santa Search*. First Santa 3, and then Santa 6, will have three minutes to tell our studio audience why he deserves their votes. Though all you wonderful, Christmas-loving viewers at home can't physically vote, we ask that you vote with your hearts."

Bobbo paused to take a breath—and, I think, to build tension.

"After each of our two *Great Santa Search* finalists has made his presentation, our studio audience will vote by pushing either the 3 or 6 button on the voting devices by their seats," he said. "Within seconds, you'll see the final totals flash on the studio monitors. At home, they'll be displayed on the lower part of your television screen. Then the official, the one and only elected Santa Claus, will be presented with a check for one million dollars to become the spokesman for LastLong Toy Company, which has so generously sponsored *The Great Santa Search* as a commercial-free broadcast."

It seemed to me, as I watched from the wings, that there was a sudden undercurrent of grumbling from the people in the theater. At least some of them found it disagreeable for Santa Claus to sell his services to Last-Long and Lucretia Pepper.

Bobbo must have heard it, too, for he hastily added, "And, of course, our officially elected Santa Claus will undoubtedly have a few last words for us before he has to jump in his sleigh and start delivering presents. Let's begin. The studio monitors and a clock on the TV screens for you at home will count down the three minutes of each finalist's presentation. And so, let's hear first from Santa 3!"

Jimmy Lee had been huddled with Lucretia Pepper, who now seemed to be coaxing rather than threatening him. Instead of pointing a red-nailed finger in his face, she patted him soothingly on the shoulder. She did this in full view of everyone backstage. She was not trying to give even the slightest appearance of impartiality.

"Remember, you *are* Santa Claus," she told him loudly enough for all of us to hear. Jimmy Lee nodded and walked out onstage. Bobbo shook his hand and walked off. As soon as he was out of camera range he turned and, like the rest of us, watched and listened intently to Jimmy Lee.

I had to give Jimmy Lee credit. He must have been badly shaken when, despite his and Lucretia Pepper's best cheating efforts, I won the cookie-eating competition. He certainly had been distracted ever since Heather Hathaway had explained to him how he might make even more money by betraying Lucretia Pepper and refusing LastLong Toy Company's million dollars to become its corporate spokesman. And, of course, there was the tremendous pressure of knowing so many people were watching him in person and on television as he stood in his red-and-white Santa costume, the hot stage lights glaring in his eyes and burning on his skin. It would have been natural for him to not only feel but look nervous, perhaps with the added discomfort of sweating profusely while words he wanted to say somehow stuck in his throat.

But instead he appeared calm, even happy. And though his three minutes had begun as soon as Bobbo Butler walked offstage and he walked on, Jimmy Lee didn't start talking right away. Instead, he stood for a moment with his hands folded comfortably in front of him, smiling and looking at the studio audience and then directly into the TV cameras so his gaze could seem to touch on everyone watching at home, too.

"Well, Merry Christmas to you all," he finally began. "We've had a wonderful evening, haven't we? Good manners are as important for Santa Claus as they are for everyone else, so let me begin by recognizing the FUN-TV network and especially its president, Mr. Bobbo Butler, for making all this possible. Please, Mr. Butler, come out and let us thank you."

Bobbo, thrilled with the record audience *The Great Santa Search* had attracted, came beaming out from the wings. He waved his arms over his head in response to the warm applause from the studio audience, then theatrically looked at his watch, tapped it to indicate time was passing, and hurried off.

"There's someone else special," Jimmy Lee continued. "She would not really want anyone to know how responsible she is for this moment. No words exist to honestly describe her goodness and generosity. The owner and president of LastLong Toy Company, Lucretia Pepper."

It was only at this moment, I realized, that Lucretia Pepper completely believed everything would turn out as she wanted. Her chosen finalist, Jimmy Lee, was going to win *The Great Santa Search*, and he was going to be a loyal, effective company spokesman, which might eventually destroy many children's belief in Santa Claus but would also earn her untold millions of dollars, which was all she really cared about.

"Thank you, Santa, thank you," she cooed as she blew kisses to the studio audience whose token clapping for her was far less enthusiastic than their genuine ovation for Bobbo Butler.

Only then did Jimmy Lee begin his plea for the studio audience's votes.

"*I* am Santa Claus," he declared. "I think most of you know that already. We know each other, you and I, because I've been in your homes each Christmas Eve as a most welcome, if not visible, guest. You've written letters to me, and I've read them. We do read your letters at the North Pole, by the way. How else would my elves know what toys to make, and how many of each?"

Elves again, I thought. *If only I could have talked to Thomas Nast and convinced him to do away with the elf business altogether!*

Jimmy Lee smiled warmly.

"So that's our bond, isn't it? The gifts I bring. They are the connection between us. When you hold that special toy in your hand, you believe in me and love me with all your heart. I can feel that love now. It's coming from everyone here tonight in New York City's Ed Sullivan Theater, and from all of you watching at home."

He waved his hand toward the wings.

"Backstage tonight I made nine new friends. I don't resent that they tried to convince you they were Santa Claus instead of me. You weren't deceived. You're about to prove it when you vote. But once you make it official, no one else should ever pretend to be me again. You won't need pretenders. You'll have the real Santa Claus. And what will that mean?"

Now Jimmy Lee hunched slightly forward, as though he was about to confide a secret.

"It will mean that from now on, you'll know for certain that I'm the one hearing which presents you want. It won't be some imitation Santa with his fake beard falling off. I know that all these years I've mostly been up at the North Pole, but after tonight I expect to be out and about much more. Don't worry—we'll still be making toys back in the North Pole shop! My elves are very efficient. And what they can't make, other companies can, like LastLong Toy Company. If you get the toys you want, I don't think you care too much who actually made them. You see, I understand that, because I understand you."

He paused again, and adopted a serious expression.

"And I understand something else. We should speak about it. We live in a terrifying world. Awful things sometimes happen. They frighten you. You don't feel safe. And then, every year for a little while, Christmas comes. And so do I, to help you forget all the other terrible things. That's what my presents are for. This is why you must vote carefully tonight. Earlier, I sang to you in English and in German. I did it so you would realize that Christmas is important all over the world. I'm needed all over the world. When you vote for me, you are doing something wonderful not only for yourselves but for others in many foreign countries who are looking to you tonight for leadership, for wisdom. Don't let them down."

Jimmy Lee craned his neck to peek at the studio clock.

"Time is precious on Christmas Eve," he said. "I won't say goodbye, because before the sun comes up in the morning I'll have been to all your houses. Now that we've officially met, we'll see much more of each other, I promise. And tonight, I know exactly what presents you want, and soon I'll be on my way to deliver them. Good night."

The applause was loud and extended. I knew that 150 members of the audience were controlled by Lucretia Pepper. They had to support and vote for Jimmy Lee to keep their jobs. That left 311 voters who were available to be persuaded by one of us. Judging from the crowd's reaction to his speech, Jimmy Lee had made a good impression on them.

Bobbo Butler hustled out onstage, clapping along with the audience as Jimmy Lee took several deep bows.

"Just wonderful, Santa 3!" he commented. "Well done indeed!"

Jimmy Lee took a final bow and walked to the wings, where he was embraced by a leering Lucretia Pepper.

I took a deep breath. Willie Skokan shook my hand. So did Felix; if Lucretia Pepper was making it obvious which finalist she favored, so could he.

Heather Hathaway hugged me, and whispered in my ear, "I think I know. I'm sure I do. I believe in you."

Those words rather than the hot studio lights warmed me as Bobbo Butler called me out onstage.

"Santa 6, take it away!" he commanded, and shook my hand on his way off. It was a firm, friendly handshake. Unlike Lucretia Pepper, Bobbo Butler would be happy with whoever won *The Great Santa Search*.

I stood onstage. Perhaps I should have felt nervous. I didn't. Thanks to Lucretia Pepper's duplicity, Jimmy Lee already had 150 votes out of a possible 461. But he wasn't Santa Claus. I was.

And that is why I began my own remarks by saying, "Good evening. It's less important for you to know *who* Santa Claus is than *why* Santa Claus is. Perhaps that sounds rather confusing. Let's talk about it."

I rubbed my chin, gently untangling white strands of beard with my fingers. I didn't try to think of words before I spoke them. I just let them come from my heart.

"By many different names—Santa Claus, St. Nicholas, Father Christmas, Kris Kringle, Père Noel, Grandfather Frost, and others—there has been widespread if not universal belief in a special holiday gift-giver for centuries," I explained. "When the legends began, like most tales they were based on some truth. If we had more time, I would tell you of my early days as a simple young boy named Nicholas, when I lived in a country called Lycia and gave my first gifts to young girls who desperately needed dowries to be married. You can find these things in history books. I promise you, the information is there.

"But in time the gift-giving was linked to me, and people began to speculate what this St. Nicholas looked like. There were paintings of me with a white beard, wearing a red cloak trimmed with white fur. In the 1860s, a very talented American artist named Thomas Nast suggested in his drawings that I lived at the North Pole, which was eventually true, and that I was helped in my gift-giving mission by elves, which wasn't. As I said, most legends begin with truth, but the tale-tellers add colorful details that have more basis in imagination than fact. And another important fact is that Dutch settlers brought their beliefs in me to America, and when their children told English-speaking children about me, the way they pronounced St. Nicholas was 'sintnicklass,' which the English children heard first as 'sinter klass' and eventually as 'Santa Claus.' That's how I got the name most of you here and watching at home tonight call me. And, over time, my friends and I—I have very special companions, though they're certainly not elves—became welcome in homes all over the world. In different places and by different names, we are expected on December 25 or December 6 or January 6. And we are glad to oblige."

I paused, not to collect my thoughts but to allow my listeners to gather theirs.

"The present confusion over who is Santa began, I believe, in 1841, when a friend of mine who owned a general store in Philadelphia hired someone to impersonate me one Christmas season. He thought having a pretend Santa in his store would boost holiday sales, and he was right. It took some time, but others eventually followed his example. Soon there were so-called Santas everywhere. How very confusing for everyone! But, always, there was really only one Santa, and that was me.

"So that's the history of who Santa is, but I mentioned earlier it is more important to know *why* Santa is. I began giving gifts in times when most people didn't have enough to eat, or sandals to wear, or blankets to keep them warm at night. So I gave these things for hundreds of years, until it was explained to me by wise friends that it was just not possible to give something to everyone. Children needed most to know they were loved, so I must concentrate on them. Something lasting and joyful was required, because food would be quickly eaten and clothes outgrown— that was how I came to bring toys."

The audience in the Ed Sullivan Theater listened in perfect silence. I hoped it was because my words touched them.

"I come to many of your homes on Christmas Eve, December 24, because on Christmas Day you celebrate the greatest gift of all, God's gift of his son," I continued. "Jesus was sent to give us comfort and hope. He was proof of God's love. There are some who do not believe in that, or in me. This is your right. But I do hope you at least believe in giving comfort to those who need it. I hope you believe in love.

"As Santa 3 has told you, this can be a terrifying world. It would be wrong to ignore its faults and its dangers. But there is no greater gift than caring for others and making sure they know you care. Yes, I bring toys, but I want you to understand that those toys are a symbol of love. They are not meant to make you forget the bad things in your lives. They are intended to remind you that goodness exists, too, and hope. My gifts are not supposed to be distractions from evil. They are proof of the goodness that exists, of the hope that is always possible, and of the dreams which might still come true. This is *why* there is Santa Claus."

Now it was my turn to peek at the studio clock. I had one minute remaining.

"Will someone please turn up the lights so I can see the audience?" I asked. "What I say next is more about you than me."

Everyone in the theater was instantly illuminated. I could see Layla and Arthur and Francis and Bill in their middle-row seats, and the various television stars much closer to the stage, and in the center of the front row Cynthia and Diana, Bobbo Butler's daughters.

"Some people believe in Santa Claus all their lives, some believe for a while, and some never believe in me at all," I said. "What few ever realize is that no matter what you do or don't believe, each of you has the ability to *be* Santa Claus. At Christmas or any other time of year, if you take it upon yourself to give a gift with the intention of reminding the recipient that someone cares, that happiness as well as sorrow can be part of each life, then you and I are the same. You, too, are extending the loving, gift-giving tradition that goes back to the original time when the Wise Men brought their gifts to the baby Jesus. The bond between us is not the gifts I give you, but the love and caring that is extended from one person to another."

I found myself gazing at ten-year-old Cynthia and eight-year-old Diana Butler. Seeing them, I knew how to conclude.

"In any of your lives, the time has come, or will come, when for one reason or another you're no longer sure that I exist," I said. "At that moment, you'll have to make your own decisions about Santa Claus. But I hope you'll remember one thing. Whether you remain a true believer, or believe for a while, or never believe at all, so long as you do your best to be a kind and caring person, Santa Claus will always believe in *you.*

"Merry Christmas."

There was total silence for one second, two seconds, three. Then, slowly at first, hands began to clap, and the clapping got louder and then there were cheers and with all the theater lights on I could see many people had tears running down their cheeks. I stood there while Bobbo raced back onstage, his own eyes shining with tears, and called a suddenly surly-looking Jimmy Lee out to stand beside me while the audience voted.

Then, by a margin of some half-dozen votes, Jimmy Lee won *The Great Santa Search.*

She rushed at Bobbo, hamlike hands extended to grab or pinch or punch, but she never reached him. Heather Hathaway stepped in front of Bobbo. The tall, rangy young woman lowered her shoulder, and Lucretia Pepper rammed her own midsection into it. The owner of LastLong Toys went sprawling.

Twenty-four

ackstage, Lucretia Pepper shrieked in triumph when the voting totals were announced. The unnerving sound reverberated through the Ed Sullivan Theater and must have been heard by all the viewers at home. A moment later *The Great Santa Search* theme song blared out instead. Jimmy Lee embraced Bobbo Butler, then walked to the front of the stage, waving at the crowd. Everyone in the theater was standing and applauding. Almost half of them would have preferred the winner to be me, but they were being good sports and showing appreciation for the victor. I could do no less.

I walked to where Jimmy Lee stood waving and tapped him on the shoulder. He'd been quite lost in his moment of triumph; he flinched as I touched him, but when he turned and saw me he threw his arms wide and we hugged.

"You can still do the right thing," I whispered in his ear.

"Watch," he whispered back.

Then, after a quick wave toward Layla and my North Pole friends in the audience, I made my way offstage.

"Let's hear it for Santa 6, a great competitor," Bobbo Butler urged, and the crowd responded with a fine ovation. Then I was off-camera in the wings, and Felix, Sarah, Heather Hathaway, and Willie Skokan greeted me with hugs and assurances that they were proud of me.

"What a lovely speech," Sarah declared. "I don't understand why Santa 3 got even one vote."

"*I* do," Heather grumbled. "He and Lucretia Pepper are such cheaters!"

"We're also *winners*," someone snarled. Lucretia Pepper was standing beside us, and the expression of evil joy on her face was frightening in its intensity. "And I'd better not read or hear suggestions from any of you that this contest wasn't on the up-and-up. If I do, you'll be hearing from my lawyers. And now, the *real* Santa Claus is about to become part of the team at LastLong Toys!"

Jimmy Lee stood with Bobbo Butler at the center of the stage. Two of the stagehands dressed as elves carried out a long, rectangular cardboard check. The amount on it was $1,000,000.00, and it was made out to Santa Claus. The LastLong Toy Company logo was prominently plastered on the upper left-hand corner.

Felix, Sarah, Heather, Willie, and I watched from the wings as Bobbo Butler raised his hand to request silence. The audience finally stopped applauding and sat back down. As they did, Oprah Winfrey shouted, "You're coming on my show first, Santa honey!" and everyone laughed.

"Just before he leaves to spend the rest of the night delivering gifts, we have a gift for Santa himself," Bobbo said. "To present our winner, the real and only official Santa Claus, with this million-dollar check is the president of LastLong Toy Company, Lucretia Pepper!"

Sarah, who has a way with words, later remarked that Lucretia Pepper slithered rather than walked out on the stage. The hulking woman rudely pulled the cardboard check away from the stagehands.

"Santa Claus, it is with the utmost pleasure that I present you with this check for one million dollars," she said. "And along with it you have my very warmest welcome as the new, year-round spokesperson for LastLong Toy Company. Santa Claus and LastLong Toys—names that as of now are linked together."

She extended her arms to present the check to Jimmy Lee. He took a step back.

"Here's your check, Santa," Lucretia Pepper said.

"Thank you, but no," Jimmy Lee replied. He turned to Bobbo. "Mr. Butler, may I have a few moments for concluding remarks?"

"Of course, Santa," Bobbo said. "But don't you want your check?"

"Actually, no," Jimmy Lee repeated. "I'll explain. Perhaps you'd escort Ms. Pepper offstage while I do."

Bobbo tried to take Lucretia Pepper's arm, but she yanked it away. Her face was twisted with rage. I'm sure she thought about attacking Jimmy Lee on the spot, but the largest audience in television history was watching, so she stormed off after leaning toward Jimmy Lee and muttering undoubtedly horrible threats that the studio microphones thankfully did not pick up and broadcast.

"What's he up to?" Felix asked me.

"Let's listen," I suggested. "I think someone's stony heart may have finally been touched by true Christmas spirit."

Jimmy Lee faced the audience, smiling warmly at them. He reached up, removed his tassled cap, and held it in front of him with both hands.

"My friends, I'm so profoundly grateful to you," he said. "I feel your love for Santa Claus, and I promise you it is mutual. My unwavering belief is that Santa Claus belongs to everyone, not just one company, and so I'm afraid I can't accept money, even such a magnificent sum, to become the spokesman for LastLong Toy Company products. But here's good news. You may have noticed Ms. Lucretia Pepper whispering to me just before she left the stage. She's too modest to make it public, so I will. She has just promised to donate the million dollars to charities that provide Christmas comfort to homeless children right here in New York City. Isn't that wonderful? Won't you please join me in thanking her?"

Lucretia Pepper had no choice but to briefly emerge from the wings and make a jerky, waving motion in the direction of the audience. She was trying to twist her furious expression into some semblance of a smile, but didn't succeed. Then, glowering at Jimmy Lee, she whirled and left the stage.

"Even Santa Claus can always learn things," Jimmy Lee continued. "I've learned a great deal tonight. If I didn't before, I know now that Santa Claus *does* belong to everyone, every girl and boy and father and mother and also to grandparents and everyone else in the world. Truly, Santa must not be affiliated with one toy company—he should share his wisdom and experience with many of them, and perhaps with other creative artists in the movie and television and book industries. Santa Claus loves them all equally."

"He means *this* Santa Claus loves everybody's *money* equally," Heather grumbled.

"Jimmy Lee doesn't completely understand Christmas and generosity of spirit yet," I agreed. "He's still anxious for the book and movie deals you suggested to him. But he's making a start, Heather. Sometimes it takes a while for holiday magic to complete its wonderful work."

Felix leaned over to me.

"Attila's brought the sleigh and reindeer out in the alley, Santa," he whispered. "All the toys are packed in it. You're ready to go."

"In a moment, Felix," I replied. "Just like Jimmy Lee, I may be learning something."

Jimmy Lee concluded his speech. He thanked everyone again, and made the audience laugh when he noted he'd be bringing toys to all of them, "even the ones who didn't vote for me." After I'd asked that the theater lights be turned up, no one in the control booth had ever turned them down again, so everyone in the audience was visible. My North Pole companions—Layla, Arthur, Francis, and Bill—were listening politely to Jimmy Lee, and everyone else, including the famous TV personalities, were simply rapt. They gazed adoringly at the man who'd just become the official Santa Claus. They were hanging on his every word.

Watching Jimmy Lee charm the crowd, I remembered how, back at Galaxy Mall, all the children were thrilled to meet Lester Sneed dressed as Santa, even though Mr. Sneed's beard was scraggly and his belly clearly wasn't of Santa-like proportions.

"Oh, why do they like him so much?" Heather murmured.

And at that moment I understood it completely. Just a few moments before, Jimmy Lee had said that even Santa Claus can always learn, and he was right.

"They like him because they truly believe in the *idea* of Santa Claus," I told Sarah. "In all these years of worrying about impostors ruining belief in me, I'd never realized that. When they see Jimmy Lee, or when anyone sees a Santa in a mall or ringing a bell on a street corner, what they're really seeing is a reminder that love and generosity still exist in this imperfect world of ours. Look at Bobbo Butler's daughters!"

Cynthia and Diana were leaning so far forward in their front-row seats that they were in danger of banging their chins on the front edge of the stage. Cynthia had her usual wide-eyed look of pleased wonder, but the previously doubting Diana appeared even more enthralled. Her smile was so wide it seemed the edges of her mouth were about to touch her ears.

"You see, it really doesn't matter which Santa Claus children believe in, so long as they believe in him at all," I continued. "If they do, then they'll eventually realize that Christmas is about caring and love and hope rather than toys, and they'll teach that to *their* children, and we'll continue to have believers and true believers and maximum true believers. Jimmy Lee is only beginning to realize that even though he's not Santa, he's still an important Santa's helper. He's going to be on television shows and in movies and have books written about him, and perhaps for a while he'll think he's doing it only for the money.

But eventually he'll understand he's also doing it for me, and for Christmas."

Up in the control booth, Mary Rogers was calling out last-second instructions. Listening on his headphones, a backstage worker held out his hand to signal Jimmy Lee—three, two, one.

"Merry Christmas!" shouted Jimmy Lee, and with that the program's theme music blared again. The hands on the studio clock read 10:00 p.m, the red lights on the cameras blinked off, and *The Great Santa Search* was now a permanent part of television history.

The curtains closed in front of the stage. Behind them, Bobbo Butler raised his arms over his head in triumph. Jimmy Lee hurried toward his dressing room, no doubt hoping there would already be messages there offering him roles in movies or publishing contracts for the *official* Santa's memoirs. But as he passed me he whispered, "I may want to talk to you soon. Where can I reach you?"

"I'll be glad to talk with you, and don't worry about reaching me," I whispered back. "When the time is right, I'll know where you are."

Jimmy Lee smiled. We shook hands. Then he disappeared into his dressing room.

"Where are you, Miss Hathaway?" Bobbo called. "Get me my girls! I want Cynthia and Diana!"

Heather rolled her eyes.

"The chief calls," she said. "I'll be back in a minute."

She darted down in front of the stage and collected Diana and Cynthia. They ran backstage and scampered into their father's arms.

"You were great, Daddy!" Cynthia gushed.

Diana said she wanted to talk to Santa Claus.

"I need to make sure he's got my present on his sleigh," she said.

"I thought you didn't believe in Santa Claus anymore," Bobbo pointed out.

"I do now," Diana declared.

Bobbo took both his daughters by the hand.

"Well, I think we can arrange——" he began, and then Lucretia Pepper made a bull-like charge in his direction.

"You *tricked* me!" she howled, which made no sense. Bobbo had nothing to do with Jimmy Lee's renunciation. But people like Lucretia Pepper must always take their anger out on someone, and she'd chosen Bobbo Butler. I really believe she intended to physically attack him right in front of his children. She rushed at Bobbo, hamlike hands extended to grab or pinch or punch, but she never reached him. Heather Hathaway stepped in front of Bobbo. The tall, rangy young woman lowered her shoulder, and Lucretia Pepper rammed her own midsection into it. The owner of LastLong Toys went sprawling.

Heather calmly walked over to where she lay gasping for air.

"You just assaulted me in front of dozens of witnesses," she said. "If you ever try to say anything different, you'll be hearing from my lawyers. Oh, and Merry Christmas."

Lucretia Pepper got slowly to her feet. She glared at everyone and left.

Bobbo, an awestruck expression on his face, walked up to Heather.

"Miss Hathaway," he began. "Um, Heather. You know, I've just realized something. You're very, well, *special*. It's been such an exciting night. I think I'd like to go out for a late meal after I take the girls home. I wonder, will you join me?"

Heather shook her head.

"I appreciate the invitation, Bobbo, but I can't. Willie Skokan is taking me to dinner."

"Who?" Bobbo asked.

"Someone I met tonight," Heather said. Bobbo looked panic-stricken, so she added, "Don't worry, Bobbo. It's only dinner. I'll see you at work next week, and you can ask me out then. Merry Christmas, Cynthia and Diana. I'm glad you believe in Santa Claus again." Heather and Willie walked away, while Bobbo stared after them.

"I swore I'd save my network, and I've done it," he muttered. "I promised I'd get the highest ratings for any show in television history, and it happened. Now I give my word that someday I'll convince Heather Hathaway to marry me. I'm going to do it. I am."

"I'm sure you will, Bobbo," said Sarah, patting the lovestruck man's arm. "Just don't take her for granted anymore. When someone is as wonderful as Heather, you can't expect that nobody else will notice."

"Well, *I've* finally noticed," Bobbo agreed. He sighed, and then remembered that his daughters were still standing at his side.

"Time to go home," he told them.

"Hurry up, Daddy," Diana urged. "Cyn and I need to get to sleep so Santa can come."

"Oh, so you and your sister do believe in me?" someone asked. Jimmy Lee had emerged from his dressing room. He still wore his costume and seemed every bit a warm, benevolent Santa. The little girls ran to him and received big hugs.

"Are *you* free for dinner after I get my girls home, Santa?" Bobbo asked.

Jimmy Lee shook his head.

"I'm afraid not, because I still have so much to do," he said. "It's Christmas Eve, don't forget, and there were also some messages in my dressing room that I need to return as soon as possible. But before I leave, I would love one last time for these pretty girls to tell me exactly what they want Santa to bring them tonight." He sat down on one of the big chairs we'd used during the cookie-eating challenge, and Cynthia and Diana scrambled up in his lap.

Turned down by Heather and Jimmy Lee, Bobbo still wanted company.

"What about you, Santa 6?" he asked. "I hope you're not too disappointed about losing. Let me buy you a consolation meal. I promise, we'll have the best food in New York City."

I declined, too. When my long night of work was done, I'd enjoy a North Pole feast prepared by Lars, and no New York City chef could match his abilities in the kitchen. With my diet now over, I hoped Lars would serve his fluffy pecan waffles, and also *huevos rancheros,* and perhaps some delicious blueberry muffins. I'd go back to eating sensibly after Epiphany—perhaps. Gift-giving is hungry work. And even before I returned home tonight, I'd also snack on cookies and milk left for me at so many houses by loving boys and girls. None of those cookies would be of the dill-and-onion variety, I was certain.

"Perhaps another time, Bobbo," I said. "Congratulations on your record-breaking program, and Merry Christmas to you."

"Merry Christmas, Santa 6," Bobbo replied. "I really don't understand why you're in such a hurry."

I told him the truth: "The reindeer are waiting."

Hot Chocolate Cake

This is one of our favorite cakes here at the North Pole, and is especially welcome on those really cold nights we have here from time to time. It's easy to make, and absolutely delicious.

DRY INGREDIENTS

1½ cups all-purpose flour

1 cup sugar

½ cup unsweetened cocoa (We use Ghirardelli.)

1 teaspoon baking soda

¼ teaspoon cayenne pepper (Use a little more if your family loves it hot, but please keep it well under 1 teaspoon.)

¼ teaspoon salt

WET INGREDIENTS

1 cup cold water

¼ cup vegetable oil

1 tablespoon balsamic vinegar

1 tablespoon vanilla extract

Glaze ingredients follow baking instructions, below.

PREPARATION

Preheat the oven to 350°F.

Lightly grease a bundt cake pan, then lightly dust it with cocoa, and set it aside.

Combine all of the dry ingredients in a mixing bowl and stir until everything is well blended. We usually don't sift the cocoa and the flour, but do break up any large clumps before they're mixed in.

Add the wet ingredients, and stir until smooth.

Pour the batter into the cake pan and bake for 25 to 35 minutes. (When it's ready, a toothpick inserted deep into the ring will come out clean.)

Leave the cake in the pan for 10 minutes, on a wire rack.

Remove the cake from the pan and let it cool completely.

After the cake has completely cooled, prepare the glaze you prefer as directed below.

CHOOSE YOUR GLAZE

Chocolate Lovers' Glaze

1 cup confectioners sugar
½ cup cocoa (We use Ghirardelli.)
2 tablespoons melted butter
5 tablespoons water
1 teaspoon vanilla extract

In a small bowl, whisk together all the ingredients until smooth. Pour the glaze over the top of the cake and let it dry (about 30 minutes).

Holiday Glaze

1½ cups confectioners sugar
2 tablespoons water
2 tablespoons melted butter
1 teaspoon vanilla extract
¼ cup dried cranberries

In a small bowl, whisk together the first 4 ingredients until smooth. Pour the glaze over the top of the cake. Sprinkle the dried cranberries on top for a tasty holiday look. Let the glaze dry (about 30 minutes).

For the Chocolate Lovers' Glaze: Just before serving, dust the slices with some powdered confectioners sugar—it will look like a light snowfall! And for more color, serve it with strawberries or raspberries.

Acknowledgments

THANKS ABOVE ALL to three special people involved in this project: Sara Carder, the brilliant senior editor at Tarcher/Penguin; Andrea Ahles Koos, the best researcher in modern-day publishing; and Jim Donovan, a literary agent who combines intelligence, heart, and unerring common sense.

I'm also grateful to Joel Fotinos, Mark McDiarmid, and Ken Siman at Tarcher/Penguin; Wes Turner, Scott Nishimura, Stephanie Owen, Paul Bourgeois, Melinda Mason, Charles and Mary Rogers, Charles Caple and Marcia Melton, Rick Press, Broc Sears, Mark Hoffer, Nancy Burford, Cynthia Wahl, Diana Andro, and Heather Landy at the *Star-Telegram*; and Felix Higgins, Robert Fernandez, Larry "Lars" Wilson, Robert Olen Butler, Zonk Lanzillo, Eri Mizobe, James Ward Lee, Carlton Stowers, Doug Perry, Mary Arendes, Del Hillen, Elizabeth Hayes, and Brian McLendon.

I found inspiration in the memories of Dot and Frank Lauden, Marie and Louis Renz, Jim Firth, Jerry Flemmons, Jack B. Tinsley, Max Lale, and Iris Chang.

Special thanks for information and cooperation from the Noerr Program.

Everything I write is always for Nora, Adam, and Grant.

"A book that deserves classic status."
—*The Dallas Morning News*

"Delightful."
—*The Commercial Appeal* (Memphis)

"Charming."
—*The Kansas City Star*

The Autobiography of Santa Claus
ISBN 978-1-58542-265-4 (hardcover) • ISBN 978-1-58542-448-1 (trade paperback)

This heartwarming family classic, set in seventeenth-century England, is narrated by the first lady of Christmas herself, as she tells the story of how she and a brave band of people saved the beloved holiday from being lost forever.

How Mrs. Claus Saved Christmas
ISBN 978-1-58542-437-5 (hardcover)
ISBN 978-1-58542-535-8 (trade paperback)